GIRL WITH
CURIOUS HAIR

GIRL WITH

DAVID FOSTER WALLACE

CURIOUS HAIR

W·W·NORTON & COMPANY
NEW YORK·LONDON

These stories are 100 percent fiction. Some of them project the names of "real" public figures onto made-up characters in made-up circumstances. Where the names of corporate, media, or political figures are used here, those names are meant only to denote figures, images, the stuff of collective dreams; they do not denote, or pretend to private information about, actual 3-D persons, living, dead, or otherwise.

Part of "Little Expressionless Animals" makes use of the third stanza of John Ashbery's "Self-Portrait in a Convex Mirror" from John Ashbery's *Selected Poems* (Viking Press, 1985, pp. 192–193).

Parts of "Westward the Course of Empire Takes Its Way" are written in the margins of John Barth's "Lost in the Funhouse" and Cynthia Ozick's "Usurpation (Other People's Stories)"; p. 294 of "Westward" contains the first seven lines of "Usurpation," from Cynthia Ozick's *Bloodshed and Three Novellas* (Afred A. Knopf, 1976, p. 132).

Acknowledgment is made to the following publications in which some of the stories in this book originally appeared: "Little Expressionless Animals" in the *Paris Review*; "Lyndon" in *Arrival*; "Here and There" in *Fiction*; "John Billy" in *Conjunctions*; "My Appearance" in *Playboy* under the title "Late Night"; "Say Never" in the *Florida Review*; "Everything Is Green" in *Puerto de Sol* and *Harper's*.

ACKNOWLEDGMENT OF SUPPORT TO:

The Trustees of the Arizona Humanities Fellowship
The Mr. And Mrs. Wallace Fund for Aimless Children
The Mrs. Giles Whiting Foundation
The Corporation of Yaddo

Printed in the United States of America.

The text of this book is composed in Garamond #3, with display type set in Avant Garde. Composition by NK Graphics. Manufacturing by The Haddon Craftsmen, Inc.

Library of Congress Cataloging in Publication Data
    Wallace, David Foster.
        Girl with curious hair : [stories] / David Foster Wallace.—1st
    ed.
            p.   cm.
        I. Title.
    PS3573.A425635G5   1989
    813'.54—dc20   89–9435

ISBN 0-393-31396-4

W. W. Norton & Company, Inc., 500 Fifth Avenue, New York, N.Y. 10110
www.wwnorton.com

W. W. Norton & Company Ltd., Castle House, 75/76 Wells Street, London W1T 3QT

3 4 5 6 7 8 9 0

FOR L——

CONTENTS

LITTLE EXPRESSIONLESS ANIMALS   1

LUCKILY THE ACCOUNT REPRESENTATIVE KNEW CPR   43

GIRL WITH CURIOUS HAIR   53

LYNDON   75

JOHN BILLY   119

HERE AND THERE   149

MY APPEARANCE   173

SAY NEVER   203

EVERYTHING IS GREEN   227

WESTWARD THE COURSE OF EMPIRE TAKES ITS WAY   231

LITTLE
EXPRESSIONLESS
ANIMALS

IT'S 1976. The sky is low and full of clouds. The gray clouds are bulbous and wrinkled and shiny. The sky looks cerebral. Under the sky is a field, in the wind. A pale highway runs beside the field. Lots of cars go by. One of the cars stops by the side of the highway. Two small children are brought out of the car by a young woman with a loose face. A man at the wheel of the car stares straight ahead. The children are silent and have very white skin. The woman carries a grocery bag full of something heavy. Her face hangs loose over the bag. She brings the bag and the white children to a wooden fencepost, by the field, by the highway. The children's hands, which are small, are placed on the wooden post. The woman tells the children to touch the post until the car returns. She gets in the car and the car leaves. There is a cow in the field near the fence. The children touch the post. The wind blows. Lots of cars go by. They stay that way all day.

It's 1970. A woman with hair like fire sits several rows from a movie theater's screen. A child in a dress sits beside her. A cartoon has begun. The child's eyes enter the cartoon. Behind the woman is darkness. A man sits behind the woman. He leans forward. His hands enter the woman's hair. He plays with the woman's hair, in the darkness. The cartoon's reflected light makes faces in the audience flicker: the woman's eyes are bright with fear. She sits absolutely still. The man plays with her red hair. The child does not look over at the woman. The theater's cartoons, previews of coming attractions, and feature presentation last almost three hours.

Alex Trebek goes around the "JEOPARDY!" studio wearing a button that says PAT SAJAK LOOKS LIKE A BADGER. He and Sajak play racquetball every Thursday.

It's 1986. California's night sky hangs bright and silent as an empty palace. Little white sequins make slow lines on streets far away under Faye's warm apartment.

Faye Goddard and Julie Smith lie in Faye's bed. They take turns lying on each other. They have sex. Faye's cries ring out like money against her penthouse apartment's walls of glass.

Faye and Julie cool each other down with wet towels. They stand naked at a glass wall and look at Los Angeles. Little bits of Los Angeles wink on and off, as light gets in the way of other light.

Julie and Faye lie in bed, as lovers. They compliment each other's bodies. They complain against the brevity of the night. They examine and reexamine, with a sort of unhappy enthusiasm, the little ignorances that necessarily, Julie says, line the path to any real connection between persons. Faye says she had liked Julie long before she knew that Julie liked her.

They go together to the *O.E.D.* to examine the entry for the word "like."

They hold each other. Julie is very white, her hair prickly short. The room's darkness is pocked with little bits of Los Angeles, at night, through glass. The dark drifts down around them and fits like a gardener's glove. It is incredibly romantic.

On 12 March 1988 it rains. Faye Goddard watches the freeway outside her mother's office window first darken and then shine with rain. Dee Goddard sits on the edge of her desk in stocking feet and looks out the window, too. "JEOPARDY!" 's director stands with the show's public relations coordinator. The key grip and cue-card lady huddle over some notes. Alex Trebek sits alone near the door in a canvas director's chair, drinking a can of soda. The room is reflected in the dark window.

"We need to know what you told her so we can know whether she'll come," Dee says.

"What we have here, Faye, is a twenty-minutes-tops type of thing," says the director, looking at the watch on the underside of her wrist. "Then we're going to be in for at least another hour's setup and studio time. Or we're short a slot, meaning satellite and mailing overruns."

"Not to mention a boy who's half catatonic with terror and general neurosis right this very minute," Muffy deMott, the P.R. co-ordinator, says softly. "Last I saw, he was fetal on the floor outside Makeup."

Faye closes her eyes.

"My husband is watching him," says the director.

"Thank you ever so much, Janet," Dee Goddard says to the director. She looks down at her clipboard. "All the others for the four slots are here?"

"Everybody who's signed up. Most we've ever had. Plus a rather scary retired WAC who's not even tentatively slotted till late April. Says she can't wait any longer to get at Julie."

"But no Julie," says Muffy deMott.

Dee squints at her clipboard. "So how many is that all together, then?"

"Nine," Faye says softly. She feels at the sides of her hair.

"We got nine," says the director; "enough for at least the full four slots with a turnaround of two per slot." The rain on the aluminum roof of the Merv Griffin Enterprises building makes a sound in this room, like the frying of distant meat.

"And I'm sure they're primed," Faye says. She looks at the backs of her hands, in her lap. "What with Janet assuming the poor kid will bump her. Your new mystery data guru."

"Don't confuse the difference between me, on one hand, and what I'm told to do," says the director.

"He won't bump her," the key grip says, shaking her head. She's chewing gum, stimulating a little worm of muscle at her temple.

Alex Trebek, looking at his digital watch, begins his pre-slot throat-clearing, a ritual. Everyone in the room looks at him.

Dee says, "Alex, perhaps you'd put the new contestants in the booth for now, tell them we may or may not be experiencing a slight delay. Thank them for their patience."

Alex rises, straightens his tie. His soda can rings out against the metal bottom of a wastebasket. He clears his throat.

"A good host and all that." Dee smiles kindly.

"Gotcha."

Alex leaves the door open. The sun breaks through the clouds outside. Palm trees drip and concrete glistens. Cars sheen by, their wipers on Sporadic. Janet Goddard, the director, looks down, pretends to study whatever she's holding. Faye knows that sudden sunlight makes her feel unattractive.

In the window, Faye sees Dee's outline check its own watch with a tiny motion. "Questions all lined up?" the outline asks.

"Easily four slots' worth," says the key grip; "categories set, all monitors on the board check. Joan's nailing down the sequence now."

"That's my job," Faye says.

"Your job," the director hisses, "is to tell Mommy here where your spooky little girlfriend could possibly be."

"Alex'll need all the cards at the podium very soon," Dee tells the grip.

"Is what your job is today." Janet stares at Faye's back.

Faye Goddard gives her ex-stepfather's wife, Janet Goddard, the finger, in the window. "One of those for every animal question," she says.

The director rises, calls Faye a bitch who looks like a praying mantis, and leaves through the open door, closing it.

"Bitch," Faye says.

Dee complains with a weak smile that she seems simply to be surrounded by bitches. Muffy deMott laughs, takes a seat in Alex's chair. Dee eases off the desk. A splinter snags and snaps on a pantyho. She assumes a sort of crouch next to her daughter, who is in the desk chair, at the window, her bare feet resting on the sill. Dee's knees crackle.

"If she's not coming," Dee says softly, "just tell me. Just so I can get a jump on fixing it with Merv. Baby."

It is true that Faye can see her mother's bright-faint image in the window. Here is her mother's middle-aged face, the immaculately colored and styled red hair, the sore-looking wrinkles that triangulate around her mouth and nose, trap and accumulate base and makeup as the face moves through the day. Dee's eyes are smoke-red, supported by deep circles, pouches of dark blood. Dee is pretty, except for the circles. This year Faye has been able to see the dark bags just starting to budge out from beneath her own eyes, which are her father's, dark brown and slightly thyroidic. Faye can smell Dee's breath. She cannot tell whether her mother has had anything to drink.

Faye Goddard is twenty-six; her mother is fifty.

Julie Smith is twenty.

Dee squeezes Faye's arm with a thin hand that's cold from the office.

Faye rubs at her nose. "She's not going to come, she told me. You'll have to bag it."

The key grip leaps for a ringing phone.

"I lied," says Faye.

"My girl." Dee pats the arm she's squeezed.

"I sure didn't hear anything," says Muffy deMott.

"Good," the grip is saying. "Get her into Makeup." She looks over at Dee. "You want her in Makeup?"

"You did good," Dee tells Faye, indicating the closed door.

"I don't think Mr. Griffin is well," says the cue-card lady.

"He and the boy deserve each other. We can throw in the WAC. We can call *her* General Neurosis."

Dee uses a thin hand to bring Faye's face close to her own. She kisses her gently. Their lips fit perfectly, Faye thinks suddenly. She shivers, in the air-conditioning.

"JEOPARDY!" QUEEN DETHRONED AFTER THREE-YEAR REIGN
—Headline, *Variety*, 13 March 1988.

"Let's all be there," says the television.

"Where else would I be?" asks Dee Goddard, in her chair, in her office, at night, in 1987.

"We bring good things to life," says the television.

"So did I," says Dee. "I did that. Just once."

Dee sits in her office at Merv Griffin Enterprises every weeknight and kills a tinkling pitcher of wet weak martinis. Her office walls are covered with store-bought aphorisms. Humpty Dumpty was pushed. When the going gets tough the tough go shopping. Also autographed photos. Dee and Bob Barker, when she wrote for "Truth or Consequences." Merv Griffin, giving her a plaque. Dee and Faye between Wink Martindale and Chuck Barris at a banquet.

Dee uses her remote matte-panel to switch from NBC to MTV,

on cable. Consumptive-looking boys in makeup play guitars that look more like jets or weapons than guitars.

"Does your husband still look at you the way he used to?" asks the television.

"Safe to say not," Dee says drily, drinking.

"She drinks too much," Julie Smith says to Faye.

"It's for the pain," Faye says, watching.

Julie looks through the remote viewer in Faye's office. "For killing the pain, or feeding it?"

Faye smiles.

Julie shakes her head. "It's mean to watch her like this."

"You deserve a break today," says the television. "Milk likes you. The more you hear, the better we sound. Aren't you hungry for a flame-broiled Whopper?"

"No I am not hungry for a flame-broiled Whopper," says Dee, sitting up straight in her chair. "No I am not hungry for it." Her glass falls out of her hand.

"It was nice what she said about you, though." Julie is looking at the side of Faye's face. "About bringing one good thing to life."

Faye smiles as she watches the viewer. "Did you hear about what Alex did today? Sajak says he and Alex are now at war. Alex got in the engineer's booth and played with the Applause sign all through "The Wheel"'s third slot. The audience was like applauding when people lost turns and stuff. Sajak says he's going to get him."

"So you don't forget," says the television. "Look at all you get."

"Wow," says Dee. She sleeps in her chair.

Faye and Julie sit on thin towels, in 1987, at the edge of the surf, nude, on a nude beach, south of Los Angeles, just past dawn. The sun is behind them. The early Pacific is lilac. The women's feet are washed and abandoned by a weak surf. The sky's color is kind of grotesque.

Julie has told Faye that she believes lovers go through three different stages in getting really to know one another. First they exchange anecdotes and inclinations. Then each tells the other what she believes. Then each observes the relation between what the other says she believes and what she in fact *does.*

Julie and Faye are exchanging anecdotes and inclinations for the twentieth straight month. Julie tells Faye that she, Julie, best likes: contemporary poetry, unkind women, words with univocal definitions, faces whose expressions change by the second, an obscure and limited-edition Canadian encyclopedia called *LaPlace's Guide to Total Data,* the gentle smell of powder that issues from the makeup compacts of older ladies, and the *O.E.D.*

"The encyclopedia turned out to be lucrative, I guess you'd have to say."

Julie sniffs air that smells yeasty. "It got to be just what the teachers tell you. The encyclopedia was my friend."

"As a child, you mean?" Faye touches Julie's arm.

"Men would just appear, one after the other. I felt so sorry for my mother. These blank, silent men, and she'd hook up with one after the other, and they'd move in. And not one single one could love my brother."

"Come here."

"Sometimes things would be ugly. I remember her leading a really ugly life. But she'd lock us in rooms when things got bad, to get us out of the way of it." Julie smiles to herself. "At first sometimes I remember she'd give me a straightedge and a pencil. To amuse myself. I could amuse myself with a straightedge for hours."

"I always liked straightedges, too."

"It makes worlds. I could make worlds out of lines. A sort of jagged magic. I'd spend all day. My brother watched."

There are no gulls on this beach at dawn. It's quiet. The tide is going out.

"But we had a set of these *LaPlace's Data Guides.* Her fourth husband sold them to salesmen who went door-to-door. I kept a few in every room she locked us in. They did, really and truly, become my friends. I got to be able to feel lines of consistency and inconsistency in them. I got to know them really well." Julie looks at Faye. "I won't apologize if that sounds stupid or dramatic."

"It doesn't sound stupid. It's no fun to be a kid with a damaged brother and a mother with an ugly life, and to be lonely. Not to mention locked up."

"See, though, it was *him* they were locking up. I was just there to watch him."

"An autistic brother simply cannot be decent company for somebody, no matter how much you loved him, is all I mean," Faye says, making an angle in the wet sand with her toe.

"Taking care of him took incredible amounts of time. He wasn't company, though; you're right. But I got so I wanted him with me. He got to be my job. I got so I associated him with my identity or something. My right to take up space. I wasn't even eight."

"I can't believe you don't hate her," Faye says.

"None of the men with her could stand to have him around. Even the ones who tried couldn't stand it after a while. He'd just stare and flap his arms. And they'd say sometimes when they looked in my mother's eyes they'd see him looking out." Julie shakes some sand out of her short hair. "Except he was bright. He was totally inside himself, but he was bright. He could stare at the same thing for hours and not be bored. And it turned out he could read. He read very slowly and never out loud. I don't know what the words seemed like to him." Julie looks at Faye. "I pretty much taught us both to read, with the encyclopedia. Early. The illustrations really helped."

"I can't believe you don't hate her."

Julie throws a pebble. "Except I don't, Faye."

"She abandoned you by a road because some guy told her to."

Julie looks at the divot where the pebble was. The divot melts. "She really loved this man who was with her." She shakes her head. "He made her leave *him*. I think she left me to look out for him. I'm thankful for that. If I'd been without him right then, I don't think there would have been any me left."

"Babe."

"*I'd* have been in hospitals all this time, instead of him."

"What, like he'd have been instantly unautistic if you weren't there to take care of him?"

Among things Julie Smith dislikes most are: greeting cards, adoptive parents who adopt without first looking inside themselves and evaluating their capacity for love, the smell of sulphur, John Updike, insects with antennae, and animals in general.

"What about kind women?"

"But insects are maybe the worst. Even if the insect stops moving, the antennae still wave around. The antennae never stop waving around. I can't stand that."

"I love you, Julie."

"I love you too, Faye."

"I couldn't believe I could ever love a woman like this."

Julie shakes her head at the Pacific. "Don't make me sad."

Faye watches a small antennaeless bug skate on legs thin as hairs across the glassy surface of a tidal pool. She clears her throat.

"OK," she says. "This is the only line on an American football field of which there is only one."

Julie laughs. "What is the fifty."

"This, the only month of the year without a national holiday, is named for the Roman emperor who . . ."

"What is August."

The sun gets higher; the blood goes out of the blue water.

The women move down to stay in the waves' reach.

"The ocean looks like a big blue dog to me, sometimes," Faye says, looking. Julie puts an arm around Faye's bare shoulders.

'We loved her like a daughter,' said "JEOPARDY!" public relations coordinator Muffy deMott. 'We'll be sorry to see her go. Nobody's ever influenced a game show like Ms. Smith influenced "JEOPARDY!"'
                                    —Article, *Variety*, 13 March 1988.

Weak waves hang, snap, slide. White fingers spill onto the beach and melt into the sand. Faye can see dark sand lighten beneath them as the water inside gets tugged back out with the retreating tide.

The beach settles and hisses as it pales. Faye is looking at the side of Julie Smith's face. Julie has the best skin Faye's ever seen on anyone anywhere. It's not just that it's so clear it's flawed, or that here in low sun off water it's the color of a good blush wine; it has the texture of something truly alive, an elastic softness, like a ripe sheath, a pod. It is vulnerable and has depth. It's stretched shiny and tight only over Julie's high curved cheekbones; the bones make her cheeks hollow, her eyes deep-set. The outlines of her face are like clefs, almost Slavic. Everything about her is sort of permeable: even the slim dark gap between her two front teeth seems a kind of slot, some recessive invitation. Julie has used the teeth and their gap to stimulate Faye with a gentle deftness Faye would not have believed.

Julie has looked up. "Why, though?"

Faye looks blankly, shakes her head.

"Poetry, you were talking about." Julie smiles, touching Faye's cheek.

Faye lights a cigarette in the wind. "I've just never liked it. It beats around bushes. Even when I like it, it's nothing more than a really oblique way of saying the obvious, it seems like."

Julie grins. Her front teeth have a gap. "Olé," she says. "But consider how very, very few of us have the equipment to deal with the obvious."

Faye laughs. She wets a finger and makes a scoreboard mark in the air. They both laugh. An anomalous wave breaks big in the surf. Faye's finger tastes like smoke and salt.

Pat Sajak and Alex Trebek and Bert Convy sit around, in slacks and loosened neckties, in the Merv Griffin Entertainment executive lounge, in the morning, watching a tape of last year's World Series. On the lounge's giant screen a batter flails at a low pitch.

"That was low," Trebek says.

Bert Convy, who is soaking his contact lenses, squints at the replay.

Trebek sits up straight. "Name the best low-ball hitter of all time."

"Joe Pepitone," Sajak says without hesitation.

Trebek looks incredulous. "Joe Pepitone?"

"Willie Stargell was a great low-ball hitter," says Convy. The other two men ignore him.

"Reggie Jackson was great," Sajak muses.

"Still is," Trebek says, looking absently at his nails.

A game show host has a fairly easy professional life. All five of a week's slots can be shot in one long day. Usually one hard week a month is spent on performance work at the studio. The rest of the host's time is his own. Bert Convy makes the rounds of car shows and mall openings and "Love Boat" episodes and is a millionaire several times over. Pat Sajak plays phenomenal racquetball, and gardens, and is learning his third language by mail. Alex, known in the industry as the most dedicated host since Bill Cullen, is to be seen lurking almost daily in some area of the MGE facility, reading, throat-clearing, grooming, worrying.

There's a hit. Sajak throws a can of soda at the screen. Trebek and Convy laugh.

Sajak looks over at Bert Convy. "How's that tooth, Bert?"

Convy's hand strays to his mouth. "Still discolored," he says grimly.

Trebek looks up. "You've got a discolored tooth?"

Convy feels at a bared canine. "A temporary thing. Already clearing up." He narrows his eyes at Alex Trebek. "Just don't tell Merv about it."

Trebek looks around, as if to see who Convy is talking to. "Me? This guy right here? Do I look like that sort of person?"

"You look like a game show host."

Trebek smiles broadly. "Probably because of my perfect and beautiful and flawless teeth."

"Bastard," mutters Convy.

Sajak tells them both to pipe down.

The dynamics of the connection between Faye Goddard and Julie Smith tend, those around them find, to resist clear articulation. Faye is twenty-six and has worked Research on the "JEOPARDY!" staff for the past forty months. Julie is twenty, has foster parents in La Jolla, and has retained her "JEOPARDY!" championship through over seven hundred market-dominating slots.

Forty months ago, game-show production mogul Merv Griffin decided to bring the popular game "JEOPARDY!" back from syndicated oblivion, to retire Art Flemming in favor of the waxily handsome, fairly distinguished, and prenominately dedicated Alex Trebek, the former model who'd made his bones in the game show industry hosting the short-lived "High Rollers" for Barris/NBC. Dee Goddard, who'd written for shows as old as "Truth or Consequences" and "Name That Tune," had worked Promotion/Distribution on "The Joker's Wild," and had finally produced the commercially shaky but critically acclaimed "Gambit," was hired by MGE as the new "JEOPARDY!"'s production executive. A period of disordered tension followed Griffin's decision to name Janet Lerner Goddard—forty-eight, winner of two Clios, but also the wife of Dee's former husband—as director of the revised show; and in fact Dee is persuaded to stay only when Merv Griffin's executive assistant puts in a personal call to New York, where Faye Goddard, having left Bryn Mawr in 1982 with a degree in library science, is doing an editorial stint at *Puzzle* magazine. Merv's right-hand man offers to put Faye on staff at "JEOPARDY!" as Category-/Question-researcher.

Faye works for her mother.

Summer, 1985, Faye has been on the "JEOPARDY!" team maybe four months when a soft-spoken and weirdly pretty young woman comes in off the freeway with a dirty jeans jacket, a backpack, and a *Times* classified ad detailing an MGE contestant search. The girl says she wants "JEOPARDY!"; she's been told she has a head for data. Faye interviews her and is mildly intrigued. The girl gets a solid but by no means spectacular score on a CBE general knowledge quiz, this particular version of which turns out to feature an important zoology section. Julie Smith barely makes it into an audition round.

In a taped audition round, flanked by a swarthy Shriner from Encino and a twig-thin Redding librarian with a towering blond wig, Julie takes the game by a wide margin, but has trouble speaking clearly into her microphone, as well as difficulty with the quirky and distinctive "JEOPARDY!" inversion by which the host "asks" the answer and a contestant supplies the appropriate question. Faye gives Julie an audition score of three out of five. Usually only fives and fours are to be called back. But Alex Trebek, who spends at least part of his free time haunting audition rounds, likes the girl, even after she turns down his invitation for a cola at the MGE commissary; and Dee Goddard and Muffy deMott pick Julie out for special mention from among eighteen other prospectives on the audition tape; and no one on the staff of a program still in its stressful initial struggle to break back into a respectable market share has anything against hauntingly attractive young female contestants. Etc. Julie Smith is called back for insertion into the contestant rotation sometime in early September 1985.

"JEOPARDY!" slots forty-six through forty-nine are shot on 17 September. Ms. Julie Smith of Los Angeles first appears in the forty-sixth slot. No one can quite remember who the reigning champion was at that time.

Palindromes, Musical Astrology, The Eighteenth Century, Famous Edwards, The Bible, Fashion History, States of Mind, Sports Without Balls.

Julie runs the board in both rounds. Every question. Never been done before, even under Flemming. The other two contestants, slack and gray, have to be helped off-stage. Julie wins $22,500, every buck on the board, in half an hour. She earns no more in this first match only because a flustered Alex Trebek declares the Final Jeopardy wagering round moot, Julie Smith having no incentive to bet any of her winnings against opponents' scores of $0 and − $400, respectively. A wide-eyed and grinning Trebek doffs a pretend cap to a blank-faced Julie as electric bongos rattle to the running of the closing credits.

Ten minutes later Faye Goddard locates a missing Julie Smith in a remote section of the contestants' dressing area. (Returning contestants are required to change clothes between each slot, conducing to the illusion that they've "come back again tomorrow.") It's time for "JEOPARDY!" slot forty-seven. A crown to defend and all that. Julie sits staring at herself in a harsh makeup mirror framed with glowing bulbs, her face loose and expressionless. She has trouble reacting to stimuli. Faye has to get her a wet cloth and talk her through dressing and practically carry her upstairs to the set.

Faye is in the engineer's booth, trying to communicate to her mother her doubts about whether the strange new champion can make it through another televised round, when Janet Goddard calmly directs her attention to the monitor. Julie is eating slot forty-seven and spitting it out in little pieces. Lady Bird Johnson's real first name turns out to be Claudia. The Florida city that produces more Havana cigars than all of Cuba is revealed to be Tampa. Julie's finger abuses the buzzer. She is on Alex's answers with the appropriate questions before he can even end-punctuate his clues. The first-round board is taken. Janet cuts to commercial. Julie sits at her little desk, staring out at a hushed studio audience.

Faye and Dee watch Julie as the red lights light and Trebek's face falls into the worn creases of a professional smile. Something happens to Julie Smith when the red lights light. Just a something. The girl who gets a three-score and who stares with no expression is gone. Every concavity in that person now looks to have come convex. The camera lingers on her. It seems to ogle. Often Julie appears on-screen while Trebek is still reading a clue. Her face, on-screen, gives off an odd lambent UHF flicker; her expression, brightly serene, radiates a sort of oneness with the board's data.

Trebek manipulates the knot of his tie. Faye knows he feels the something, the odd, focused flux in the game's flow. The studio audience gasps and whispers as Julie supplies the Latin name for the common radish.

"No one knows the Latin word for radish," Faye says to Dee. "That's one of those deadly ones I put in on purpose in every game."

The other two contestants' postures deteriorate. Someone in the audience loudly calls Julie's name.

Trebek, who has never before had an audience get away from him, gets more and more flustered. He uses forty expensive seconds relating a tired anecdote involving a Dodgers game he saw with Tom Brokaw. The audience hoots impatiently for the game to continue.

"Bad feeling, here," Faye whispers. Dee ignores her, bends to the monitor.

Janet signals Alex for a break. Moist and upstaged, Alex promises America that he'll be right back, that he's eager to inquire on-air about the tremendous Ms. Smith and the even more tremendous personal sacrifices she must have made to have absorbed so much data at such a tender age.

"JEOPARDY!" breaks for a Triscuit advertisement. Faye and Dee stare at the monitor in horror. The studio audience is transfixed as Julie Smith's face crumples like a Kleenex in a pocket. She begins silently to weep. Tears move down the clefs of her cheeks and drip into her mike, where for some reason they hiss faintly. Janet, in the booth, is at a loss. Faye is sent for a cold compress but can't make the set in time. The lights light. America watches Julie Smith murder every question on the Double Jeopardy board, her face and vinyl jacket slickered with tears. Trebek, suddenly and cumbrously cool, pretends he notices nothing, though he never asks (and never in hundreds of slots does he ask) Julie Smith any of the promised personal questions.

The game unfolds. Faye watched a new, third Julie respond to answer after answer. Julie's face dries, hardens. She is looking at Trebek with eyes narrowed to the width of paper cuts.

In Final Jeopardy, her opponents again cashless, Julie coolly overrides Trebek's moot-motion and bets her entire twenty-two-five on the fact that the first part of Peking Man discovered was a parenthesis-shaped fragment of mandible. She ends with $45,000. Alex pretends to genuflect. The audience applauds. There are bongos. And in a closing moment that Faye Goddard owns, captured in a bright glossy that hangs over her iron desk, Julie Smith, on television, calmly and deliberately gives Alex Trebek the finger. A nation goes wild. The switchboards at MGE and NBC begin jangled two-day symphonies. Pat Sajak sends three-dozen long-stemmed reds to Julie's dressing table. The market share for the last segment of "JEOPARDY!" slot forty-seven is a fifty—on a par with Super Bowls and assassinations. This is 17 September 1985.

"My favorite word," says Alex Trebek, "is *moist*. It is my favorite word, especially when used in combination with my second-favorite word, which is *induce*." He looks at the doctor. "I'm just associating. Is it OK if I just associate?"

Alex Trebek's psychiatrist says nothing.

"A dream," says Trebek. "I have this recurring dream where I'm standing outside the window of a restaurant, watching a chef flip pancakes. Except it turns out they're not pancakes—they're faces. I'm watching a guy in a chef's hat flip faces with a spatula."

The psychiatrist makes a church steeple with his fingers and contemplates the steeple.

"I think I'm just tired," says Trebek. "I think I'm just bone weary. I continue to worry about my smile. That it's starting to maybe be a tired smile. Which is *not* an inviting smile, which is professionally worrying." He clears his throat. "And it's the *worry* I think that's making me tired in the first place. It's like a vicious smiling-circle."

"This girl you work with," says the doctor.

"And Convy reveals today that he's getting a discolored tooth," Trebek says. "Tell me *that* augurs well, why don't you."

"This contestant you talk about all the time."

"She lost," Trebek says, rubbing the bridge of his nose. "She lost yesterday. Don't you read papers, ever? She lost to her own brother, after Janet and Merv's exec snuck the damaged little bastard in with a rigged five audition and a board just crawling with animal questions."

The psychiatrist hikes his eyebrows a little. They are black and angled, almost hinged.

"Queer story behind that," Trebek says, manipulating a broad bright cufflink to produce lines of reflected window-light on the ceiling's tile. "I got it about fourth-hand, but still. Parents abandoned the children, as kids. There was the girl and her brother, Lunt. Can you imagine a champion named Lunt? Lunt was autistic. Autistic to where this was like a mannequin of a kid instead of a kid. Muffy said Faye said the girl used to carry him around like a suitcase. Then finally he and the girl got abandoned out in the middle of nowhere somewhere. By the parents. Grisly. She got adopted and the brother was institutionalized. In a state institution. This hopelessly autistic kid, who it turns out he's got the whole *LaPlace's Data Guide* memorized. They were both forced to somehow memorize this thing, as kids. And I thought *I* had a rotten childhood, boy." Trebek shakes his head. "But he got put away, and the girl got adopted by some people in La Jolla who were not, from the sense I get, princes among men. She ran away. She got on the show. She kicked ass. She was fair and a good sport and took no crapola. She used her prize money to pay these staggering bills for Lunt's autism. Moved him to a private hospital in the desert that was supposed to specialize in sort of . . . *yanking* people outside themselves. Into the world." Trebek clears his throat.

"And I guess they yanked him OK," he says, "at least to where he could talk. Though he still hides his head under his arm whenever things get tense. Plus he's weird-looking. And but he comes and bumps her off with this torrent of zoology data." Trebek plays with the cufflink. "And she's gone."

"You said in our last hour together that you thought you loved her."

"She's a lesbian," Trebek says wearily. "She's a lesbian through and through. I think she's one of those political lesbians. You know the kind? The kind with the anger? She looks at men like they're unsightly stains on the air. Plus she's involved with our ditz of a head researcher, which if you don't think the F.C.C. took a dim view of *that* little liaison you've got another. . . ."

"Free-associate," orders the doctor.

"Image association?"

"I have no problem with that."

"I invited the girl for coffee, or a Tab, years ago, right at the start, in the commissary, and she gave me this haunting, moisture-inducing look. Then tells me she could never imbibe caffeine with a man who wore a digital watch. The hell she says. She gave me the finger on national television. She's practically got a crewcut. Sometimes she looks like a vampire. Once, in the contestant booth—the contestant booth is where we keep all the contestants for all the slots—once one of the lights in the booth was flickering, they're fluorescent lights—and she said to get her the hell out of that booth, that flickering fluorescence made her feel like she was in a nightmare. And there *was* a sort of nightmary quality to that light, I remember. It was like there was a pulse in the neon. Like blood. Everybody in the booth got nervous." Trebek strokes his mustache. "Odd girl. Something odd about her. When she smiled things got bright, too focused. It took the fun out of it, somehow.

"I love her, I think," Trebek says. "She has a way with a piece of data. To see her with an answer . . . Is there such a thing as an intellectual caress? I think of us together: seas part, stars shine spotlights. . . ."

"And this researcher she's involved with?"

"Nice enough girl. A thick, friendly girl. Not fantastically bright. A little emotional. Has this adoration-versus-loathing thing with her mother." Trebek ponders. "My opinion: Faye is the sort of girl who's constantly surfing on her emotions. You know? Not really in control of where they take her, but not quite ever wiping out, yet, either. A psychic surfer. But scary-looking, for so young. These black, bulging, buggy eyes. Perfectly round and black. Impressive breasts, though."

"Mother-conflicts?"

"Faye's mother is one very tense production exec. Spends far too much time obsessing about not obsessing about the fact that our director is her ex-husband's wife."

"A woman?"

"Janet Lerner Goddard. Worst director I've ever worked with. Dee hates her. Janet likes to play with Dee's head; it's a head that admittedly tends to be full of gin. Janet likes to put little trinkety reminders of Dee's ex in Dee's mailbox at the office. Old bills, tie clips. She plays with Dee's mind. Dee's obsessing herself into stasis. She's barely able to even function at work anymore."

"Image associated with this person?"

"You know those ultra-modern rifles, where the mechanisms of aiming far outnumber those of firing? Dee's like that. God am I worried about potentially ever being like that."

The psychiatrist thinks they have done all they can for today. He shows Trebek the door.

"I also really like the word *bedizen*," Trebek says.

In those first fall weeks of 1985, a public that grows with each Nielsen sweep discerns only two areas of even potential competitive vulnerability in Ms. Julie Smith of Los Angeles. One has to do with animals. Julie is simply unable to respond to clues about animals. In her fourth slot, categories in Double Jeopardy include Marsupials and Zoological Songs, and an eidetic pharmacist from Westwood pushes Julie all the way to Final Jeopardy before she crushes him with a bold bet on Eva Braun's shoe size.

In her fifth slot (and what is, according to the game's publicized rules, to be her last—if a winner, she'll be retired as a five-time champion), Julie goes up against a spectacularly fat Berkeley mailman who claims to be a co-founder of the California chapter of MENSA. The third contestant is a neurasthenic (but gorgeous— Alex keeps straightening his tie) Fullerton stenographer who wipes her lips compulsively on the sleeve of her blouse. The stenographer quickly accumulates a negative score, and becomes hysterically anxious during the second commercial break, convinced by the skunked, vengeful, and whispering mailman that she will have to pay "JEOP-ARDY!" the nine hundred dollars she's down before they will let her leave the set. Faye dashes out during Off-Air; the woman cannot seem to be reassured. She keeps looking wildly at the exits as Faye runs off-stage and the red lights light.

A bell initiates Double Jeopardy. Julie, refusing to meet the audience's eye, begins pausing a bit before she reponds to Alex.

She leaves openings. Only the mailman capitalizes. Julie stays ahead of him. Faye watches the stenographer, who is clearly keeping it together only through enormous exercise of will. The mailman closes on Julie. Julie assumes a look of distaste and runs the board for several minutes, down to the very last answer, Ancient Rome For A Thousand: author of *De Oratore* who was executed by Octavian in 43 B.C. Julie's finger hovers over the buzzer; she looks to the stenographer. The mailman's eyes are closed in data-search. The stenographer's head snaps up. She looks wildly at Julie and buzzes in with Who is Tully. There is a silence. Trebek looks at his index card. He shakes his head. The stenographer goes to − $1,900 and seems to suffer something resembling a petit mal seizure.

Faye watches Julie Smith buzz in now and whisper into her mike that, though Alex was doubtless looking for the question Who is Cicero, in point of fact one Marcus Tullius Cicero, 106–43 B.C., was known variously as both Cicero *and* Tully. Just as Augustus's less-common appellation is Octavian, she points out, indicating the card in the host's hand. Trebek looks at the card. Faye flies to the Resource Room. The verdict takes only seconds. The stenographer gets the credit and the cash. Out of the emotional red, she hugs Julie on-camera. The mailman fingers his lapels. Julie smiles a really magnificent smile. Alex, generally moved, declaims briefly on the spirit of good clean competition he's proud to have witnessed here today. Final Jeopardy sees Julie effect the utter annihilation of the mailman, who is under the impression that the first literature in India was written by Kipling. The slot pulls down a sixty-five share. Hardly anyone notices Julie's and the stenographer's exchange of phone numbers as the bongos play. Faye gets a tongue-lashing from Muffy deMott on the inestimable importance of researching all possible questions to a given answer. The shot of Julie buzzing in with the correction makes the "Newsmakers" column of *Newsweek*.

That night Merv Griffin's executive assistant calls an emergency policy meeting of the whole staff. MGE's best minds take counsel. Alex and Faye are invited to sit in. Faye calls downstairs for coffee and Cokes and Merv's special seltzer.

Griffin murmurs to his right-hand man. His man has a shiny face and a black toupee. The man nods, rises:

"Can't let her go. Too good. Too hot. She's become the whole show. Look at these figures." He brandishes figures.

"Rules, though," says the director. "Five slots, retire undefeated, come back for Champion's Tourney in April. Annual event. Tradition. Art Flemming. Fairness to whole contestant pool. An ethics type of thing."

Griffin whispers into his shiny man's ear. Again the man rises.

"Balls," the shiny man says to the director. "The girl's magic. Figures do not lie. The Triscuit people have offered to double the price on thirty-second spots, long as she stays." He smiles with his mouth but not his eyes, Faye sees. "Shoot, Janet, we could just call this the Julia Smith Show and still make mints."

"Julie," says Faye.

"Absolutely."

Griffin whispers up at his man.

"Need Merv mention we should all see substantial salary and benefit incentives at work here?" says the shiny man, flipping a watch fob. "A chance here to be industry heroes. Heroines. MGE a Camelot. You, all of you, knights." Looks around. "Scratch that. Queens. Entertainment Amazons."

"You don't get rid of a sixty share without a fight," says Dee, who's seated next to Faye, sipping at what looks to Faye a little too much like water. The director whispers something in Muffy deMott's ear.

There's a silence. Griffin rises to stand with his man. "I've seen the tapes, and I'm impressed as I've never been impressed before. She's like some lens, a filter for that great unorganized force that some in the industry have spent their whole lives trying to locate and focus." This is Merv Griffin saying this. Eyes around the table are lowered. "What is that force?" Merv asks quietly. Looks around. He and his man sit back down.

Alex goes to the door to relieve a winded gofer of refreshments.

Griffin whispers and the shiny man rises. "Merv posits that this force, ladies, gentleman, is the capacity of facts to transcend their internal factual limitations and become, in and of themselves, meaning, feeling. This girl not only kicks facts in the ass. This girl informs trivia with import. She makes it human, something with the power to emote, evoke, induce, cathart. She gives the game the simultaneous transparency and mystery all of us in the industry have groped for, for decades. A sort of union of contestantorial head, heart, gut, buzzer finger. She is, or can become, the game show incarnate. She is mystery."

"What, like a cult thing?" Alex Trebek asks, opening a can of soda at arm's length.

Merv Griffin gives Trebek a cold stare.

Merv's man's face gleams. "See that window?" he says. "That's where the rules go. Out the window." Feels at his nose. "Does your conscientious entertainer retain—and here I say think about all the implications of 'retention,' here"—looking at Janet—"I mean does he cling blindly to rules for their own sake when the very goal and purpose and *idea* of those rules walks right in off the street and into the hearts of every Triscuit consumer in the free world?"

"Safe to say not," Dee says drily.

The man: "So here's the scoop. She stays till she's bumped. We cannot and will not give her any help on-air. Off-air she gets anything within what Merv defines as reason. We get her to play a little ball, go easy on the board when strategy allows, give the other players a bit of a shot. We tell her we want to play ball. DeMott here is one of our carrots."

Muffy deMott wipes her mouth on a commissary napkin. "I'm a carrot?"

"If the girl plays ball, then you, deMott, you start in on helping the kid shelter her income. Tell her we'll give her shelter under MGE. Take her from the seventy bracket to something more like a twenty. Kapisch? She's got to play ball, with a carrot like that."

"She sends all her money to a hospital her brother's in," Faye says softly, next to her mother.

"Hospital?" Merv Griffin asks. "What hospital?"

Faye looks at Griffin. "All she told me was her brother was in Arizona in a hospital because he has trouble living in the world."

"The world?" Griffin asks. He looks at his man.

Griffin's man touches his wig carefully, looks at Muffy. "Get on that, deMott," he says. "This hospitalized brother thing. If it's good P.R., see that it's P.'d. Take the girl aside. Fill her in. Tell her about the rules and the window. Tell her she's here as long as she can hang." A significant pause. "Tell her Merv might want to do lunch, at some point."

Muffy looks at Faye. "All right."

Merv Griffin glances at his watch. Everyone is instantly up. Papers are shuffled.

"Dee," Merv says from his chair, absently fingering a canine tooth. "You and your daughter stay for a moment, please."

Idaho, Coins, Truffaut, Patron Saints, Historical Cocktails, Animals, Winter Sports, 1879, The French Revolution, Botanical Songs, The Talmud, 'Nuts to You.'

One contestant, slot two-eighty-seven, 4 December 1986, is a bespectacled teenage boy with a smear of acne and a shallow chest in a faded Mozart T-shirt; he claims on-air to have revised the Western solar calendar into complete isomorphism with the atomic clocks at the U.S. Bureau of Time Measurement in Washington. He eyes Julie beadily. Any and all of his winnings, he says, will go toward realizing his father's fantasy. His father's fantasy turns out to be a spa, in the back yard of the family's Orange County home, with an elephant on permanent duty at either side of the spa, spouting.

"God am I tired," Alex intones to Faye over a soda and handkerchief at the third commercial break. Past Alex, Faye sees Julie, at her little desk, looking out at the studio audience. People in the audience vie for her attention.

The boy's hopes for elephants are dashed in Final Jeopardy. He claims shrilly that the Islamic week specifies no particular sabbath.

"Friday," Julie whispers.

Alex cues bongos, asks the audience to consider the fact that Californians never ("*never*," he emphasizes) seem to face east.

"Just the facts on the brother who can't live in the world is all I want," Merv Griffin says, pushing at his cuticles with a paper clip. Dee makes soft sounds of assent.

"The kid's autistic," Faye says. "I can't really see why you'd want data on a damaged person."

Merv continues to address himself to Dee. "What's wrong with him exactly. Are there different degrees of autisticness. Can he talk. What's his prognosis. Would he excite pathos. Does he look too much like the girl. And et cetera."

"We want total data on Smith's brother," iterates the gleaming face of Merv's man.

"Why?"

Dee looks at the empty glass in her hand.

"The potential point," Merv murmurs, "is can the brother do with a datum what she can do with a datum." He switches the paper clip to his left hand. "Does the fact that he has, as Faye here put it, trouble being in the world, together with what have to be impressive genetics, by association," he smiles, "add up to mystery status? Game-show incarnation?" He works a cuticle. "Can he do what she can do?"

"Imagine the possibilities," says the shiny man. "We're looking way down the road on this thing. A climax type of deal, right? Antigone-thing. If she's going to get bumped sometime, we obviously want a bumper with the same kind of draw. The brother's expensive hospitalization at the sister's selfless expense is already great P.R."

"Is he mystery, I want to know," says Merv.

"He's *austistic*," Faye says, staring bug-eyed. "Meaning they're like trying to teach him just to talk coherently. How not to go into convulsions whenever somebody looks at him. You're thinking about maybe trying to put him on the air?"

Merv's man stands at the dark office window. "Imagine sustaining the mystery beyond the individual girl herself, is what Merv means. The mystery of total data, that mystery made a sort of antic, ontic self-perpetuation. We're talking fact sustaining feeling, right through the change that inevitably attends all feeling, Faye."

"We're thinking perpetuation, is what we're thinking," says Merv. "Every thumb over at Triscuit is up, on this one."

Dee's posture keeps deteriorating as they stand there.

"Remember, ladies," Merv's man says from the window. "You're either part of the solution, or you're part of the precipitate." He guffaws. Griffin slaps his knee.

Nine months later Faye is back in the office of Griffin's man. The man has different hair. He says:

"I say two words to you, Faye. I say F.C.C., and I say separate apartments. We do not I repeat not need even a whiff of scandal. We do not need a "Sixty-Four-Thousand-Dollar-Question"–type-scandal kind of deal. Am I right? So I say to you F.C.C., and separate pads.

"You do good research, Faye. We treasure you here. I've personally heard Merv use the word *treasure* in connection with your name."

"I don't give her any answers," Faye says. The man nods vigorously.

Faye looks at the man. "She doesn't need them."

"All I'm saying to you is let's make our dirty linen a private matter," says the shiny man. "Treasure or no. So I say keep your lovely glass apartment, that I hear so much about."

That first year, ratings slip a bit, as they always do. They level out at incredible. MGE stock splits three times in nine months. Alex buys a car so expensive he's worried about driving it. He takes the bus to work. Dee and the cue-card lady acquire property in the canyons. Faye explores IRAs with the help of Muffy deMott. Julie moves to a bungalow in Burbank, continues to live on fruit and seeds, and sends everything after her minimal, post-shelter taxes to the Palo Verde Psychiatric Hospital in Tucson. She turns down a *People* cover. Faye explains to the *People* people that Julie is basically a private person.

It quickly gets to the point where Julie can't go out anywhere without some sort of disguise. Faye helps her select a mustache and explains to her about not too much glue.

Extrapolation from LAX Airport flight-plan data yields a scenario in which Merv Griffin's shiny man, "JEOPARDY!" director Janet Goddard, and a Mr. Mel Goddard, who works subsidiary rights at Screen Gems, board the shiny man's new Piper Cub on the afternoon of 17 September 1987, fly nonstop to Tucson, Arizona, and enjoy a three-day stay among flying ants and black spiders and unimaginable traffic and several sizzling, carbonated summer monsoons.

> Dethroning Ms. Smith after 700-plus victories last night was one 'Mr. Lunt' of Arizona, a young man whose habit of hiding his head under his arm at crucial moments detracted not at all from the virtuosity with which he worked a buzzer and board that had, for years, been the champion's own.
>
> —Article, *Variety*, 13 March 1988.

> WHAT NEXT FOR SMITH?
>
> —Headline, *Variety*, 14 March 1988.

Los Angeles at noon today in 1987 is really hot. A mailman in mailman shorts and wool knee socks sits eating his lunch in the black guts of an open mailbox. Air shimmers over the concrete like fuel. Sunglasses ride every face in sight.

Faye and Julie are walking around west L.A. Faye wears a bathing suit and rubber thongs. Her thongs squeak and slap.

"You did *what?*" Faye says. "You did *what* for a living before you saw our ad?"

"A psychology professor at UCLA was doing tests on the output of human saliva in response to different stimuli. I was a professional subject."

"You were a professional salivator?"

"It paid me, Faye. I was seventeen. I'd had to hitch from La Jolla. I had no money, no place to stay. I ate seeds."

"What, he'd like ring bells or wave chocolate at you and see if you'd drool?"

Julie laughs, gap-toothed, in mustache and sunglasses, her short spiked hair hidden under a safari hat. "Not exactly."

"So what, then?"

Faye's thongs squeak and slap.

"Your shoes sound like sex," Julie says.

"Don't think even one day doesn't go by," says veteran reference-book sales representative P. Craig Lunt in the office of the game-show production mogul who's looking studiously down, manipulating a plastic disk, trying to get a BB in the mouth of a clown.

Dee Goddard and Muffy deMott sit in Dee's office, overlooking the freeway, today, at noon, in the air-conditioning, with a pitcher of martinis, watching the "All New Newlywed Game."

"It's the 'All New Newlywed Game'!" says the television.

"Weak show," says Dee. "All they do on this show is humiliate newlyweds. A series of low gags."

"I like this show," Muffy says, reaching for the pitcher that's refrigerating in front of the air-conditioner. "It's people's own fault if they're going to let Bob Eubanks embarrass them on national daytime just for a drier or a skimobile."

"Cheap show. Mel got a look at their books once. A really . . . a really chintzy operation." Dee jiggles a lemon twist.

Bob Eubanks' head fills the screen.

"Jesus will you look at the size of the head on that guy."

"Youthful-looking, though," Muffy muses. "He never seems to age. I wonder how he does it."

"He's traded his soul for his face. He worships bright knives. He makes sacrifices to dark masters on behalf of his face."

Muffy looks at Dee.

"A special grand prize chosen just for you," says the television.

Dee leans forward. "Will you just look at that head. His forehead simply *dominates* the whole shot. They must need a special lens."

"I sort of like him. He's sort of funny."

"I'm just glad he's on the inside of the set, and I'm on the outside, and I can turn him off whenever I want."

Muffy holds her drink up to the window's light and looks at it. "And of course you never lie there awake in the dark considering the possibility that it's the other way around."

Dee crosses her ankles under her chair. "Dear child, we are in this business precisely to make sure that that is *not* a possibility."

They both laugh.

"You hear stories, though," Muffy says. "About these lonely or somehow disturbed people who've had only the TV all their lives, their parents or whomever started them right off by plunking them down in front of the set, and as they get older the TV comes to be their whole emotional world, it's all they have, and it becomes in a way their whole way of defining themselves as existents, with a distinct identity, that they're outside the set, and everything else is inside the set." She sips.

"Stay right where you are," says the television.

"And then you hear about how every once in a while one of them gets on TV somehow. By accident," says Muffy. "There's a shot of them in the crowd at a ball game, or they're interviewed on the street about a referendum or something, and they go home and plunk right down in front of the set, and all of a sudden they look and they're *inside* the set." Muffy pushes her glasses up. "And sometimes you hear about how it drives them mad, sometimes."

"There ought to be special insurance for that or something," Dee says, tinkling the ice in the pitcher.

"Maybe that's an idea."

Dee looks around. "You seen the vermouth around here any-place?"

Julie and Faye walk past a stucco house the color of Pepto-Bismol. A VW bus is backing out of the driveway. It sings the high sad song of the Volkswagen-in-reverse. Faye wipes her forehead with her arm. She feels moist and sticky, something hot in a Baggie.

"But so I don't know what to tell them," she says.

"Being involved with a woman doesn't automatically make you a lesbian," says Julie.

"It doesn't make me Marie Osmond, either, though."

Julie laughs. "A cross you'll have to bear." She takes Faye's hand.

Julie and Faye take walks a lot. Faye drives over to Julie's place and helps her into her disguise. Julie wears a mustache and hat, Bermuda shorts, a Hawaiian shirt, and a Nikon.

"Except what if I am a lesbian?" Faye asks. She looks at a small child methodically punching a mild-faced father in the back of the thigh while the father buys Häagen-Dazs from a vendor. "I mean, what if I am a lesbian, and people ask me why I'm a lesbian?" Faye releases Julie's hand to pinch sweat off her upper lip. "What do I say if they ask me why?"

"You anticipate a whole lot of people questioning you about your sexuality?" Julie asks. "Or are there particular people you're worried about?"

Faye doesn't say anything.

Julie looks at her. "I can't believe you really even care."

"Maybe I do. What questions I care about aren't really your business. You're why I might be a lesbian; I'm just asking you to tell me what I can say."

Julie shrugs. "Say whatever you want." She has to keep straightening her mustache, from the heat. "Say lesbianism is simply one kind of response to Otherness. Say the whole point of love is to try to get your fingers through the holes in the lover's mask. To get some kind of hold on the mask, and who cares how you do it."

"I don't want to hear mask theories, Julie," Faye says. "I want to hear what I should really tell people."

"Why don't you just tell me which people you're so worried about."

Faye doesn't say anything. A very large man walks by, his face red as steak, his cowboy boots new, a huge tin star pinned to the lapel of his business suit.

Julie starts to smile.

"Don't smile," says Faye.

They walk in silence. The sky is clear and spread way out. It shines in its own sun, glassy as aftershave.

Julie smiles to herself, under her hat. The smile's cold. "You know what's fun, if you want to have fun," she says, "is to make up explanations. Give people reasons, if they want reasons. Anything you want. Make reasons up. It'll surprise you—the more improbable the reason, the more satisfied people will be."

"That's fun?"

"I guarantee you it's more fun than twirling with worry over the whole thing."

"Julie?" Faye says suddenly. "What about if you lose, sometime? Do we stay together? Or does our being together depend on the show?"

A woman in terry-cloth shorts is giving Julie a pretty brazen look.

Julie looks away, in her hat.

"Here's one," she says. "If people ask, you can give them this one. You fall totally in love with a man who tells you he's totally in love with you, too. He's older. He's important in terms of business. You give him all of yourself. He goes to France, on important business. He won't let you come. You wait for days and don't hear from him. You call him in France, and a woman's voice says a French hello on the phone, and you hear the man's electric shaver in the background. A couple days later you get a hasty French postcard he'd mailed on his first day there. It says: 'Scenery is here. Wish you were beautiful.' You reel into lesbianism, from the pain."

Faye looks at the curved side of Julie's face, deep skin of a perfect white grape.

Julie says: "Tell them this man who broke your heart quickly assumed in your memory the aspects of a political cartoon: enormous head, tiny body, all unflattering features exaggerated."

"I can tell them all men everywhere look that way to me now."

"Give them this one. You meet a boy, at your East Coast college. A popular and beautiful and above all—and this is what attracts you most—a terribly *serious* boy. A boy who goes to the library and gets out a copy of *Gray's Anatomy*, researches the precise location and neurology of the female clitoris—simply, you're convinced, to allow him to give you pleasure. He plays your clitoris, your whole body, like a fine instrument. You fall for the boy completely. The intensity of your love creates what you could call an organic situation: a body can't walk without legs; legs can't walk without a body. He becomes your body."

"But pretty soon he gets tired of my body."

"No, he gets obsessed with your body. He establishes control over your own perception of your body. He makes you diet, or gain weight. He makes you exercise. He supervises your haircuts, your make-overs. Your body can't make a move without him. You get muscular, from the exercise. Your clothes get tighter and tighter. He traces your changing outline on huge sheets of butcher's paper and hangs them in his room in a sort of evolutionary progression. Your friends think you're nuts. You lose all your friends. He's introduced you to all his friends. He made you turn slowly around while he introduced you, so they could see you from every conceivable angle."

"I'm miserable with him."

"No, you're deliriously happy. But there's not much you, at the precise moment you're feeling most complete."

"He makes me lift weights while he watches. He has barbells in his room."

"Your love," says Julie, "springs from your incompleteness, but also reduces you to another's prosthetic attachment, calcified by the Medusa's gaze of his need."

"I told you I didn't want abstractions about this stuff," Faye says impatiently.

Julie walks, silent, with a distant frown of concentration. Faye sees a big butterfly beat incongruously at the smoke-black window of a long limousine. The limousine is at a red light. Now the butterfly falls away from the window. It drifts aimlessly to the pavement and lies there, bright.

"He makes you lift weights, in his room, at night, while he sits and watches," Julie says quietly. "Pretty soon you're lifting weights nude while he watches from his chair. You begin to be uneasy. For the first time you taste something like degradation in your mouth. The degradation tastes like tea. Night after night it goes. Your mouth tastes like tea when he eventually starts going outside, to the window, to the outside of the window at night, to watch you lift weights nude."

"I feel horrible when he watches through the window."

"Plus, eventually, his friends. It turns out he starts inviting all his friends over at night to watch through the window with him as you lift weights. You're able to make out the outlines of all the faces of his friends. You can see them through your own reflection in the black glass. The faces are rigid with fascination. The faces remind you of the carved faces of pumpkins. As you look you see a tongue come out of one of the faces and touch the window. You can't tell whether it's the beautiful serious boy's tongue or not."

"I reel into lesbianism, from the pain."

"You still love him, though."

Faye's thongs slap. She wipes her forehead and considers.

"I'm in love with a guy and we get engaged and I start going over to his parents' house with him for dinner. One night I'm setting the table and I hear his father in the living room laughingly tell the guy that the penalty for bigamy is two wives. And the guy laughs too."

An electronics shop pulls up alongside them. Faye sees a commercial behind the big window, reflected in the fly's-eye prism of about thirty televisions. Alan Alda holds up a product between his thumb and forefinger. Smiles at it.

"You're in love with a man," says Julie, "who insists that he can love you only when you're standing in the exact center of whatever room you're in."

Pat Sajak plants lettuce in the garden of his Bel Air home. Bert Convy boards his Lear, bound for an Indianapolis Motor Home Expo.

"A dream," says Alex Trebek to the doctor with circumflex brows. "I have this dream where I'm standing smiling over a lectern on a little hill in the middle of a field. The field, which is verdant and clovered, is covered with rabbits. They sit and look at me. There must be several million rabbits in that field. They all sit and look at me. Some of them lower their little heads to eat clover. But their eyes never leave me. They sit there and look at me, a million bunny rabbits, and I look back."

"Uncle," says Patricia ("Patty-Jo") Smith-Tilley-Lunt, stout and loose-faced behind the cash register of the Holiday Inn Restaurant at the Holiday Inn, Interstate 70, Ashtabula, Ohio:
    "Uncle uncle uncle uncle."

"No," says Faye. "I meet a man in the park. We're both walking. The man's got a tiny puppy, the cutest and most beautiful puppy I've ever seen. The puppy's on a little leash. When I meet the man, the puppy wags its tail so hard that it loses its little balance. The man lets me play with the puppy. I scratch its stomach and it licks my hand. The man has a picnic lunch in a hamper. We spend all day in the park, with the puppy. By sundown I'm totally in love with the man with the puppy. I stay the night with him. I let him inside me. I'm in love. I start to see the man and the puppy whenever I close my eyes.
    "I have a date with the man in the park a couple days later. This time he's got a different puppy with him, another beautiful puppy that wags its tail and licks my hand, and the man's hand. The man says it's the first puppy's brother."

"Oh Faye."

"And but this goes on, me meeting with the man in the park, him having a different puppy every time, and the man is so warm and loving and attentive toward both me and the puppies that soon I'm totally in love. I'm totally in love on the morning I follow the man to work, just to surprise him, like with a juice and Danish, and I follow him and discover that he's actually a professional cosmetics researcher, who performs product experiments on puppies, and kills them, and dissects them, and that before he experiments on each puppy he takes it to the park, and walks it, and uses the beautiful puppies to attract women, who he seduces."

"You're so crushed and revolted you become a lesbian," says Julie.

Pat Sajak comes close to skunking Alex Trebek in three straight games of racquetball. In the health club's locker room Trebek experiments with a half-Windsor and congratulates Sajak on the contract renewal and iterates hopes for no hard feeling re that Applause-sign gag, still. Sajak says he's forgotten all about it, and calls Trebek big fella; and there's some towel-snapping and general camaraderie.

"I need you to articulate for me the dynamics of this connection between Faye Goddard and Julie Smith," Merv Griffin tells his shiny executive. His man stands at the office window, watching cars move by on the Hollywood Freeway, in the sun. The cars glitter.

"You and your mother happen to go to the movies," Faye says. She and Julie stand wiping themselves in the shade of a leather shop's awning. "You're a child. The movie is *Son of Flubber*, from Disney. It lasts pretty much the whole afternoon." She gathers her hair at the back of her neck and lifts it. "After the movie's over and you and your mother are outside, on the sidewalk, in the light, your mother breaks down. She has to be restrained by the ticket man, she's so hysterical. She tears at her beautiful hair that you've always admired and wished you could have had too. She's totally hysterical. It turns out a man in the theater behind you was playing with your mother's hair all through the movie. He was touching her hair in a sexual way. She was horrified and repulsed, but didn't make a sound, the whole time, I guess for fear that you, the child, would discover that a strange man in the dark was touching your mother in a sexual way. She breaks down on the sidewalk. Her husband has to come. She spends a year on antidepressants. Then she drinks.

"Years later her husband, your stepfather, leaves her for a woman. The woman has the same background, career interests, and general sort of appearance as your mother. Your mother gets obsessed with whatever slight differences between herself and the woman caused your stepfather to leave her for the woman. She drinks. The woman plays off her emotions, like the insecure and basically shitty human being she is, by dressing as much like your mother as possible, putting little mementos of your stepfather in your mother's In-box, coloring her hair the same shade of red as your mother does. You all work together in the same tiny but terrifyingly powerful industry. It's a tiny and sordid and claustrophobic little community, where no one can get away from the nests they've fouled. You reel into confusion. You meet this very unique and funny and sad and one-of-a-kind person."

"The rain in Spain," director Janet Goddard says to a huge adolescent boy so plump and pale and vacant he looks like a snowman. "I need you to say 'The rain in Spain' without having your head under your arm.

"Pretend it's a game," she says.

It's true that, the evening before Julie Smith's brother will beat Julie Smith on her seven-hundred-and-forty-first "JEOPARDY!" slot, Faye tells Julie about what Merv Griffin's man and the director have done. The two women stand clothed at Faye's glass wall and watch distant mountains become Hershey kisses in an expanding system of shadow.

Faye tells Julie that it's because the folks over at MGE have such respect and admiration for Julie that they want to exercise careful control over the choice of who replaces her. That to MGE Julie is the mystery of the game show incarnate, and that the staff is understandably willing to do pretty much anything at all in the hopes of hanging on to that power of mystery and incarnation through the inevitability of change, loss. Then she says that that was all just the shiny executive's bullshit, what she just said.

Julie asks Faye why Faye has not told her before now what is going to happen.

Faye asks Julie why Julie sends all her sheltered winnings to her brother's doctors, but will not talk to her brother.

Julie isn't the one who cries.

Julie asks whether there will be animal questions tomorrow.

There will be lots and lots of animal questions tomorrow. The director has personally compiled tomorrow's categories and answers. Faye's been temporarily assigned to help the key grip try to repair a defectively lit *E* in the set's giant "JEOPARDY!" logo.

Faye asks why Julie likes to make up pretend reasons for being a lesbian. She thinks Julie is really a lesbian because she hates animals, somehow. Faye says she does not understand this. She cries, at the glass wall.

Julie lays her hands flat on the clean glass.

Faye asks Julie whether Julie's brother can beat her.

Julie says that there is no way her brother can beat her, and that deep down in the silence of himself her brother knows it. Julie says that she will always know every fact her brother knows, plus one.

Through the window of the Makeup Room Faye can see a gray paste of clouds moving back over the sun. There are tiny flecks of rain on the little window.

Faye tells the makeup lady she'll take over. Julie's in the makeup chair, in a spring blouse and faded cotton skirt, and sandals. Her legs are crossed, her hair spiked with mousse. Her eyes, calm and bright and not at all bored, are fixed on a point just below her own chin in the lit mirror. A very small kind smile for Faye.

"You're late I love you," Faye whispers.

She applies base.

"Here's one," Julie says.

Faye blends the border of the base into the soft hollows under Julie's jaw.

"Here's one," says Julie. "To hold in reserve. For when you're really on the spot. They'll eat it up."

"You're not going to get bumped. He's too terrified to stand up, even. I had to step over him on the way down here."

Julie shakes her head. "Tell them you were eight. Your brother was silent and five. Tell them your mother's face hung tired from her head, that first men and then she herself made her ugly. That her face just hung there with love for a blank silent man who left you touching wood forever by the side of the road. Tell them how you were left by your mother by a field of dry grass. Tell them the field and the sky and the highway were the color of old laundry. Tell them you touched a post all day, your hand and a broken baby's bright-white hand, waiting for what had always come back, every single time, before."

Faye applies powder.

"Tell them there was a cow." Julie swallows. "It was in the field, near where you held the fence. Tell them the cow stood there all day, chewing at something it had swallowed long ago, and looking at you. Tell them how the cow's face had no expression on it. How it stood there all day, looking at you with a big face that had no expression." Julie breathes. "How it almost made you need to scream. The wind sounds like screams. Stand there touching wood all day with a baby who is silence embodied. Who can, you know, stand there forever, waiting for the only car it knows, and not once have to understand. A cow watches you, standing, the same way it watches anything."

A towelette takes the excess powder. Julie blots her lipstick on the blotter Faye holds out.

"Tell them that, even now, you cannot stand animals, because animals' faces have no expression. Not even the possibility of it. Tell them to look, really to look, into the face of an animal, sometime."

Faye runs a gentle pick through Julie's moist spiked hair.

Julie looks at Faye in a mirror bordered with bulbs. "Then tell them to look closely at men's faces. Tell them to stand perfectly still, for time, and to look into the face of a man. A man's face has nothing on it. Look closely. Tell them to look. And not at what the faces do—men's faces never stop moving—they're like antennae. But all the faces do is move through different configurations of blankness."

Faye looks for Julie's eyes in the mirror.

Julie says, "Tell them there are no holes for your fingers in the masks of men. Tell them how could you ever even hope to love what you can't grab onto."

Julie turns her makeup chair and looks up at Faye. "That's when I love you, if I love you," she whispers, running a finger down her white powdered cheek, reaching to trace an angled line of white onto Faye's own face. "Is when your face moves into expression. Try to look out from yourself, different, all the time. Tell people that you know your face is least pretty at rest."

She keeps her fingers on Faye's face. Faye closes her eyes against tears. When she opens them Julie is still looking at her. She's smiling a wonderful smile. Way past twenty. She takes Faye's hands.

"You asked me once how poems informed me," she says. Almost a whisper—her microphone voice. "And you asked whether we, us, depended on the game, to even be. Baby?"—lifting Faye's face with one finger under the chin—"Remember? Remember the ocean? Our dawn ocean, that we loved? We loved it because it was like us, Faye. That ocean was *obvious*. We were looking at something obvious, the whole time." She pinches a nipple, too softly for Faye even to feel. "Oceans are only oceans when they move," Julie whispers. "Waves are what keep oceans from just being very big puddles. Oceans are just their waves. And every wave in the ocean is finally going to meet what it moves toward, and break. The whole thing we looked at, the whole time you asked, was obvious. It was obvious and a poem because it was us. See things like that, Faye. Your own face, moving into expression. A wave, breaking on a rock, giving up its shape in a gesture that *expresses* that shape. See?"

It wasn't at the beach that Faye had asked about the future. It was in Los Angeles. And what about the anomalous wave that came out of nowhere and broke on itself?

Julie is looking at Faye. "See?"

Faye's eyes are open. They get wide. "You don't like my face at rest?"

The set is powder-blue. The giant "JEOPARDY!" logo is lowered. Its *E* flickers a palsied fluorescent flicker. Julie turns her head from the sick letter. Alex has a flower in his lapel. The three contestants' names appear in projected cursive before their desks. Alex blows Julie the traditional kiss. Pat Sajak gives Faye a thumbs-up from stage-opposite. He gestures. Faye looks around the curtain and sees a banana peel on the pale blue carpet, carefully placed in the tape-marked path Alex takes every day from his lectern to the board full of answers. Dee Goddard and Muffy deMott and Merv Griffin's shiny man hunch over monitors in the director's booth. Janet Goddard arranges a shot of a pale round boy who dwarfs his little desk. The third contestant, in the middle, feels at his makeup a little. Faye smells powder. She watches Sajak rub his hands together. The red lights light. Alex raises his arms in greeting. There is no digital watch on his wrist.

The director, in her booth, with her headset, says something to camera two.

Julie and the audience look at each other.

LUCKILY THE ACCOUNT REPRESENTATIVE KNEW CPR

A N Account Representative, newly divorced, finished another late evening of work at his office, in Accounts. It was well past ten. In another office, at the opposite end of a different floor, the firm's Vice President in Charge of Overseas Production, married for almost thirty years, grandfather of one, also finished working late. Both men left.

There were between these last two executives to leave the Building the sorts of similarities enjoyed by parallel lines. Each man, leaving, balanced his weight against that of a heavily slender briefcase. Monograms and company logos flanked handles of leathered metal, which each man held. Each man, on his separate empty floor, moved down white-lit halls over whispering and mealy and monochromatic carpet toward elevators that each sat open-mouthed and mute in its shaft along one of the large Building's two accessible sides. Each man, passing through his department's hall, felt the special subsonic disquiet the overtime executive in topcoat and unfresh suit and loosened tie feels as he moves in nighttime through areas meant to be experienced in, and as, daytime. Each received, to the varying degrees their respective pains allowed, an *intuition of the askew* as, in the neatly stacked slices of lit space between the executive and the distant lament of a custodian's vacuum, the Building's very silence took on expression: they sensed, almost spinally, the slow release of great breath, a spatial sigh, a slight sly movement of huge lids cracked in wakened affinity with the emptiness that was, after all, the reasonable executive realizes, half the Building's total day. Realizes that the Building not only took up but organized space; contained the executive and not vice versa. That the Building was not, after all, comprised of or by executives. Or staff.

Particularly the divorced Account Representative, who remarked, silently, alone, as his elevator dropped toward the Executive Garage, that, at a certain unnoticed but never unheeded point in every corporate evening he worked, it became Time To Leave; that this point in the overtime night was a fulcrum on which things basic and unseen tilted, very slightly—a pivot in hours unaware— and that, in the period between this point and the fresh-suited working dawn, the very issue of the Building's ownership would become, quietly, in their absence, truly an issue, hung in air, unsettled.

The Account Representative hung in air, dropping on his elevator's wire. This again-single junior executive was spare, lithe, had about him an air of extreme economy, was young for an executive (almost literally a junior executive), was most at ease with those he countenanced at a distance of several feet, and had a professional manner, with respect to the accounts he represented for the firm, describable along a continuum from smoothly capable to cold. His elevator descended with a compact hum that was usually hard to hear.

The Account Representative's imported and clean-white motor scooter leaned at the angle of its kickstand beside a solid and equally clean broad Brougham of a car. These were the only vehicles left in the empty Executive Garage below the Staff Garage below the Building's basement maintenance level. Now, well past ten, the Building's deepest plane seemed very distant from everything else. The empty Executive Garage was enormous, broad, long, its ceiling a claustrophobic eight-and-a-quarter feet, its (barely) overhead lights harshly yellow, its surfaces' cement the tired color of much exhaust. The ding, trundle, and sigh of the Account Representative's elevator's closure produced echoes and echoes of echoes against and between the Executive Garage's gray stone planes, as did the click of the Account Representative's dress shoes and the jangled separation of his keys from his change. The silence of the place, complete and sensitive to disturbance, discouraged whistling. The Executive Garage smelled of: automobile exhaust, something vaguely but thoroughly rubber, and the Account Representative. A humid stir of air moved through the Garage: it came from the curving orifice of the Exit Ramp, located next to the Reserved Spaces— reserved for Directors and Operating Officers—perhaps half a terranean city block from the centrally parked Brougham and cycle. The Exit Ramp spiraled darkly around and out of sight, up through the Staff level and toward the silent, empty, municipally lit street above it.

The Account Representative rounded the keel of the shiny black Brougham and was at his scooter when an elevator on the Executive Garage's opposite side trundled and sighed.

His safety helmet was attached and locked to the cycle's tail clamp, was thus for now the cycle's own safety helmet; and the Account Representative, whose wife, from whom he was now legally separate, had been into the combined and confabulated sides of things, had a temporary experience of the helmeted scooter as Shetland centaur, sprite-ridden, emptily and tinily owned—tonight's experience very temporary, because the junior executive looked almost immediately past the cycle and across the Garage toward the echoed ding of its opposite elevator. The elevator disgorged the Vice President in Charge of Overseas Production, who moved stiffly, flushed, into the open, low yellowed space of the Executive Garage.

The Account Representative and the Vice President in Charge of Overseas Production knew each other only slightly, and only by sight, and the Account Representative had removed his contact lenses in the men's room in Accounts before settling down into a long evening of close reading by white light. But since the Vice President in Charge of Overseas Production was such a large man— tall, large, broad and blunt, his back a slow-moving hull in Production's daytime hallways, was also florid, craggy, an executive old enough to be literally senior—the Account Representative recognized almost instantly that it was the Vice President in Charge of Overseas Production who emerged from the Executive Garage's opposite elevator and clicked and jangled hs way, stiffly, toward the Account Representative's focus, the big older man's head cocked as at an unheard pitch, distracted, his quite large body queerly and slantedly slowed, halting, listing, failing to satisfy a clear disposition to briskness, moving only via a shift of weight from side to side, a humanoid balloon with too much air, bearing his heavy slender leather-handled case toward the solid black Brougham that sat next to the Account Representative's "spritely" and helmeted cycle, all the while feeling at something in the front of his topcoat with a hand full of tissues and keys.

The Account Representative bent back to the involved removal of his securely clamped helmet. He was preparing to feel that male and special feeling associated with the conversational imperative faced by any two men with some professional connection who meet in nighttime across an otherwise empty and silent but fragilely silent underground space far below the tall and vaguely pulsing site of a long and weary day for both: the obligation of conversation without the conversational prerequisites of intimacy or interests or concerns to share. They shared pain, though of course neither knew.

Bent to the decapitation of his cycle, the Account Representative was choosing words neither dismissive nor inviting, neither terse nor intrusive; he was composing a carefully casual face, narrowing salutatory options toward a sort of landlocked "Halloo" that contained already an acknowledgment of distance and an easy willingness to preserve same. Bent, he composed the flesh of his face, shaped a cool but respectfully cool and by no stretch of the imagination pained eye with which to meet the inevitable eye of the Vice President in Charge of Overseas Production. The opposite elevator's door trundled shut; things inside ascended, sounding.

The Vice President in Charge of Overseas Production was still distant enough to produce echoes, but was, peripherally, still bearing down, slowly, a balloon, a glacier, on the Account Representative, who lifted his face's composition from the (at last) amputated helmet and turned from the white cycle to the approach of the senior executive.

The Vice President in Charge of Overseas Production, he saw, having been bearing down, his jangled hand to his topcoat's front, had now stopped; he now stood, stock-still, lifting his thick neck and large head to nothing, as an animal keens to the waft of a warning scent.

The Account Representative looked, then watched, as the Vice President in Charge of Overseas Production stood—frozen, inflated—and grimaced; the senior executive grimaced at a point behind and apparently just above the Account Representative, as if parsing an auto antenna's rune on the scratched eight-foot-three-inch clearance of the Executive Garage's ceiling.

The Vice President in Charge of Overseas Production stood, grimaced, rooted just beyond perfect astigmatic focus. He balanced heavily, grimaced again, dropped a noisy slender briefcase, and placed both hands over a vague concavity that seemed, a bit blurrily, to have appeared in the double-breasted front of his topcoat. He grabbed at himself as do those in pain; he seemed to fold himself in two, his whole big body curving out and around the apparent pain of his coat's front's divot. He emitted what sounded like a gargle, trebled by echo.

The Account Representative watched as the Vice President in Charge of Overseas Production pirouetted, raked a raw clean streak in a cement pillar's soot and clipped a WRONG WAY sign's weighted concrete doughnut with a roundabout heel as he pirouetted, reached out at air, hunched, crumpled, and fell. He seemed to fall, the Account Representative remarked, watching, surprised out of time, at about half the rate the average thing takes to fall.

The Vice President in Charge of Overseas Production, gargling, holding his chest's recession, fell with a slow grace to the exhausted floor of the Executive Garage, where he proceeded to writhe.

Luckily the Account Representative knew CPR. In time, alert, composed, svelte, lithe, well-kept, independent, now a lone wolf—

though an efficient wolf—in life's gray forest, less cold by far than smoothly efficacious, he was, in a samaritan shot, across the stony yardage between his slender case and unhelmeted cycle and the Vice President in Charge of Overseas Production, straddling the writhing huge blunt older man, who was, at this new close emergency range, now revealed to the Account Representative to have large facial pores, blankly kind eyes, and a delicate capillary web of red in his jowls, his mouth fishily agape, forehead toad-white and sickly sour, chin lost in a pool of his own throat's meat, hands rattling a rhythmless beat against the breasts of his clothes, faint mewed gargles lost in the trebled echoes of the Account Representative's immediate and repeated calls for help from above. Clothes, coat, gray knit suit seemed to be spreading, loose, from the supine senior executive—spreading like water, thought the Account Representative, an inveterate thrower of stones at the skins of ponds—spreading as water retreats in rings from what's disturbed its center.

The Account Representative, throughout this interval, from the moment the pillar and sign were streaked and clipped, had been shouting for help in the empty Executive Garage. His shouts, the supine Vice President in Charge of Overseas Production's gargles, and attendant echoes were making for a sum-noise-total whose dimensions, seemingly limitless here in the enclosed Executive Garage, were such that the Account Representative would have been nonplussed and surprised to the point of outright denial—as he tilted the big, craggy large-pored head back over a fulcrum of palm and used a clean slender finger to clear the stricken executive's cervically pink throat of tongue and foreign matter—at how little of the cacophonous and seemingly total sound of his calls for help was carrying curved up the tiny Exit Ramp and oozing through rare chinks in the bunkered ceiling of the Executive Garage and sounding on the vacant Staff level, to say nothing of negotiating the now reversed spiral of the Ramp or escaping the quite thick concrete walls of the Staff Garage into the silent but well-lit business-district street above, across which two lovers walked, stately, pale as dolls, arms woven, silent, listening for but hearing always no real difference in the city's constant distant nighttime traffic's hiss and sigh.

Meanwhile, below the Staff Garage below the street, in the hugely echoing and deserted Executive Garage, the Account Representative had ripped the spreading cloth from the queer recession and was positively *having at* the Vice President in Charge of Overseas Production's defective heart. He administered CPR, beating at the soft dent of a chest's breastbone, alternating quartered beatings with infusions of breath down through the senior stricken executive's full but faintly blue lips and tilted head and into the rising sunken chest, the chest falling, the Account Representative taking affordable time and breath at every possible fourth-beat pause to call "Help" in the directions of the quiet street as, using CPR, he kept the Vice President in Charge of Overseas Production minimally alive, until help could arrive, as he had been trained and certified by the petite new-Bohemian almond-eyed Red Cross volunteer instructor—by whom, he remembered, all the students had volunteered to be straddled and infused, and whom the Account Representative had, one spontaneous and quartz-lit evening, bought a cup of coffee and a slice of nine-grain toast, and had asked to the Sales Trainees' Annual Formal, and had married—certified by her to do, one never knowing when it could save a life, he seduced utterly by his fiancee's dictum that you erred, in doubt, always on the side of prepared care and readiness to preserve minimal life-function, until help could arrive, his arms and lumbar beginning now to burn as he beat, bent, at the supine senior executive, pausing to call "Help" again and loosen his own stiff collar, sweat moving oily on the tight skin beneath his own newer lined topcoat and gray knit clothes, his own breath coming harder as he kept the incapacitated Vice President in Charge of Overseas Production minimally alive, pending the arrival of help, at well past ten, amid complete emptiness, calling "Help" unheard, the happily married and blankly kind grandfather of one person's own life now literally the junior executive's, to have and to hold, for a lifetime, amid swirls of forgotten exhaust, beneath the composed and watchful eye of his decapitated cycle's light.

"*Help*," the Account Representative continued to call, during affordable fourths in the artificial circulatory maintenance of the supine, straddled and infused Vice President in Charge of Overseas Production, stricken amid a flat swirl of disturbed cloth spreading out, still, slowly against the cemented monoxide floor.

"Help," the working Account Representative called, feeling the stir of a tinily remembered humid wind and pausing, again, to look behind him, past the Brougham's black hood and the carelessly dropped safety helmet beside the white cycle, at the Ramp that spiraled up out of sight toward a street, empty and bright, before the Building, empty and bright, dispossessed, autonomous and autonomic. Bent to what two lives required, below everything, he called for help again and again.

GIRL WITH
CURIOUS HAIR

For William F. Buckley
and Norman O. Brown

GIMLET dreamed that if she did not see a concert last night she would become a type of liquid, therefore my friends Mr. Wonderful, Big, Gimlet and I went to see Keith Jarrett play a piano concert at the Irvine Concert Hall in Irvine last night. It was such a good concert! Keith Jarrett is a Negro who plays the piano. I very much enjoy seeing Negroes perform in all areas of the performing arts. I feel they are a talented and delightful race of performers, who are often very entertaining. I especially enjoy watching Negroes perform from a distance, for close up they frequently smell unpleasant. Mr. Wonderful unfortunately also smells unpleasant, but he is a good fellow and a sport and he laughs when I state that I dislike his odor, and is careful to remain at a distance from me or else position himself downwind. I wear English Leather Cologne which keeps me smelling very attractive at all times. English Leather is the men's cologne with the television commercial in which a very beautiful and sexy woman who can play billiards better than a professional makes the assertion that all her men wear English Leather or they wear nothing at all. I find this woman very alluring and sexually exciting. I have the English Leather Cologne commercial taped on my new Toshiba VCR and I enjoy reclining in my horsehair recliner and masturbating while the commercial plays repeatedly on my VCR. Gimlet has observed me masturbating while I watch the English Leather Cologne commercial and she agrees that the woman is very alluring and states that she would like to lick the woman's vagina for her. Gimlet is a bisexual who is keen as anything on oral sex.

We had to stand in the dumb line for a long time at the Irvine Concert Hall in order to see Keith Jarrett in concert because we were late in arriving and did not beat the rush. We were late in arriving because Big had to stop off to sell LSD to two people in Pasadena and to two women in Brea, and even in the long line to see Keith Jarrett he sold some LSD to two fellows, Grope and Cheese, who had driven by motorcycle all the way up to Irvine to be his LSD customers. Big is a skillful punkrocker musician who also makes LSD in his room in my friends' house, and sells it. I like to beat the rush for lines and do not prefer being late, but Gimlet fellated me instantly the instant she and Big and Mr. Wonderful picked me up in their used milk truck at my new home in Altadena, and I had an orgasm on Highway 210, and it felt very good, so Gimlet made me not mind being late in arriving or paying for the tickets, which were very expensive, even to see a Negro.

Grope and Cheese instantaneously placed the LSD they'd purchased on their tongues and decided to stay and go to the Keith Jarrett concert with us after Gimlet offered to make me pay for their tickets. Gimlet introduced me to Grope and Cheese, who were of roughly high school age.

Gimlet introduced me to Grope and Cheese; she said Grope, Cheese: Sick Puppy. And she introduced Grope and Cheese to me, as well. My name is Sick Puppy even though my name is really not. All my good friends are punkrockers and rarely have names except names like Tit and Cheese and Gimlet. Gimlet's real name is Sandy Imblum and she is from Deming, New Mexico. Cheese asked Gimlet if he could touch the tip of her hair and she invited him to sit on a picket fence instead, causing me to react with laughter.

Cheese looked very immature for a true blue punkrocker and was unfortunately not attractive. He was bald-headed but displayed whiskers of hair here and there and he wore spectacles which were pink and had a thin neck but he seemed like a good egg, but Grope did not like my new suit which I had purchased in Rodeo's on Rodeo Drive or my Top-Siders or my tie from my prep school which had Westminster Military Academy on it and an American flag as well. He stated that I did not seem like a fine fellow or a good egg and that my clothes were unattractive. He also disliked the smell of my English Leather Cologne.

Grope's utterances peeved Gimlet and she told Mr. Wonderful to harm Grope, therefore Mr. Wonderful kicked Grope in the mid section with his heavy black boots, for Contra combat in Central America, with studs in the toes. Grope became in extreme pain and was forced to sit on the curb smack dab in the middle of the line to see Keith Jarrett, holding his kicked mid section. Gimlet placed fingers in each of Grope's nose's nostrils and asked him to apologize to me or she would try to pull the nose from amid Grope's features. Pain and unpleasantness are very unpleasant for people with LSD on their tongue, and Grope apologized instantaneously without even having to look at me.

I informed Grope that his apology was totally accepted and that he seemed like an A-OK sort of person to me, and I shook Grope's hand to let him know that Sick Puppy was no spoilsport, and Big helped him up and let him lean on him while I paid the face behind the window of the Irvine Concert Hall for six tickets to see Keith Jarrett, which cost one hundred-and-twenty dollars. Grope told Big that his LSD was numero uno while we all entered the balmy and comfortable and tastefully decorated interior lobby of the Irvine Concert Hall. Gimlet whispered to my ear that in return for paying for the tickets to see Keith Jarrett and keeping her from liquidating, she would attempt to keep my erect penis in her mouth for several minutes without having an orgasm, and that she would let me burn her with several matches on the backs of her legs, as well, and this made me very happy, and Gimlet and I placed our tongues in each other's mouths while all our friends formed a circle around us and indicated their vocal approval. The other crowds coming to see Keith Jarrett's concert were in approval of our bunch's happy go luckiness and gave us a generous amount of room and privacy in the Concert Hall's spacious lobby.

Mr. Wonderful and Big and Gimlet had all taken a large amount of Big's LSD, which is a special kind he manufactures for concerts and is free of amphetamines which might make a fellow fidget, and Grope and Cheese had taken LSD also, therefore they were all under the influence of LSD, which made them super amounts of fun to be with. I had not taken any LSD because LSD and other controlled substances unfortunately do not affect me or my state of normal consciousness. I cannot become high from ingesting drugs, and all my friends who are punkrockers find this very fascinating and a lot of fun. I was a very popular and outgoing peer in prep school and college and business school and law school but could not become affected by controlled substances in these environments either. My friends the punkrockers like me to buy very large amounts of drugs and take them and not become high while they are all affected. Last month for my birthday they made me place over two paper squares of Big's LSD on my tongue and then we all went joy riding in the new sports car I received from my mother for my birthday. It is a Porsche with six forward gears and two reverses and a leather interior. And turbo-charged! Gimlet and Big placed drugs on their tongues also and we went driving like greased lightning down the Pacific Coast Highway in reverse until a policeman pulled us over and I was forced to give him a gift of a thousand dollars not to incarcerate Gimlet when she determined that his revolver was in reality a radioactive chemical waste product and attempted to pull it out of his holster and throw it at a palm tree in order to kill it. The officer was a fine and gentlemanly man, however, and was very happy to receive a cash gift of a thousand dollars. We went away in a forward gear and Big began to laugh at Gimlet for temporarily believing that she could kill a service revolver by throwing it at a palm tree, and he laughed so heartily that he wet his pants and could have damaged some of the leather interior of my new Porsche, and I have to admit that I got peeved, and gave Big the cold shoulder, but Gimlet let me burn one of Big's nipples with my gold lighter at a rest stop, so I became happy and felt that Big was a fine individual once more.

Last night we arrived at our row of six seats in the Irvine Concert Hall and sat in our seats. My new friend Grope sat down far away from me next to Big, and Mr. Wonderful sat beside Big also. I sat between Cheese and Gimlet who sat at the end of our row of six seats. Far down on stage in the Irvine Concert Hall was a piano with a bench. The woman seated behind Gimlet tapped me on the padded shoulder of my new sportcoat and complained that Gimlet's hair was creating problems for her vision of the piano and bench on the stage. Gimlet told the woman to Fuck You, but good old Cheese was concerned at the situation and politely traded to Gimlet's outside seat so as to solve the vision problems of the woman, who was coughing at what Gimlet said. Cheese was a shrimp and he had very little hair to ascend from his head into the air so he was a good fellow to sit behind. Gimlet only has hair at the center of her round head, and it is very skillfully sculptured into the shape of a giant and erect male penis, otherwise she is bald like Cheese. The penis of her hair is very large and tumescent, however, and can introduce problems in low spaces or for those people behind her who wish to see what she can see. Her friend and confidante Tit sculptures Gimlet's hair and provides her with special haircare products from her career as a hair stylist which makes Gimlet's hair sculpture rigid and realistic at all times. I have my hair maintained at Julio's Unisex Fashion Cut Center in West Hollywood, with an attractive part on the right side of my hair and a feathering technique on the sides so that my ears, which are extremely well shaped and attractive, show at all times. I saw the fine hairstyle I have in *Gentleman's Quarterly* and clipped the picture to show Julio my hairstyle. Mr. Wonderful has a mohawk which last night was a very light shade of violet, but which on many occasions is orange, as well. Big's hair is extremely long and thick and black and covers his head and shoulders and chest and back, including his face. Big has a plastic facemask for vision which he has had woven into his hair at eye level, utilizing the skill of Tit. The hair in the vicinity of what is probably Big's mouth often tends to be unattractive because food passes through this area when he dines. I do not remember how Grope wore his hair.

Cheese leaned across me and told Gimlet she was a real trouper for trading seats so the coughing woman could enjoy the performance, because Keith Jarrett was an outstanding Negro performer whom everyone should get to see for their own musical good, and he asked me to agree. I was happy to agree with Cheese and calm down Gimlet so she would not be a pain in the neck, and Cheese was indeed correct when the Negro Keith Jarrett appeared on stage in slacks and shoes and a velour shirt which hung loose because it was too large for him, and sat on his bench at his piano. Like many Negroes, Keith Jarrett had an afro of hair; from where our six seats were located in the Irvine Concert Hall all I could see of Keith Jarrett was the back of him and his hair's afro while he played.

But he played awfully well! I told Gimlet I thought this performer was swell for a performer who was not a punkrocker like Gimlet and Big and Mr. Wonderful, who together comprise an excellent and skillful punkrock band known far and wide as Mighty Sphincter, and Gimlet who was very affected from the LSD at this juncture looked at me as if there was something extremely interesting behind me. She licked my cheek with her tongue for over thirty seconds but soon stopped and directed my attention to a small and young blond girl in a lower row, and stated that the girl's hair was a fascinating and curious thing to observe. She stared at the small girl below us with great intensity while Keith Jarrett played some of his concert.

As my friends and I listened to Keith Jarrett play the piano in the Irvine Concert Hall last night I was thinking what a super bunch of guys and gals my friends were and how glad I was that I had gotten to be friends with such fine and fun persons! They are very unique and different from my past friends whom I had growing up in Alexandria, Virginia and attending fine schools and universities such as the Westminster Military Academy, Brown University, the Wharton School of Business at the University of Pennsylvania, and the Law School at the University of Yale. All my past friends have real names and wear clothes similar to mine, and are very attractive and skillful and often fun but never the barrel of monkeys which my new friends in the Los Angeles area are! I met all my new punkrocker friends at a party which occurred shortly after I arrived here in the Los Angeles area for my new job which pays me over a hundred thousand dollars per year.

At the party in Los Angeles for the Los Angeles Young Republicans I was there with Ms. Paisley Campbell-Greet, a fine gal whom I was trying to convince to fellate me and subsequently let me burn her, and I was talking and quipping for several hours with her and several Young Republicans when several punkrockers in leather and metal clothing, who were at political odds with the Young Republicans on many social issues, spontaneously showed up out of nowhere and gate crashed and began to eat the expensive refreshments the Young Republicans' Ladies Auxiliary had prepared, and to take drugs and break objects. The host of the party received a finger in his eye when he complained to the largest punkrockers, who were Big and Big's chums Death and Boltpin, that they should be more sporting and well-bred fellows.

And slightly after this time of the finger in the eye at the party I became embroiled in a fracas with a Young Democrat at the party who had gone to Law School in Berkeley, California (why did they even let him in is what I want to know!?!). Paisley Campbell-Greet knew this fellow and we were all chatting in an amiable manner when I innocently and proudly broached the subject of my father and my brother and my brother's recent promotion and responsibility and honor.

Cheese leaned toward my body and made the assertion that the Negro Keith Jarrett was such a skillful and pleasurable musician because his jazz music performance was in reality *improvisational*, that Keith Jarrett was in reality composing his performance as he performed it. Gimlet began to cry because of this and because of the small girl's curious hair and I lent her one of my silk handkerchiefs which complements the color and design of several of my wardrobe ensembles.

At the Young Republican get together I stated that my family on my maternal side owns a company which manufactures high quality Pharmaceutical Products, while my family on my paternal side is true blue military aristocracy. My father is one of the highest-ranking individuals in the United States Marine Corps, and he and my brother and I are related to the finest fighting general the American nation has had since Ulysses S. Grant. My brother is thirty-four and is now a Lieutenant Colonel in the United States Marine Corps and has the honor of serving as the carrier of the Black Box of nuclear codes for the President of the United States. At the outset my brother was merely the night officer on this duty and merely sat at attention in a chair with the Black Box attached to his wrist outside the private bedroom of the nation's President at night, but now he has proven such a fine carrier of nuclear codes that he is the day officer on this duty, therefore he can be frequently seen on television and in all types of media, standing at attention at all times closer than ten feet to the President, carrying the Black Box of nuclear codes which are important to the balance of power of our country.

The Young Democrat who had sneaked into the party became off the wall about my statements about my brother the day officer for the Codes and he began to be awfully impolite and to speak loudly and to gesture Democratically in the air with his arms in his corduroy sportcoat, then one time he poked me in the chest with his finger. Paisley Campbell-Greet stated that he was drunk as well as passionate about the issues of our nation's defensive policies but being poked in the chest really gets my goat and I took my gold lighter and set the Democrat from Berkeley Law School's beard on fire. He got super upset and began running here and there and hitting at his beard with his hand, and Paisley was really ticked as well, however I was happy that I had set his beard on fire with my gold lighter.

And how I met my new punkrocker friends and became Sick Puppy is Gimlet and her friend Tit had been bobbing for lemon slices in the Young Republicans' punch bowl from Tiffany's and the attorney whose beard I had lit was on fire in the region of his head, and he pushed them aside from the punch bowl to extinguish his head in liquid. Gimlet got angry at him for this action and attempted to hold his head under the surface of the punch so he would be deprived of oxygen. Paisley Campbell-Greet attempted to pull Gimlet off the Democratic attorney and this got under Tit's skin so she tore Paisley's expensive taffeta dress down the front, so that the appearance of Paisley Campbell-Greet's breasts was demonstrated to many people at the party. It made me happy that Gimlet had tried to hurt the burning attorney, and I began to predict that Paisley Campbell-Greet would refuse to fellate me to get even for igniting her friend from Berkeley, plus her breasts turned out to be extremely small and pointy, so I laughed heartily at the exposed sight of Paisley's cocktail gown and greeted Gimlet and complimented her penis of hair and told her I was happy that she had tried to Pecos the attorney who had poked me because my brother carried the Black Box of nuclear codes for the President of the United States. And when Gimlet and her clique of Tit and Death and Boltpin and Big and Mr. Wonderful learned that my brother carried the nuclear codes for our nation's President and that it made me happy to ignite attorneys who get my goat, they caucused and decided I was the most outstanding and fine Young Republican in the history of the planet earth, and they spirited me away from the Republican cocktail party in their black second hand milk truck with Druidic symbols painted skillfully on the paint before the police whom Paisley and the lit attorney called could come and make trouble for me that could lose me my job that pays me a great deal of money.

That night Gimlet and Tit fellated me, and Boltpin did as well. Gimlet and Tit made me happy but Boltpin did not, therefore I am not a bisexual. Gimlet allowed me to burn her slightly and I felt that she was an outstanding person. Big acquired a puppy from the alley behind their house in East Los Angeles and he soaked it with gasoline and they allowed me set it on fire in the basement studio of their rented home, and we all stood back to give it room as it ran around the room several times.

At the Irvine Concert Hall last night Grope nursed his mid section and began to opine that Keith Jarrett was firing forms of electricity at him from the outer regions of his Negro afro, and he became a nervous Nellie. Gimlet no longer cried but did become even more interested and fascinated with the blond and curled hair of the young child sitting with an older man in a very attractive sportcoat two rows of concert seats below our six seats. Gimlet stated that the girl's curious hair represented radioactive chemical

waste product anti-immolation mojo and that if Gimlet could cut
it off and place it in her vagina beneath the porch of her stepfather's
house in Deming, New Mexico, she could be burned and burned
and never feel pain or discomfort. She was crying and beating at
fictitious flames, and subsequently tried to rise and run pell mell
over concert seats down to the hair of the girl, but Mr. Wonderful
held Gimlet back and offered her his assurances that he would
attempt to get her some of the curious hair at an intermission, and
placed something in Gimlet's mouth courtesy of Big.

Next to me at the end of our row of concert seats Cheese became
very interested in me as a person and began to talk to me as we
listened to Keith Jarrett improvise his performance right on the
spot on his bench. Cheese stated that while it was evident that I
was a swell individual he wondered how I had come to become
friends with my punkrocker friends in Los Angeles, Big and Gimlet
and Mr. Wonderful, since I did not look like them nor did I dress
like them or have a distinctive punkrocker hairstyle, nor was I poor
or disaffected or nihilistic. Cheese and I began a deep conversation
which was very fascinating and I told him several facts about myself
which he found interesting and compelling. We talked in depth
while Mr. Wonderful restrained Gimlet and Big restrained the
nervous Grope, quietly so as to be able to hear the very good
melodies our entertaining Negro performer was putting forth at
all times.

I informed Cheese that my punkrocker friends and I were thick
as thieves and that although I could not dress like them for reasons
of my job and family traditions I admired my friends' fashion sense
like all get out. Since Gimlet knows that my excellent job and well
to do family are what provide me with lots of capital at all times,
she is not unhappy that I cannnot dress in leather and metal or
shave my head or sculpture my hair like a true blue punkrocker.
My job is very fascinating and pleasurable and I have had it for less
than a year. At the law firm where I am an Associate I am a corporate
liability trouble shooter. Sometimes the products certain manufac-
turers manufacture have bugs and defects in them which might
injure a consumer, and when a consumer gets a wild hair about

being injured and attempts to litigate against one of my firm's clients, I am called in to trouble shoot. This often happens with such products as children's toys and power tools. I am an extremely effective corporate liability trouble shooter because I enjoy a challenge very much and enjoy jumping in there with the old Corps spirit and licking the competition! I am especially pleased and challenged in my career when it really happens that a manufacturer's product has a bug and has injured a consumer, because then it is even more challenging to try to convince a jury or a jurist that what really happened didn't really happen and the manufacturer's product did not injure the consumer. It is more challenging still when the consumer is right there at the proceedings and is injured, for a jury tends often to feel sorry for an injured person, especially if the person is a racial minority and has swarms of small children, as racial minorities when they appear in court tend to. But although I have already had many corporate liability cases to trouble shoot I have only failed to bring home the bacon once or twice, because I enjoy a good competition in which I am part of the process, and also because people naturally like me out of instinct, because of my appearance. The average layman would be surprised to know how much juries are impressed by appearances. I am fortunately an entirely handsome devil and appear even younger than twenty-nine. I look like a clean cut youth, a boy next door, and a good egg, and my mother stated at one time that I have the face of a heaven's angel. I have the eyes of an attractive marsupial, and I have baby-soft and white skin, and a fair complexion. I do not even have to shave, and I have finely styled hair without any of dandruff's unsightly itching or flaking. I keep my hair perfectly groomed, neat, and short at all times. I have exceptionally attractive ears.

I explained to Cheese that dressing in an accepted manner and looking a lot like an angel helps me in my career and that Gimlet comprehended this fact. My career pays me over a hundred thousand dollars per annum, and my mother also sends me checks from her personal wealth, so I have a great deal of liquidity on hand, which makes Gimlet and Big and Mr. Wonderful a very happy bunch of punkrockers.

Before I got angry at Cheese I liked him a lot. Unlike Gimlet and Grope, LSD-taking made Cheese a quite happy go lucky fellow last night at Keith Jarrett's concert. He did not see false events or get fidgety, but instead merely recounted that the paper on his tongue made it possible for him to discern the Negro Keith Jarrett's music with many different of his five senses. He could hear it, but see and smell and taste the music, as well. Cheese stated that some of the music smelled like old velvet in a trunk in an attic, or like vitamins, or medicine, or morning. He asserted that he could see Keith Jarrett's improvisational compositions as well. He gamely tried to describe in his own terms what a sunset looks like through fire, apricot and blue, and through smoke, plum and black. He said sometimes the music resembled weak light behind ice. I became happy merely listening to the sensual recountings of Cheese, and when Gimlet placed her hand on my penis in my gabardine slacks and claimed that there were secret worms and snakes in the small blond child's curious hair which were incessantly moving and spelling out the names of Gimlet's family of Imblums in Deming, New Mexico, I gave her a big buss.

Cheese knew a great deal about many other genres of music besides punkrock. He felt that Keith Jarrett was a very talented negro performer. He stated that only a genius could have a seat on his bench before thousands of distant spectators and begin to play any old melodies which were floating around inside his head with its afro. Cheese posited that for Keith Jarrett there are billions of these ditties, that he plays, and subsequently marveled to me that Keith Jarrett not only played the little tunes with skill but also joined them together in unique and interesting ways, improvisationally, so that each of his piano concerts was different from all the others. The manner in which the little melodies were linked was arranged by Keith Jarrett's sub conscious, stated Cheese, thus his concerts were linear, Keith Jarrett's piano performance was a line instead of a composed and round circle. The line was like a little life story of the Negro's special experiences and feelings. I informed Cheese that I did not know that Negroes had sub consciousnesses but enjoyed the sound of the music a great deal, and

Cheese frowned. Gimlet began to moan in a way that got me very sexually excited and Gimlet did not even tell the coughing woman behind Cheese to Fuck You after the woman behind Cheese requested that we all please keep our voices subdued so that everyone in the audience in the Irvine Concert Hall could enjoy the concert, but Cheese was frowning yet and he informed the woman that he would stomp her husband if she did not get out of our face so she zipped her lip and I held Gimlet's hand and put one of her fingers with white nail polish that tastes like vanilla, which I enjoy, inside my mouth.

The small girl with the yellow hair Gimlet felt was chemical and occult appeared to be drowsing and leaning against the shoulder of the older man's finely tailored sportcoat. I admired the sportcoat and wished that it belonged to me instead of the man. I wanted the man to turn around in his concert seat so that I could see who owned the sportcoat and I began to decide whether to throw a penny at the back of the fellow's head to induce him to turn around.

However besides being a fine all around bald punkrocker with pink glasses Cheese could also be intelligent and clever. He was extremely interested in yours truly as a person, and without me even noticing the fact Cheese took us from discussing musical genres and Keith Jarrett's negro experiences and emotions to no music and my white experiences and emotions. Cheese betrayed that he was anxious to learn why I had such satisfactory relations with my punkrocker friends. He said he wished to understand a Sick Puppy like me. He began to look very serious on his LSD trip but he became funny in a way which I found entertaining and engaging. He divulged his position that punkrockers were children born into a very tiny space, with no windows, plus walls all around them made of concrete and metal, often despoiled with graffiti, and that as adults they were trying to cut their way out of the walls. They were attempting to move quickly along the very thin edge of something and accomplished this feat by failing to care if they fell over the edge or not. Cheese stated that my punkrocker clique all felt as if they had nothing and would always have nothing therefore they made the nothing into everything. However Cheese stated

that I was a Sick Puppy who already had everything, thus he wished
to inquire as to why I traded my big everything for a big nothing.
Cheese was being curious and amusing from his seat on the edge,
but he persisted in looking at the side of my fair face, and had his
hand on the sleeve of my new sportcoat, which I did not like, for
his fingernails were unclean. He asked me why I was Sick Puppy.

I proposed to Cheese that he was a fine fellow and that I was
enjoying having an in depth conversation with him a lot and that
I admired his earring. His earring was composed of bone. At these
statements Cheese became a grump once more and I told him to
turn that frown upside down.

Gimlet observed my penny in my hand while I was gazing at the
back of the older man's head, and she read me like a book. She
requested into my ear that I throw my penny at the girl with the
curious hair so that the girl would be hurt and turn around in her
seat and Gimlet would utilize the opportunity to observe the face
of the girl with the curious hair. She said she predicted the girl's
face would be the face of an absolute giant, with planets rotating
in the sockets of her eyes, and that her breath would smell like
apples. She stated that the curious hair when removed from the
child and placed in Gimlet's LSD-influenced vagina would alter
Gimlet from a Sandy Imblum to an area of fire with arms and legs
and vagina of proper heat. Cheese politely asked Gimlet whether
she would care to take some tablets of Vitamin B_{12} in order to tone
down the strength of her dosage of her controlled substance, however Gimlet had stopped being aware of Cheese. She placed her
hand in the vicinity of my gabardine penis and thereupon stated
that when she was full of curious active hair and fire she would pay
a little visit to my father at his office in the United States Marine
Corps and throw herself into his warrior's arms and commit the
sexual act with him and when he had his orgasm he would catch
on fire from Gimlet and immolate while she cut open his warrior's
throat and allowed me to bathe in his blood. Gimlet's a first rate
gal but I have to admit that these statements got under my skin,
Gimlet talking about my father and the sexual act in public in the
Irvine Concert Hall. Cheese hypothesized that Gimlet was having

an unpleasant LSD experience and advised Mr. Wonderful to keep his well developed arm around her for various persons' protection, and Big told Cheese to zip the old lip and mind his own business.

I was royally peeved at Gimlet and as the back of Keith Jarrett's afro head began to move in a side-to-side fashion and as his music became louder and more like punkrock, I crossed my arms and began breathing through the nostrils of my nose with anger at Gimlet. Subsequently I got her in a stare-down and stared at her with anger. Gimlet's black pupils in her eyes became so large that they obscured her eyes' color and she began to become frightened of yours truly and to cry, which made me a small amount happier. Cheese put his unclean hand on my new sportcoat's sleeve once more and I turned to him with my arms previously crossed and must have appeared extremely ticked off at him, as well, for putting his hand on my sleeve, for his immature eyes as well became extremely wide and purple behind his pink glasses and he felt at the whiskers on his head and stated quietly that we had to step into the interior lobby of the Concert Hall and have a chat with each other for a moment, and wait for the other kids to join us in the lobby in a moment at the hour's intermission. I was mad and on the horns of a dilemma about whether I wanted to throw my penny at the girl with the hair's head or burn Cheese with my lighter in the lobby, and I decided to burn Cheese and I trailed him up the stairs of the aisle and into the pleasant and cool lobby of the Irvine Concert Hall. Gimlet asked me Sick Puppy where are you going? but I gave her the cold shoulder.

Except when we entered the lobby I failed to want to burn Cheese because it would not have been any fun because when we entered the lobby Cheese spontaneously sat down on a pleasant bench owned by the Concert Hall in his leather pants and black combat boots and leather shirt with amounts of chain and ammunition strapped across his poorly developed chest and back and bald head with bristles and whiskers and began to cry, so that tears of Cheese's began to run out from underneath his rose-colored spectacles. Cheese began to look as young as he truly was, which was a minor. I knew that Big's LSD on the tongue was having an effect

upon good old Cheese and that, unlike me, his consciousness became affected by controlled substances.

While crying, Cheese stated that he did not understand me and
that I frightened him. I claimed that that was a riot of amusement:
a punkrocker with ammunition such as Cheese being frightened of
a dapper and handsome civilian like Sick Puppy. I said no harm no
foul and offered to ask Gimlet to fellate him very skillfully, however
Cheese ignored my offer and took the hand I proffered in friendship
and with his poorly maintained hand pulled me down on the attractive bench beside him. It was difficult to hear Keith Jarrett from
the lobby.

Cheese restated that he was unable to conceptualize a Sick Puppy
such as myself, and stated that he also did not understand the
happiness that was exuded by me at virtually all moments. It took
him time to verbally grope for the word happy. Do you know what
I mean, he inquired. There is something about you that is so totally
happy, Sick Puppy. I patiently explained to Cheese once more about
my great amount of income and clothing and fine home entertainment products, however Cheese shook his predominantly bald head
and claimed that he meant a different word by the word happy
which he had groped for. I wish to know why you are so *happy*,
he said. After he kept asking me why I was happy he asked me if
I loved Gimlet. I put the arm of my new sportcoat around Cheese's
leather shoulders and informed him that Gimlet was aces in my
book, and that on many occasions I was made happy by Gimlet
because she fellated me and gave me pleasurable orgasms, and
allowed me to burn parts of her body. Tears ceased to crawl from
behind Cheese's pink lenses but he persisted in looking and staring
at me in a fashion that made me want to hurt him until I hypothesized that he had entered a type of substance-induced hypnosis in
which a person often stares at objects as if they were too large to
comprehend, often for a long time. I did not know if I should leave
Cheese in the lobby in a state of hypnosis but I wanted to hear
Keith Jarrett play music, therefore I forgot Cheese and went away
from him to the public drinking fountain and then to the doors of
the auditorium. However before I could enter the doors of the

auditorium I heard Cheese's voice call and I remembered Cheese once more and he no longer blindly stared like a bunny in my headlights when I arrived back at his bench and did not even have to look or stare transfixed at me in order to say that if I would tell him what was the nature of the happiness I exuded at all times he would allow me to burn him a little and also allow me to burn his fiancée, who was part Negro.

I stated to Cheese that he had made me an offer I couldn't refuse but that, however, his question stymied yours truly because I had already patiently explained to him that there were myriads of times and occasions when things made me happy. The fact of the matter is that there have only been a few things that historically have ever made me unhappy and gotten me down in the dumps. Exemplum gratia, one thing was the time in college at Brown University when I went to proudly enlist in the United States Marine Corps R.O.T.C. program to continue to follow in the footsteps of my father and brother who serve with honor in the military and the Recruiting Colonel made us take a dumb personality test and I flunked and later when I went back to politely complain they gave me another dumb test and said I flunked it, as well, and then made me speak to a Dr. who came in the R.O.T.C. office and then the Recruiting Colonel for Brown University called my father who was busy with important work in Washington, D.C., and my father was super peeved at the whole incident. The Colonel repeatedly addressed my father as Sir, and apologized for interrupting his work, however I never got to enlist in any R.O.T.C. programs for officer training at Brown University or elsewhere. And exemplum gratia, another thing was the occasion in Alexandria, Virginia, when I was eight and my sister was ten and my brother who now carries the nuclear codes for the President was at Westminster Military Academy and my sister and myself were in my brother's room playing in his desk and we came upon magazines in low drawers and the magazines, which were erotic, were full of men and women committing sexual acts and we read the magazines and witnessed pictures of men placing their penises in holes between the women's legs and the men and the women looking very happy and I took my sister's underpants off and my underpants off as well and placed my penis which was very excited from the magazines into a hole my sister and I found between her legs, which was her vagina, but having me place my penis in her vagina failed to make my sister happy and my father entered the room when she called him and saw us committing a sexual act and he took me down into his workshop by our playroom in our home's basement and burned my penis with his gold lighter from the United States Corps and stated that if I ever touched his little girl again he would burn my penis off with his gold lighter and I had to go to a Dr. and obtain ointment for my burned penis, and was unhappy and down in the dumps.

If it were not a sign of ill breeding to discuss private family matters in public as my parents taught me as a child I would have filled Cheese in on examples of times I was historically unhappy and state to him as well that in my book Gimlet is aces and frequently makes me happy by fellating me and letting me burn her, for these are the only two events which make me become happy in matters of the birds and the bees. Unfortunately, even though I am one handsome dude and desirable on the part of many girls throughout my school and life, my penis declines to become erect when they want to commit the sexual act, and will only be erect if they fellate me, and if they fellate me I wish to burn them with matches or my lighter very much and most women dislike this event and are unhappy when burned and thus are chicken to fellate me and only wish to commit the sexual act.

However Gimlet is not chicken and she will. Furthermore Gimlet knows that what would make me the happiest corporate liability trouble shooter in the history of the planet earth would be to kill my father and that I will kill my father and bathe in his blood as soon as I can do it without maybe getting caught or found guilty at it, maybe when he is retired and my mother is weak, and Gimlet promises to help me and to kill her stepfather as well and she fellates me and lets me burn her sometimes.

I conversed with Cheese and my voice sounded slowly thick to my ears because recalling historical events from the past frequently affects my state of normal consciousness in the manner controlled substances affect other persons, and influences me. I stated to Cheese that I could not regrettably answer his question, yet I would give him a cash gift of a thousand dollars in return for Cheese making his negro fiancée bathe thoroughly and then fellate me and then allow me to burn her with matches on the backs of her legs.

Cheese glanced at yours truly in a semi hypnotized fashion for a long period, and I became confident that he was going to agree to accept the gift and that we would consummate a deal, however at this time Keith Jarrett's jazz piano concert had its hour's intermission and persons began to enter the lobby of the Irvine Concert Hall. The persons were moving slowly and my heart in my chest was beating slowly. The people were exiting the auditorium doors and conversing, utilitizing motions which were in slower motion even than the NFL Highlights Show, a show which frequently shows the commercial in which the beautiful and sexy woman playing billiards asserts that all her men wear English Leather Cologne or they wear nothing at all. My state of normal consciousness became historically affected even further as Cheese persisted in staring at me and people in the lobby proceeded to mill and purchase refreshments and drink from the public drinking fountain and enter the restroom facilities extremely slowly, and the air in the Irvine Concert Hall became similiar to lit ice, and Cheese's voice as he began to decline my initial offer of a deal came from distances, and his pink glasses began to have the appearance of two dull sunrises through ice.

From the attractive bench in the slow lobby I began to attempt to see if Gimlet and Big and Mr. Wonderful and Grope were coming out to help me persuade old Cheese to accept my offer of a gift, yet I instead found myself noting with extreme interest the slow running of the older and distinguished gray-haired and athletic man in the sportcoat. The sportcoat had appeared to be the real McCoy from above his back in the Irvine Concert Hall, however now in the lobby it appeared to have unattractive narrow lapels and also nonEuropean tailoring, which are fashion features I dislike. The man was running with amusing slowness, carrying the young girl with the curious hair, and was being pursued through the slow and crowded lobby by Mr. Wonderful and Gimlet, who had left Grope and Big in the dust in their pursuit of the man and the girl with the curious hair. The mouths of my friends Mr. Wonderful and Gimlet were open wide in a laughing and excited manner and Mr. Wonderful had something metal and bright in his hand and Gimlet's hair's penis sculpture was becoming disordered at the tip and her eyes continued to be all dark black pupil rather than white and color and pupil and she was running slowly in her leather and plastic and reaching out with her hand for the curious hair of the girl with the curious hair who was asleep in the protective arms of the distinguished older man running slowly past me in narrow lapels, and when I saw the beautiful and pale face of the sleeping girl over the bouncing shoulder of the running man the face slowly made me extremely joyful and excited, and as Gimlet and Mr. Wonderful slowly caught the man by the rear portion of his unattractive sportcoat near the front of the lobby of the Irvine Concert Hall and as Gimlet's hands with vanilla nails and Mr. Wonderful's bright object were almost in her curious hair the girl with the hair seemed to awaken in the older man's arms and she gazed incessantly and directly at yours truly, sitting at attention on Cheese's bench and removing Cheese's hand and unsightly nails from the wrist of the sleeve of my sportcoat, and I slowly assumed a happy and comforting and reassuring expression at the young blond girl and rose to my feet from the bench as Gimlet's hands became even slower yet and were moving in the girl's radiant hair and Mr. Wonderful was doing something with the bright thing to the man who was the girl's father. And here's what I did.

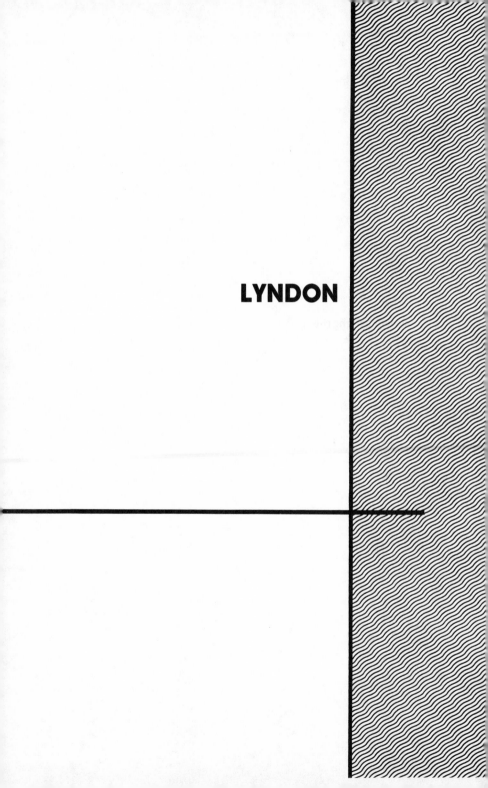

LYNDON

"Hello down there. This is your candidate, Lyndon Johnson."
— Campaigning by helicopter for U.S. Senate, 1954

'**M**Y name is Lyndon Baines Johnson. I own the fucking floor you stand on, boy.'

There was also an aide in the office, in one corner, a skinny man with big ears, working at a long pinewood table, doing something flurried between a teletype and a stack of clipped newspapers, but Lyndon was talking to me. It was the Fifties and I was young, burned-out cool, empty. I slouched emptily where I stood, before his desk, my hands in the pockets of my topcoat, flapping the coat a little. I stood hip-shot and looked at the scarlet floor tile under my shoes. Each red square tile was decorated with a lone gold star.

He leaned over his desk at me. He looked like a big predatory bird.

'My name is Lyndon Baines *Johnson*, son. I am the Senator to the United States Senate from the state of Texas, U.S.A. I am the twenty-seventh richest personal man in the nation. I got the biggest wazoo in Washington and the wife with the prettiest name. So I don't care who your wife's Daddy knows—don't you slouch at this Senator, boy.'

The way he looked, when I looked at him, was always the same.

He looked like eyes, the eyes of a small person, looking trapped from behind the lined hooked jutting face of a big bland bird of prey. His eyes are the same in pictures.

I apologized nervously. 'I'm sorry, sir. I think maybe I'm nervous. I was just sitting out there, filling out application forms, and all of a sudden here I am speaking to you, directly, sir.'

He produced a nasal inhaler and an index card. He put the inhaler to a nostril and squeezed, inhaling. He squinted at the card.

' "Every prospective part of the personnel in the office of the United States Senator from Texas shall be interviewed"—I'm reading this, boy, off this card here—"interviewed with the potential of being interviewed by *any* part of the personnel of the office he shall potentially work under." I wrote that. I don't care who your wife's Daddy's wife's internist knows—you're potentially under me, boy, and I'm interviewing you. What do you think of that?'

The big-eared aide sighted down his shears at a news clipping, making sure the cut lines were clean and square.

'A senator who interviews low-level office help?' I said. I listened to oak-muffled, far-away sounds of telephones and typewriters and teletypes. I was beginning to think I had filled out forms for an inappropriate job. I had no experience. I was young, burned out. My transcript was an amputee.

'This must be a very conscientious office,' I said.

'Goddamn right it's conscientious, boy. The president of this particular stretch of the Dirksen Building is me, Lyndon Johnson. And a president views, interviews, and reviews everything he presides over, if he's doing his job in the correct manner.' He paused. 'Say, write that down for me, boy.'

I looked to the jughead of an aide, but he was laying down long ribbons of Scotch tape along a straightedge. 'Plus "previews," ' Lyndon said. 'Stick in "previews" there at the start, son.'

Pores open, I patted at my jacket and topcoat tentatively, trying to look as if this might have been the one just-my-luck day I wasn't carrying anything connected to writing down aphorisms for inspired Senators.

But Lyndon didn't notice; he had turned his leather chair and was continuing, facing the office window, facing the regiments of autographed photos, civic awards, and the headless cattle horns, curved like pincers, those weird disconnected horns that projected from the wall behind his big desk. Lyndon probed at his teeth with a corner of the card he'd read from, his chair's square back to me. He said:

'If there's even a pissing chicken's chance that the ass of some sorry slouching boy who can't even button up his topcoat is going to cross my path in the office of this particular United States Senator, I'm interviewing that boy's ass.'

His scalp shone, even in the Fifties. The back of his head was rimmed with a sort of terrace of hair. His head was pill-shaped, tall, with the suggestion of a huge brain cavity. His hands, treed with veins, were giant. He pointed a limb-sized finger slowly at the thin aide:

'Piesker, you keep me waiting for a news summary again and I'll kick your ass all down the hall.'

The thin aide was clipping out a complicatedly shaped newspaper article with unbelievable speed.

I cleared my throat. 'May I ask what whatever job I seem to have applied for consists of, sir.'

Lyndon remained facing the decorated wall and big window. The window had limp United States and Texas flags flanking it. Out the window was a sidewalk, a policeman, a street, some trees, a black iron fence with sharp decorative points like inverted Valentines. Beyond that was the bright green and scrubbed white of Capitol Hill.

Lyndon inhaled again from his nasal inhaler. The bottle wheezed a bit. I waited, standing, on the starred tile, while he looked through the onion-skin forms I'd completed.

'This boy's name is David Boyd. Says here you're from Connecticut. Connecticut?'

'Yes sir.'

'But your wife's Daddy is Jack Childs?'

I nodded.

'Speak up Boyd goddamnit. Black Jack Childs, of the Houston Childses? And Mrs. Childs and my own lovely wife share a internist, at the doctor's, back home, in Texas?'

'So I'm told, sir.'

He rotated his chair toward me, noiseless, still fondling the policy card he'd written, tracing his lip's outline with it as he scanned forms.

'Says here you went and dropped out of Yale Business School, does it.'

'I did that, sir, yes. I left Yale.'

'Yale is in Connecticut, also,' he said thoughtfully.

I fluttered my coat pockets. 'It is.' I paused. 'In all honesty sir I was asked to leave,' I said.

'Met Jack Childs's little girl at Yale, then? Kicked in the butt by love? Dropped them books and picked up a loved one? Admirable. Similar.' He had his boots, two big boots with sharp shining toes, up on his desk. The eyes behind that big face were looking at something far away.

'*Had* to get married did you? *Had* to leave?'

'Sir, in all honesty, I was asked to leave.'

'Yale up there in Connecticut asked you to leave?'

'Yes sir.'

He had rolled the card into a tight cylinder and had it deep inside his ear, probing at something, looking past me.

"Tomorrow will be drastically different from today."
            —Speech to National Press Club, Washington, D.C.,
        April 17, 1959

"The President is a restless man."
                                —Staff member, 1965

"The President is a wary man."
                                —Staff member, 1964

"I doubt if Lyndon Johnson ever did anything impulsive in his life, he was such a cautious, canny man."
                    —The Honorable Sam Rayburn, 1968

'I committed indiscretions,' I told Lyndon. 'Indiscretions were committed, and I was asked to leave.'

Lyndon was looking pointedly from Piesker to his wristwatch. Piesker, the aide, whimpered a little as he collated sheets at that very long knotty-pine table beneath a painting of scrub and dead-brown hills and a dry riverbed under a blue sky.

'I was asked by Yale to leave,' I said. 'That's why my postgraduate transcript appears as it does.'

He was always right there, but you had the sense that his side of a conversation meandered along its own course, now toward yours, now away.

'Me personally,' he said, 'I worked my ass all *through* college. I shined some shoes in a barber's. I sold pore-tightening cream door-to-door. I was a printer's devil at a newspaper. I even herded goats, for a fellow, one summer.' I saw him make that face for the first time. 'Jesus I hate the smell of a goat,' he said. 'Fucking Christ. Ever once smelled a goat, boy?'

I tried my best to shake my head regretfully. I so wish I could summon the face he made. I was laughing despite myself. The face had seemed to settle into itself like a kicked tent, his eyes rolling back. My laughter felt jagged and hysterical: I had no clue how it would be taken. But Lyndon grinned. I had not yet even been asked to sit. I stood on this great red echoing floor, separated from Lyndon and his boots by yards of spur-scuffed mahogany desktop.

'Probably heard rumors about what it smells like, though,' he mused.

'Some grapevine or other, having to do with animal smells, I'm sure I . . .'

But he sat up suddenly straight, as if he'd remembered something key and undone. The suddenness of it made Piesker drop his shears. They clattered. Lyndon looked me up and down closely.

'Shit, son, you look about twenty.'

> "Remember that one of the keys to Lyndon Johnson is that he is a perfectionist—a perfectionist in the most imperfect art in the world: politics. Just remember that."
>
> —An old associate, 1960

I finally got to sit. My back had been starting to get that sort of museum stiffness. I sat in a corner of Lyndon's broad office for four hours that cool spring day. I watched him devour Piesker's collected, clipped, and collated packet of important articles from the nation's most influential newspapers. I watched aides and advisors, together and separate, come and go. Lyndon seemed to forget I was here, in an outsized chair, in the corner, my coat puddled around my lap as I sat, watching. I watched him read, dictate, sign and initial all at once. I watched him ignore a ringing phone. I noticed how rarely such a busy man's phone seemed to ring. I watched him speak to Roy Cohn for twenty solid minutes without once answering Cohn's question about whether Everett Dirksen could be shown to be soft on those who were soft on Communism. Lyndon looked over at my corner only once, when I lit a smoke, baring his teeth until I put the long cigarette out in a low ceramic receptacle I prayed was an ashtray. I watched the Senator receive an elegantly accented Italian dignitary who wanted to talk about sales of Texas cotton to the Common Market, the two men sitting opposite on slim chairs in the waxed red floor's center, drinking dark coffee out of delicate saucer-and-spoon complexes brought in by Lyndon's personal secretary, Dora Teane, a heavily rouged, eyebrowless woman with a kind face and a girdle-roll. I watched Lyndon leave the slender spoon in his cup and reach casually down into his groin to ease his pants as he and the dignitary talked textiles, democracy, and the status of the lira.

The light in the office reddened.

I think I was drowsing. I heard a sudden: 'Yo there in my *corner*.'

'Don't just sit there with your mind in neutral, boy,' Lyndon was saying, rolling down his shirtsleeves. We were alone. 'Go and talk to Mrs. Teane out front. Go get orientated. I once see a disorientated boy on Lyndon Baines Johnson's staff, that boy's ass gets introduced to a certain sidewalk.'

'I'm hired, then? The interview's over?' I asked, standing, stiff.

Lyndon seemed not to hear. 'The man that invented specially convened sessions of the United States Senate, *that*'s the man ought to be made to herd goats,' drawing his jacket on carefully, easing into it with a real grace. He fastened his cuff studs as he crossed the floor, his walk vaguely balletic, his boots clicking and jingling. I followed.

He stopped before his door and looked at his topcoat, on its coat hook. He looked to me.

The coat hook was the same ornately carved wood as the office door. I held Lyndon's coat up as he slipped back into it, snapping the lapels straight with a pop.

'May I ask what exactly I'm to be hired to do?' I asked, stepping back to give him room to rotate in front of the mirror, checking his coat.

Lyndon looked at his watch. 'You're a mailboy.'

I didn't parse. 'Isn't that a little redundant?'

'You deliver mail, boy,' he said, bearing down on the door's handle. 'You think you can deliver some mail in this office do you?' I trailed him through the noise and fluorescence of the staff's office complex. There were cubicles and desks and *Congressional Record*s and gray machines. The harsh doubled overhead lights threw the range of his shadow over every desk he passed.

'The Senator places great importance on communication with citizens and constituents at all times,' Dora Teane told me. I was handed an index card. Its heading, bold-face, read SAME DAY DI-RECTIVE. "It is an office regulation for the staff that every piece of mail the Senator receives must be answered that same day it came in.' She put her hand on my arm. I got a faint odor of luncheon meat. The card was filled with numbered instructions, the hand-writing spiky and almost childish. I was sure it was not the pen-manship of a secretary.

'That'—Mrs. Teane indicated the index card—'is an un*prece*-dented regulation for offices of Senators.'

She showed me the Dirksen Building's basement mailroom, the mail boxes, mail bags, mail carts. Lyndon Johnson received seas of mail every day.

"I'm a compromiser and a maneuverer. I try to *get* something. That's the way our system in the United States works."
—In *The New York Times*, December 8, 1963

Margaret and I found a pleasant walk-up apartment on T Street NW. I was able to walk to the Dirksen Building. Margaret, who had gumption and drive, landed a part-time job teaching composition to remedials at Georgetown. I quickly became familiar with a good many of the huge number of young staffers who swarmed yearly from eastern colleges to the Hill. I established a regular relationship with a shy, smooth young press aide to another senior Southern Senator in the Building. Peter, who lasted four months, had a marvelous Carolinian manner and was as interested in discretion as I.

And I delivered mail. I emptied, thrice daily, gold-starred boxes, wire baskets, and dull-white sacks of mail into carts with canvas sides, trundled them over gray cellar stone into the freight elevator, and brought them up to Lyndon's maze of wooden offices and glass cubicles. I sorted mail in the sweet-smelling mimeo room. I got to know quickly what classes of mail there were and which went to whom for response. I got to know Lyndon's circle of assistants and researchers and aides and secretaries and public relations people, the whole upper-subordinate staff: Hal Ball, Dan Johnson, Walt Peltason, Jim Johnson, Coby Donagan, Lew N. Johnson, Dora Teane and her pool of typists—all pleasant, Southern, deeply tense, hardworking, dedicated to the constituency of Texas, the Democratic Party, and united in a complicated, simultaneous suspension of fear, hatred, contempt, awe, and fanatical loyalty to Lyndon Baines Johnson.

"Every night when I go to bed I ask myself: 'What did we do today that we can point to for generations to come, to say that we laid the foundations for a better and more peaceful and more prosperous and less-suffering world?'"
—Press Conference, Rose Garden
White House
April 21, 1964

"Oh he could be a bastard. He had it in him to be a beast, and it was widely known. He'd hide paper-clips on the floor beneath his desk, to test the night custodian. He'd scream. One day he'd be as kind as you please and the next he'd be screaming and carrying on and cursing you and your whole family tree, in the most vile language, in front of your public co-workers. We became accustomed to this and all stopped, gradually we stopped being embarrassed by it, because it happened to all of us at one time or another. Except Mr. Boyd. We had a policy of trying to stay out of the Vice President's peripheral vision. He would go into rages for days at a time. But they were quiet rages. But oh that only made them more frightening. He prowled the offices the way a prowling storm will prowl. You never knew when it would hit, or where, or who. Rages. It was not a working environment I enjoyed, sir. We were all terrified much of the time. Except Mr. Boyd. Mr. Boyd, sir, never received an unkind public word from the Vice President from the first day he came to work when the Vice President was still a Senator. We believed that Mr. Boyd was a close relative at the time. But I wish to say Mr. Boyd never abused his position of immunity to the rages, however. Whether as a messenger all the way up to executive assistant, oh he worked as hard as we did, sir, and was as devoted to the Vice President as one man can be devoted to another. These are only the opinions of one typist, of course."

—Former typist in the office of LBJ
November, 1963

The truth made the truth's usual quick circuit around the offices, the Building, the Hill. I was a homosexual. I had been a homosexual at Yale. In my last year before matriculating to the Business College, I met and became intimate with a Yale undergraduate, Jeffrey, a wealthy boy from Houston, Texas, who was beautiful, often considerate, wistful, but passionate, possessive, and a sufferer from periodic bouts of clinical depression so severe he had to be medicated. It was the medication, I discovered, that made him wistful.

My lover Jeffrey ran with a group of synthetic but pleasant Texas socialites, one of whom was Margaret Childs, a tall, squarely built girl who eventually claimed, from unknown motive, to be in love with me. Margaret pursued me. I declined her in every sensitive way I knew. I simply had no interest. But Jeffrey grew inflamed. He revealed that his friends did not and must not know he was a homosexual. He pushed me to avoid Margaret altogether, which was hard: Margaret, gritty, bright enough to be chronically bored, had become puzzled, suspicious, of Jeffrey's (quite unsubtle) attempts to shield me from her. She smelled potential drama, and kept up the pursuit. Jeffrey became jealous as only the manic can. In my first year in Business, while I was shopping for my father's annual Christmas golf balls, Jeffrey and Margaret had it out, publicly, dramatically, in a Beat New Haven coffeehouse. Jeffrey put his foot through a doughnut counter. Certain information became public. Bits of this public information got back to my parents, who were close to the parents of two of my housemates. My parents came to me, personally, at Yale, on campus. It was snowing. At dinner with my parents and housemates, at Morty's, Jeffrey became so upset that he had to be taken to the men's room and calmed. My father swabbed Jeffrey's forehead with moist paper towels in a cold stall. Jeffrey kept telling my father what a kind man he was.

Before my parents left—their hands literally on the handles of the station wagon's doors—my father, in the snow, asked me whether my sexual preferences were outside my own control. He asked me whether, were I to meet the right woman, I might be capable of heterosexual love, of marriage and a family and a pillar-type position in the community of my choice. These, my father explained, were his and my mother's great and only wishes for me, their one child, whom they loved without judgment. My mother did not speak. I remember a distanced interest in the steam of my own breath as I explained why I thought I could not and so would not do as my father wished, invoking Fifties' wisdom about deviancy, invoking a sort of god of glands as a shaman might blame vegetable spirits for a lost harvest. My father nodded continually throughout this whole very serious and civil conversation while my mother checked maps in the glove compartment. When I failed to present for next week's holiday, my father sent me a card, my mother a check and leftovers in foil.

I saw them only once more before my father dropped dead of

something unexpected. I had left Jeffrey's company, and had been befriended in my upset by a still grimly determined Margaret Childs. Jeffrey unfortunately saw, in all this, cause to take his own life, which he did in an especially nasty way; and he left, on the table beneath the heating pipes from which he was found suspended, a note—a document—neatly typed, full enough of absolute truth concatenated with utter fiction that I was asked by the administration of the Business College to leave Yale University. Weeks after my father's wake I married Margaret Childs, under a mesquite tree, the blue stares of my mother and a Houston sky, and a system of vows, promises of strength, denial, trial, and compassion far beyond the Childs' Baptist minister's ritual prescriptions.

The truth, to which there was really no more than that, and which made its way through the Senator's staff, the Dirksen and Owen Buildings, and the Little Congress of the Hill's three-piece-suited infantry remarkably focused and unexaggerated, concluded with the fact that Margaret's father, Mr. Childs, less wealthy than outright powerful by the standards of 1958's Texas, had lines of political influence that projected all the way into the U.S. Senate, and that he, Mr. Childs, in a gesture that was both carrot and stick, slung his son-in-law on one line of that influence and had me hand-over-hand it into the offices of a risen and rising, uncouth and ingenious senior Senator, a possible Democratic candidate in the next Presidential election. Lyndon.

I categorized and delivered mail. Business mail, official mail, important or letterheaded mail was all put into the hands of one or another of Lyndon's eight closest advisors and aides. Intra-Senate mail went to one of three administrative assistants.

All envelopes addressed by hand—automatically classified as letters from constituents—were doled out by Mrs. Teane and me among secretaries, interns, typists, low-level staffers. There was often far more of this constituents' mail, these Voices of the People, full of invective or adulation or petition for redress or advantage, far, far more than the low-level personnel could handle in a physical day. I developed and got approval for a few standardized replies, form letters made to look personal, responding to some one or another major and predictable theme in some of this mail, but we were still barely ahead of the Same Day Directive's demands. Backlogs threatened. I began staying at the offices late, telephoning Margaret or Peter to release me from the evening's plans, working to finish up assembling the Senator's replies to his people's every voice. I enjoyed the night's quiet in the staff room, one lamp burning, cicadas thrilling in rhythm out on the grounds. The staffers who handled mail began to appreciate me. A typist kept bringing me loaves of banana bread. Best, I now got access to Mrs. Teane's dark and deeply bitter East Texas coffee; she'd leave me a chuckling percolator of it as she made the closing rounds, plump and clucking, turning off lights and machines. I enjoyed the offices' night.

And, most nights, Lyndon's lights would glow from the seams in his heavy office door. I could sometimes hear the muffled tinniness of the transistor radio he listened to when alone. He rarely left the building before ten, sometimes later, slinging his coat over a shoulder, sometimes speaking to someone absent, sometimes jogging toward an abrupt halt that let him slide the length of the slick staffers' floor, not a glance in my direction as I read crudely cursived letters, advancing a few to Mrs. Teane's attention, determining which of the pre-prepared responses were appropriate for which of the others, applying the Senator's signature stamp, moistening, fastening, metering, stacking, smoking.

And one night I looked up in a lean shadow to find him stopped, puzzled, before my desk in the big empty staff room, as if I were a person unknown to him. It's true we'd rarely spoken since that first interview four months ago. He stood there, cotton sportcoat over shoulder, impossibly tall, inclined slightly over me.

'What on God's green earth you doing, boy?'

'I'm finishing up on some of this mail, sir.'

He checked his wrist. 'It's twelve midnight at night, son.'

'You work yourself pretty hard, Senator Johnson.'

'Call me Mr. Johnson, boy,' Lyndon said, twirling a watchless fob that hung from his vest. 'You can just go on ahead and call me mister.'

He hit another lamp and settled tiredly behind the desk of Nunn, a summer intern from Tufts.

'This isn't your job, boy.' He gestured at the white castle of stacks I'd made. 'Do we pay you to do this?'

'Someone needs to do it, sir. And I admire the Same Day Directive.'

He nodded, pleased. 'I wrote that.'

'I think your concern with the mail is admirable, sir.'

He made that thoughtful, clicking sound with his mouth. 'Maybe not if it keeps some sorry red-eyed boy up licking all night without renumeration it isn't.'

'Someone needs to do it,' I said. Which was true.

'Words to live my life by, son,' he said, throwing a boot up onto Nunn's blotter, opening an envelope or two, scanning. 'But damned if most wives who had minds in their head would let most husbands stay out this late, leave them lonesome till twelve midnight at night.'

I looked at my own watch, then at the heavy door to Lyndon's office.

Lyndon smiled at my point. He smiled gently. 'I carry my Miss Claudia "Lady Bird" Johnson in here, boy,' he said, tapping at his chest, the spot over the scar from his recent bypass (he'd shown the whole office his scar). 'Just like my Bird carries me in her own personal heart. You give your life to other folks, you give your bodily health and your mind in your head and your intellectual concepts to serving the people, you and your wife got to carry each other inside, 'matter from how far away, or distant, or alone.' He smiled again, grimacing a little as he scratched under an arm.

I looked at him over a government postal meter.

'You and Mrs. Johnson sound like a very lucky couple, sir.'

He looked back. He put his glasses back on. His glasses had odd clear frames, water-colored, as if liquid-filled.

'My Lady Bird and me have been lucky, haven't we. We have.'

'I think you have, sir.'

'Damn right.' He looked back to the mail. 'Damn right.'

We stayed that night, answering mail, for hours, mostly silent. Though, before the air around the distant Monument got mauve and a foggy dawn lit the Hill, I found Lyndon looking at me, hunched in my loosened three-piece, staring at me, over me, somehow, nodding, saying something too low to hear.

'Excuse me, sir?'

'I was saying to keep it up, boy, is what. Keep it up. I kept it up. You keep it up.'

'Can you elaborate on that?'

'Lyndon Baines Johnson never elaborates. It's a personal rule I have found advantageous. I never elaborate. Folks distrust folks who elaborate. Write that down, boy: "Never elaborate." '

He rose slowly, using Nunn's little iron desk for support. I reached for my little notebook and pen as he shook the wrinkles out of his topcoat.

> "I never saw a man with a deeper need to be loved than LBJ."
> —Former aide, 1973

> "He hated to be alone. I mean he *really* hated it. I'd come into his office when he was sitting alone at his desk and even though you could tell it wasn't me he wanted to see, his eyes would get this relieved light . . . He carried a little pocket radio, a little transistor radio, and sometime's we'd hear it playing in his office, while he worked in there alone. He wanted a little noise. Some voice, right there, talking to him, or singing. But he wasn't a sad man. I'm not trying to give you that impression of him. Kennedy was a sad man. Johnson was just a man who *needed* a lot. For all he gave out, he needed things back for himself. And he knew it."
> —Former research aide Chip Piesker
> April, 1978

I began doing much of my quieter busywork in Lyndon's inner office, on the red floor, among the stars. I sorted and categorized and answered mail on the floor in the corner, then on the long pine table when Piesker was remanded to my desk outside to put together Lyndon's daily news summary. I answered more and more of the personal mail. Lew N. Johnson said I lent a special, personal touch. Mrs. Teane began to forward things to my attention instead of vice versa.

Lyndon often asked me to jot things down for him—thoughts, turns of phrase, reminders. He showed, even then, a passion for rhetoric. He'd ask to see the little notebook I carried, and review it.

He did run in 1960, or rather canter, in the primaries, while still a Senator. His determination not to shirk duties in the Senate meant that he couldn't really run more than halfway. But his Dirksen Building office still tripled its staff and came to resemble a kind of military headquarters. I took orders directly from Lyndon or from Dora. Mail became more and more a priority. I did some crude 1960-era mass mailings for the campaign, working with P.R. and the weird shiny-eyed men in Demographics.

Aides and advisors and friends and rivals and colleagues came and went and came and went. Lyndon hated the telephone. Dora Teane would put only the most urgent calls through. Those who knew Lyndon well always came by personally for 'chats' that sometimes made or ended careers. They all came. Humphrey looked like the empty shell of a molted locust. Kennedy looked like an advertisement for something you ought not to want, but do. Sam Rayburn reminded me of an untended shrub. Nixon looked like a Nixon mask. John Connally and John Foster Dulles didn't look like anything at all. Chet Huntley's hair looked painted on. DeGaulle was absurd. Jesse Helms was unfailingly polite. I often brought, to whoever had to wait a few minutes, some of Mrs. Teane's dark special blend. I sometimes chatted for a few moments with the visitor. I found my new French useful with the general.

Margaret Childs Boyd, my wife of almost two years, had found undershorts of mine, in the laundry, ominously stained, she said, from the very beginning of our time on T Street. She threatened to tell Mr. Jack Childs, now of Austin, that certain elaborate and philosophical pre-nuptial arrangements seemed to have fallen through. She had entered into an ill-disguised affair with a syndicated cartoonist who drew Lyndon as a sort of hunched question mark of a man with the face of a basset. She enjoyed, besides mechanical missionary congress, drinking imported beer. She had always enjoyed the beer—the first image her name summons to me involves her holding a misted mug of something Dutch up to the New Haven light—but now she got more and more enthusiastic about it. She drank with the cartoonist, with her remedial colleagues, with other election widows. Drunk, she accused me of being in love with Lyndon Johnson. She asked whether some of my stained shorts should be tucked away for posterity. I made her some good strong East Texas blend and went to my room, where by now I frequently worked into the morning on itineraries, mail, mailings, the organization and editing of some of Lyndon's more printable observations and remarks for possible inclusion in speeches. I became, simultaneously, a paid member of Lyndon's secretarial, research, and speech-writing staffs. I drew a generous enough salary to keep my new companion, M. Duverger, a young relation to the Haitian ambassador to the United States, in a pleasant, private brownstone unit that seemed ours alone. Duverger too admired the autographed portrait of Vice President and Mrs. Johnson I had hung, with his permission, in one of our rooms.

> "So let's just don't talk, and let's just don't brag. Let's talk to our kinfolks and our uncles and our cousins and our aunts, and let's go do our duty November third and vote Democratic."
> —Speech to Senior Class
> Chesapeake High School,
> Baltimore, Maryland
> October 24, 1960

> "So you tell them what you do is just reach up there and get that lever and just say, 'All the way with LBJ.' Your Mamas and your Papas and your Grandpas, some of them are going to forget this. But I am depending on you youths who are going to have to fight our wars, and who are going to have to defend this country, and who are going to get blown up if we have a nuclear holocaust—I am depending on you to have enough interest in your future which is ahead of you to get up and prod mama and papa and make them get up early and go vote."
> —Speech to Fourth-grade Class
> Mansfield Elementary School,
> Mansfield, Ohio
> October 31, 1964

"Boyd and Johnson? There wasn't one of us could really say we understood Dave's relationship with LBJ. None of us knew what kind of hold the boy had on Johnson. But we knew he had one."

"That's for sure."

"But it worked the other way, too, didn't it? Boyd worshipped the hell out of LBJ."

"I would've said 'worshipped' wasn't the right word."

"Loved?"

"Now let's not get off on that again, boys. Those rumors, we knew those were just rumorous lies, even at the time. There wasn't a homosexual bone in Lyndon Johnson's body. And he loved Lady Bird like an animal."

"There *was* something animalistic about LBJ, wasn't there? He confirmed animalism for me, in a way. His time in the limelight, that time seemed to confirm for the whole country that a man was nothing more than a real sad and canny animal. He could hope to be no more. It was a dark time."

"That's what those radicals hated so much about him. They were scared that all they were was animals, and that LBJ was just a cannier and more powerful animal. That's all there was to it."

"God knows what that bodes for the political future of this nation right here."

"LBJ was a genius and a gorilla at the same time."

"And Boyd liked that."

"I think Dave was certainly drawn to it, don't you all? Dave was not one bit like an animal. No way."

"Too refined to ever be animalistic, maybe."

"You could say he was refined, I suppose. But I never trusted him. Not enough of his personality or his character was ever out there for me to see for me to really call him refined. A refined what?"

"A lot of times Dave could be in a room with you and you'd never even notice him in the room."

"Almost refined right out of existence, somehow."

"Whereas a whole giant ballroom or convention hall would know if Johnson was in it. He made the whole air in a room different."

"Johnson *needed* to have people know he was in their room."

"Was that it, then? Johnson needed an audience, and Boyd

was an audience that Johnson knew was just barely there? That he didn't ever even have to acknowledge or feel any responsibility to?"

"I'm still not sold on it being impossible they were involved."

"I'm sure sold on it."

"I'm sold, also. Being homosexual would have been too delicate or human for LBJ to even dream of. I doubt if LBJ even had himself any ability to even try to imagine what being homosexual was like. Being homosexual is kind of abstract, to my way of thinking, and LBJ hated abstractions. They were outside his ken."

"He hated anything outside his ken. He'd totally ignore it, or else hate it."

"Boyd lived with that third-world French nigger that wore high heels. He lived with that nigger for years."

"Johnson had to have had some kind of hold over him."

"Did LBJ ever even know, though? About Boyd and that Negro? Even as close as him and LBJ were?"

"I never knew of anybody who had any inklings as to that."

"No one knew if he knew."

"How could he not know?"

—From Dr. C. T. Peete, ed.
Dissecting a President:
Conversations with LBJ's Inner Circle
1970

Lyndon as Vice President still kept his Dirksen Building office, the red tile with gold stars, the huge cubicled staff complex, the big window and the knotty-pine table where my new assistants sorted mail under my supervision.

'There was just one goddamned job I'd of picked up and moved that whole real carefully put-together system of offices and technology and personnel for. One goddamned job, boy,' he told me in the freezing open-air limousine on the way to his running mate's inauguration. 'And it seems like some good folks in their wisdom didn't want to give Lyndon Baines Johnson that job. So I say fuck off to all them, is what I say. Am I right Bird?' He knuckled at Claudia Johnson's ribs under her furs and taffeta.

'Now you just hush, now, Lyndon,' the lady said with a mock severity Lyndon clearly adored, a code between them. Lady Bird patted Lyndon's lined topcoat's thick arm and leaned across his red hooked profile, resting her other gloved hand on my knee.

'Now Mr. Boyd, I'm holding you responsible for making this rude and evil force of a man behave.'

'I'll try, Ma'am.'

'That's right boy, make me *behave*,' whooped the Vice President, waving to crowds he really looked at. 'I'll just tell you now, I have to blow my nose, or fart up there on that platform, I'm farting. I'm blowing my nose. Don't care how many *e*lectronic eyes are on that handsome little shit up there. Hope all this wind messes with his hair some.' He paused, looking around, surprised. 'Shoot, I *do* have to fart.'

He farted deeply into his coat and the limousine's cold hard leather seat.

'Whoo*ee*.'

'What is to be *done* with you, Lyndon?' Lady Bird laughed, cheerfully horrified, shaking her head at the crowd's waving line. I again remember white plumes of breath from everyone's mouth. It was freezing.

I first met Claudia Alta 'Lady Bird' Taylor Johnson at a summer barbecue on the banks of the Perdenales River that bordered Lyndon's ranch in Texas. Close friends and staff had been flown down to help Lyndon blow off steam and prepare for an upcoming Convention that already belonged, mathematically, to another man.

Lyndon had me shake hands with his dog.

'I'm telling Blanco to shake, not you, boy,' he reassured me. He turned to Lew N. Johnson. 'I *know* this boy will shake. Don't even have to say it to him.' Lew N. had pushed up his horn-rims and laughed.

'And this here is my unnatural wife, Mrs. Lyndon Baines Johnson,' he said, presenting to me a lovely, elegant woman with a round face and a sharp nose and a high hard hairdo. 'This is the Lady Bird, boy,' he said.

I'm very pleased to meet you, Ma'am.'

'This pleasure is mine, Mr. Boyd,' she murmured, a soft Texan.

I touched my lips to the small warm knuckles of the hand she proffered. Everyone around us could see the way Lyndon hung on the sound of his wife's voice, saw the tiny curtsies, her social motions, as though each movement of Lady Bird gently burst a layer of impediment between her and him.

'Lyndon has spoken to me of you with affection and gratitude,' she said, as Lyndon draped himself over her from behind and used his mouth to make a noise against the bare freckled shoulder just inside her gown's strap.

'Mr. Johnson is too kind,' I said, as Blanco slid against my shins and the hem of my Bermudas and then ran toward the smoking barbecue pit.

'That's *it* boy, I'm *too* kind!' Lyndon blared, knocking his head with his hand in revelation. 'Write that down for me, son: "Johnson *too* kind." ' He turned, making a bullhorn of his hands. 'Say!' he shouted. 'Is that there *band* going to play some songs, or did you boys' asses get connected onto your chairs?' A cluster of men with instruments and checked shirts and cowboy hats began to fall all over themselves rushing toward the small bandstand.

We listened, ate from paper plates. Lyndon stomped his boot in time to the band.

I felt a hand's tininess on my wrist. 'Perhaps you would do me the honor of calling to take tea and refreshment at some time.' Mrs. Johnson smiled, holding my gaze only as long as was needed to communicate something. I shivered slightly, nodding. Mrs. Johnson excused herself and moved off, turning heads and parting crowds, radiating some kind of authority that had nothing to do with power or connection or the ability to harm.

I hitched up my shorts, which tended even then to sag.

'Quit mooning around and go get you some barbecue!' Lyndon shouted in my ear, tearing at an ear of corn, stomping.

Lyndon had his second serious and first secret coronary in 1962. I was driving him home from the office, late. We moved east through Washington and toward his private ocean-side home. He began gasping in the passenger seat. He couldn't breathe properly.

The nasal inhaler had no effect. His lips blued. Mr. Kutner of the Secret Service and I had a hard time of it even getting him into the house.

Lady Bird Johnson and I stripped Lyndon down and massaged his bypass-scarred chest with isopropyl alcohol. Lyndon had wheezed that this usually helped his breathing. We massaged him. He had the sort of tired, bulblike breasts old men have.

His lips continued to cyanidize. He was having his second serious coronary, he gasped. Lady Bird massaged him all over. He refused to let me ask Kutner to call an ambulance. He wanted no one to know. He said he was the Vice President. It took Lady Bird's veto finally to get him to Bethesda Naval in a black-windowed Service sedan. Kutner ignored traffic lights. It took both Lady Bird's hands to hold Lyndon's hand as he fought for breath and clutched his shoulder. He was plainly in great pain.

'Shit,' he kept saying, baring his teeth at me. 'Shit, boy. *No.*'

'Yes, *no,*' Mrs. Johnson said soothingly into his giant blue ear.

The Vice President of the United States was in Bethesda for eighteen days. For routine tests, we had Salinger tell the press. Somehow, toward the end of his stay, Lyndon persuaded a surgeon to remove his healthy appendix. Pierre talked to the media at length about the appendectomy. Lyndon showed people the appendectomy scar at every public opportunity.

'Damn appendix,' he would say.

He began to take prescribed digitalis. Lady Bird forced him to stop eating the fried pork rind he kept in his top right desk drawer alongside his silver-handled revolver. I tried hard to stop smoking in Lyndon's office.

I received a note on plain pink stationery. 'My husband and I wish to thank you for your kind and discreet attention to our needs during my husband's recent illness.' The note smelled wonderful; M. Duverger said he wanted to smell the way *L'Oiseau's* note smelled.

    "I graduated from the Johnson City High School back in Texas in a class of six. For some time I had felt that my father was not really as smart as I thought he ought to be, and I thought that I could improve on a good many of my mother's approaches to life, as well. So when I got my high school diploma I decided to follow the old philosopher Horace Greeley's advice and 'Go West, Young Man,' and seek my fortune. With twenty-six dollars in my pocket and a T-Model Ford automobile, five of my schoolmates and I started out early one morning on our way to the Golden West, the great state of California. We got there in due time, minus most of my twenty-six dollars, and I got a very well-paying job of ninety dollars a month running an elevator up and down. But I found at the end of the month, after I paid for three meals and paid for my room and my laundry that I was probably better off back there eating Mama's food than I was in California. So I went back to Texas and I got a job with the Highway Department. We didn't have to get to work until sunup, and we got to quit every night at sundown. We did have to get to work on our own time. We had to be at work at sunup, and that was usually twenty or thirty miles down the Highway, and we had to ride home on our own time after sundown. I got paid the magnificent salary of a dollar a day. After a little over a year of that at the Highway Department, I began to think that my father's advice that I should go and take some more training and not be a school drop-out— maybe he was wiser than I had thought a year before. In other words, he became a lot smarter while I was gone in California and on the Highway. And with the help of the good Lord, and with a mother persistently urging to me to go back to school and get some training, I hitchhiked fifty miles to get back into the classroom, where I spent four long years. But I have been reasonably well-employed ever since. I now have a contract that runs until January 20, 1965.

—Speech to Graduating Class
Amherst College,
Amherst, Massachusetts
May 25, 1963

Mother came to Washington just once in those ten years to visit; she and Margaret kept in very good touch.

The day my mother visited, Duverger cooked all morning, a crown roast, yams in cream, and Les Jeux Dieux, a Haitian dessert, a specialty, airy and painfully sweet. He fussed nervously around the kitchen all morning in only an apron and heels while I vacuumed under furniture and worked surfaces over with oil soap.

Over drinks in the spotless room redolent of spiced pork, mother talked about Margaret Childs and how mother and Jack and Sue-Bea Childs so hoped that Margaret's hospitalization for alcohol dependency would mean a new lease on life for a dear girl who'd never once done anything to hurt anybody. Duverger kept fidgeting in the sportcoat I'd lent him.

It was the only completely silent dinner party I've ever experienced. We listened to the sounds of our knives against our plates. I could hear differences in our styles of mastication.

Our housewarming gift from her was a false cluster of grapes, the grapes purple marbles on a green glass stem.

My mother did not look old.

'*Elle a tort,*' Duverger kept repeating, later, as he applied the gel. He had little English he was proud of; we spoke a kind of pidgin when alone.

'*Elle a tort, cette salope-là.* She has wrong. She has wrong.'

I asked what he meant as he spread cold gel on himself and then me. He opened me roughly, rudely. I winced into the pattern of the bed's headboard.

'About what is Mother wrong?'

'She hates me because she believes you *love* me.'

He sodomized me violently, without one thought to my comfort or pleasure, finally shuddering and falling to weep against me. I had cried out several times in pain.

'*Ce n'est pas moi qui tu aimes.*'

'Of course I love you. We share a life, René.'

He was having difficulty breathing. '*Ce n'est* not I.'

'Whom, then?' I asked, rolling him off. 'If you say I do not love you, whom do I love?'

'*Tu m'en a* besoin,' he cried, rending dark bedroom air with his nails. 'You *need* me. You feel the responsibility for me. But your love it is not for me.'

'My love is for you, Duverger. Need, responsibility: these are part of love, in this nation.'

'Elle a tort.' He turned himself away, curling fetal on his side of the bed. 'She believes we are not lonely.' I said nothing.

'Why must it be lonely?' he said. He said it as if it were a statement. He kept repeating it. I woke once, very late, to his broad brown back, moving, a rhythm, his open hand to his face, still repeating.

> "He sees life as a jungle. No matter how long a rein you think you're on, he's always got the rein in his hands."
> —Former associate, 1963

> "Most of his worries are of his own making. He sees troubles where none exist. He's liable to wake up in the morning and think everything's got loose during the night."
> —Close friend, 1963

Lyndon spent the fourteen-minute ride to Parkland Hospital on the floor of the open-air limousine's back seat, his nose jammed against the sole of Senator Yarbrough's shoe. On top of them, covering them and holding them down as they struggled, was a Secret Serviceman whose cologne alone could have caused the confused panic I saw ripple through the Dallas streets' crowds as I lay on top of them all, riding their struggle, watching from my perch three Servicemen, in the convertible ahead, restraining the First Lady as she struggled and screamed, imploring them to let her go back to the site and retrieve something I could not quite hear.

We were jammed together in that back seat, a tumble of limbs, Yalies stuffing a phone booth. Lyndon's pantcuff and white hairless ankle and low-cut dress boot waved around in front of my face as we rode. I could hear him, beneath the overpoweringly scented Serviceman, cursing Yarbrough.

The hospital was choreographed madness. Lyndon, handkerchief to his bruised nose, was besieged by cameras, microphones, doctors, Servicemen, print media, and, worst, all those Presidentially appointed officials and staffers, eyes narrowed with self-interest, who knew enough to jump hosts before the political animal they had ridden had even cooled.

I telephoned Lady Bird Johnson—Lyndon's teeth had bared at even the suggestion that he use the telephone now—to reassure her and advise her to arrange travel to Dallas as quickly as possible. I called Hal Ball to facilitate quick transportation for Mrs. Johnson. I saw Lyndon trapped by the mob in the lobby's corner, his slack cheeks flushed hot, his nose redly purple, his small person's eyes dull with shock and a dawning realization. His little eyes sought mine above the roiling coil of press and lackeys, but he could not get through, even as I waved from the phone-bank.

'You get that mike out my face or it's gonna be calling your personal ass home,' was edited from the special newscasts. Dan Rather had reeled away, pale, rubbing his crew cut.

The crowd slowly dissolved as news from doctors and Service upstairs failed to forthcome. We were able to huddle with Lyndon in a small waiting room off the lobby. The meeting was grimly efficient. An ad hoc transition team was assembled on the spot. Service had set up a line to Ball back at the office. Bunker and Califano and Salinger were filling note cards furiously. Cabinet appointments were hashed out with the kind of distanced heat reserved for arguments about golf. Lyndon said little.

I took Lyndon up to the First Lady's room. Lyndon parted the crowd around her bed. He felt her tranquilized forehead with a hand that almost covered her face. Her color was good. A flashbulb popped. I saw the First Lady's drugged eyes between Lyndon's fingers.

No one had any news even about who in the hospital might have news. We all huddled, conferred, smoked, blew the smoke away from Lyndon, waited. Lyndon was so savage to those young Bostonians who came snuffling up both to commiserate and congratulate that our group was soon left to itself. Connally, his arm in a sling, hovered pacing at the perimeter of our circle, drinking at a bottled seltzer whose volume seemed to remain somehow constant.

I called Duverger, who had been home with bronchitis, watching the news on television and out of his mind with worry. I called Mrs. Teane at her home in Arlington. I tried to call Margaret at her treatment center in Maryland and was informed that she had checked out weeks ago. My mother's line remained busy for hours.

Our huddle ended, too, long before the official word came. Everyone had a hundred things to do. The small room emptied little by little. Flanked by Pierre and me, Lyndon finally had a few minutes to slouch and reflect in his waiting-room chair. He applied the inhaler to his swollen passages. His spurs made lines on the floor as he stretched out long legs. He held his own forearm, opening and closing his fist. The skin below his eyes was faintly blue. I dispensed some digitalis and all but had to force him to swallow.

We sat. We stared for a time at the little room's white walls. Connally studied the concession machines.

'Everything,' Lyndon was murmuring.

'Excuse me sir?'

He looked out absently over his own legs. 'Boy,' he said, 'I'd give every fucking thing I have not to have to stand up there and take a job ain't mine by right or by the will of folks. Your thinking man, he avoids back doors to things. Charity. Humiliation. Distrust. Responsibility you didn't never get to get ready to expect.'

'Natural to feel that way, LB,' Connally said, feeding a candy machine coins.

Lyndon stared hard at a point I could not see, shaking his great pill of a head.

'I'd give every fucking thing I have, boy.'

Salinger shot me a look, but I had already clicked out my pen.

There was transition. Two hurried mass mailings. Boxes to be packed and taped. Burly movers to be supervised.

Duverger's health declined. He seemed unable to shake the bronchitis and the coincident infections it opened him to. He lost the strength to climb stairs and had to give up his job at the boutique. He lay in bed, listening to scratched Belafonte records and raising in our linen a daily mountain of colorful used Kleenex. He lost weight and had fevers. I learned that malaria was endemic in Haiti, and obtained quinine from Bethesda. Whether from empathy or exposure, I felt my own health getting more delicate as the time with Duverger passed. I caught every sore throat that went around the White House. I got used to having a sore throat.

The White House systems for receiving and distributing and answering mail were huge, hugely staffed, time-tested, honed to a hard edge of efficiency. Lyndon's Same Day Directive presented these quick furtive career mailboys small challenge. I became little more than a postal figurehead, responsible for drafting and updating the ten or so standardized reply letters that were printed and signature-stamped by the gross and flowed out in response to the growing number of letters and telegrams from people in every state. By 1965 the incoming mail was on the whole negative, and it was hard to prevent the formulated responses from sounding either artificial or defensive and shrill.

Duverger and I were formally married in a small civil ceremony outside a Mount Vernon suburb. The service was attended by a few close mutual friends. Peter came all the way from Charlotte. Duverger had to sit for the ceremony, dressed in mute silks that deemphasized, or maybe complemented, the sick weak gray of his complexion.

> "I especially appreciate your coming here because I feel I have a rapport with you and they won't let me out of the gate so I am glad they let you in."
>> —To White House Tour Group
>> May 14, 1966

> "This is not a change in purpose. It is a change in what we believe that purpose requires."
>> —To Young Democrats' Council
>> Columbia University, New York
>> May 21, 1966

> "He seemed to get obsessed with his health. He began to seem robust in the way delicate people seem robust."
> "Boyd got delicate and obsessed, too. He wore his topcoat all the time. He perspired. As if he followed LBJ's lead in everything."
> "Boyd barely even had a formal function. That army of

career mail-boys of Kennedy's was all over the SDD before we even got the transition over with."

"He'd just sit there holding the radio while Lyndon worked. Who knows what he did in there."

"They'd both wander around constantly. Walk around the grounds. Look out the fence."

"Sometimes just the President alone, except there wandering a ways behind him'd be Boyd, with all those Secret Service folks."

"But who knows what they walked over in that office, hour after hour."

"The radio stopped, when they were in there."

"Who knows how many decisions he was in on. Tonkin. Cambodia. The whole Great Big Society."

"We'll never know that about Lady Bird, either. She was one of those behind-the-scenes types of First Ladies. Influence impossible to gauge."

"We know Boyd helped write some of the later speeches."

"But no one even knows which ones were whose."

"They were all thick as thieves over there."

"Nobody who knows anything is even alive anymore."

"That summary-boy with the ears had that gruesome office pool going about whether Dave would outlive Lyndon.

—From *Dissecting*

"Now you folks come on and be happy, God damn it."
—Televised address
Oval Office,
White House
November 1967

Most of the stories about those last months, about Lyndon refusing sometimes ever to leave the Oval Office, are the truth. I sat in the oversized corner chair, my lap full of tissues and lozenges, and watched him urinate into the iron office wastebasket Mrs. Teane would quietly empty in the morning. Sounds in the office were hushed by thick Truman carpet, lush furnishings. The office was dark except for passing headlights and the orange flicker of the protesters' bonfire in the park across the street.

The office window facing Pennsylvania was dappled and smeared with the oil of Lyndon's nose. He stood, face touching the window, an ellipse of his breath appearing and shrinking and appearing on the glass as he whispered along with the protesters' crudely rhymed chants. Helicopters circled like gulls; fat fingers of spotlight played over the park and the White House grounds and the line of Kutner's Servicemen ranged along the black iron fence. Things were occasionally thrown at the fence, and clattered.

Lyndon applied his nasal inhaler, inhaling fiercely.

'How many kids did I kill today, boy?' he asked, turning from the window.

I sniffed deeply, swallowing. 'I think that's neither a fair nor a healthy way to think about a question like that, sir.'

'Goddamn your pale soul boy I asked you how *many*.' He pointed at a window full of yam-colored bonfire light. 'They're sure the mother-fuck asking. I think Lyndon Johnson should be allowed to ask, as well.'

'Probably between three and four hundred kids today, sir,' I said. I sneezed wetly and miserably into a tissue. 'Happy now?'

Lyndon turned back to the window. He had forgotten to rebutton his trousers.

'Happy,' he snorted. The best way to tell he'd heard you was to listen for repetition. 'You think they're happy?' he asked.

'Who?'

He twitched his big head at the bonfire, listening for the tiny loudness of the distant bullhorns and the plaintive hiss of crowds' response. He slouched, his hands on the sill for support. 'Those youths of America over across there,' he said.

'They seem pretty upset, sir.'

He hitched up his sagging pants thoughtfully. 'Boy, I get a smell of happiness off their upset, however. I think they enjoy getting outraged and vilified and unjustly ignored. That's what your leader of this here free world thinks, boy.'

'Could you elaborate on that, sir?'

Lyndon horselaughed a big misted circle onto the window, and we looked together at the big hand-lettered sign on the Oval Office wall, beside the cattle horns, behind the Presidential desk. I'd made it. It read NEVER ELABORATE.

He was shaking his head. 'I believe . . . I believe I am out of touch with the youth of America. I believe that they cannot be touched by me, or by what's right, or by intellectual concepts on what's right for a nation.'

I sneezed.

He touched, with big brown-freckled fingers, at the window, leaving more smears. 'You'll say this is easy for me to say, but I say they've had it too goddamned easy, son. These youths that are yippies and that are protesters and that use violence and public display. We gave it to them too easy, boy. I mean their Daddies. Men that I was youths with. And these youths today are pissed *off*. They ain't never once had to worry or hurt or suffer in any real way whatsoever. They do not know Great Depression and they do not know desolation.' He looked at me. 'You think that's good?'

I looked back at him.

'I think I'm gettin' to be a believer in folks' maybe needing to suffer some. You see some implications in that belief? It implies our whole agenda of domestic programs is maybe possibly bad, boy. I'm headed for thinking it's smelling bad right at the heart of the whole thing.' He inhaled nasally, watching protesters dance around. 'We're taking away folks' suffering here at home through these careful domestic programs, boy,' he said, 'without giving them nothing to replace it. Take a look at them dancing across over there, boy, shouting *fuck you* like they invented both fucking and me, their President, take a look over across, and you'll see what I see. I see some animals that need to suffer, some folks that need some suffering to even be Americans inside, boy; and if we don't give them some suffering, why, they'll just go and hunt up some for themselves. They'll take some suffering from some oriental youths who are caught in a great struggle between sides, they'll go and take those other folks' suffering and take it inside themselves. They're getting stimulation from it, son. I'm believing in the youths of America's need for some genuine stimulation. Those youths are out there making their own stimulation; they're making it from scratch off oriental youths wouldn't squat to help your Mama take a leak. We as leaders haven't given them shit. They think prosperity and leadership is dull. God bless the general patheticness of their souls.' He pressed his nose against the glass. I had a quick vision, as he stood there, of children and candy stores.

I squinted as a helicopter's passing spot brightened the Oval Office to a brief blue noon. 'So you think there's something right about what they're doing out there?'

' "Something *right*," ' Lyndon snorted, motionless at the blue window. 'No, 'cause they got no notion of right and wrong. Listen. They got no notion whatsoever of right and wrong, boy. Listen.'

We listened to them. I sniffed quietly.

'To them, right and wrong is *words,* boy.' He came away and eased himself into his big desk chair, sitting straight, hands out before him on the unscarred presidential cherrywood. 'Right and wrong ain't words,' he said. 'They're feelings. In your guts and intestines and such. Not words. Not songs with guitars. They're what make you feel like you do. They're inside you. Your heart and digestion. Like the folks you personally love.' He felt at his forearm and clenched his fist. 'Let them sad sorry boys out across there go be *responsible* for something for a second, boy. Let them go be responsible for some folks and then come back and tell their President, me, LBJ, about right and wrong and so forth.'

We took his pulse together. We measured his pressure. There were no pains in his shoulder or side, no blue about his mouth. We reclined him for blood flow, placed his boots on the window's sill. My chest and back were soaked with perspiration. I made my way back to my chair in the corner, feeling terribly faint.

'You all right, boy?'

'Yes, sir. Thank you.'

He chuckled. 'Some pair of federal functionaries right here, I got to say.'

I coughed.

We listened, quiet, unwell, to the songs and chants and slogans and to the chop of Service helicopters and the clang and clatter of beer cans. Minutes passed in the faint bonfire glow. I asked Lyndon whether he was asleep.

'I ain't sleeping,' he said.

'Could I ask you to tell me what it feels like, then, sir.'

A silence of distant chant. Lyndon picked at his nose deeply, his eyes closed, head thrown back.

'Does what feel like?'

I cleared my throat. 'Being responsible, as you were saying, I meant. Being responsible for people. What does it feel like, if you are?'

He either chuckled or wheezed, a deep sound, almost subsonic, from the recesses of his inclined executive chair. I stared at his profile, a caricaturist's dream.

'You and Bird,' he said. 'Damned if you and my Bird don't always ask the same things of Lyndon Johnson, son. It's queer to me.' He brought himself upright to face my bit of the office's darkness. 'I done told Bird just last week how responsibility, why, it is not even like a feeling at all,' he said quietly.

'You can't feel what responsibility feels like? It numbs you?'

He administered the inhaler, played with his fob against the bad light of the window.

'I told Bird it's like the sky, boy. Is what I told her. How about if I come and ask you what does the sky *feel* like to you? The sky ain't a feeling, boy.'

We both coughed.

He pointed upward, vaguely up at the horns, nodding as if at something familiar. 'But it's there, friend. The sky is there. It's there, over your ass, every fucking day. 'Matter where you go, boy, look on up, and on top of every goddamned thing else she's there. And the day there ain't no sky . . .'

He squeezed and worked the last bits of inhalant out of his nasal inhaler. It was a hideous sound. Before long I had to help Lyndon back over to the office wastebasket full of urine. We stood there, together, on the plain white marble Presidents' floor.

"Mr. Lyndon 'LBJ' Johnson, like all men in public service, was driven both by a great and zealous personal ambition and by a great and zealous compassion for the well-being of his fellow man. He was, like all great men, hell, like all men, a paradox of mystery. He will not and cannot ever be completely or totally understood. But for those of us gathered today under these great lone-star skies to try and understand a man we must try to understand if we are to do him the honor he deserves, I say this. I say to go west. I say the further you go west, the nearer you get to Lyndon Baines Johnson."

> —Texas State Senator Jack Childs
> Eulogy on the Passing of LBJ
> Austin, Texas, 1968

When I received the pink, plainly inscribed invitation to take tea and refreshment with Claudia 'Lady Bird' Johnson, I was prostrate in our big bed, down with a violent flu.

Duverger had been gone almost a week. I had come home from some mass-mailing work in New Hampshire to find him gone. He had left no word and had packed none of his several pieces of luggage. His money and several of my small black office notebooks were gone.

I can offer no better testimony to my feelings for Lyndon's career than my panic that René had either defected to or been shanghaied by some Other Side. Most of the entries in the notebooks were verbatim. One had recounted a Joint Chiefs briefing session held on sinks and hampers and the lip of a claw-footed tub while Lyndon had been moving his bowels on the commode. There was enough truth in those tiny records to embarrass Lyndon beyond repair; he had ordered that everything that was written be written. I admit, with pain, that my first day's thoughts were of Lyndon and betrayal and the masklike Republican we'd all grown to fear.

Three days of frantic searching for Duverger had taken me as far north as the New Hampshire camps of Humphrey, McCarthy, Lindsay and Percy—and that man—and as far south as the dark lounges of Chevy Chase. It left me weak beyond description, and I came down with a violent flu. Lyndon, too, had been sick, out of the office and news for a week. He had not contacted me. No one from either office or White House had called for the three days I had been home ill. And I hadn't the character to call anyone.

'Our husbands and I inquire as to whether you would do us the

honor of taking tea and refreshment at our Shore home this evening,' read the note on colored stationery, without letterhead. I
had become so trained to look for the letterhead first that the
blankness of the First Lady's notes seemed almost high-handed.

And it was well-known scuttlebutt—scuttle, I suspected, from
the butt of Margaret's old cartoonist, who had sketched me as a
W.C.-Fields-nosed flower girl, holding the '68 train of Johnson as
bride—that Mrs. Johnson wanted Lyndon out, and saw his office/
me as the rival she'd never had in life. 'Our husbands,' then, fit
what I would hear.

Too, we could never name the heady perfume that had risen
from Mrs. Johnson's notes and seduced Duverger from the first.
He had shopped, sniffing, for days, and had fixed the central scent
as essence of bluebonnet before he had become unable to leave
our home altogether.

Duverger was dying of something that was not malaria. All four
of my salaries went to Bethesda, where Duverger was not covered
and where the staff, like Aquinas before God, could think of nothing to do but define his decline via what it was not. The doctors
between whom I had shuttled my seated, coughing husband could
isolate nothing but a pattern in his susceptibility to the uncountable
diseases that came and thrived in the petri dish that was Washington.

For these last many months I had lain at nighttime holding a man
dying of a pattern, encircling with my white arm gray ribs that
became more and more defined, feeling pulses through a wrist too
wasted narrow to support the length of its long-nailed hand, watching his stomach cave and his hips flare like a woman's and his knees
bulge like balls from his legs' receding meat.

'Suis fatigue. M'aimes-tu?'
'Tais-toi. Bois celui-ci.'
'M'aimes-tu?'

An ever weaker me, blinking the cornered translucence of all
my connections, I saw Lyndon himself fading before a carnivorous
press corps; a war as nasty and real and greenly-broadcast as it was
statistical and fuzzily bordered to those of us who read and acted

on the actual reports; a reversal of his presidential resolve that the
government's *raison* was before all to reduce sum totals of suffering;
a growing intuition of his own frailty as two more well-concealed
infarctions left him gaunt and yellow and blotched, his eyes seeming
to grow to fit the face that settled into itself around them.

Duverger, who hadn't the strength to leave, was gone. He had
taken my notes and left none of his own. Nothing in the vase below
the mantel's autographed photo and little Klee. Amid tissues and
the popped aluminum shells of antinauseants, I read the finely
penned note from Mrs. Johnson, hand-delivered by one of my own
distant subordinates in Mail. I breathed at what rose from the note.

'Wardine has prepared some praline mix which I find to com-
plement camomile tea very nicely, Mr. Boyd.'

'Thank you, Ma'am.'

'Thank you that will be all Wardine.'

The black servant in black stockings and a doilied apron wiped
away the last of the cold cream that had masked the First Lady's
round sharp face. She adjusted the pillow under Mrs. Johnson's
feet and withdrew, her back always to me.

I coughed faintly. I wiped my forehead.

'My own husband is near death, child.'

I had arrived late by taxi at the Johnsons' private home, retained
from his days as a Senator, a turreted post-plantation thing on the
very eastern shore of the Potomac delta that pouted lip-like out
into the Atlantic. I could hear ocean and see lightning bubbling
over a cloud roof far out to the east's sea. A horn in a channel
moaned. I felt at the glands in my throat.

'You don't look well at all yourself, Mr. Boyd.'

I looked about. 'Will the President be able to join us, Ma'am?'

She looked at me over her cup of steam. 'Lyndon is dying, child.
He has had great and additional . . . trouble with the illness that
has been troubling him all these years.'

'He infarcted again?'

'He has asked not to be alone on this night.'

'He's supposed to die tonight, you're saying?'

She readjusted the hem of her robe. 'It's a great trial for all of us who are close to the President.' She looked up. 'Don't you agree?'

I was wary. There were no doctors. I'd seen only the ordinary number of Kutner's men at the gate. I sniffed meatily. 'So then why aren't you with him, Ma'am, if he doesn't want to be alone?'

Lady Bird took a tiny bite of praline. She smiled the way elegant ladies smile when they chew. 'I am with Lyndon every moment of every day, dear child. As he told you. President Johnson and I are too close, we believe, to afford one another real company or comfort.' She took another little bite. 'Perhaps those come from others?'

I sipped at the sweet tea in the wafer-thin china cup. The cup was almost too delicate to hold. A wave of complete nausea went over me. I hunched and closed my eyes. My ears rang, from medicine. I wanted to tell Mrs. Johnson that I didn't believe what she, who had flown to Dallas in a *fighter-jet,* was sitting there calmly eating a cookie and telling me. I really wanted to tell her I had troubles of my own. I didn't want to tell her what they were. I wanted to talk to Lyndon.

'So I'm to go sit up with him, Ma'am?'

'Are you all right, Mr. Boyd?'

'Not exactly. But I'd be honored to sit with President Johnson.' I tried to swallow. 'But I very much doubt, with all due respect, that the President is actually dying, Ma'am. No two consecutive presidents have ever died in office, Mrs. Johnson.' I had researched this for a form letter reassuring citizens who'd written for reassurance in 1963.

Mrs. Johnson adjusted her robe under herself on the pink sofa. Everything about the room was as a First Lady's personal private parlor should be. From the mirrors with frames carved like tympana to the delicate oriental statuary to the crystal place settings spread out upright for display on white shelves to the spiraled rug whose pattern swirled into itself in a kind of arabesque between my couch and Mrs. Johnson's. I closed my eyes.

'You too, Mr. Boyd,' she said, snapping a cookie, 'seem marked for a . . . a kind of frailty by the evident love and responsibility you feel toward others.'

I heard an expensive clock tick. I decided what this was about
and somehow just withdrew my thoughts from Duverger and the
books. I swallowed against a hot flash. 'I'm not in love with the
President,' I said.

She smiled wonderfully as what I'd said hung there. 'I beg your
pardon, Mr. Boyd.'

'I'm sure it looks bad, my being sick just when he's sick,' I said.
I held onto the arm of my sofa. 'I'm sure you've heard several
stories about me and about how I'm supposedly in love with Mr.
Johnson and follow him around like a love-starved animal and want
to be intimate with him and enjoy such a close working relationship
with him because I love him.' I'm afraid I retched the bit of the
camomile and praline refreshment I'd taken. It hung in a dusky
line of retch over my topcoat and slowly collected itself in my lap.
'Well I'm not,' I said, wiping my mouth. 'And please excuse me
for retching just now.'

'Mr. Boyd,' she said. 'Dear Mr. Boyd, I have no reservations
about your feelings for Lyndon. I appreciate beyond my poor power
to express it your devotion to my husband, to the responsibility
and tasks the Lord has seen fit to assign him. I appreciate your
feelings toward my husband more than I can say. And I believe I
understand what those feelings are.' She looked delicately away
from my lap. 'I was speaking of *your* husband.'

I was dabbing at the puddle, swirled with praline. 'And this my-
husband-your-husband business, Ma'am. I'd just ignore as much
scuttlebutt as you can. Rumors are seldom all true,' I said. I stood,
to facilitate my dabbing.

Mrs. Johnson's forehead furrowed and cleared. '*Your* husband,
Mr. Boyd.' She produced a sort of pink index card as I stood there.
'M. Duverger,' she read, 'a Caribbean Negro with diplomatic immunity, civilly married by you in 1965.' She looked up from the
card. 'He has been kind enough to provide Lyndon the company
and attention he has required during his illness.'

I tried to focus on the rug. 'Duverger is here?'

'As you were north, doing what Mr. Donagan described as integral
postal work for our organization in New Hampshire,' she said,

tidying the cookie tray. 'He arranged for Mr. Kutner of the Service to bring your husband to our home to be presented to the President. Who is dying.'

I sneezed. She sipped. I looked for something in her face. I had an unreasonable need to see whose script was on the index card she'd produced. These balanced off urges both to race to Duverger's side—though the Shore home was huge, and I'd never been past the rear hall—and to know how on earth Coby Donagan could have said the work I'd been north doing was important. I wanted so many different things all at once that I could not move. The First Lady sipped. 'So Mr. Johnson knows I have a husband?' I said.

'How, child, could he not know?' Lady Bird smiled kindly. 'How could he not know the heart of a young man who has emptied his life and his own heart into the life and work of Lyndon Baines Johnson?'

I began to feel for Mrs. Johnson a dislike beyond anything I'd ever felt for Margaret. She sat there, coiffed, in a robe, eating pralines. I felt simply awful. 'Is Duverger all right?' I said hoarsely. 'Where is he? Has he died? He's been dying, is the thing. Not Mr. Johnson. That's why I think I'm sick. Not Mr. Johnson.'

'They have been conversing together, Mr. Boyd.'

'René has hardly any English.'

She shrugged as at the irrelevant. 'They have had several conversations of great length, Lyndon has told me. And preserved them, as you two did.'

'How could Duverger not have said he was coming here? Is he dead?'

'M. Duverger has impressed Lyndon as a truly singular Negro, Mr. Boyd. They have discussed such issues close to Lyndon's heart as suffering, and struggles between sides, and Negroness. It was the best my husband has felt since you and Mrs. Teane finally removed him from his office, he told me.'

'Is he dead, I said,' I said.

She ate. 'Are you as privy as I to what my husband feels, David?' She looked for response. I wasn't giving any if she wasn't. 'My husband,' she continued, 'feels responsibility as you and I feel our own weight. The responsibility has eaten at him. You have watched him. You have been his sole comfort for almost a decade, child.'

'So you really are afraid he's in love with me.'

Whether from resemblance or real grief, I noticed, she answered questions as Lyndon did; she answered them as tangents, on a kind of curve that brought her now in close, now out on her own course. Now she tittered Southernly, a white hand to her mouthful of refreshment. Her hair was confined in a kind of net.

'Lyndon cannot, he insists, for the life of him understand why new generations such as your own see everything of importance in terms of love, David. As if it explained feelings lasting years, that word.'

I could see Kutner's shadow, and another, move from foyer to kitchen. I rose.

She said 'Love is simply a word. It joins separate things. Lyndon and I, though you would disagree, agree that we do not properly *love* one another anymore. Because we ceased long ago to be enough *apart* for a 'love' to span any distance. Lyndon says he shall cherish the day when *love* and *right* and *wrong* and *responsibility,* when these words, he says, are understood by you youths of America to be nothing but arrangements of distance.'

'Is that Kutner and Coby Donagan I saw going into the kitchen?'

'Please sit.'

I sat.

She leaned in. 'Lyndon is haunted by his own conception of distance, David. His hatred of being alone, physically alone, no matter atop what—the area of his hatred in which your own devoted services have been so invaluable to us—his hatred of being alone is a consequence of what his memoir will call his great intellectual concept: the distance at which we see each other, arrange each other, love. That love, he will say, is a federal highway, lines putting communities, that move and exist at great distance, in touch. My husband has stated publicly that America, too, his own America, that he loves enough to conceal deaths for, is to be understood in terms of distance.'

'So we don't even love each other, then?' I stared at her crystal place settings, arranged and never used, hot with nausea. 'Two close people can't love each other, even in a sort of Platonic way?'

'You stand in relations, my husband says. You contain one another. He says he owns the floor you stand on. He says you are the sky whose presence and meaning have become everyday.'

I coughed.

'Surely love means less?'

I realized, again, what Mrs. Johnson was talking about. I almost retched again.

'Mrs. Johnson,' I said, 'I was talking about Duverger and me.' I tried to lean as she had. 'Does Mr. Johnson know that Duverger and I love each other? That my first thoughts, when I found the notebooks and him gone, were for him? Does he know that I love?'

The shadow apart from Kutner's was Wardine, the First Lady's Negro servant, who was skilled with cold cream.

'And who wrote that card, about me, you read from?' I said.

'Someone in the room above us,' Mrs. Johnson said, not pointing, 'where the two husbands inside us have withdrawn,' not looking at me once, 'have removed themselves to positions of distance, must know that we love, child. He simply must. Don't you agree?' She inclined to the china pot, lifted its wafery lid to let Wardine check its contents. Upstairs. I was on my feet. She could tell me to sit as much as she liked.

'The President won't die, Ma'am.'

'Don't you agree?'

Wardine poured for her mistress, then came for my cup.

'Ma'am?'

She leaned, dispensing sugar, speaking to her own sharp bird's face as it trembled on the surface of her tea like the moon on water. 'I asked you, boy, whether or not you agreed.'

The smell of my soiled topcoat was the smell that came, faint, from under that door. The gently feminine clink of Lady Bird Johnson's willow-necked spoon was the masculine sound of my heavy old undergraduate ring rapping firmly against the carved panel of that great bedroom door. I rapped. A spasm passed through me, my gut, and I held until it passed. Something else moaned, businesslike, in the harbor.

The big door was silent, tonight, in November, 1968.

Forget the curved circle, for whom distance means the sheer size of what it holds inside. Build a road. Make a line. Go as far west as the limit of the country lets you—Bodega Bay, not Whittier, California—and make a line; and let the wake of the line's movement be the distance between where it starts and what it sees; and keep making that line, west, farther and farther; and the earth's circle will clutch at that line, keep it near to what it holds, like someone greedy with a praline; and the giant curve that informs straight lines will bring you around, in time, to the distant eastern point of the country behind you, that dim master bedroom on the dim far eastern shore of the Atlantic; and the circle you have made is quiet and huge, and everything the world holds is inside: the bedroom: a toppled trophy has punched a shivered star through the glass of its case, a swirling traffic-flickered carpet and massed wooden fixtures smelling of oil soap and the breath of the ill. I saw the big white Bufferin of the President's personal master bed, stripped to sheets, variously shadow-colored by the changing traffic light at the Washington and Kennedy Streets' intersection below and just outside. On the stripped bed—neatly littered with papers and cards, my notecards, a decade of stenography to Lyndon—lay my lover, curled stiff on his side, a frozen skeleton X ray, impossibly thin, fuzzily bearded, his hand outstretched with dulled nails to cover, partly, the white face beside him, the big white face attached to the long form below the tight clean sheets, motionless, the bed flanked by two Servicemen who slumped, tired, red, green. Duverger's spread cold hand partly covered that Presidential face as in an interrupted caress; it lay like a spider on the big pill of the man's head, the bland, lined, carnivore's mouth, his glasses with clear frames, his nasal inhaler on the squat bedside table, the white Hot Line blinking, mutely active, yellow in a yellow light on Kennedy. Duverger's hand was spread open over the face of the President. I saw the broad white cotton sheet, Duverger above and

Johnson below, the sharp points of Johnson's old man's breasts against the sheet, the points barely moving, the chest hardly rising, the sheet pulsing, ever so faintly, like water at great distance from its source.

I wiped mucus from my lip and saw, closer, the President's personal eyes, the eyes of not that small a person, eyes yolked with a high blue film of heartfelt pain, open and staring at the bedroom's skylight through Duverger's narrow fingers. I heard lips that kissed the palm of a black man as they moved together to form words, the eyes half-focused on the alien presence of me, leaning in beside the bed.

Duverger's hand, I knew, would move that way only if the President was smiling.

'Hello up there,' he whispered.

I leaned in closer.

'Lyndon?'

JOHN BILLY

1. WAS ME SUPPOSED TO TELL SIMPLE RANGER

Was me supposed to tell Simple Ranger how Chuck Nunn Junior done wronged the man that wronged him and fleen to parts unguessed. Brought up the Ranger to date on Chuck and Mona May Nunn's boy Chuck Junior, closest thing to handsome and semi-divine we got here in Minogue Oklahoma, good luck bad luck man, who everything that hit him stuck and got valuable, but on whom of this late time the vicissitudes of human relatings had wrought grief and retinal aggravation to such a extreme that C. Nunn Jr. lost his temper to a nameless despair and got him some vengeance.

Told Nunn's tale to Simple Ranger, the damaged dust-scout, who is a old man, watched his farm blow away in the hard and depressed highwindy days of the Bowl, got farmless, but however angled some job out of F. Delano R.'s WPA and set himself up in a plywood shack on the Big Dirt between here and El Reno, drawing government pay as a watcher for major or calamitous dust. Stayed out there near on forty years til looking at the dust made him damaged. Now he's too old not to be back, roving the streets in a kind of crazy d.j. vu, Minogue Oklahoma's own toothless R. Winkle, wants to re-know the lives of his people and their children after forty alone years of trying to make out the shape of his farm in the air. Buys me my personal beers with the checks some Washington D.C. computer sends him too much of, and I tell Simple Ranger things about Minogue only he don't know.

Told him some facts about Chuck Nunn Junior, with whom even the high winds decline to mess. How the prodigiousness of his 1948 birth tore up his Momma Mona May's innards so bad that even today the woman can only fall asleep after hot pads and loud opera, and requires institutional caring. How Chuck Junior was swarthy and pubic by ten, bearded and bowlegged and randy by twelve; how his late Daddy tried to whip him just once, like to broke his belt to smithers on Chuck Junior's concrete behind. How C. Jr. flipped his cherry on our seventh-grade music teacher, a pale, jagged woman, but highly scented, who even today passes through Minogue Oklahoma in a Trailways bus ever leap year, needlepointing and humming vacant tunes of love's non-requiting. How Chuck Nunn Junior's color was that of the land and how his sweat smelled like copper and how the good ladies of Minogue got infallibly behooved to sit down whenever he passed, walking as walks a man who is in communion with Forces, legs bandy and boots singing with the Amarillo spurs he won himself at the '65 State Fair in O. City for kicking the public ass of a bull without but one horn, but a sharp one.

Told Simple Ranger, whose rate of beer is scary on account of no teeth to hinder a maximal swallow, told Ranger how, while he was out on Big Dirt watching skies and eating peas out of cans, Minogue Oklahoma H.S. won the state H.S. football title two years back to back with Chuck Nunn Junior at quarterback and defense and myself at Equipment Manager. How in '66, in the state final versusing Minogue Oklahoma and Enid Oklahoma, our sworn and fatal foes for all time, how in the final game's final few competitive seconds Enid, down by five, granted the ball to their giant ringer nameless nigra wingback, who took off from the Enid eleven with the ball in his hands and wrongness in his eyes, meaning harm to Minogue Oklahoma's very heart and self-perception, this nigra blowing through Minogue boys like grit on big wind, plus getting interferences run by two cow-punchers' boys of human form but

geologic size, plus a Canadian martial arts expert in a padded bath-
robe and metal cleats, who played dirty and low. How (I'm seeing
this now, mind) how after a climactic and eternal chase-down-the-
field and catch-from-behind, a swift cruel red-bearded and glitter-
eyed C. Nunn Jr. brought down the whole stadium house, solved
the runner-plus-interference problem at our ten's Enid sideline by
tackling the huge cow-boys, the low Canadian kicker, the inhumanly
fast nigra, three Enid cheerleaders, a referee, and one ten-gallon
cooler of Enid Gatorade, all at one cataclysmic time. Busted a
igneous leg on a interferer's spine and healed up in just weeks,
bandier than before. Got a hall of Minogue Oklahoma H.S. named
Chuck Nunn Junior Hall.

2. CHUCK NUNN JUNIOR MORE GOD THAN NOT

Told Simple Ranger some data on how Chuck Nunn Junior, more
God than not to those of us peers that lived for a whiff of his jet
trail, ate up his school and town, left us bent and in mid-yearn
his eighteenth year and moved on to Oklahoma University, Norman, at whence he was observable throwing high-altitude televised
spirals and informing his agriculture and range-management teachers of facts they did not know. Then how Nunn chucked it all to
give time as a volunteer in The United States' Involvement in
Vietnam, whence trickled down rumors of the glory and well-armed
mightiness of Nunn: how he toted his unit's fifty-calibers up sheer
and cliff-like impediments to conflict; how he declined to duck,
never once crawled or ate mud, however never even once smelled
lead in his cranial vicinity; how he got alone and surrounded by
VCR's (Viet Cong Regulars) in '71, and through sheer force of
personality and persuasion persuaded the whole battalion of sly
slanted Charlies to turn their own guns on their selves. How etc.
etc. How he sent me a postcard with a red bloom of napalmed
jungle on the front, wrote how he wished my personal vision was

better so I could leave the feed store and get over there to watch and whiff the trail of his jet.

Simple Ranger's eyes is the color of the sky. There's speculation hereabouts concerning if you look at something long enough does your eyes take its color.

I profess to telling the grey-eyed Ranger, plus a Nunn-happy group of Minogue civilians, how Chuck Nunn Junior returned home from OU Norman and South East Conflict more theory than man. How there was a welcome parade, fussy and proud, with a tuba. How the immoderate and killer twister that hit in '74 (this twister old Simple Ranger, by then more than a tinch damaged, chased for twelve helter and skelter miles in his DeSoto, said he smelled his aloft land in every revolution, finally wound up upside down in phone lines and no sign of his car evermore. Didn't never come down) that hit in spring, '74, the day after Nunn's returning and parade, how that sucker ripped the roof off Nunn's late Daddy's machine shed, sucked two N. Rockwell prints and Nunn's late Daddy out a busted ranchhouse window to follow Simple Ranger's DeSoto in a straight-up, and how it took up the Nunns' TV's aerial antenna off the house roof and flew the electric javelin out a fair quarter mile, flung the pole down into Nunn land like a mumblepeg, and how up from this TV-speared ground, just inherited *ex officio* by Chuck Nunn Junior, come a bubbling crude. Black gold. Texas tea. How Nunn paid off his late missing Daddy's sheep ranch's mortgage with revenues, put his scrambled and operatic Momma Mona May into institutional caring, and took over the Nunn sheep business with such a slanderous cunning and energy, plus oil money, that soon amounts of CNJ-brand sheep was bulging straining and bleating against the barbed wire limit of Nunn's spread, mating in frenzies, plus putting out wool hand over hoof, plus fighting over which one got to commit suicide whenever Nunn looked like he even might

(*"Might,"* I told Simple Ranger)

be hungry.

Was telling the dust-watcher how C. Nunn Jr. passed up multitudes of come-hitherish cheerleaders and oriental princesses to return to Minogue and enter into serious commitment with his childhood sweetheart, the illegally buxom and tall Glory Joy duBoise, closest thing to femininity and pulchritude that to date exists in Minogue Oklahoma, eyes like geometry and a all-around bodily form of high allure and near-religious implication, and just as I was commencing a analogy relating the shape of Glory Joy's hips to the tight curve of the distant Big Dirt horizon, the door to the Outside Minogue Tavern busted inward and there against the dusty sunlight was framed the tall, angstified, and tortured frame of Glory Joy duBoise, hand to her limpid and Euclidean eyes, hips (that was similar to horizons) brushing the trauma-struck frame of the busted-inward door. She stood like that for time, looking at me, then come over at the table we was all at. Whereupon she stood, staggered, dropped and flopped in a floor-direction, her wracked and convulsively semi-conscious frame moving in directions like the Minogue Oklahoma H.S. half-time band, spelling out Kicked In The Butt By Love, or, Forlorn And Subject To Devastation Following The Loss Of Chuck Nunn Junior Due To The Hurtful Precariousness Of His Post-Accident Temper.

3. NUNN'S PERSONAL UNDOING WAS THE DAY IT RAINED SHEEP

Nunn's personal undoing was the day it rained sheep, I outlined to Simple Ranger as me and several civilians carried the forlornly swooned and flopping frame of Glory Joy duBoise to our table, smeared cold Rolling Rock on her pulse-points, and propped her up in a splinterless chair to come round to the outlining of our mutual Minogue sadnesses and troubles.

Told Simple Ranger how the success of the Nunn sheep ranch, plus the devotion of the near-beautiful Glory Joy, had aroused the ire and jealousy of T. Rex Minogue, the antique and hermitically reclusive, also malignant and malevolent, Minogue Oklahoma sheep mogul, plus the manufacturer of the illegal and chemically unstable sweet-potato whiskey that kept our neighboring reservation's Native Americans glazed and politically inactive; and how following the spectacular rise of the Nunn sheep operation under the energy and Agriculture Degree of Chuck Junior, who was, remember, a-shtuppin' the little lady T. Rex himself had wanted to a-shtup since she was twelve,

how in light of all this it's comprehensible how T. Rex Minogue repeatedly and with above-average vigor attempted to financially acquire, legally finagle, then violently appropriate the Nunn sheep operation from Chuck Nunn Junior; how Nunn was too petroleumly rich, well and savvily educated, and martially formidable, respective, for any of the attempts to fructify; how Nunn took all Minogue's shit with good humor, even the complimentary and ribboned jelly jars of yam liquor that T. Rex kept sending Glory Joy, each attached to a note headed NOTICE OF FORMAL WOOING, all with great and superior humor, until finally T. Rex, a man wholly allergic to any distance between himself and his way (least here in this town his own Daddy built before getting fatally harmed by some politically active Native Americans), until T. Rex arranged for his younger antique brother V.V. Minogue—a benign however treatably alcoholic rangehand and poet (his stuff rhymed, I'm told) who was under the thumb of dependency on T. Rex's secret sweet-potato recipe, I informed the ranger—for V.V. and two humungous out-of-town cow-punchers' boys from Enid (yes the old interferers from the climax of the state football title game in '66), for them to explosively dynamite a large and bulk-like portion of Chuck Nunn Junior's ranch's flock-infested grazing land; how whereupon the land was in fact dynamited by V.V. and the geologic Enid boys; and how it rained various percentages of sheep in Minogue Oklahoma for one whole nauseous afternoon two years ago next Ascension.

As Simple Ranger sat up straight at this and informed myself and the civilians that he himself had heard a far-off thunder booming off the dome of Big Dirt space, plus seen a singular pink-white rain from clear out in his shack on Dirt two Ascensions back, and had attributed the experiences to theology, plus the effects of damage, Glory Joy duBoise fluttered her way into consciousness and arousal, smoothed her brass-colored and towering hair with a hand-motion of such special sensuousness that two civilians tipped back over in their chairs and was largely lost for the rest of the duration, and entered into the therapy of it all, getting on the outside of several beers and detailing for the Ranger how it had been, that dark, fluffy, and rusty day, running with C. Nunn Jr. through the blasted heaths of exploded former pasture, ruining her best silk umbrella for all time, watching her man move through turf, mutton, and gore like the high wind of madness itself, floundering bow-legged through gruesome fields of gruesomer detonated wool, catching plummeting major percentages of particular favorite sheep in a shearing-basket, Glory Joy watching his mood and attitude getting more and more definable in terms of words such as grief, sorrow, loss, disorientation, suspicion, anger, and finally *unambiguous and unequivocal rage.* How as coyotes and buzzards began to sweep in off Big Dirt and commence a scavengerial orgy unsurpassed in modern Oklahoma in terms of pure and bilious nasty, how C. Nunn Jr. unhitched his '68 souped-entirely-up Italian Sports Car from his OU Norman quarterback career and fairly flew off the ranch east on rickety two-lane 40 toward the gigantic and private T. Rex Minogue spread, without so much as a kiss my foot to Glory Joy, who watched her man inject his vehicle of light into the chewed-up straight-shot road to TRM, his mind on the noun T. Rex Minogue, the near-gerunds confrontation, reparation, possibly even reciprocation (i.e. detonation).

4. SO IT WENT BACK AND FORTH

So it went back and forth, myself and Glory Joy, Simple Ranger gumming his bottle, his expression moving between vacant and preoccupied, the odd and frequent passing civilian patron getting pulled into the table, beer in hand, whenever Glory Joy rose her six-foot self up to tell what it had been similar to, those lonesome days of trying to run off carrionizers and mop up sheep percentages and run a ranch—admittedly now a smaller spread by a good measure—all herself; she'd rise up in her purple satin midi- and pay public tribute to the resemblance the days after Nunn's undoing and accident bore to hell right up on the grey and psoriatic skin of this world's land.

So it went back and forth, me handling the historical and observational, Glory Joy the personal and emotive. Was me revealed to Simple Ranger how, after the rain of sheep, Nunn was fairly flying in his little Italian Sports Car east on 40 to present to T. Rex Minogue the gift of T. Rex's own personal ass, and how meanwhile, back at Nunn's ranch, a good part of Minogue Oklahoma commenced to arrive and gawk and Kodak and catch mutton-cuts in receptacles ("Honey," this one old Mrs. Peat in yellow rain boots and slicker and a pince nez told me as she adjusted her hairnet she told me "Honey, when it rains bread and fishes, you get yourself a bucket, is what you do.") And how but *mean*-meanwhile, T. Rex Minogue's benign but sub-digital brother V.V., steeped in post-explosion guilt and self-loathing, plus not a little eau d'sweet potato, was speeding away from T. Rex's enormous spread for the Deep Dirt of Oklahoma's interior to commune with himself, guilt, pain, and a whole big truck full of jelly jars of distilled yam, and was accordingly fairly flying west on rickety 40 in this huge old truck, and at a ominous and coincidental point in time V.V. subconsciously decided, in some dark and pickled back part of his oceanic head, to see just what it was like driving his gargantular three-ton IH home-modified yam liquor transport truck on the left side of the hills, valleys, and sinewing curves of two-lane 40, V.V.'s left side being Chuck Nunn Junior's by right, course; and how here come Chuck Nunn Junior ripping up the highwayed hill right dab equidistant center between the two ranches, and here's V.V., driving in a pickled manner and a inappropriate lane up the hill's other side, and how there was impact at high speed, of a head-on kind, between the two.

"Impact," I said to Simple Ranger. "Plus damage, in no small measure."

And Glory Joy duBoise testified to the feelings she felt upon arriving in my pickup upon the accident scene, some pathetically

few miles down 40, and seeing her Chuck Nunn Junior literally
wearing his little impacted car; how there was white steam whistling
out of his tires, out of the accordion that had been his engine, and
out of Nunn's head, which looked on first look to be minus a jaw,
consciousness, and two healthy eyes, in that order. How red lights
and sirens come emergencying out across Dirt; how the Emergency
Folks had to cut Chuck Junior out of his car with torches; how they
was scared to move him on account of spinal considerations; how
Minogue Sheriff Onan L. Axford announced to some press and
media that wearing a safety belt, which Nunn was, had been all
that come between Chuck Nunn Junior and eternal flight out a
punctured windshield.

She told how Nunn come more or less to, in his little wrap-
around car, his torch-lit busted eyes in blood like bearings in deep
oil;

"Remember the eyes of Nunn," I interjaculated, and Simple
Ranger give me a watching look

; and as Glory Joy finished up communicating the anger and jus-
ticelessness she felt, upon seeing T. Rex's brother V.V. Minogue,
listing far to port up against the largely unharmed cab of his IH
liquor truck, weepy, shitfaced, scratchless; how V.V.'s accidental
ass had been immunized and preserved by how some old International Harvester trucks turned out had one of them air bags in
them, that nobody knew about, from a IH experiment in the 1960's
that didn't make the economic wash. But so the whole accident
that was V.V.'s pickled fault and that impacted Nunn's hairy jaw
and busted both his eyes, plus a pelvis, plus concussed the sucker
into moral comatosity and undoing—the whole damaging calamity
had consisted for V.V. Minogue of just a jillionth-of-a-second sen-
suous experience of soft and giant marshmallow (the white foaming
lumpy bag was still filling up the big truck's cab, at this time, I
remember, starting to jut and ooze out the busted windows, looking
dire and surreal), of a marshmallow instant, plus a upcoming year
of subsequent legalities. As Glory Joy climaxed telling how it felt,
and took a deserved grief-intermission, a certain palate-clefted but
upstanding civilian turn to me and he say,

"Sucker busted his eyes?" being real interested in physical damage, birth defects, accidental maimings, and the like.

"Sucker busted his eyes?" the Simple Ranger repeated in a rich gritty voice that croaked of advanced Grey Lung, the disease most specially feared by us who spend our lives on Big Dirt.

Out of a consideration for Glory Joy duBoise, who was wearing her pain like a jacket, now, I lowered my voice as I invited civilian and Ranger to picture what two cantaloupe melons dropped from a high height would resemble, if they wanted the picture of how Nunn's eyes got busted out his head via general impact and collision, hanging right out his head, ontojolly insecure.

And was me told the table how except for the eyes, the jaw, and the pelvis, which to our community relief all healed up, *prime face,* in just weeks, leaving good luck bad luck Chuck Junior a sharper shot, wickeder dancer, and nearer to handsome than before, how except for that, the major impact and damage from the accident had turned out to be to Nunn's head, mind, and sensibility. How right there in the post-accidental car he suddenly got conscious but evil,

"evil," I emphasized, and there was shudders from civilians and Glory Joy,

and how a evil Chuck Nunn Junior fought and cussed and struggled against his spinal restraints, invected against everything from the Prime Mobile to OU Norman's head football coach Mr. Barry B. Switzer hisself; how even slickered in blood, and eyes hanging ominous half out their holes, Nunn'd laid out two paramedics and a deputy and shined up my personal chin when we tried to ease him into a ambulance; how right there on rickety two-lane 40 Nunn publicly withdrew his love from his Momma Mona May, me, the whole community of Minogue Oklahoma, and especially from Glory Joy, who he loudly accused of low general spirits and what he called a lack of horizontal imagination.

"Chuck Junior was just in a moral coma from the accident, is all it was," declared a Glory Joy known from here to next door for the deepness of her loyalty toward Nunn. She told Simple Ranger how C. Nunn Jr. suffered six evil and morally comatose post-damage

days, his sense of right and wrong and love and hate smithered
to chaotic, but how the subsequent Nunn thankfully remembered
none of those six dark and devilish days of screaming and vandal-
izing in the Minogue County Hospital, where he was at, as restrained as was possible given the personality and persuasiveness
of Nunn vis à vis orderlies. How Nunn woke up familiar and normal
on the seventh day and asked about location, which is always a real
good medical sign. How we was all relieved.

5. NUNN'S SURFACE HEALED UP, BUT WITH SOMETHING INTERIOR ASKEW

Got dark outside, gritty afternoon dark that means serious wind
through high dirt, movement of soil in sky, a swirl that fakes twister
once a week and keeps the tourists minimal, and there was a peculiar but occasional black flutter at some of the tavern windows,
and Simple Ranger got aroused, disquiet. Me and G.J. was telling
the Ranger how Chuck Nunn Junior's surface healed up as fast
and fine as the town could expect, how he was back on his post-
explosion ranch and inside Glory Joy's affections and limbs by six
weeks time; how his broke cantaloupe eyes got put back together
via skill and laser by Drs., paid for through V.V. Minogue's subsequent legalities (V.V. was in institutional caring and de-tox up in
El Reno, by this time), how the eyes healed together so right and
improved that Nunn could claim to spot dust-movement against
the sky's very curve. No small claim.

But how something inside Nunn got left by the impact askew,
his interior self messed with, hurting, under strain, all due to the
lingering insecurity of the previously busted Nunn temper and
moral sense.

"We got frightened of his temper and moral sense," Glory Joy
told from a window she was at, standing, curious and distracted,
looking out against dark at something against the seam of land and
air that stretched tight across the Dirt. "Chuck Junior got scared
of hisself."

Ever get scared of your own self? Painful. Glory Joy had mummed up to Nunn, from concern and such, but Chuck Jr. got subsequently informed by friends and civilians about his six-day moral coma, about things he'd done, said, and implied in the privacy of a special padded Hospital wing, things he did not recollect; got told of a unnameable evil and rage directed at the universe in general, one that was diarrhetic and fearsome to see in a previous semi-demiurge, larger than life. It got known around Minogue Oklahoma that while his quality Italian seatbelt had saved his exterior, the impact with V.V. following the rain of sheep had knocked something loose in the center of Nunn. Chuck Junior got informed on this fact, and it chewed at him.

"His temper got scary," Glory Joy said. "It got precious and valuable to us, like only something you is scared to death to lose can get." She'd got to caressing the peeling frame of the window she was at with a mournfulness and musing that repercussed among the civilians piling up in circles at our little table. "His temper got insecure. We lived in around-the-clock fear of when Chuck Junior might possibly lose his temper."

"Focus in on that verb *lose*, S.R.," I told Simple Ranger. "The lady means it special. Whenever C. Nunn Jr. lost his post-accident temper, he lost the sucker real and true. It became gone. Absent. Elsewhere. Blew away to unfindable locations. A state of nameless and potential eternal rage and evil ever time he but stub his toe or some such shit." I put a earnest hand on the Ranger's deep grey sleeve, tried to get his eyes off the air outside the window. "Chuck Nunn Junior lived in fear of, plus alienation from, his own personal temper."

Was Glory Joy duBoise told us in emotive terms how collision and concussion and coma had left Nunn's interior bent. How the bowlegged pride of Minogue Oklahoma had to scrutinize and rein his own emotional self each minute, for fear that upset or anger could loop him back into a blank white comality of evil and meanness. How his tender gentleness toward G.J. duBoise got so extreme as to crowd pitiful, so scared was he that if he stopped loving her for a second he'd never get it back. How the rare times when a vicissitude of human relating, sheep-shearing, or pasture-status pissed him off, he'd get positively other-, under-worldly with anger, a bearded unit of pure and potent rage, ranging his sheep's ranges like something mythopoeic, thunderous, less man or thing than sudden and dire force, will, ill. How the bright blank evil'd stay on him for a day, two, a week; and Glory Joy'd shut herself in the storm cellar Chuck Nunn Junior hisself had lined with impregnable defensive steel, and she'd stay put, drinking bottled water and watching out for Nunn-activity through a emergency periscope Chuck Jr. had punctured through the storm cellar's roof for just such episodic periods; and how, after time, Nunn would come back out of the blind nameless hate, the objectless thirst for revenge against whole planets; how he'd find his spent and askew temper on some outer range of detonated Nunn land and return, pale and ignorant, to a towering, quivering, forgiving Glory Joy.

"Chuck Junior steered way clear of even thinking about T. Rex Minogue's place for fear he'd kill the old man," I told the Ranger. "Got terrified of even the concept of what T. Rex might could do to his emotions and sensibilities."

"The tenderness and caring Chuck Nunn Junior showed me were inhuman," Glory Joy semi-sobbed, her eyes resembling a St. Vitus of red threads. "Superhuman; not of this landed earth."

Simple Ranger got moved, here, at something.

6. WAS BUZZARDS THAT HAD STAYED ON

Now, the peculiar darkness and peculiarer fluttering outside the Outside Minogue Bar was in fact buzzards, two civilians at the busted-inward bar door told us. Glory Joy and the Ranger nodded absent to theirselves. We took looks outside. There was buzzard-presence and -activity of thought-provoked scope. The air was dark and agitated with wings, beaks, soft bellies. The suckers soared round. The air around the Outside Minogue Bar was swirling and influenced by regiments of the buzzards that had got drawn to Big

Dirt by the rain of Nunn mutton two Ascensions past, and had stayed on.

It was like something giant was coming out of the Dirt to die, the Ranger said in a gravelly whisper, staring his eyes past civilians, door, into a swirling soiled grey, looking for signals, his land, his car.

"This sucker's damaged," whispered a civilian, low.

But I commenced to revelate to Simple Ranger about Chuck Nunn Junior's special and secret post-accident strain.

"You knew about the secret post-accident strain when I didn't til it was too late and Chuck Junior was temperless and gone?" asked a disbelieving Glory Joy, pale, tight of lip, hip-shot. She come back over, toting menace.

I sympathied Glory Joy, told her how Chuck Junior had suffered a spell of his optical dislocation over to the feed store once after I once slapped him on his back over a humorous joke, and how he'd dislocated, and I'd seen, and how he'd swore me to a eternity of silence about his secret,

a sworn promise I kept til he wronged T. Rex Minogue and vameesed. I told Simple Ranger and the civilians about the hidden and subterranean strain, suffered by a already askew C. Nunn Jr., caused by his post-impact-with-V.V.-Minogue-spontaneously-detachable eyes. Told some historic facts: how the Drs. sewed up Nunn's busted ball-bearing melon eyes with laser and technocracy and left him farther down the line from blindness and blear than ever, but with a hitch: those eyes, sewed with light, was left smaller. Ain't hard to see that the Drs. at the Hospital had to take them some slack up from Nunn's ball-busted eyes to laser-stitch the busts with, and how the deslacking of the eyes left them tight, small, rattling in the sockets, insecure.

"They'd fall out his head," I told the company of men that was round our table about three deep, countless bottles of Rolling Rock already dealt with, stacked in a pyramid and headed for ceiling. "Be like the accidental impact all over again, at times: slap Chuck Junior on the back, or maybe he'd bend down after a untied lace, or
(worst)

if he'd sneeze at all—ever see the man sneeze, personally, a post-accident sneeze, Glory Joy?"

Glory Joy's powdered and geometry-eyed face got singular, loose, looked like Walter Matthau a second, out of my stimulating of a old but sudden recognition (unclear but true). She got smaller in her chair, too interested by half in the label on her ninth Rolling Rock.

Was me told Simple Ranger, who kept coughing and sniffing, nervous at the special smell of interested buzzard, how Chuck Nunn Junior commenced to buckle under the emotive strain of two little post-accidental eyes that exited their sockets and dangled by cords down his bearded and near-handsome face at the slightest gravitational invitation. How the twin pressures of fear that the possible sight of his insecure and A.W.O.L. eyes could repulse the love clear out of Glory Joy duBoise, plus how the fragileness of his coma-inclined and skittish temper might at any time dust from Nunn's concussed head any sense of ought, right, love, or concern for men, man, woman, or Glory Joy, how all this shit wore on Chuck Nunn Junior. How he got wore: thinned out, legs bandier, skin loose and paler than land, copper sweat verdigrised, rattling eyes milky and other-directed.

"Interior and progressing damage," I summed.

7. AND, PENCLIMACTICALLY,

Glory Joy revealed how, some weeks back, the infamous pollenated dust of pre-Ascension springtime Minogue Oklahoma brought on a hay fever that had Chuck Junior woolly and writhen with secret strain, plus mysteriously excusing himself from her every few minutes to go out to the privy to sneeze,

"And to reinsert his recalcitrant and threnodic eyes," she moaned, "I understand the total picture now, God bless his soul and mine together,"

(tears, by this point in time)

GIRL WITH CURIOUS HAIR

; and how, the torpid grey three-days-past morning of Nunn's temper's final debarkation into vengeance and fleeing, Glory Joy revealed, a fit of uncontrollable and pollenated sneezing had reared up out of the dusty land its own self and overtook a tired, tattered Chuck Nunn Junior there at breakfast, at the table, and how to Glory's combined horror and pathos he'd sneezed his keen but tiny eyes right out into his bowl of shredded wheat, and milk and fiber covered his sight, and Glory Joy'd rushed over to his sides but he was already up, horrified and swinging the balls, the twin cords the color of innards, Nunn fumbling in a wild manner to refit his lariatic eyes, healthy ears keen to the sound of the horror, pathos of the gasps of Glory Joy, temper bidding adios altogether to the flat grey world of the limited but steady-keeled mortal mind.

"And off he flew for the second recent-historic time," I climaxed, "this time in the impact-proof and souped-up used cement mixer he'd bought with V.V.'s legalities, off he flew east on rickety two-lane 40, blank with hate and optical mortification, to reciprocally wrong old T. Rex and V.V. Minogue."

"Who'd malignantly through willful and explosive machinations and vehicularism caused Nunn the twin insecurities of eye and moral temper," Simple Ranger finished up for me, in a curious plus haunting voice that was not

(more I reflected there the more I got convinced that those polysyllables were not of his gravelly Grey Lung voice, somehow) his own, somehow.

Was telling Simple Ranger how C. Nunn Jr., blood in his eye, plus cereal, roared out on that military mixer, in mood and stature similar to a demiurge, a banshee, a angry mythopoeum, roared out east on four-O to deprive T. Rex Minogue and wretched V.V. of their animate status, how he left the tall, forlorn, and quivering Glory Joy duBoise to watch the ever-tinier fog of his thunderous exhaust, his dusty final jet trail, three days past, and how Nunn never got seen no more. How the rumorous talk around town was that he'd forcibly detached the Minogue brothers' malignant/benign, reclusive/alcoholic asses, reattached them in inappropriate and harm-conducive locations, left the two of them twisted, bent, wronged, full of gnash and rue and close to expiration, and fleen the state and nation in his unimpactable mixer, taken on down the last road to fullness, redemption, and temper.

Any old civilian at all can conceptualize Glory Joy duBoise's crumpled Walter Matthauness by this revelational and recapitulatory time, but it's something just other to visualize how she refilled, smooth and animated, in a negative manner, toward the sight that now half-filled the busted frame of the door of the Outside Minogue Bar, appeared against the swirling swooping light through soil outside. The sight, dressed and draped in a dusty black, was the ancient and all-around ravaged frame of T. Rex Minogue, appearing publicly for the first time since the wool-price crisis of '67. He was seated in a dirt-frosted wicker and electricity-powered wheelchair, which hissed a low electric hiss as T. Rex made, first entry, then his way over to near the plywood bar and the combined and uncharitably disposed sight of our whole crowded three-deep pyramidded table. Was me whispered to Simple Ranger, "Minogue, T. Rex, first public display since '67, crisis, wool," and the Ranger nodded, his eyes more full of knowing than sky, a second.

Glory Joy duBoise, here, was getting hostiler-looking as she stared at old T. Rex, by the bar in his chair, covered by a black blanket, with crumbled old cheesy brown boots protruding from under, a white National Cancer Society cap on his skull-shaped skull, a curved and immense and hopefully domesticated buzzard on one shoulder, plus besides all this a device for electronic talking he was trying to put to his throat in just the right spot, for folks with throat dysfunctions. One of the civilians Glory Joy had proned to the floor swears later how he seen out-of-town dirt caked on the tattery soles of T. Rex's boots, seen a tiny and scripted IMPENDING glowing fire in T. Rex's one eye, a also tiny DOOM, CANCER burning cursive in the other; and this supine civilian was the first saw the rich orange of the jelly jars of illegal unstable sweet-potato whiskey that T. Rex commenced to pull out of a soft sheepskin satchel he had with him under that unwholesome blanket. Got the jars out and tossed them to the Ranger, who passed them around.

We passed the jars around and unscrewed Minogue's bootleg lids.

We was silent at our table, expected T. Rex dead, or at least twisted, traumatized, Nunn-struck.

"Hi," he said.

8. WAS THE MALIGNANT AND MALIGNIFIED T. REX MINOGUE

told us and Simple Ranger how Chuck Nunn Junior did flee to unknown and foreign locales. Manipulated his wicker-chaired plus disease-ridden self to where we all couldn't avoid but look right at him and his bird. Held his little vibrator-esk talking tube to his gizzardy (liver-spotted to hell) throat. Lifted a jar of potato whiskey to the dusty light. Told us some facts on how C. Nunn Jr. pulled up at the lush and isolated Minogue homestead in his heavy cement mixer, freshly re-fit eyes, moral unconsciousness, and a fine fettle, not respective; how Nunn right off laid out the two geologic Enid ranchhands, who was on their way off the TRM spread to take their women skeetshooting, how Nunn laid them out, kicked them where they laid, and rogered their women; how subsequently (not very), Nunn manufactured a unarchitectural and spontaneous entryway in the bay window of the front of T. Rex's spread's Big House; and then how Nunn, on the spot, performed for T. Rex Minogue, in his wheelchair, in his front parlor, a uncontrolled and optically hazardous dance of blank white mindless rage that turned out to be one complex and complete charade for some words bore semantic kin to Wrath, Damage, Retaliation. So on.

Now the buzzards outside the Outside Minogue Oklahoma Bar was down, sitting row on straight and orderly row on the edge-of-Minogue land stretching off toward dirt. Appeared to us through the windows like fat bad clerics, soft and plump, teetery, red-eyed, wrapped up tight in soft black coats of ecumenism and observation. Had orange beaks and claws. Was a good thousand orange beaks out there. Double on the claws. Lined up.

T. Rex Minogue was asking us to drink to his death;
"To death, gents, lady, civilians, Ranger,"
he said in a rich electricity of mechanical voicebox. He hefted a jar
of yam liquor up, and Glory Joy grinned unpleasant and right off
lifted hers up with a enthusiasm I got to call sardonic. Upright
civilians commenced to lift too, and finally myself, and under the
pyramid of bottles on our table there was a quiet community toast
to the publicity and temporariness of T. Rex Minogue, who explained while he poured rounds—his IMPENDING-DOOM-
ravaged face dry brown and wrinkled as a circus peanut, hair hanging
out his cap thin and white as linen off the deeply unwell—explained
that when Chuck Nunn Jr. come three days past to damage and
maim T. Rex and V.V., he got informed in the parlor by T. Rex
that the benign and pliable V.V. had already previously ceased and
succumbed, in a institutional-caring facility in El Reno, months
back, to hostility of the liver and smoothness of the brain. That
Nunn, in mid-rage-charade, declined to show either sympathy for
the late V.V. or any sort of compassion or Christianity to the soon-
to-be-late T. Rex; expressed, instead, through interpretive amoral
dance, his own personal attitude toward T. Rex Minogue, plus some
strong personal desires that had to do with the nullifying cancel-
lation of T. Rex's happiness, gender, life.

Jelly jars or no, we was objectively and deeply unclear on how
Chuck Junior and T. Rex got spared iniquitous criminality and
grievous harm, respective; and was me asked T. Rex Minogue, who
was attending a itch between his buzzard's wings with the corner
of a tie clip, how and where Nunn had spared T. Rex and gone,
plus whether the moral coma and eye-and-T.-Rex-centered rage
and *vengeancelüst* still now had hold of the fleen and missing Chuck
Nunn Junior.

"A titanic plus miraculous scene to see," grated T. Rex's vibrator. He detailed the titanic plus miraculous struggle of minds and
wills that proceeded to take place in Minogue's front parlor that
vengeful dancing day: Nunn cataloguing such T.-Rex-offenses as
jealousy, neighbor's-wife-coveting, avarice, manipulation, illegality,
explosions of turf and lamb, loosenings of eyes and consciousness,

desecurings of abilities to love and requite; T. Rex, in his wicker chair and blanket, countering with a list of Nunn's putative virtuous qualities headlined by charity-via-might, -main, altruism, Christian regard and duty, forgiveness, other-cheek-turning, *eudaimonia, sollen, devoir,* ⟨symbols⟩. Told how he, T. Rex, due for consumption by his own malignancy in just time, anyhow, refused to yield up fear or resignation to Nunn's blood-eyed blankness. How T. Rex's ravagedness, will, and wind-blown statuses saved his life from a thoroughly amoral and fatal-minded Nunn.

Now "To life," intoned the Ranger, nose full of dust and buzzard, eyes to quartz glitter by vegetable hooch, face shining with a odd and ignorant presence. Voice was still different, smoother. Young. Also familiar.

T. Rex Minogue and his personal fowl looked at Simple Ranger. Asked him some soft and intimately acquainted questions about the variable various shapes of the dusted Big Dirt air patterns. Asserted he could hear the special whistle of the Ranger's aloft land in certain storms of darkness, grey. Ranger done nodded. His face come and went.

"But not a bad career, Ranger," T. Rex continued, referring here to the governmental dust-watcher job Simple Ranger had had for a solid forty. But except T. Rex said wasn't actually the Ranger who had got hisself the cushy WPA angle; fellow with the real cushiony arrangement was a certain old and hold-out government clerk in Washington, D.C., who'd got his antique job under the original F. Delano R.   Clerk was the one had himself the cush: his entire and salaried career was just sending Simple Ranger, plus this certain blind octogenerial Japanese sub-sentry in Peuget, Wash., their checks ever month. Clerk lived in big-city Washington and owned TV, T. Rex revelated. Simple Ranger commenced to feeling along his own jaw, thrown by new fits down into a jelly jar of introversion and temporary funk. And just internal theorizing on how T. Rex Minogue possessed these far-off historical facts sent some civilians into a state of shivering that had T. Rex's vulture agitated and hissing, plus opening and closing its clerical wings, thus hiding and revealing by turns the spectral and disquieting (calm, though) face of T. Rex Minogue, making his IMPENDING eye show red fire. The rows of audobonial Dirt-scavengers was still outside, now a tinch closer to the bar windows, watching, lined up.

Things was threatening to get surreal until Glory Joy duBoise rose up, tall and shaky, looking the worse for a mixture of Rolling Rock and yam whiskey, which your thinking person don't want to mix, and proclamated in a falsetto of disbelief and anger that: one) she disbelieved T. Rex's sitting here, leguminous cool and un-scathed, if her own Chuck Nunn was as desirous to scathe him right there in his parlor as T. Rex implied; and that: two) she was angry as a animal, plus forlorn and subject to devastation follow-ing the loss of Chuck Nunn Junior due to the hurtful precarious-ness of his post-accident temper, plus eyes, angry as a animal at the galaxy in general and T. Rex in especial for his causal part in the above precariousness, forlornness, and devastation; and that the malignant T. Rex Minogue just better come out clean about the whereabouts of Nunn if he didn't want his wrinkled and senescent butt to make the acquaintance of Glory Joy's high-heeled shoe, but good. And T. Rex, whose historical thirst for the self and corpo-reality of Glory Joy duBoise is the stuff of Minogue Oklahoma myth—a whole nother story, I informed the funked and othered Ranger

—T. Rex, whose passion for our town's lone arm-wave at beauty is legend, glanced, gazed, and stared at Glory Joy, til we all of us got skittery. T. Rex and G. Joy faced each other cross ten feet of plywood room like fields of energy, all energetic with lust mixed up with regret, on one hand, rage and repulsion mixed up with a dire need for knowledge of Nunn, on the other. Simple Ranger's face had checked entirely out: the old and historical and adental man was dreaming out through the window into the geometry of bird and soil that stretched to the sky's tight burlap seam.

"I took the boy upstairs," T. Rex croaked into his box. "Took him upstairs to my own boodwar and to the window and I showed

the boy what was outside, is how I come out of the titantic plus
miraculous struggle." Addressed himself to Glory Joy, plus to Simple Ranger, who besides looking checked-out now was looking also
strangely odd, bigger, eyes both here and not, his head's outline
too focused, some deep wrinkles in his face, stained by dust for all
time, like slashes of No. 1 pencil. T. Rex touched his fowl's claw
with speculation, rue:

"Took the boy to my own window and opened her up. It was
mornin. Three months exact since we buried my brother, who got
consumed by my liquor, by poetic burnings and yearnings, by grief
and legalities on account of under-influence driving and the eyes
and mind of Chuck and Mona May Nunn's boy."

"What I see," whispered the big sharp clear new Ranger in a
smooth new clear young voice, his paperskinned hands steady
around his jar of liquor. There was non-spectral colors in his eyes.

"Ranger?"

"What was outside?" said Glory Joy.

"Was and is," vibrated T. Rex Minogue. "Showed the boy where
it all blew to. Showed him what his seatbelt done left him to look
at and be." Looked around. "Made the sucker sniff and see." Drank
up.

"Made him smell death on your own wind? Death he'd missed
by a impacted whisker, zif that was a prize? Made him read IM-
PENDING and DOOM, CANCER? Introduced him to buzzards
and such fowl?"

The birds was at the windows, now. All over them. Ranks broke.
Bar all dark. Each window covered and pocked with a mabusity of
cold red observational buzzard eyes. Dry rasp of orange claws going
for purchase on the dusty frames and panes. We was on exhibit to
animals.

"Miss Glory Joy," T. Rex said, "I knocked that boy upside the
back. Out come the eyes, hangin. The eyes Drs. me and V.V. paid
for put back together after they was busted."

"Made him think he owed you his eyes?" I incredulized.

"Ranger, tell John Billy here he's missin a point," said T. Rex.

"Don't owe my eyes to nought but the clean high wind," whispered Simple Ranger.

Glory Joy stared. *"Your* eyes?"

"Knocked that boy's eyes loose, out they come, hangin'," recollected Minogue. "I lean his puppy ass out the window so he's dangling his eyes out over the land. Wind blows them eyes around. Sucker can see straight down into everything there is."

We was all looking at the new Ranger, tall and straight and other. Each window a smeared tray of cold red watching marbles. Glory Joy took back her seat, dizzy with mix. T. Rex Minogue lifted his jar of deep orange up to the fly-speckled overhead light, swirled it round.

"You brought Chuck Nunn Junior's eyes out his head and made him look at dirt and brush and soil and fowls?" I said. I was pissed off. "You show him the waist-deep shit we all grew up in, like it's a gift from you to him? Grey sights and greyer smells we can't get out our own heads, and for that he declines to scathe you?"

"Something like that."

"Don't believe it for nothing," Glory Joy wailed. (Woman could *wail.*) "T. Rex done something sinister to Chuck Junior, is what happened."

I agreed loudly. Plus two civilians, as well, with the sinister part.

The ceiling commenced to creak and precipitate dust, on account of the immense and shifting clerical weight on top. We was in the belly of something black and orange and numerous.

Now: "Where it all blew to," whispered the smooth steely Ranger. I remarked how his jelly jar's colors was overhung with lush and various floras. Was me asked Simple Ranger how floras got in his liquor.

"Gents, lady," smiled T. Rex, "in regard for your community selves I'm here today public to say that me and Chuck and Mona May's boy's struggle ended where all things titanic end. In meadowphysics. We done some together, that day. Some macrocosmic speculation."

This one previous civilian, cleft palate, red iron hair, up and levitates. We look up at his Keds. He asks the air in front of him: "Where did Minogue Oklahoma blow to?"

Commenced to just *rain* ceiling-dust.

"Boys, wrap yourselves around something affirmative," said T. Rex, his domestic bird now holding his box to his throat with one savvy claw. "Remember what's the next world and what ain't. Minogue blew to Minogue, neighbors. See you selves. You, me, the corporeally phenomenal Glory Joy, the Ranger especial, we been swirlin and blowin in and out Minogue land since twinkles commenced in our Daddies' eyes."

"Minogue is you, Minogue?" slurred Glory Joy duBoise. I couldn't say skank. We was all sleepy with vegetable fuss.

"Minogue blew to Minogue," Minogue said. "Under Dirt's curve she's whirled and fertilized her own self into a priceless poor. Lush, dead, elsewhere."

"So where is it at, Minogue," asks the palatal man, aloft in a cumulus of webs and dust and creak. "Where's the meat of the bones we crawl on, plus eke out of, plus die and sink back in without no sound."

"Ain't no difference," sighed the Ranger. He'd growed him half a beard in just time. He sniffed at his liquor.

"Where you at, there, Ranger?" smiled a uncertain and far-off T. Rex.

"At the window," whispered the Ranger, at the window. He stared into a wormy and boiling black peppered with eyes, red. "Me and Mr. Minogue is at the window looking down at what the life and death of every soul from Comanche to Nunn done gone to fertilize and plenish."

"Showed him what we own," said T. Rex. He smelled at his old hands. "Showed what we all done gave via the planetarial actions of movement, wind, top-soil artistics, to the landed spread my own personal Daddy first plowed. That I first fertilized to humud black with the juices of his arrow-punctured self and my grief-withered Momma."

"Ain't no Chuck Nunn from Minogue Oklahoma that ain't eternal and aloft," sighed the Ranger at the window. The cleft rigger got levitationally joined by some more civilians.

Things was dark and singular.

"Aloft," intoned the damaged man. "My eyes are free of my head and flat grey temper and I am able to see directly below my dangling self the plumed and billowing clusters of the tops of trees of meat, dressed and heavy with the sweet white tissued blossoms indigenous to Minogue, fertilized by the wind-blown fruit of the toneless Curve on which me, my woman, my people move."

"Indigenous?" I slurred.

"That voice there, John Billy, that voice there is Chuck Junior's voice," said Glory Joy, flat, toneless, curved, Klan-white.

"When the high winds blew off Country," the Ranger said, "I was able to hear the infinitely many soft sounds of the millions of delicate petals striking and rubbing together. They joined and clove together in wind. My eyes was blowing everywhere. And the rush of perfume sent up to me by the agitation of the clouds of petals nearly blew me out that window. Delighted. Aloft. Semi-moral. New."

Glory Joy duBoise up and levitated. Also myself. Soon we was all uncommitted except to air and vision. T. Rex stayed where he was at, under us, by our pyramid of bottles studded with jars.

"Shit," he said.

Buzzards was gone. Flown home with a violence that set the edge-of-Minogue soil to lifting and tearing, twisted and grey, only to get beat down by a sudden plus unheard-of rush of clean rain from a innocent and milk-white sky. It fell like linen-wear, strings of technical light. Other such things. Windows ran smeared, then clear, then the rain shut down as abruptly as it had etc. etc.

The land commenced to look wounded. Dimpled puddles stretched off into nothing, outside—coins of water bright and clean and looking like open cancres in the red light of the low hurt red sun.

"Fore I die," whispered the malignified T. Rex, "I need to know where y'all think you live." He looked up. Around. "It's why I'm public today. Think what this is costing me. I need to know where y'all think you *live* at," he wailed. (Sucker could wail, too, gravelly vibrator or no.) His fowl got ornery.

"Maybe we'll just have us some fine new liquor first," whispers a aloft Ranger beside me, old, unbearded, sky-eyed. I saw for the first time how cataracted he was.

T. Rex commenced to hand up jars. "Tell me, Ranger," he said.

"Lord but don't it look clean," I was saying over and over.

"Show me the Chuck Nunn Junior I love, plus need," Glory Joy petitioned to a T. Rex maneuvering into a position for looking up her dress.

I grappled with some unsayably fearsome temptations to tell Chuck Nunn Junior's loyal and near-lovely woman who in all this landed world I loved.

"What's all that again?" said the Ranger in a flat grey gurgle.

"Have some liquor."

"Tell me where y'all think you live at."

Should of seen me grapple.

9. MY NAME IS JOHN BILLY.

Was me supposed to tell you how, on that one fine dark day a pentecost's throw from Ascension, we all of us got levitationally aloft, moving around the seated form of Minogue Oklahoma's expired T. Rex Minogue. How we passed, hand over hand, jar after jar of his unstable sweet-potato medicine, each jar deeper in color, duskier, til it got like the washed and bleeding land in the colored outside. How we all, even and especially Glory Joy, got glazed and apolitical, also torpid, docile, our minds in a deep loose neutral gear; how I started the story how Chuck Nunn Junior done wronged the man that wronged him all over again; and how at a point in time,

which is where we lived at, if the sucker'd asked me,

we all, me and civilians and Woman and old lone listening sky-eyed Ranger, we all crossed the thin line and slept. Aloft. How we dreamed a community dream of Chuck and Mona May Nunn's good luck boy Chuck Junior, riding his own mixer and might and absent purpose high, chasing a temper, a Daddy, Simple Ranger's DeSoto and farm, an everything of flora, sheep, soil, light, elements, through the windy fire of Oklahoma's roaring, watching stars. Now go on and ask me if we wasn't sorry we ever woke up. Go on.

HERE AND THERE

For K. Gödel

'**H**ER photograph tastes bitter to me. A show of hands on the part of those who are willing to believe that I kiss her photo? She'd not believe it, or it would make her sad, or rather it would make her angry and she would say you never kissed me the way you kiss my chemically bitter senior photo, the reasons you kiss my photo all have to do with you, not me.'

'He didn't really like to kiss me.'

'On the back of the photo, beneath the remains of the reversible tape I had used to attach it carefully to the wall of my room at school, are written the words: "Received 3 February 1983; treasured as of that date." '

'He didn't like to kiss me. I could feel it.'

'No contest to the charge that kissing an actual living girl is not my favorite boy-girl thing to do. It's not a squeamishness issue, has nothing to do with the fact, noted somewhere, that kissing someone is actually sucking on a long tube the other end of which is full of excrement. For me it's rather a sort of silliness issue. I feel silly. The girl and I are so close; the kiss contorts our mouths; noses get involved, bent; it's as if we're making faces at each other. At the time, with her, yes, I'd feel vaguely elsewhere, as a defense against myself. Admittedly this has to do with me, not her. But know that when I wasn't with her I dreamed of the time I could kiss her again. I thought about her constantly. She filled my thoughts.'

'What about my thoughts?'

'And then let's be equally candid about the utter lack of self-consciousness with which I'd kiss her elsewhere, slowly and in a way I'd found too soon she loved, and she'd admit she loved it, she does not lie, she'd admit to the pillow over her face to keep her quiet for the people in the other apartments. I knew her. I knew every curve, hollow, inlet and response of a body that was cool, hard, tight, waistless, vaguely masculine but still thoroughly exciting, quick to smile, quick to arch, quick to curl and cuddle and cling. I could unlock her like a differential, work her like an engine. Only when I was forced to be away at school did things mysteriously "change." '

'I felt like there was something missing.'

'I kiss her bitter photo. It's cloudy from kisses. I know the outline of my mouth from her image. She continues to teach me without knowing.'

'My feelings changed. It took time, but I felt like there was something missing. He just works all the time on well-formed formulas and poems and their rules. They're the things that are important to him. He'd tell me he missed me and then stay away. I'm not angry but I'm selfish, I need a lot of attention. All the time apart gave me a chance to do some thinking.'

'All the time apart I thought of her constantly—but she says "My feelings have changed, what can I do, I can't with Bruce anymore." As if her feelings controlled her rather than vice versa. As if her feelings were something outside her, not in her control, like a bus she has to wait for.'

'I met someone I like to spend time with. Someone here at home, at school. I met him in Stats. We got to be really good friends. It took time, but my feelings changed. Now I can't with Bruce anymore. It doesn't all have to do with him. It's me, too. Things change.'

'The photo is a Sears Mini-Portrait, too large for any wallet, so I've bought a special receptacle, a supporting framing folder of thick licorice cardboard. The receptacle is now wedged over the sun visor, along with a toll ticket, on the passenger side of my mother's car. I keep the windows rolled up to negate any possibility of the photo's blowing around, coming to harm. In June, in a car without air-conditioning, I keep the windows rolled up for the sake of her photo. What more should anyone be required to say?'

"Bruce here I feel compelled to remind you that fiction therapy in order to be at all effective must locate itself and operate within a strenuously yes some might even say harshly limited defined structured space. It must be confronted as text which is to say fiction which is to say project. Sense one's unease as you establish a line of distraction that now seems without either origin or end."

'This kind of fiction doesn't interest me.'

"Yes but remember we decided to construct an instance in which for once your interests are to be subordinated to those of another."

'So she's to be reader, as well as object?'

"See above for evidence that here she is so constructed as to be for once subject as well."

'A relief of contrivance, then? The therapeutic lie is to pretend the truth is a lie?'

"Affording you a specular latitude perspective disinterest the opportunity to be emotionally generous."

'I think he should get to do whatever makes him feel better. I still care about him a lot. Just not in that way anymore.'

'By late May 1983 her emotional bus has pulled out. I find in myself a need to get very away. To do a geographic. I am driving my mother's enclosed car on hot Interstate 95 in southern Maine, moving north toward Prosopopeia, the home of my mother's brother and his wife, almost at the Canadian border. Taking I-95 all the way from Worcester, Mass., lets me curve comfortably around the west of Boston, far from Cambridge, which I don't wish ever to see again. I am Bruce, a hulking, pigeon-toed, blond, pale, red-lipped Midwestern boy, twenty-two, freshly graduated in electrical engineering from MIT, freshly patted on the head by assorted honors committees, freshly returned in putative triumph with my family to Bloomington, Indiana, there to be kicked roundly in the psychic groin by a certain cool, tight, waistless, etcetera, Indiana University graduate student, the object of my theoretical passion, distant affection and near-total loyalty for three years, my prospective fiancée as of Thanksgiving last.'

'All I said to him then was do you think we could do it. He had asked me if he could ask me someday.'

'I was home again for Christmas: as of the evening of 27/12 we were drinking champagne, lying on her leopard-skin rug.'

'I told him a hundred times it wasn't a leopard-skin rug: the last tenant just had a dog.'

'We were discussing potential names for potential children. She said for a girl she might like "Kate." '

'And then all of a sudden it's like he suddenly wasn't there.'

'At this point she'd bring up how I seemed suddenly distant. I would explain in response that I had gotten, suddenly, over champagne, an idea for a truly central piece on the application of state variable techniques to the analysis of small-signal linear control systems. A piece that could have formed the crux of my whole senior year's thesis, the project that had occupied and defined me for months.'

'He went to his Dad's office at the University and I didn't see him for two days.'

'She claims that's when she began to feel differently about things. No doubt this new Statistics person comforted her while I spent two sleepless, Coke-and-pizza-fueled days on a piece that ended up empty and unfeasible. I went to her for comfort and found her almost hostile. Her eyes were dark and she was silent and trying with every fiber to look Unhappy. She practically had her forearm to her forehead. It was distressed-maiden/wronged-woman scenario.'

'He only came to my apartment to sleep. He spent almost all Christmas break either working or sleeping, and he went back to Cambridge a week before he had to, to work on his thesis. His honors thesis is an epic poem about variable systems of information- and energy-transfer.'

'She regarded the things that were important to me as her enemy, not realizing that they were, in fact, the "me" she seemed so jealously to covet.'

'He wants to be the first really great poet of technology.'

'I see it like I see weather coming.'

'He thinks art as literature will get progressively more mathematical and technical as time goes by. He says words as "correlative signifiers" are withering up.'

'Words as fulfillers of the function of signification in artistic communication will wither like the rules of form before them. Meaning will be clean. No, she says? Assuming she cares enough even to try to understand? Then say that art necessarily exists in a state of tension with its own standards. That the clumsy and superfluous logos of all yesterdays gives way to the crisp and proper and satisfactory of any age. That poetry, like everything organized and understood under the rubric of Life, is dynamic. The superfluous always exists simply to have its ass kicked. The Norbert Wiener of today will be triumphant in the Darwinian arena of tomorrow.'

'He said it was the most important thing in his life. What does that make me feel like?'

'It's Here. It's Now. The next beauties will and must be new. I invited her to see a crystalline renaissance; cool and chip-flat; fibers of shine winking in aesthetic matrices under a spreading sodium dawn. What touches and so directs us is what *applies*. I sense the impending upheaval of a great cleaning, a coming tidiness foaming at every corner of meaning. I smell change, and relief at cost, like the musty promise of a summer rain. A new age and a new understanding of beauty as range, not locus. No more uni-object concepts, contemplations, warm clover breath, heaving bosoms, histories as symbol, colossi; no more man, fist to brow or palm to decolletage, understood in terms of a thumping, thudding, heated Nature, itself conceived as colored, shaped, invested with odor, lending meaning in virtue of qualities. No more qualities. No more metaphors. Gödel numbers, context-free grammars, finite automata, correlation functions and spectra. Not sensuously here, but causally, efficaciously here. Here in the most intimate way. Plasma electronics, large-scale systems, operational amplification. I admit to seeing myself as an aesthetician of the cold, the new, the right, the truly and spotlessly *here*. Various as Poisson, morphically dense:

pieces whose form, dimension, character, and implication can spread like sargasso from a single structured relation and a criterion of function. Odes to and of Green, Bessel, Legendre, Eigen. Yes there were moments this past year when I almost had to shield my eyes before the processor's reflection: I became in myself axiom, language, and formation rule, and seemed to glow filament-white with a righteous fire.'

'He said he'd be willing to take me with him. And when I asked him where, he got mad.'

'I was convinced I could sing like a wire at Kelvin, high and pale, burn without ignition or friction, shine cool as a lemony moon, mated to a lattice of pure meaning. Interferenceless transfer. But a small, quiet, polite, scented, neatly ordered system of new signals has somehow shot me in the head. With words and tears she has amputated something from me. I gave her the intimate importance of me, and her bus pulled away, leaving something key of mine inside her like the weapon of a bee. All I want to do now is drive very away, to bleed.'

"Which is neither here nor there."

'No, the thing to see is exactly that it's *there*. That Maine is different from, fundamentally other than both Boston and Bloomington. Unfamiliar sights are a balm. From the hot enclosed car I see rocks veined with glassy color, immoderate blocks of granite whose cubed edges jut tangent to the scraggled surface of hills; slopes that lead away from the highway in gentle sine curves. The sky is a study in mint. Deer describe brown parabolae by the sides of the forested stretches.'

"I sense feeling being avoided not confronted Bruce. Maybe here we might just admit together that if one uses a person as nothing more than a receptacle for one's organs, fluids, and emotions, if one never regards her as more than and independent from the feelings and qualities one is disposed to invest her with from a distance, it is wrong then to turn around and depend on her feelings for any significant part of one's own sense of wellbeing. Bruce why not just admit that what bothers you so much is that she has given irresistible notice that she has an emotional life with features that

you knew nothing about, that she is just plain different from whatever you might have decided to make her into for yourself. In short
a person Bruce."

'Look: a huge black bird has curved through the corner of my
sight and let loose a strangely lovely berry rainbow of guano on
the center of the windshield near Smyrna, Maine; and under the
arc of this spectrum from a remote height a unit of memories is
laid out and systematized like colored print on the gray, chewed-
looking two-lane road ahead of me. The trip I took with my family
here to Prosopopeia, just two summers ago, and how she braved
her own stone-faced parents' disapproval to come along, how she
and my sister discovered they could be friends, how she and I
touched knees instead of holding hands on the airplane because
my mother was seated next to her and she felt embarrassed. I
remember with my gut the unbreachable promise of a whole new
kind of distance implicit in the dizzying new height we all seemed
to reach in the airplane on this long, storm-threatened flight, up to
where the sky first turned cold and then darkened to cadet and we
smelled space just above. How the shapes of a whole terrain of
clouds, from inside the sky, took on the modal solidity of the real:
shaggy buffalo heads; tattered bridges; the topology of states; political profiles; intricately etched turds. We flew away over the flat
summer board games of Indiana and Ohio. Thunderstorms over
Pennsylvania were great anvils that narrowed darkly to rain on
counties. We had a steel belly. I remember a jutting, carbuncular
ruby ring on the finger of an Indian woman in the seat across the
aisle, a dot stained into her forehead, robes so full they seemed to
foam. Her dark husband, in a business suit, with white eyes and
white teeth and impossibly well-combed hair.'

"And this place you would 'take' the girl to, someday? And why
now that she is forever absent does she become that place, the loss
of which summons images of decapitation and harm?"

'Little I-95 proceeds north to Houlton, Maine, then curves east
into New Brunswick. I exit the highway at Houlton, pay my toll,
and, via a side street that leads between the Hagan Cabinet Company and the Atrium Supper Club, come out on County Route 1,

again heading due north, through dense farmland, toward Mars Hill and then Prosopopeia. The sun sets gradually to my left over ranges of pale purple earth I learned two years ago are colored by the young potato plants they feed. An irrigation generator howls and clanks by the road a few miles out of Mars Hill, and in this purple now an intricate circuit of tiny rivers runs red in the late light. Just farther up 1 is a hand-lettered sign announcing hubcaps for sale, spoils of war with the rutted road, the improbable wares displayed in long rows on my right, glinting dull pink on a fence and the side of a barn-red barn, looking like the shields of an army of dwarfs. About everything there is an air of age, clocks running slow on sluggish current.'

"The sun setting to the left means to the west, meaning even here you remember things west Bruce, meaning one becomes uncomfortable at this new silence from a subject in a west we have evidence you remember. One voice cannot just *shut off* another, even in a structure of lies, if light is to be shed the way we profess to—"

'Perhaps I should mention that at the toll booth for the Houlton exit her photo's receptacle came free when I pulled down the visor to get at the ticket, and curved airborne over to me in the backwash from the window I had to roll down, and ended half-wedged between the brake and the floor. In reaching for it I dropped my money and somehow touched the accelerator with my foot. The car moved forward and nudged the controlled gate that lowers to stop a vehicle until its debt to the state is discharged. The woman in the toll booth was out like a shot; a policeman in his cruiser by the road looked over and put down something he was eating. I had to scoop up my money and fork it over at the gate. The receptacle was bent and dusted with floor-dirt and cracker crumbs. The toll-taker was polite but firm. There was honking.'

'The trip Bruce and his parents and his sister invited me for to Maine year before last was the last time I think everything was totally good between us. On the trip he pointed at things out of the airplane window and made his Mom and I laugh. We kept our legs touching and he'd touch my hand too, very gently, so his Mom wouldn't see him. At his aunt and uncle's house we went to a lake, and swam, and could of gone waterskiing if we wanted. Sometimes we took long walks all day down back roads and got dusty and sometimes lost, but we always got back because Bruce could tell times and directions by the sun. We drank water with our hands out of little streams that were really cold. Once Bruce was picking us blueberries for lunch and got stung by a bee on the hand and I pulled the stinger out, because I had nails, and put a berry on the sting and he laughed and said he didn't care about anything, really. I had a wonderful time. It was really fun. It was when Bruce and I felt right. It felt right to be with him. It was maybe the last time it felt to me like there was both a real me and a real him when we were together. It was at his uncle's house, on some sweatshirts and clothes on the ground in some woods at night by a potato field, that I gave Bruce something I can't ever get back. I was glad I did it. But I think maybe that's when Bruce's feelings began to change. Maybe I'm wrong, but I think it kind of drove him away a little that I did it finally. That I finally wanted to, and he could see that I did. It's like he knew he really had me, and it made him go down inside himself, to have, instead of just want. I think he really likes to want. That's OK. I think maybe we were just meant to be friends the whole time. We knew each other ever since high school. We swam in the quarry where they made that movie. We had driver's education together, and took our tests for our driver's licenses in the same car, is how we got to really know each other. Except we didn't get really close until a long time after that, when we were both already in different colleges and only saw each other at vacations.'

'I hit Prosopopeia just as the sun goes seriously down and all sorts of crepuscular Maine life begins rustling darkly in a spiny old section of forest I am happy to leave behind at the corporation limit. I detour briefly to stop at an IGA and buy some cold Michelob as a bit of a housewarming present, something my mother had suggested and financed. Michelob is a beer my uncle loves and does not really drink so much as inhale. It's practically the only thing he can inhale. He has emphysema now, advanced, at fifty-five.

Even the few steps from a chair to the kitchen door and a hearty handshake and the appropriation of one of my light bags is enough to make him have to begin his puffing exercise. He sits heavily back in his chair and begins to breathe, rhythmically, with concentration, between pursed lips, as my aunt hugs me and makes happy sounds punctuated by "Lord" and "Well" and then whisks all my luggage upstairs in one load. There's not much luggage. I keep my bent receptacle with me. My uncle goes for a wheezer of adrenaline spray and resumes puffing as hard as he can, smiling tightly and waving away both my concern and his discomfort. He blows as though trying to extinguish a flame—which is perhaps close to what it felt like for him. He has dropped more weight, especially in his legs; his legs through his pants have a sticklike quality as he sits, breathing. Even thin and crinkled, though, he is still an eerie, breastless copy of my mother, with: gray-white hair, an oval high-cheekboned face, and blue pecans for eyes. Like my mother's, these eyes can be sharply lit as a bird's or sad and milky as a whale's; while my uncle puffs they are blank, unfocused, away. My aunt is an unreasonably pretty sixty, genuinely but not cloyingly nice, a lady against whom the only indictment might be hair dyed to a sort of sweet amber found nowhere in nature. She has put my portable life in my bedroom and asks whether I'd eat some supper. I'd eat anything at all. A television is on, with no sound, by an ancient electric stove of chipped white enamel and a new brown dishwasher. My uncle says I look like I was the one carried the car out here rather than the other way around. I know I do not look good. I've driven straight for almost thirty hours, a trip punctuated only by the filling and emptying of various tanks. My shirt is crunchy with old sweat, I have a really persistent piece of darkened apple skin between my two front teeth, and something has happened to a blood vessel in one of my eyes from staring so long at distance and cement—there is a small nova of red at the corner and a sandy pain when I blink. My hair needs a shampoo so badly it's almost yellow. I say I'm tired and sit down. My aunt gets bread from an actual bread box and takes a dish of tuna salad out of the refrigerator and begins stirring it up with a wooden spoon. My uncle eyes the beer on the kitchen counter, two tall silver six-packs already spreading a bright puddle of condensation on the linoleum. He looks over at my aunt, who sighs to herself and gives a tiny nod. My uncle is instantly up, no invalid; he gets two beers loose and puts one in front of me and pops the other and drains probably half of it in one series of what I have to say are unattractively foamy swallows. My aunt asks whether I'd like one sandwich or two. My uncle says I'd better just eat up that tuna salad, that they've had it twice now and if it hangs around much longer they're going to have to name it. His eyes are completely back, they are in him, and he uses them to laugh, to tease, to express. Just like his sister. He looks at the Sears receptacle by my place at the table and asks what I've got there. My aunt looks at him. I say memorabilia. He says it looks like it had a hard trip. The kitchen smells wonderful: of old wood and new bread and something sharply sweet, a faint tang of tuna. I can hear my mother's car ticking and cooling out in the driveway. My aunt puts two fat sandwiches down in front of me, pops my tall beer, gives me another warm little hug with a joy she can't contain and I can't understand, given that I have more or less just *appeared* here, with no explicable reason and little warning other than a late-night phone call two days ago and some sort of follow-up conversation with my parents after I'd hit the road. She says it's a wonderful surprise having me come visit them and she hopes I'll stay just as long as I'd like and tell her what I like to eat so she can stock up and didn't I feel so good and *proud* graduating out of such a good school in such a hard subject that she could never in a dog's age understand. She sits down. We begin to talk about the family. The sandwiches are good, the beer slightly warm. My uncle eyes the six-packs again and goes into his shirt pocket for the disk of snuff he dips since he had to stop smoking. There is cool, sweet, grassy air through the kitchen screens. I am too tired not to feel good.'

'I felt so sorry when he said he was going to have to go out of town, maybe for the whole summer. But I got mad when he said now we were even, summer for summer. Because him leaving this summer is his choice, just like last summer was all his choices, too.

He stayed in Cambridge, in Boston, last summer, to work on starting his project, and he got a research job in his engineering lab,
and he didn't even ever really explain why he didn't want to come
be in Bloomington for the summer, even though I'd just got my
B.A. here. But he sent me a big arrangement of roses and said for
me to come live with him and be his love in Boston that summer,
that he missed me so much he couldn't endure it, and I went through
a lot deciding, but I did, I used my graduation present money to
fly to MIT and got a job as a hostess in Harvard Square at a German
restaurant, the Wurst House, and we had an apartment in the Back
Bay with a fireplace that was really expensive. But then after some
time passed, Bruce acted like he really didn't want me to be there.
If he'd said something about it that would be one thing, but he just
started being really cold. He'd be away at the lab all the time, and
he never came in to see the Wurst House, and when we were alone
at home he didn't touch me for a week once, and he'd snap sometimes, or just be cold. It was like he was repulsed by me after a
while. I'd started taking birth control pills by then. Then in July
once he didn't come home or call for a day and a night, and when
he did he got mad that I was mad that he didn't. He said why
couldn't he at least have some vestige of his own life every once
in a while. I said he could, but I said it just didn't feel to me like
he felt the same anymore. He said how dare you tell me what I
feel. I flew back home a few days later. We decided that's what I
better do, because if I stayed he'd feel like he had to be artificially
nice all the time, and that wouldn't be any fun for either of us. We
both cried a little bit at Logan airport when he took me on the bus.
In Bloomington my family threw confetti on me when I got home,
they were glad to have me back, and I felt good to be home, too.
Then a day later Bruce sent arranged roses again and called and
said he'd made a ghastly error, and he flew back home, too, and
said he was very sorry that he had got obsessional about all sorts
of exterior things, and he tried to make me understand that he felt
like he was standing on the cusp between two eras, and that however
he'd acted I should regard as evidence of his own personal short-
comings as a person, not as anything about his commitment to me

as a lover. And I guess I had so much invested in the relationship by then that I said OK that's OK, and he stayed in Bloomington over a week, and we did everything together, and at night he made me feel wonderful, it could really be wonderful being close with him, and he said he was making me feel wonderful because he wanted to, not because he thought he had to. Then he went back to Boston and said wait for me till Thanksgiving, don't sit under apple trees, and I'll come back to you, so I did, I even turned down friendly lunch invitations and football tickets from guys in my classes. And then Thanksgiving and Chrstmas felt to me like the exact same thing as that bad part of the summer in the Back Bay. My feelings just started to change. It wasn't all him. It took time, but after time passed I felt something was missing, and I'm selfish, I can only feel like I'm giving more than I'm getting for so long, then things change.'

"Bruce perhaps here is the opportunity to confront the issue of your having on four separate occasions late last fall slept with a Simmons College sophomore from Great Neck, New York. Perhaps you'd care to discuss a certain Halloween party."

'Last summer was no fun, and when I'd tell him that at Christmas, he'd get mad, and tell me not to bring it up unless I was trying to really tell him something. I'd already started to be friends with the guy from Stats, but I wouldn't have even been interested in hanging around with him if things had been OK with Bruce and me.'

'I sleep and eat and sit around a great deal, and the red in my eye slowly fades. I wash insects' remains from my mother's windshield. For a time I devote most of my energy to immersing myself in the lives and concerns of two adults for whom I have a real and growing affection. My uncle is an insurance adjuster, though he's due for early retirement at the end of the year because of the state of his wind: the family worries about the possibility of his car breaking down on one of the uncountable Aroostook County roads he crisscrosses every day, adjusting claims. The winters here are killers. I have the feeling that when my uncle retires he will do nothing but watch television and tease my aunt and relate stories about the claims he adjusts. His stories are not to be believed. They all start with, "I had a loss once . . ." He talks to me, in the living room, over the few beers he's allowed each day. He tells me that he's always been a homebody and a family man, that he loved spending time with his family—the children now grown and gone south, to Portland and Augusta and Bath—that there have been plenty of fools in his agency who spent all their time on their careers or their hunting or their golf or their peckers, and then what did they have, when winter came and the world got snowed in, after all? My aunt teaches third grade at the elementary school across town, and has the summer off, but she's taking two courses, a French and a Sociology, at the University of Maine's Prosopopeia branch downtown. For a few days after I'm rested I ride over with her to the little college and sit in the campus library while she's in class. The library is tiny, cute, like the children's section of a public facility, with carpet and furniture and walls colored in the muted earth-tones of autumn rot. There is hardly anyone in the summer library except two very heavy women who inventory the books at the tops of their lungs. It is at once too noisy and too quiet to do any real work, and I have no ideas that do not seem to me shallow and overwrought. I really feel, sitting, trying to extrapolate on the equations that have informed the last two years of my life, as though I'd been shot in the head. I end up writing disordered pieces, or more often letters, without direction or destination. What is to prove? It seems as though I've disproved everything. I soon stop going to the UMP library. Days go by, and my aunt and uncle are impeccably kind, but Maine becomes another here instead of a there.'

"Explain."

'Things become bad. I now have a haircut the shadow of which scares me. It occurs to me that neither my aunt nor my uncle has once asked what happened to the pretty little thing that came visiting with us last time we were up, and I wonder what my mother has said to my aunt. I begin to be anxious about something I can neither locate nor define. I have trouble sleeping: I wake very early every morning and wait, cold, for the sun to rise behind the gauzy white curtains of my cousins' old room. When I sleep I have unpleasant, repetitive dreams, dreams involving leopards, skinned knees, a bent old cafeteria fork with crazy tines. I have one slow dream in which she is bagging leaves in my family's yard in Indiana and I am pleading with her magically to present with amnesia, to be for me again, and she tells me to ask my mother, and I go into the house, and when I come out again, with permission, she is gone, the yard knee-deep in leaves. In this dream I am afraid of the sky: she has pointed at it with her rake handle and it is full of clouds which, seen from the ground, form themselves into variegated symbols of the calculus and begin to undergo manipulations I neither cause nor understand. In all my dreams the world is windy, disordered, gray.'

"Now you stop kissing pictures and tearing up proofs and begin to intuit that things are, and have been, much more general and in certain respects sinister all along."

'I begin to realize that she might never have existed. That I might feel this way now for a different—maybe even no—reason. The loss of a specific referent for my emotions is wildly disorienting. Two and a half weeks have passed since I came here. The receptacle is lying on the bureau in my room, still bent from the tollbooth. My affections have become a sort of faint crust on the photo, and the smell when I open the receptacle in the morning is chemically bitter. I stay inside all day, avoid windows, and cannot summon hunger. My testicles are drawn up constantly. They begin to hurt. Whole periods of time now begin to feel to me like the intimate, agonizing interval between something's falling off and its hitting the ground. My aunt says I look pale. I put some cotton in my ear, tell her I have an earache, and spend a lot of time wrapped in a scratchy blanket, watching Canadian television with my uncle.'

"This sort of thing can be good."

'I begin to feel as though my thoughts and voice here are in some way the creative products of something outside me, not in my control, and yet that this shaping, determining influence outside me is still me. I feel a division which the outside voice posits as the labor pains of a nascent emotional conscience. I am invested with an urge to "write it all out," to confront the past and present as a community of signs, but this requires a special distance I seem to have left behind. For a few days I exercise instead—go for long, shambling runs in jeans and sneakers, move some heavy mechanical clutter out of my uncle's backyard. It leaves me nervous and flushed and my aunt is happy; she says I look healthy. I take the cotton out of my ear.'

"All this time you're communicating with no one."

'I let my aunt do the talking to my parents. I do, though, have one odd and unsatisfactory phone conversation with my eldest brother, who is an ophthalmologist in Dayton. He smokes a pipe and is named Leonard. Leonard is far and away my least favorite relative, and I have no clue why I call him one night, collect, very late, and give him an involved and scrupulously fair edition of the whole story. We end up arguing. Leonard maintains that I am just like our mother and suffer from an unhappy and basically silly desire to be perfect; I say that this has nothing constructive to do with anything I've said, and that furthermore I fail to see what's so bad about wishing to be perfect, since being perfect would be . . . well, perfect. Leonard invites me to think about how *boring* it would be to be perfect. I defer to Leonard's extensive and hard-earned knowledge about being boring, but do point out that since being boring is an imperfection, it would by definition be impossible for a perfect person to be boring. Leonard says I've always enjoyed playing games with words in order to dodge the real meanings of things; this segues with suspicious neatness into my intuitions about the impending death of lexical utterance, and I'm afraid I indulge myself for several minutes before I realize that one of us has severed the connection. I curse Leonard's pipe, and his wife with a face like the rind of a ham.'

"Though of course your brother was only pointing out that perfection, when we get right down to the dark, cheese-binding heart of the matter, is impossible."

'There is no shortage of things that are perfect for the function that defines them. Peano's axioms. A chameleon's coat. A Turing Machine.'

"Those aren't persons."

'No one has ever argued pursuasively that that has anything to do with it. My professors stopped trying.'

"Could we possibly agree on whom you might ask now?"

'He said real poetry won't be in words after a while. He said the icy beauty of the perfect signification of fabricated nonverbal symbols and their relation through agreed-on rules will come slowly to replace first the form and then the stuff of poetry. He says an epoch is dying and he can hear the rattle. I have all this in letters he sent me. I keep all my letters in a box. He said poetic units that allude and evoke and summon and are variably limited by the particular experience and sensitivity of individual poets and readers will give way to symbols that both are and stand for what they're about, that both the limit and the infinity of what is real can be expressed best by axiom, sign, and function. I love Emily Dickinson. I said I wasn't going to pretend like I understood and disagreed but it seemed like what he thought about poetry was going to make poetry seem cold and sad. I said a big part of the realness that poems were about for me, when I read them, was feelings. I wasn't going to pretend to be sure, but I didn't think numbers and systems and functions could make people feel any way at all. Sometimes, when I said it, he felt sorry for me, and said I wasn't conceiving the project right, and he'd play with my earlobes. But sometimes at night he'd get mad and say that I was just one of those people that are afraid of everything new and unavoidable and think they're going to be bad for people. He came so close to calling me stupid that I almost got really mad. I'm not stupid. I graduated college in three years. And I don't think all new things and things changing are bad for people.'

"How could you think this was what the girl was afraid of?"

'Today, a little over three weeks in Prosopopeia, I am sitting in my relatives' living room, with the cotton back in my ear, watching the lunchtime news on a Canadian station. I suspect it's nice outside. There is trouble in Quebec. I can hear my aunt saying something, in the kitchen. In a moment she comes in, wiping her hands on a small towel, and says that the stove is acting up. Apparently she can't get the top of the stove to heat, that sometimes it acts up. She wants to heat some chili for my uncle and me to eat when he comes home for lunch. He'll be home in the early afternoon. There's not much else for a good lunch in the house, and she's not fussy for going to the IGA because she has to prepare for a French quiz, and I'm certainly not going to go out in the wind with that ear acting up like it's been, and she can't get the stove to work. She asks me if I could maybe have a quick look at the stove.'

'I'm not afraid of new things. I'm just afraid of feeling alone even when there's somebody else there. I'm afraid of feeling bad. Maybe that's selfish, but it's the way I feel.'

'The stove is indeed officially acting up. The stovetop burners do not respond. My aunt says it's an electrical thingummy in the back of the stove, that comes loose, that my uncle can always get it working again but he won't be home until she's already in class, and the chili won't be able to simmer, reblend, get tasty. She says if it wouldn't make my ear hurt could I try to get the stove going? It's an electrical thingummy, after all. I say no problem. She goes for my uncle's toolbox in the closet by the cellar door. I reach back and unplug this huge, ugly old white stove, pull it away from the wall and the new dishwasher. I get a Phillips out of my uncle's box and remove the stove's back panel. The stove is so old I can't even make out the manufacturer's name. It is possibly the crudest piece of equipment ever conceived. Its unit cord is insulated in some sort of ancient fabric wrap with tiny red barber-spirals on it. The cord simply conducts a normal 220 house AC into a five-way distributor circuit at the base of the stove's guts. Bundles of thick, inefficient wires in harness lead from each of the four burner controls and from the main oven's temperature setting into outflow jacks on the circuit. The burner controls determine temperature level at the selected point through straightforward contact and conduction of AC to the relevant burner's heating unit, each of which units is simply a crudely grounded high-resistance transformer circuit that conducts heat, again through simple contact, into the black iron spiral of its burner. Energy-to-work ratios here probably sit at no better than 3/2. There aren't even any reflecting pans under the burners. I tell my aunt that this is an old and poor and energy-inefficient stove. She says she knows and is sorry but they've had it since before Kennedy and it's got sentimental value, and that this year it came down to either a new stove or a new dishwasher. She is sitting at the sunlit kitchen table, reviewing verb tenses, apologizing about her stove. She says the chili needs to go on soon to simmer and reblend if it's going to go on at all; do I think I can fix the thingummy or should she run to the store for something cold?'

'I've only gotten one letter since he left, and all it says is how much he's taking care of a picture of me, and would I believe he kisses it? He didn't really like to kiss me. I could feel it.'

'The harnessed bundles of insulated wires all seem well connected to their burners' transformers, so I have to disconnect each bundle from its outflow jack on the distributor circuit and look at the circuit itself. The circuit is just too old and grimy and crude and pathetic to be certain about, but its AC-input and hot-current-outputs seem free of impediment or shear or obvious misconnection. My aunt is conjugating French ir-verbs in the imperfect. She has a soft voice. It's quite pretty. She says: *"Je venais, tu venais, il venait, elle venait, nous venions, vous veniez, ils venaient, elles venaient."* I am deep in the bowels of the stove when she says my uncle once mentioned that it was just a matter of a screw to be tightened or something that had to be given a good knock. This is not especially helpful. I tighten the rusted screws on the case of the distributor circuit, reattach the unit cord to the input jack, and am about to reattach the bundles of wire from the burners when I see that the harnesses, bundle casings, and the outflow jacks on the circuit are so old and worn and be-gooed that I can't possibly tell which bundle of wires corresponds to which outflow jack on the circuit. I am afraid of a fire hazard if the current is made to cross improperly in the circuit, and the odds are $(1/2)^{4!}$ that anyone could guess the proper jack for each bundle correctly. *"Je tenais,"* my aunt says to herself. *"Tu tenais, il tenait."* She asks me if everything is going all right. I tell her I've probably almost got it. She says that if it's something serious it would really be no trouble to wait until my uncle gets home, that he's an old hand with that devil of a stove and could have a look; and if neither he nor I could get the thing going we two could just go out and get a bite. I feel my frightening haircut and tell her I've probably almost got it. I decide to strip some of the bundles of their old pink plastic casings for a few inches to see whether the wires themselves might be color-coded. I detach the bundles from their harnesses and strip down the first two, but all the wires reveal themselves to be the same dull, silverfish-gray, their conduction elements so old and frayed that the wires begin to unravel and stick out in different directions, and become disordered, and now I couldn't get them back in the distributor circuit even if I could tell where they went, not to mention the increased hazard inherent in crossing current in bare wires. I begin to sweat. I notice that the stove's unit cord's cloth insulation is itself so badly worn that one or two filaments of copper 220-wire are protruding. The cord could have been the trouble all along. I realize that I should have tried to activate the main oven unit first to see whether the power problem was even more fundamental than the burner bundles or the circuit. My aunt shifts in her chair. I begin to have trouble breathing. Stripped, frayed burner wires are spread out over the distributor like gray hair. The wires will have to be rebound into bundles in order to be reinserted and render the burners even potentially workable, but my uncle has no tool for binding. Nor have I ever personally bound a system of wire. The work that interests me is done with a pencil and a sheet of paper. Rarely even a calculator. At the cutting edge of electrical engineering, almost everything interesting is resolvable via the manipulation of variables. I've never once been stumped on an exam. Ever. And I appear to have broken this miserable piece-of-shit stove. I am unsure what to do. I could attach the main oven's own conduction bundle to a burner's outflow jack on the distributor circuit, but I have no idea how hot the resultant surge would render the burner. There is *no way to know* without data on the resistance ratios in the metal composition of the burners. The current used to heat a large oven even to WARM could melt a burner down. It's not impossible. I begin almost to cry. My aunt is moving on to ir/iss verbs. *"Je partissais, tu partissais, il partissait, elle partissait."* '

"You're unable to fix an electric stove?"

'My aunt asks again if I'm sure it's no problem and I don't answer because I'm afraid of how my voice will sound. I carefully disconnect the other end of each bundle from each burner's transformer and loop all the wire very neatly and lay it at the bottom of the stove. I tidy things up. Suddenly the inside of this stove is the very last place on earth I want to be. I begin to be frightened of the stove. Around its side I can see my aunt's feet as she stands. I hear the refrigerator door open. A dish is set on the counter above me and something crinkly removed; through the odors of stove-slime and ancient connections I can smell a delicate waft of chili. I rattle a screwdriver against the inside of the stove so my aunt thinks I'm doing something. I get more and more frightened.'

'He told me he loved me lots of times.'

"Frightened of what?"

'I've broken their stove. I need a binding tool. But I've never bound a wire.'

'And when he said it he believed it. And I know he still does.'

"What does this have to do with anything?"

'It feels like it has everything to do with it. I'm so scared behind this dirty old stove I can't breathe. I rattle tools.'

"Is it that you love this pretty old woman and fear you've harmed a stove she's had since before Kennedy?"

'But I think feeling like he loved somebody scared him.'

'This is a crude piece of equipment.'

"Whom else have you harmed."

'My aunt comes back behind the stove and stands behind me and peers into the tidied black hollow of the stove and says it looks like I've done quite a bit of work! I point at the filthy distributor circuit with my screwdriver and do not say anything. I prod it with the tool.'

"What are you afraid of."

'But I don't think he needs to get hurt like this. No matter what.'

'I believe, behind the stove, with my aunt kneeling down to lay her hand on my shoulder, that I'm afraid of absolutely everything there is.'

"Then welcome."

MY APPEARANCE

I AM a woman who appeared in public on "Late Night with David Letterman" on March 22, 1989.

In the words of my husband Rudy, I am a woman whose face and attitudes are known to something over half of the measurable population of the United States, whose name is on lips and covers and screens. And whose heart's heart is invisible, and unapproachably hidden. Which is what Rudy thought could save me from all this appearance implied.

The week that surrounded March 22, 1989 was also the week David Letterman's variety-and-talk show featured a series of videotaped skits on the private activities and pastimes of executives at NBC. My husband, whose name is better known inside the entertainment industry than out of it, was anxious: he knew and feared Letterman; he claimed to know for a fact that Letterman loved to savage female guests, that he was a misogynist. It was on Sunday that he told me he felt he and Ron and Ron's wife Charmian ought to prepare me to handle and be handled by Letterman. March 22 was to be Wednesday.

On Monday, viewers accompanied David Letterman as he went deep-sea fishing with the president of NBC's News Division. The executive, whom my husband had met and who had a pappus of hair sprouting from each red ear, owned a state-of-the-art boat and rod and reel, and apparently deep-sea fished without hooks. He and Letterman fastened bait to their lines with rubber bands.

"He's waiting for the poor old bastard to even think about saying holy mackerel," Rudy grimaced, smoking.

On Tuesday, Letterman perused NBC's chief of Creative Development's huge collection of refrigerator magnets. He said: "Is this entertainment ladies and gentlemen? Or what?"

I had the bitterness of a Xanax on my tongue.

We had Ramon haul out some videotapes of old "Late Night" editions, and watched them.

"How do you feel?" my husband asked me.

In slow motion, Letterman let drop from a rooftop twenty floors above a cement lot several bottles of champagne, some plump fruit, a plate-glass window, and what looked, for only a moment, like a live piglet.

"The hokeyness of the whole thing is vital," Rudy said as Letterman dropped a squealing piglet off what was obviously only a pretend rooftop in the studio; we saw something fall a long way from the original roof to hit cement and reveal itself to be a stuffed piglet. "But that doesn't make him benign." My husband got a glimpse of his image in our screening room's black window and rearranged himself. "I don't want you to think the hokeyness is real."

"I thought hokeyness was pretty much understood not to be real," I said.

He directed me to the screen, where Paul Shaffer, David Letterman's musical sidekick and friend, was doing a go-figure with his shoulders and his hands.

We had both taken Xanaxes before having Ramon set up the videotapes. I also had a glass of chablis. I was very tired by the time the refrigerator magnets were perused and discussed. My husband was also tired, but he was becoming increasingly concerned that this particular appearance could present problems. That it could be serious.

The call had come from New York the Friday before. The caller had congratulated me on my police drama being picked up for its fifth season, and asked whether I'd like to be a guest on the next week's "Late Night with David Letterman," saying Mr. Letterman would be terribly pleased to have me on. I tentatively agreed. I have few illusions left, but I'm darn proud of our show's success. I have a good character, work hard, play her well, and practically adore the other actors and people associated with the series. I called my agent, my unit director, and my husband. I agreed to accept an appearance on Wednesday, March 22. That was the only interval Rudy and I had free in a weekly schedule that denied me even two days to rub together: my own series tapes Fridays, with required read-throughs and a Full Dress the day before. Even the 22nd, my husband pointed out over drinks, would mean leaving L.A.X. very early Wednesday morning, since I was contracted to appear in a wiener commercial through Tuesday. My agent had thought he could reschedule the wiener shoot—the people at Oscar Mayer had been very accommodating throughout the whole campaign—but my husband had a rule for himself about honoring contracted obligations, and as his partner I chose also to try to live according to this rule. It meant staying up terribly late Tuesday to watch David Letterman and the piglet and refrigerator magnets and an unending succession of eccentrically talented pets, then catching a predawn flight the next morning: though "Late Night"'s taping didn't begin until 5:30 E.S.T., Rudy had gone to great trouble to arrange a lengthy strategy session with Ron beforehand.

Before I fell asleep Tuesday night, David Letterman had Teri Garr put on a Velcro suit and fling herself at a Velcro wall. That night his NBC Bookmobile featured a *1989 Buyer's Guide to New York City Officials;* Letterman held the book up to view while Teri hung behind him, stuck to the wall several feet off the ground.

"That could be you," my husband said, ringing the kitchen for a glass of milk.

The show seemed to have a fetish about arranging things in lists of ten. We saw what the "Late Night" research staff considered the ten worst television commercials ever. I can remember number five or four: a German automobile manufacturer tried to link purchase of its box-shaped car to sexual satisfaction by showing, against a background of woodwinds and pines, a languid Nordic woman succumbing to the charms of the car's stickshift.

"Well I'm certainly swayed," Letterman said when the clip had ended. "Aren't you, ladies and gentlemen?"

He offered up a false promo for a cultural program PBS had supposedly decided against inserting into next fall's lineup. The promo was an understated clip of four turbaned Kurdistani rebels, draped in small-arms gear, taking time out from revolution to perform a Handel quartet in a meadow full of purple flowers. The bud of culture flourishing even in the craggiest soil, was the come-on. Letterman cleared his throat and claimed that PBS had finally submitted to conservative PTA pressure against the promo. Paul Shaffer, to a drum roll, asked why this was so. Letterman grinned with an embarrassment Rudy and I both found attractive. There were, again, ten answers. Two I remember were Gratuitous Sikhs and Violets, and Gratuitous Sects and Violins. Everyone hissed with joy. Even Rudy laughed, though he knew no such program had ever been commissioned by PBS. I laughed sleepily and shifted against his arm, which was out along the back of the couch.

David Letterman also said, at various intervals, "Some fun now, boy." Everyone laughed. I can remember not thinking there was anything especially threatening about Letterman, though the idea of having to be peeled off a wall upset me.

Nor did I care one bit for the way the airplane's ready, slanted shadow rushed up the runway to join us as we touched down. By this time I was quite upset. I even jumped and said *Oh* as the plane's front settled into its shadow on the landing. I broke into tears, though not terribly. I am a woman who simply cries when she's upset; it does not embarrass me. I was exhausted and tense. My husband touched my hair. He argued that I shouldn't have a Xanax, though, and I agreed.

"You'll need to be sharp," was the reason. He took my arm.

The NBC driver had put our bags far behind us; I heard the trunk's solid sound.

"You'll need to be both sharp and prepared," my husband said. He judged that I was tense enough to want simply to agree; Rudy did know human nature.

But I was irritable by now. Part of my tension about appearing knew where it came from. "Just how much preparation am I supposed to need?" I said. Charmian and I had already conferred long-distance about my appearance. She'd advised solidity and simplicity. I would be seen in a plain blue outfit, no jewelry. My hair would be down.

Rudy's concerns were very different. He claimed to fear for me.

"I don't see this dark fearful thing you seem to see in David Letterman," I told him. "The man has freckles. He used to be a local weatherman. He's witty. But so am *I*, Rudy." I did want a Xanax. "We both know me. I'm an actress who's now forty and has four kids, you're my second husband, you've made a successful career change, I've had three dramatic series, the last two have been successful, I have an Emmy nomination, I'm probably never going to have a feature-film career or be recognized seriously for my work as an actress." I turned in the back seat to look at him. "So so *what?* All of this is known. It's all way out in the open already. I honestly don't see what about me or us is savageable."

My husband ran his arm, which was well-built, out along the back seat's top behind us. The limousine smelled like a fine purse; its interior was red leather and buttery soft. It felt almost wet. "He'll give you a huge amount of grief about the wiener thing."

"Let him," I said.

As we were driven up through a borough and extreme southeast Manhattan, my husband became anxious that the NBC driver, who was young and darkly Hispanic, might be able to hear what we were saying to one another, even though there was a thick glass panel between us in back and the driver up front, and an intercom in the panel had to be activated to communicate with him. My husband felt at the glass and at the intercom's grille. The driver's head was motionless except to check traffic in mirrors. The radio was on for our enjoyment; classical music drifted through the intercom.

"He can't hear us," I said.

". . . if this were somehow taped and played back on the air while you looked on in horror?" my husband muttered as he satisfied himself about the intercom. "Letterman would eat it up. We'd look like absolute idiots."

"Why do you insist that he's mean? He doesn't seem mean."

Rudy tried to settle back as serious Manhattan began to go by. "This is the man, Edilyn, who publicly asked Christie Brinkley what state the Kentucky Derby is run in."

I remembered what Charmian had said on the phone and smiled. "But was she or wasn't she unable to answer correctly?"

My husband smiled, too. "Well she was *flustered*," he said. He touched my cheek, and I his hand. I began to feel less jittery.

He used his hand and my cheek to open my face toward his. "Edilyn," he said, "meanness is not the issue. The issue is *ridiculousness*. The bastard feeds off ridiculousness like some enormous Howdy-Doodyesque parasite. The whole show feeds on it; it swells and grows when things get absurd. Letterman starts to look gorged, dark, shiny. Ask Teri about the Velcro. Ask Lindsay about that doctored clip of him and the Pope. Ask Nigel or Charmian or Ron. You've heard them. Ron could tell you stories that'd curl your toes."

I had a compact in my purse. My skin was sore and hot from on-air makeup for two straight days. "He's likeable, though," I said. "Letterman. When we watched, it looked to me as though he likes to make himself look ridiculous as much as he does the guests. So he's not a hypocrite."

We were in a small gridlock. A disheveled person was trying to clean the limousine's windshield with his sleeve. Rudy tapped on the glass panel until the driver activated the intercom. He said we wished to be driven directly to Rockefeller Center, where "Late Night" taped, instead of going first to our hotel. The driver neither nodded nor turned.

"That's part of what makes him so dangerous," my husband said, lifting his glasses to massage the bridge of his nose. "The whole thing feeds off *everybody's* ridiculousness. It's the way the audience can tell he *chooses* to ridicule himself that exempts the clever bastard from real ridicule." The young driver blew his horn; the vagrant fell away.

We were driven west and slightly uptown; from this distance I could see the building where Letterman taped and where Ron worked in an office on the sixtieth floor. Ron used to be professionally associated with my husband before Rudy made the decision to go over to Public Television. We were all still friends.

"It will be on how your ridiculousness is *seen* that whether you stand or fall depends," Rudy said, leaning into my compact's view to square the knot of his tie.

Less and less of Rockefeller's skyscraper was visible as we approached. I asked for half a Xanax. I am a woman who dislikes being confused; it upsets me. I wanted after all, to be both sharp and relaxed.

"Appear," my husband corrected, "both sharp and relaxed."

"You will be made to look ridiculous," Ron said. He and my husband sat together on a couch in an office so high in the building my ears felt as they'd felt at take-off. I faced Ron from a mutely expensive chair of canvas stretched over steel. "That's not in your control," Ron said. "How you respond, though, is."

"Is what?"

"In your control," Ron said, raising his glass to his little mouth.

"If he wants to make me look silly I guess he's welcome to try," I said. "I guess."

Rudy swirled the contents of his own glass. His ice tinkled. "That's just the attitude I've been trying to cultivate in her," he said to Ron. "She thinks he's really like what she sees."

The two of them smiled, shaking their heads.

"Well he isn't really like that, of course," Ron told me. Ron has maybe the smallest mouth I have ever seen on a human face, though my husband and I have known him for years, and Charmian, and they've been dear friends. His mouth is utterly lipless and its corners are sharp; the mouth seems less a mouth than a kind of gash in his head. "Because no one's like that," he said. "That's what he sees as his great insight. That's why everything on the show is just there to be ridiculed." He smiled. "But that's our edge, that we know that, Edilyn. If you know in advance that you're going to be made to look ridiculous, then you're one step ahead of the game, because then you can make *yourself* look ridiculous, instead of letting *him* do it to you."

Ron I thought I could at least understand. "I'm supposed to make myself look ridiculous?"

My husband lit a cigarette. He crossed his legs and looked at Ron's white cat. "The big thing here is whether we let Letterman make fun of you on national television or whether you beat him to the punch and join in the fun and do it yourself." He looked at Ron as Ron stood. "By *choice*," Rudy said. "It's on that issue that we'll stand or fall." He exhaled. The couch was in a patch of sunlight. The light, this high, seemed bright and cold. His cigarette hissed, gushing smoke into the lit air.

Ron was known even then for his tendency to fidget. He would stand and sit and stand. "That's good advice, Rudolph. There are definite do's and don't's. Don't look like you're trying to be witty or clever. That works with Carson. It doesn't work with Letterman."

I smiled tiredly at Rudy. The long cigarette seemed almost to be *bleeding* smoke, the sunlight on the couch was so bright.

"Carson would play along with you," Rudy nodded. "Carson's *sincere.*"

"Sincerity is out," Ron said. "The joke is now *on* people who're sincere."

"Or who are sincere-seeming, who think they're sincere, Letterman would say," my husband said.

"That's well put," Ron said, looking me closely up and down. His mouth was small and his head large and round, his knee up, elbow on his knee, his foot on the arm of another thin steel chair, his cat swirling a lazy figure-eight around the foot on the floor. "That's the cardinal sin on 'Late Night.' That's the Adidas heel of every guest that he mangles." He drank. "Just be aware of it."

"I think that's it: I think being seen as being *aware* is the big thing, here," my husband said, spitting a sliver of drink-ice into his hand. Ron's cat approached and sniffed at the bit of ice. The heat of my husband's proffering fingers was turning the sliver to water as I looked at my husband blankly. The cat sneezed.

I smoothed the blue dress I'd slipped on in Letterman's putty-colored green room. "What I want to know is is he going to make fun of me over the wiener spots," I told Ron. I had become truly worried about at least this. The Mayer people had been a class act throughout the whole negotiations and campaign, and I thought we had made some good honest attractive commercials for a product that didn't claim to be anything more than occasional and fun. I didn't want Oscar Mayer wieners to be made to look ridiculous because of me; I didn't want to be made to look as though I'd prostituted my name and face and talents to a meat company. "I mean, will he go beyond making fun? Will he get savage about it?"

"Not if you do it first!" Rudy and Ron said together, looking at each other. They laughed. It was an in-joke. I laughed. Ron turned and made himself another small drink. I sipped my own. My cola's ice kept hitting my teeth. "That's how to defuse the whole thing," Ron said.

My husband ground out his cigarette. "Savage yourself before he can savage you." He held out his glass to Ron.

"Make sure you're seen as making fun of yourself, but in a self-aware and ironic way." The big bottle gurgled as Ron freshened Rudy's drink.

I asked whether it might be all right if I had just a third of a Xanax.

"In other words, appear the way Letterman appears, on Letterman," Ron gestured as if to sum up, sitting back down. "Laugh in a way that's somehow deadpan. Act as if you knew from birth that everything is clichéd and hyped and empty and absurd, and that that's *just* where the fun is."

"But that's not the way I am at all."

The cat yawned.

"That's not even the way I act when I'm acting," I said.

"Yes," Ron said, leaning toward me and pouring a very small splash of liquor on my glass's ice cubes, furred with frozen cola.

"Of *course* that's not you," my husband said, lifting his glasses. When tense, he always rubbed at the red dents his frames imposed on his nose. It was a habit. "That's why this is serious. If a you shows its sweet little bottom anywhere near the set of 'Late Night,' it'll get the hell savaged out of it." He tamped down another cigarette, looking at Ron.

"At least she's looking terrific," Ron said, smiling. He felt at his sharp little mouth, his expression betraying what looked to me like tenderness. Toward me? We weren't particularly close. Not like Ron's wife and I. The liquor tasted smoky. I closed my eyes. I was tired, confused and nervous; I was also a bit angry. I looked at the watch I'd gotten for my birthday.

I am a woman who lets her feelings show rather than hide them; it's just healthier that way. I told Ron that when Charmian had called she'd said that David Letterman was a little shy but basically a nice man. I said I felt now as though maybe the *extreme* nervousness I was feeling was my husband's fault, and now maybe Ron's; and that I very much wanted either a Xanax or some constructive, supportive advice that wouldn't demand that I be artificial or empty or on my guard to such an extent that I vacuumed the fun out of what was, when you got right down to it, supposed to be nothing more than a fun interview.

Ron smiled very patiently as he listened. Rudy was dialing a talent coordinator. Ron instructed Rudy to say that I wasn't really needed downstairs for makeup until after 5:30: tonight's monologue was long and involved, and a skit on the pastime of another NBC executive would precede me.

My husband began to discuss the issue of trust, as it related to awareness.

It turned out that an area of one wall of Ron's office could be made to slide automatically back, opening to view several rows of monitors, all of which received NBC feeds. Beneath a local weatherman's set-up and the March 22 broadcast of "Live at Five," the videotaping of "Late Night"'s opening sequence had begun. The announcer, who wore a crewneck sweater, read into an old-fash-

ioned microphone that looked like an electric razor with a halo:
"Ladies and gentlemen!" he said. "A man who is, even as we
speak, *checking his fly: DaVID LETTERMAN!*"

There was wild applause; the camera zoomed in on a tight shot
of the studio's APPLAUSE sign. On all the monitors appeared the
words LATE NIGHT APPLAUSE–SIGN–CAM. The words flashed on
and off as the audience cheered. David Letterman appeared out of
nowhere in a hideous yachting jacket and wrestling sneakers.

"What a *fine* crowd," he said.

I felt at the fuzz of Pepsi and fine rum on my ice. My finger left
a clear stripe in the fuzz. "I *really* don't think this is necessary."

"Trust us, Edi."

"Ron, talk to him," I said.

"Testing," said Ron.

Ron stood near the couch's broad window, which was no longer
admitting direct sunlight. The window faced south; I could see
rooftops bristling with antennae below, hear the tiny sounds of
distant car horns. Ron held a kind of transmitting device, compact
enough to fit in his soft palm. My husband had his head cocked
and his thumb up as Ron tested the signal. The little earplug in
Rudy's ear was originally developed to allow sportscasters to take
direction and receive up-to-the-minute information without having
to stop talking. My husband had sometimes found it useful in the
technical direction of live comedy before he made the decision to
leave commercial television. He removed the earplug and cleaned
it with his handkerchief.

The earplug, which was supposed to be flesh-colored, was really
prosthesis-colored. I told them I emphatically did *not* want to wear
a pork-colored earplug and take direction from my husband on not
being sincere.

"No," my husband corrected, "being *not-sincere*."

"There's a difference," Ron said, trying to make sense of the
transmitter's instructions, which were mostly in Korean.

But I wanted to be both sharp and relaxed, and to get downstairs
and have this over with. I did want a Xanax.

And so my husband and I entered into negotiations.

"Thank you," Paul Shaffer told the studio audience. "Thank you so much." I laughed, in the wings, in the long jagged shadows produced by lights at many angles. There was applause for Shaffer. The APPLAUSE sign was again featured on camera.

From this distance Letterman's hair looked something like a helmet, I thought. It seemed thick and very solid. He kept putting index cards in the big gap between his front teeth and fiddling with them. He and the staff quickly presented a list of ten medications, both over-the-counter and 'scrip, that resembled well-known candies in a way Letterman claimed was insidious. He showed slides side by side, for comparison. It was true that Advils looked just like brown M&M's. Motrin, in the right light, were SweetTarts. A brand of MAO inhibitor called Nardil looked just like the tiny round Red Hots we'd all eaten as children.

"Eerie or what?" Letterman asked Paul Shaffer.

And the faddish anti-anxiety medication Xanax was supposed to resemble miniatures of those horrible soft pink-orange candy peanuts that everyone sees everywhere but no one will admit ever to having tasted.

I had gotten a Xanax from my husband, finally. It had been Ron's idea. I touched my ear and tried to drive the earplug deeper, out of sight. I arranged my hair over my ear. I was seriously considering taking the earplug out.

My husband did know human nature. "A deal's a deal" kept coming into my ear.

The florid young aide with me had told me I was to be the second guest on the March 22 edition of "Late Night with David Letterman." Appearing first was to be the executive coordinator of NBC Sports, who was going to be seen sitting in the center of a circle of exploding dynamite, for fun. Also on the bill with me was the self-proclaimed king of kitchen-gadget home sales.

We saw a short veterinary film on dyspepsia in swine.

"Your work has gone largely unnoticed by the critics, then," the videotape showed Letterman saying to the film's director, a veterinarian from Arkansas who was panicked throughout the interview because, the electric voice in my ear maintained, he didn't know whether to be serious about his life's work with Letterman, or not.

The executive coordinator of NBC Sports apparently fashioned perfect rings of high explosive in his basement workshop, took them into his backyard, and sat inside explosions; it was a hobby. David Letterman asked the NBC executive to please let him get this straight: that somebody who sat in the exact center of a perfect circle of dynamite would be completely safe, encased in a vacuum, a sort of storm's eye—but that if so much as one stick of dynamite in the ring was defective, the explosion could, in theory, kill the executive?

"Kill?" Letterman kept repeating, looking over at Paul Shaffer, laughing.

The Bolsheviks had used the circle ceremoniously to "execute" Russian noblemen they really wanted to spare, the executive said; it was an ancient and time-honored illusion. I thought he looked quite distinguished, and decided that sense played no part in the hobbies of men.

As I waited for my appearance, I imagined the coordinator in his Westchester backyard's perfect center, unhurt but encased as waves of concussed dynamite whirled around him. I imagined something tornadic, colored pink—since the dynamite piled on-stage was pink.

But the real live explosion was gray. It was disappointingly quick, and sounded flat, though I laughed when Letterman pretended that they hadn't gotten the explosion properly taped and that the executive coordinator of NBC Sports, who looked as though he'd been given a kind of cosmic slap, was going to have to do the whole thing over again. For a moment the coordinator thought Letterman was serious.

"See," Ron had said as it became time for me to be made up, "there's no way he *can* be serious, Edilyn. He's a millionaire who wears wrestling sneakers."

"One watches him," my husband said, bent to check the fit of the cold pink plug in my ear, "and one envisions a whole nation, watching, nudging each other in the ribs."

"Just get in there and nudge," Ron said encouragingly. I looked at his mouth and head and cat. "Forget all the rules you've ever learned about appearing on talk shows. This kid's turned it inside out. Those rules of television humor are what he makes the most fun of." His eyes went a bit cold. "He's making money ridiculing the exact things that have put him in a position to make money ridiculing things."

"Well, there's been a kind of parricidal mood toward rules in the industry for quite some time," my husband said as we waited for the elevator's ascent. "He sure as hell didn't invent it." Ron lit his cigarette for him, smiling sympathetically. We both knew what Rudy was talking about. The Xanax was beginning to take effect, and I felt good. I felt psyched up to appear.

"You could say it's like what happened over at 'Saturday Night Live,' " Ron said. "It's the exact same phenomena. The cheap sets that are supposed to look even cheaper than they are. The home-movie mugging for the cameras, the backyard props like Monkey-Cam or Thrill-Cam or coneheads of low-grade mâché. 'Late Night,' 'SNL'—they're *anti*-shows."

We were at the back of the large silent elevator. It seemed not to be moving. It seemed like a room unto itself. Rudy had pressed 6. Both my ears were crackling. Ron was speaking slowly, as if I couldn't possibly understand.

"But even if something's an anti-show, if it's a hit, it's a *show*," Ron said. He got his cat to lift its head, and scratched its throat.

"So just imagine the strain the son of a bitch is under," my husband muttered.

Ron smiled coolly, not looking at Rudy.

My husband's brand of cigarette is a foreign sort that lets everyone know that something is on fire. The thing hissed and popped and gushed as he inhaled, looking steadily at his old superior. Ron looked at me.

"Remember how 'SNL' had those great parodies of commercials right after the show's opening, Edilyn? Such great parodies that it always took you a while to even realize they were parodies and not commercials? And how the anti-commercials were a hit? So *then* what happened?" Ron asked me. I said nothing. Ron liked to ask questions and then answer them. We arrived on Letterman's floor. Rudy and I got out behind him.

"What happened," he said over his shoulder, "is that the sponsors started putting commercials on 'SNL' that were almost like the *parodies* of the commercials, so that it took you a while to realize that these were even real commercials in the first place. So the sponsors were suddenly guaranteed huge audiences that watched their commercials very, very closely—hoping, of course, that they'd be parodies." Secretaries and interns rose to attention as Ron passed with us; his cat yawned and stretched in his arms.

"*But,*" Ron laughed, still not looking at my husband, "But instead, the sponsors had turned the anti-commercials' joke around on 'SNL' and were *using* it, using the joke to manipulate the very same audience the parodies had made fun of them for manipulating in the first place."

Studio 6-A's stage doors were at the end of a carpeted hall, next to a huge poster that showed David Letterman taking a picture of whoever was taking his picture for the poster.

"So really being a certain way or not isn't a question that can come up, on shows like this," Rudy said, tapping an ash, not looking at Ron.

"Were those great days or what?" Ron whispered into the ear of the cat he nuzzled.

The locked studio doors muffled the sounds of much merriment. Ron entered a code on a lit panel by the Letterman poster. He and Rudy were going back upstairs to watch from Ron's office, where the wall of monitors would afford them several views of me at once.

"You'll just have to act, is all," my husband said, brushing the hair back from my ear. He touched my cheek. "You're a talented and multifaceted actress."

And Ron, manipulating the cat's white paw in a pretend goodbye, said, "And she *is* an actress, Rudolph. With you helping her we'll help you turn this thing just the right way."

"And she appreciates it, sir. More than she knows right now."

"So I'm to be a sort of anti-guest?" I said.

Terribly nice to see you," is what David Letterman said to me. I had followed my introduction on-stage; the sweatered attendant conducted me by the elbow and peeled neatly away as I hit the lights.

"Terribly, nay, *grotesquely* nice to see you," Letterman said.

"He's scanning for pretensions," crackled my ear. "Pockets of naïve self-importance. Something to stick a pin in. Anything."

"Yas," I drawled to David Letterman. I yawned, touching my ear absently.

Close up, he looked depressingly young. At most thirty-five. He congratulated me on the series' renewal, the Emmy nomination, and said my network had handled my unexpected pregnancy well on the show's third year, arranging to have me seen only behind waist-high visual impediments for thirteen straight episodes.

"That was fun," I said sarcastically. I laughed drily.

"Big, *big* fun," Letterman said, and the audience laughed.

"Oh Jesus God let him see you're being sarcastic and dry," my husband said.

Paul Shaffer did a go-figure with his hands in response to something Letterman asked him.

David Letterman had a tiny label affixed to his cheek (he did have freckles); the label said MAKEUP. This was left over from an earlier joke, during his long monologue, when Letterman had returned from a commercial air-break with absolutely everything about him labeled. The sputtering fountain between us and the footlights was overhung with a crudely lettered arrow: DANCING WATERS.

"So then Edilyn any truth to the rumors linking that crazy thing over at your husband's network and the sort of secondary rumors. . . ." He looked from his index card to Paul Shaffer. "Gee you know Paul it says 'secondary rumors' here; is it OK to go ahead and call them secondary rumors? What does that mean, anyway, Paul: 'secondary rumors'?"

"We in the band believe it could mean any of . . . really any of hundreds of things, Dave," Shaffer said, smiling. I smiled. People laughed.

The voice of Ron came over the air in my ear: "Say *no*." I imagined a wall of angles of me, the wound in Ron's head and the transmitting thing at the wound, my husband seated with his legs crossed and his arm out along the back of wherever he was.

". . . secondary or not, about you and Tito's fine, fine program perhaps, ah, leaving commercial television altogether at the end of next season and maybe moving over to that other, unnamed, uncommercial network?"

I cleared my throat. "Absolutely every rumor about my husband is true." The audience laughed.

Letterman said, "Ha *ha*." The audience laughed even harder.

"As for me," I smoothed my skirt in that way prim women do, "I know next to nothing, David, about the production or business sides of the show. I am a woman who *acts*."

"And, you know, wouldn't that look terrific emblazoned on the T-shirts of women everywhere?" Letterman asked, fingering his tiepin's label.

"And was it ever a crazy thing over at his network, Dave, from what I heard," said Reese, the NBC Sports coordinator, on my other side, in another of these chairs that seemed somehow disemboweled. Around Reese's distinguished eyes were two little raccoon-rings of soot, from his hobby's explosion. He looked to Letterman. "A power struggle in public TV?"

"Kind of like a . . . a bloody *coup* taking place in the League of Women Voters, wouldn't you say, Edilyn?"

I laughed.

"Riot squads and water-cannon moving in on a faculty tea."

Letterman and Reese and Shaffer and I were falling about the place. The audience was laughing.

"Polysyllables must just be *flying*," I said.

"Really . . . really *grammatically correct* back-stabbing going on all over. . . ."

We all tried to pull ourselves together as my husband gave me some direction.

"The point is I'm afraid I just don't know," I said, as Letterman and Shaffer were still laughing and exchanging looks. "In fact," I said, "I'm not even all that aware or talented or multifaceted an actress."

David Letterman was inviting the audience, whom he again called ladies and gentlemen (which I liked) to imagine I AM A WOMAN WHO *ACTS* emblazoned on a shirt.

"That's why I'm doing those commercials you're seeing all the time now," I said lightly, yawning.

"Well, and now hey, I wanted to ask you about that, Edilyn," Letterman said. "The problem, ah, is that"—he rubbed his chin—"I'll need to ask you what they're commercials *for* without anyone of course mentioning the fine . . . fine and may I say delicious?"

"Please do."

"Delicious product by name." He smiled. "Since that would be a commercial itself right there."

I nodded, smiled. My earplug was silent. I looked around the stage innocently, pretending to stretch, whistling a very famous jingle's first twelve-note bar.

Letterman and the audience laughed. Paul Shaffer laughed. My husband's electric voice crackled approvingly. I could also hear Ron laughing in the background; his laugh did sound deadpan.

"I think that probably gives us a good clear picture, yes," Letterman grinned. He threw his index card at a pretend window behind us. There was an obviously false sound of breaking glass.

The man seemed utterly friendly.

My husband transmitted something I couldn't make out because Letterman had put his hands behind his head with its helmet of hair and was saying "So then I guess *why,* is the thing, Edilyn. I mean we *know* about the dollars, the big, *big* dollars over there in, ah, prime time. They scribble vague hints, *allusions,* really, is all, they're such big dollars, about prime-time salaries in the washrooms here at NBC. They're amounts that get discussed only in low tones. Here you are," he said, "you've had, what, three quality television series? *Countless* guest-appearances on other programs . . . ?"

"A hundred and eight," I said.

He looked aggrieved at the camera a moment as the audience laughed. ". . . Virtually *countless* guest-credits," he said. "You've got a critically acclaimed police drama that's been on now, what, three years? four years? You've got this . . ." he looked at an index card ". . . talented daughter who's done several fine films and who's currently in a series, you've got a husband who's a mover and a shaker, basically a legend in comedy development. . . ."

"Remember 'Laugh-In'?" said the NBC Sports coordinator. " 'Flip Wilson'? 'The Smothers'? Remember 'Saturday Night Live' back when it was good, for a few years there?" He was shaking his head in admiration.

Letterman released his own head. "So series, daughter's series, Emmy nomination, husband's virtually countless movings and shakings and former series, one of the best marriages in the industry if not the Northern, ah, Hemisphere . . ." He counted these assets off on his hands. His hands were utterly average. "You're *loaded,* sweetie," he said. "If I may." He smiled and played with his coffee mug. I smiled back.

"So then Edilyn a nation is wondering what's the deal with going off and doing these . . . *wiener* commercials," he asked in a kind of near-whine that he immediately exaggerated into a whine.

Rudy's small voice came: "See how he exaggerated the whine the minute he saw how—?"

"Because I'm not a great actress, David," I said.

Letterman looked stricken. For a moment in the angled white lights I looked at him and he looked stricken for me. I was positive I was dealing with a basically sincere man.

"Those things you listed," I said, "are assets, is all they are." I looked at him. "They're my assets, David, they're not me. I'm an actress in commercial television. Why not act in television commercials?"

"Be honest," Rudy hissed, his voice slight and metallic as a low-quality phone. Letterman was pretending to sip coffee from an empty mug.

"Let's be honest," I said. The audience was quiet. "I just had a very traumatic birthday, and I've been shedding illusions right and left. You're now looking at a woman with no illusions, David."

Letterman seemed to perk up at this. He cleared his throat. My earplug hissed a direction *never* to use the word "illusions."

"That's sort of a funny coincidental thing," Letterman was saying speculatively. "I'm an illusion with no *women*; say do you . . . detect a sort of parallel, there, Paul?"

I laughed with the audience as Paul Shaffer did a go-figure from the bandstand.

"Doom," my husband transmitted from the office of a man whose subordinates fished without hooks and sat in exploding circles. I patted at the hair over my ear.

I said, "I'm *forty,* David. I turned forty just last week. I'm at the point now where I think I have to know what I am." I looked at him. "I have four kids. Do you know of many working commercial-television actresses with four kids?"

"There are actresses who have four kids," Letterman said. "Didn't we have a lovely and talented young lady with four kids on, recently, Paul?"

"Name ten actresses with four kids," Shaffer challenged.

Letterman did a pretend double-take at him. *"Ten?"*

"Meredith Baxter Birney?" Reese said.

"Meredith Baxter Birney," Letterman nodded. "And Loretta Swit has four kids, doesn't she, Paul?"

"Marion Ross?"

"I think Meredith Baxter Birney actually has *five* kids, in fact, Dave," said Paul Shaffer, leaning over his little organ's microphone. His large bald spot had a label on it that said BALD SPOT.

"I guess the point, gentlemen"—I interrupted them, smiling— "is that I've got kids who're already bigger stars than I. I've appeared in two feature films, total, in my whole career. Now that I'm forty, I'm realizing that with two films, but three pretty long series, my mark on this planet is probably not going to be made in features. David, I'm a television actress."

"You're a *woman who acts* in television," Letterman corrected, smiling.

"And now a woman in television commercials, too." I shrugged as if I just couldn't see what the big deal was.

Paul Shaffer, still leaning over his organ, played a small but very sweet happy-birthday tune for me.

Letterman had put another card between his teeth. "So what I think we're hearing you saying, then, is that you didn't think the wiener-commercial thing would hurt your career, is the explanation."

"Oh no, God, no, not at all," I laughed. "I didn't mean that at *all*. I mean this *is* my career, right? Isn't that what we were just talking about?"

Letterman rubbed his chin. He looked at the Sports coordinator. "So then fears such as . . . say maybe something like compromising your integrity, some, ah, art factor: not a factor in this decision, is what you're saying."

Ron was asking Rudy to let him have the remote transmitter a moment.

"But there *were* art factors," I said. "Ever try to emote with meat, David?" I looked around. "Any of you? To dispense mustard like you *mean* it?"

Letterman looked uncomfortable. The audience made odd occasional sounds: they couldn't tell whether to laugh. Ron was beginning to transmit to me in a very calm tone.

"To still look famished on the fifteenth frank?" I said as Letterman smiled and sipped at his mug. I shrugged. "Art all over the place in those commercials, David."

I barely heard Ron's little voice warning me to be aware of the danger of appearing at all defensive. For Letterman appeared suddenly diffident, reluctant about something. He looked stage-left, then at his index card, then at me. "It's just Edilyn I guess a cynic, such as maybe Paul over there"—Shaffer laughed—"might be tempted to ask you . . . I mean," he said, "with all those assets we just listed together, with you being quote unquote, ah, loaded . . . and now this is just something someone like Paul gets curious about, certainly not our business," he felt uncomfortably at his collar; "this question then with all due respect of how *any* amount of money, even vast amounts, could get a talented, if not great then certainly we'd both agree acclaimed, and above all *loaded* actress . . . to emote with meat."

Either Ron or Rudy whispered Oh my God.

"To be *famished* for that umpteenth frank she's putting all that . . . *mustard* on," Letterman said, his head tilted, looking me in what I distinctly remember as the right eye. "And this is something we'll certainly understand if you don't want to go into, I mean . . . am I right Paul?"

He did look uncomfortable. As if he'd been put up to this last-minute. I was looking at him as if he were completely mad. Now that he'd gotten his silly question out I felt as if he and I had been having almost separate conversations since my appearance's start. I genuinely yawned.

"Just be honest," Ron was saying.

"Go ahead and tell him about the back taxes," Rudy whispered.

"Look," I said, smiling, "I think one of us hasn't been making themselves clear, here. So may I just be honest?"

Letterman was looking stage-left as if appealing to someone. I was sure he felt he'd gone too far, and his discomfort had quieted the audience like a death.

I smiled until my silence got his attention. I leaned toward him conspiratorially. After an uncertain pause he leaned over his desk toward me. I looked slowly from side to side. In a stage whisper I said *"I did the wiener commercials for nothing."*

I worked my eyebrows up and down.

Letterman's jaw dropped.

"For nothing," I said, "but art, fun, a few cases of hot dogs, and the feeling of a craft well plied."

"Oh, now, come now, really," Letterman said, leaning back and grabbing his head. He pretended to appeal to the studio audience: "Ladies and gentlemen . . ."

"A feeling I'm sure we all know well here." I smiled with my eyes closed. "In fact, I called *them*. I volun*teered*. Almost *begged*. You should have seen it. You should have been there. Not a pretty sight."

"What a kid," Paul Shaffer tossed in, pretending to wipe at an eye under his glasses. Letterman threw his index card at him, and the Sound man in his red sweater hit another pane of glass with his hammer. I heard Ron telling Rudy this was inspired. Letterman seemed now suddenly to be having the time of his life. He smiled; he said ha *ha*; his eyes came utterly alive; he looked like a very large toy. Everyone seemed to be having a ball. I touched my ear and heard my husband thanking Ron.

We talked and laughed for one or two minutes more about art and self-acceptance being inestimably more important than assets. The interview ended in a sort of explosion of good will. David Letterman made confetti out of a few of his body's labels. I was frankly sorry it was over. Letterman smiled warmly at me as we went to commercial.

It was then that I felt sure in my heart all the angst and conference, Rudy's own fear, had been without point. Because, when we cut to that commercial message, David Letterman was still the *same way*. The director, in his cardigan, sawed at his throat with a finger, a cleverly photographed bumper filled all 6-A's monitors, the band got funky under Shaffer's direction, and the cameras' lights went dark. Letterman's shoulders sagged; he leaned tiredly across his obviously cheap desk and mopped at his forehead with a ratty-looking tissue from his yachting jacket's pocket. He smiled from the depths of himself and said it *was* really grotesquely nice having me on, that the audience was cetainly getting the very most for its entertainment dollar tonight, that he hoped for her sake my daughter Lynnette had even one half the stage presence I had, and that if he'd known what a thoroughly engaging guest I'd be, he himself would have moved molehills to have me on long before this.

"He really said that," I told my husband later in the NBC car. "He said 'grotesquely nice,' 'entertainment dollar,' and that I was an engaging guest. And no one was listening."

Ron had gotten a driver and gone ahead to pick up Charmian and would meet us at the River Café, where the four of us try to go whenever Rudy and I are able to get into town. I looked at our own driver, up ahead, through the panel; his hat was off, his hair close-clipped, his whole head as still as a photo.

My husband in the back seat with me held my hand in his hands. His necktie and handkerchief were square and flush. I could almost smell his relief. He was terribly relieved when I saw him after the taping. Letterman had explained to the audience that I needed to be on my way, and I'd been escorted off as he introduced the self-proclaimed king of kitchen-gadget home sales, who wore an Elks pin.

"Of course he really said that," my husband said. "It's just the sort of thing he'd say."

"Exactly," I maintained, looking at what his hands held.

We were driven south.

"But that doesn't mean he's really that way," he said, looking at me very directly. Then he too looked at our hands. Our three rings were next to each other. I felt a love for him, and moved closer on the soft leather seat, my face hot and sore. My empty ear did feel a bit violated.

"Any more than you're really the way you were when we were handling him better than I've ever seen him handled," he said. He looked at me admiringly. "You're a talented and multifaceted actress," he said. "You took direction. You kept your head and did us both credit and survived an appearance on an anti-show." He smiled. "You did good work."

I moved away from my husband just enough to look at his very clean face. "I wasn't acting, with David Letterman," I told him. And I was sincere. "It was more you and Ron that I had to . . . handle." Rudy's smile remained. "I would've taken Ron's earplug out altogether, agreement or not, if Charmian hadn't had me wear my hair down. It would have hurt the man's feelings. And I knew the minute I sat across that silly desk from him I wasn't going to need any direction. He wasn't savage." I said. "He was *fun*, Rudy. I had fun."

He lit a long Gauloise, smiling. "Did it just for fun?" he asked wryly. He pretended almost to nudge my ribs. A high-rent district that I had remembered as a low-rent district went by on both sides of us.

And I'll say that I felt something dark in my heart when my husband almost nudged me there. I felt that it was a sorry business indeed when my own spouse couldn't tell I was being serious. And I told him so.

"I was just the way I am," I maintained.

And I saw in Rudy's face what my face must have betrayed when I hadn't a clue about what he and Ron or even David had been talking about. And I felt the same queer near-panic I imagine now he must have felt all week. We both listened as something sweetly baroque filtered through the limousine intercom's grille.

"It's like my birthday," I said, holding my second husband's hand in mine. "We agreed, on my birthday. I'm forty, and have both grown and tiny children, and a husband who is dear to me, and I'm a television actress who's agreed to represent a brand of wiener. We drank *wine* to that, Rudy. We held the facts out and looked, together. We agreed just last week about the way I am. What other way is there for me to be, now?"

My husband disengaged his hand and felt at the panel's grille. The Spanish driver's hatless head was cocked. A part of his neck was without pigment, I saw. The lighter area was circular; it spiraled into his dark hair and was lost to me.

"He leaned across right up to me, Rudy. I could see every little part of his face. He was freckled. I could see little pinheads of sweat, from the lights. A tiny mole, near that label. His eyes were the same denim color Jamie and Lynnette's eyes get in the summer. I looked at him. I *saw* him."

"But we told you, Edilyn," my husband said, reaching into his jacket pocket. "What put him there, here and now, for you to see, is that he *can't* be seen. That's what the whole thing's about, now. That no one is really the way they have to be seen."

I looked at him. "You really think that's true."

His cigarette crackled. "Doesn't matter what I think. That's what the show is about. They make it true. By watching him."

"You believe that," I said.

"I believe what I see," he said, putting his cigarette down to manipulate the bottle's cap. The thing's typed label read TAKE SEVERAL, OFTEN. "If it wasn't true, could he use it the way he does . . . ?"

"That strikes me as really naïve."

". . . The way we used to?" he said.

Certain pills are literally bitter. When I'd finished my drink from the back seat's bar, I still tasted the Xanax on the back of my tongue. The adrenaline's ebb had left me very tired. We broke out of the tall buildings near the water. I watched the Manhattan Bridge pass. The late sun came into view. It hung to our right, red. We both looked at the water as we were driven past. The sheet of its surface was wound-colored under the March sunset.

I swallowed. "So you believe no one's really the way we see them?"

I got no response. Rudy's eyes were on the window.

"Ron doesn't really have a mouth, I noticed today. It's more like a gash in his head." I paused. "You needn't defer to him in our personal lives just because of your decisions in business, Rudy." I smiled. "We're loaded, sweetie."

My husband laughed without smiling. He looked at the last of the sun-colored water as we approached the Brooklyn Bridge's system of angled shadow.

"Because if no one is really the way we see them," I said, "that would include me. And you."

Rudy admired the sunset out loud. He said it looked explosive, hanging, all round, just slightly over the water. Reflected and doubled in that bit of river. But he'd been looking only at the water. I'd watched him.

"Oh, *my*," is what David Letterman said when Reese the coordinator's distinguished but raccoon-ringed face had resolved out of a perfect ring of exploded explosives. Months later, after I'd come through something by being in its center, survived in the stillness created by great disturbance from which I, as cause, perfectly circled, was exempt, I'd be struck all over again by what a real and simply *right* thing it was for a person in such a place to say.

And I have remembered and worked hard to show that, if nothing else at all, I am a woman who speaks her mind. It is the way I have to see myself, to live.

And so I did ask my husband, as we were driven in our complimentary limousine to join Ron and Charmian and maybe Lindsay for drinks and dinner across the river at NBC's expense, just what way he thought he and I really were, then, did he think.

Which turned out to be the mistake.

SAY NEVER

LABOV

A THING that is no fun? *Stomach trouble.* You don't believe me, you ask Mrs. Tagus here, she'll illuminate issues. Me: no stomach trouble. A stomach of hardy elements, such as stone. Arthritis yes, stomach trouble no.

The tea is not helping Mrs. Tagus's stomach trouble. "Such discomfort Mr. Labov!" she says to me in my kitchen of my apartment, where we are. "Excuse me for the constant complaining," she says, "but it seems that to me anything that is the least little worry these days means the automatic making of my stomach into a fist!" She makes with a fist in the air, in her coat, and bends to blow on the very hot tea, which is steaming with violence into the cold air of my kitchen. "And now such worry," Mrs. Tagus says. She is making an example of a fist in the air in a firm manner I envy, because of the arthritis I have in my limbs every day, especially in these winters; but I only express sympathy to the stomach of Mrs. Tagus, who has been my best and closest friend since my late wife and then her late husband passed away inside three months of each other seven years ago may they rest in peace.

I am a tailor. Labov the North-side tailor who can make anything. Now retired. I chose, cut, fit, stitched and tailored the raccoon coat Mrs. Tagus has been wearing for years now and is inside of now in my kitchen which my landlord keeps cold, like the rest of this apartment, which my late wife Sandra Labov and I first rented in the years of President Truman. The landlord wants Labov out so he can raise rent to a younger person. But he should know who should know better than a tailor how it's no trouble to wear finely stitched coats and wait for spring. An ability to wait has always been one of my abilities.

I made the heavy raincoat with lining of various fur Mrs. Tagus's late husband and my close friend Arnold Tagus was interred in eight years ago this August.

"Lenny," Mrs. Tagus has murmured to her tea. There is no more fist in the air; she is warming her hands on the emergency cup of tea. "Lenny," she says, distracted from me by the warmth she holds in her dry hands.

Lenny is Mr. and Mrs. Tagus's son, Lenny Tagus. Also there is a younger son, Mike Tagus. Me: no children. Mrs. Labov had reproduction troubles which I loved her no less when we found out. But no children. But Labovs and all the Taguses are like this. Close. I watched the Tagus boys grow up, Lenny and Mike, prides and joys.

You know the type who comes right out with it? Mrs. Tagus is not such a type of person. Something is on her mind: she beats around it, a gesture here, a word there, a sigh maybe; she shapes it inside her like with a soft medium, for instance clay, and you have to patiently work the medium with her to get the something out in the open.

Me: I come right out with it, when there's something.

MIKEY AND LOUIS

"You want to still date her?"

"Are you fucking kidding? I want to strangle her."

"Uh-huh."

"I'd love to still date her."

"Just stay away. She seems like bad news. She seemed like she was really into it."

"She blew me off. I didn't blow her off."

"How, exactly?"

"Carlina blew *me* off."

"So how, Tagus?"

"She just said how she didn't want to go out no more. It didn't feel so good, either. I can maybe see why they cry, when you blow them off."

"She said that? Just like that?"

"Just like after I'd rammed about half a gram up her nose and bought her drinks all night."

"Bad news."

"I must of rammed about a gram up her nose."

"I bet you didn't have to ram anything up anything. I bet her nose didn't need much persuading."

"It started out nice. It was her and Lenny, who I want her to hit it off with, and me. Her and him do my whole gram while I'm over at the bar getting us drinks. Then he takes off to like tuck his kids into bed. He's dribbling the shit out his nose, he's bouncing off walls, and he's going to tuck in his kids. And then me and her have an argument about it. I don't even remember what about. And then later she just blows me off."

"Want a beer?"

"She just left me sitting there. I don't even know how she got back home."

" . . . . "

"I think I feel like killing her."

"Not worth it. Have a beer."

"Two months, man. That's two months down the tube. I had her meet everybody. Mom, Labov. I told her personal shit. Shit about who I was."

"Bad news."

"You bet your sweet ass bad news, Lou."

" 'Does Lenny have to say about it? You talk this out with Lenny?"

"He'd condescend. He's a pecker in situations like this. He talks down to me. Big brother little brother. And plus he's out like all day. Bonnie says she don't even know where, office, bar, where.

She's half crying herself the whole time. Her and Len got their own problems. They're both like this about something. Shaky. Pissed off. Lenny was on the drinks and the toot like a last meal. I go to the bar to get them drinks, they just do it without me. Who's gonna figure on that?"

"Nobody, man."

"And then I bought her drinks all night."

"Open the beer."

"I think I might kill her."

"Nobody's killing anybody, Mikey."

"Try to think of somebody for me to hit, at least."

LEN

Cinnamon girl, spiced cream, honey to kiss, melt hot around the center of me.

LABOV

"Lenny is your pride and joy," I say to Mrs. Tagus. I say: "What could be with Lenny that makes for stomach trouble for a proud and joyful mother such as you Mrs. Tagus?"

"If you had gotten a letter and then a call on the telephone like I got today Mr. Labov, even your perfect stomach would make for itself a knot, a fist. And for me, with stomach trouble . . ." She shakes her head in her well-made coat.

I press Mrs. Tagus to eat a saltine.

"Lenny trouble," she murmurs, beating around the something. While a saltine is being carefully chewed she murmurs also: "Bonnie."

So I can gather there are troubles between Lenny Tagus, Mrs. Tagus's son, a teacher, in college, who wrote a book about Germans before Hitler (in a print so tiny who could read it?) that got called

Solid and Scholarly in a Review Mrs. Tagus has taped onto her refrigerator with the kind of invisible tape you don't get off in a hurry. There is trouble between Mrs. Tagus's Lenny and Lenny Tagus's Bonnie, his wife of eight, nine years, a sweeter and better girl than even as perfect a catch as Len could hope for, who has borne him healthy and polite children, and who makes a knish so good it is spelled s-i-n.

Mrs. Tagus is whispering unhearable things, sipping her tea which is now cooler and has stopped its steaming violently into the cold air of my apartment's kitchen.

"So how do letters and telephones and your children I love like my own make for such stomach trouble?" I say. I place four stacked crackers next to Mrs. Tagus's saucer.

"If you had gotten the call I got from Bonnie," Mrs. Tagus says. "From this girl who who would want to hurt her? Who who would want to not give her feelings weight on the scale?"

I can see the whiteness of my breath a little in the kitchen air. I find a reassurance in how I can see it. I put my hand on Mrs. Tagus's fist of a hand on my cold kitchen table. The skin of the knuckles of Mrs. Tagus is drawn tight and dry, and when she unfists the fist to let me comfort the hand I feel the skin crinkle like paper. Me: unfortunately also skin like paper. I look at our two hands. If my late Sandra were here with us this night I would say, to her only, things concerning oldness, coldness, trouble with stairs, paper-dry skin with brown sprinkles and yellowed nails, how it seems to Labov we get old like animals. We get claws, the shape of our face is the shape of our skull, our lips retreat back from big teeth like we're baring to snarl. Sharp, snarling, old: who should wonder at how nobody cares if I hurt, except another snarler?

Sandra Labov: the type everybody could say things to concerning issues like this. I miss her with everything. The loss of Sandra Labov is what makes my kitchen's clock's black hands go around, telling me when to do what.

Me and Mrs. Tagus have gotten close, like if you'll excuse me I think old people need to in this city these days. Her husband and me were like this, we were so close. For Mr. Tagus and the Taguses: tailored clothes at discounts. For me and Mrs. Labov: insurance at cost. Taguses and Labovs are close. So close I all of a sudden look at my clock and press Mrs. Tagus to tell me the cause of her stomach trouble straight out.

"Lay it on the line, Mrs. Tagus," I say.

She sighs and feels at herself in the cold. I watch her breath. She leans close and lays it on the line, whispering to me the words: "Infidelity, Mr. Labov." She looks with her cloudy eyes from operated-on cataracts behind her thick spectacles into my eyes and says, with a cleared throat: "Betrayal, also."

I let silence collect around this thing that's finally out in the open's hard medium and then ask Mrs. Tagus to clear me up on what's all this about betrayal.

"He's going to kill Bonnie by making her die of the pain of the shame of it. Or Mikey could justly raise hands against him, his own blood," is what Mrs. Tagus says she is having the awful stomach trouble over tonight, this some sort of triangular problem between the three children that I still don't feel like I'm cleared up on.

Mrs. Tagus fights against some tears. Her tea has gotten cold and lighter in color than tea, and I get up to my feet for the can of tea and the hot water in the copper kettle my wife Sandra and I received from Arnold and Greta Tagus on the day of our wedding when Roosevelt passed away may he rest, and Mrs. Tagus clears her throat some more and feels at her stomach through her coat I stitched together, using fine gut thread to weld the pelts.

She says the call on the phone from her daughter-under-law Bonnie Tagus today that has her in her condition had also to do with half a Xeroxed letter from Lenny, her son and pride, a half a letter which Mrs. Tagus received in her postal box, also today, but before the call on the phone from Bonnie Tagus. It all comes in a rush. The half a letter from Lenny she says was a Xerox (not even personal?). He had mailed several Xerox copies of the letter, by Express Mail. A rush job. " 'An outpouring' he says," Mrs. Tagus says, " 'to all friends and family.' " Illuminating all issues for everybody. She looks at me at the kettle on the stove which only one big burner still has gas. Did I, Mr. Labov, also get such a first half of a letter? But I get my mail once a week only, on Tuesday (today is almost Friday, by the clock), on account of my box here at my building has been broken into, and I feel it is insecure, and my check for Social Security from the government comes by mail, so I have a secure box I got at the Post Office but the Post Office is half an hour by El or seven dollars by taxicab and let's not even discuss bus routes and in this weather who needs the more than once a week bother? So it could be in my box. Mrs. Tagus has confidence in the security of her postal box here in the building, which she and Arnold Tagus first moved in starting with the weekend they electrocuted the Rosenbergs because of Nixon.

I put some more hot and dark freshened tea before Mrs. Tagus, in a specially gotten mug, from the Mug House in Marshall Fields, with a lid on it, to keep the heat in the tea, which I got with emergencies like this one maybe in the back of my mind. The night years ago when Mikey Tagus swallowed his tongue in high school football, cup after cup Arnold and Greta drank out of some emergency mugs, with lids, that I'd brought, at the Emergency Room. We all sat close with tea and prayed with worry. That night was the first time Mrs. Tagus's stomach made like a fist. And she is making with the fist with her hand in the air again, and in the fist are crinkled paper pages, from a letter, smeared like Xeroxes get when wet, from Lenny. She rocks in my kitchen chair and looks across the alley at the fire escape which is the view, speaking.

LEN'S HALF AN OPEN LETTER SENT TO "THAT COMMUNITY OF MY FAMILY AND INTIMATE FRIENDS—LETTER APPROPRIATELY CONCEIVED ALSO AS AN INFORMATIONAL SATELLITE, A PROBE LAUNCHED INTO THE EMOTIONAL CONSTELLATION SURROUNDING AND INFORMING THIS CORRESPONDENT'S PERSONAL ORBIT—EXCLUDING THE PARTIES BONNIE FLUTTERMAN TAGUS AND MICHAEL

ARNOLD TAGUS—REGARDING THIS CORRESPONDENT AND
THE ABOVE TWO EXCLUDED PARTIES"

21-2

Beloved fathers and teachers,

Please know that the party Leonard Shlomith Tagus, Gent.,
Ph.D., author of *Motion in Poetry: The Theme of Momentum in
Weimar Republic Verse,* a monograph from which royalties in
excess of three figures are forecast to accrue in fiscal 1985,
Northwestern University's lone blade-burnished Teutonist,
student, teacher, son, father, brother; that wiliest of connubial
mariners, that L. S. Tagus, having for nine years navigated
successfully between the Scylla and Charybdis of Inclination
and Opportunity, has, as of today, 21 February 1985, committed *adultery,* on four occasions, with one *Carlina Rentaria-
Cruz,* former significant other of my *brother, Michael Arnold
Tagus;* that the party anticipates further episodes of such
adultery; and that such past and highly probable future episodes will be brought to the attention of the party's *wife,* Ms.
Bonnie Flutterman Tagus, between 1:00 and 2:00 pm (lunch)
this date.

Know further that it is neither the desire & intention of L.
Tagus, nor the project of an openly probing letter, either: (a)
to *excuse* those libidinal/genital activities on the part of this
party likely to excite disfavor or -ease within his intimate
constellation; or: (b) to *explain* same, since the explanation of
any transgression inevitably metastasizes into *excuse* (see (a));
but rather merely: (c) to *inform* those parties on whom my
existence and the behavior that defines same can be expected
to have an effect of the events outlined above and discussed,
as usual, below; and: (d) to *describe,* probably via the time-
tested heuristic pentad, the W's of why those events have taken
and do and will take place; and: (e) to *project* the foreseeable
consequences of such activities for this correspondent, for
those other parties (B.F.T., M.A.T.) directly affected by his

choices, and for those other other parties whose psychic fortunes are, to whatever extent, bound up with our own.

(a) and (b) conceded, then, and (c) killed in the telling:

Cinnamon girl. Full-lipped, candy-skinned, brandy-haired South-American-type girl. A type: a girl the color of dirty light, eyes a well-boiled white and hair like liquor, scintillant and smoky; precisely pointed breasts that shimmy when her chest caves in, when her chest caves in and hand flutters worried about the breastbone, from the laughter. Which is constant. This is a merry girl. Laughs at any stimuli not macabre or political, *avoid* abortion controversy; but otherwise a weather without change, a thing that carries her from place to place rather than obversely, a laugh of the piercing sort that resembles a possessed state, helpless, crumpled in around her perception of anomaly or embarrassment, harmless harm to anyone in a world that is only a violent cartoon, wet eyes darting around for assistance, some invitation to gravity, the detumescence of a nipple scraped in shimmy by cotton, some distraction to let her decontort. A merriment that is almost on the edge of pain.

And I watched her crumple, eyes the color of cream squeezed tight, over a tall and sonorous Graphix water-pipe, at the apartment of Mikey Tagus; and a wax-deaf man in a city of sirens heard one siren's fatal call; and the malignant, long-slalomed rocks mated with a crunch through the dry eggshell prow of my careful character. Carlina Rentaria-Cruz, secretarial aide at North Side offices of Chicago Park District. *Twenty,* lovely, light and dark, hair sticky with gin, our lady of wet rings on album covers, Spanish lilt, pointed boots, a dairy sheen to redly white skin, lips that gleam, shine a light—shine without aid of tongue—they *manufacture their own moisture.*

Contrast—please, neither offense nor explanation intended—contrast a wide-bottomed, solid, pale-as-all-indoors woman of thirty-four. Known in milliscopic detail. Large squash-shaped mole on left arm sports a banner of black hair. Nipples like pencil erasers, hard and corrective against wide shallow breasts whose broad curves I know like the Lake's own tired sweep. A woman ever armed with hemorrhoid pillow in one of only two stages of inflation, an obscene pink doughnut of hardened plastic, cushioning with her own dioxides the woman's legacy from the long and labored birth of Saul Tagus. A woman whose lips are chronically dry (bad sebum flow) and collect a white paste at the corners. Whose posture, I confess, has always been a *little too good* for my complete peace of mind. And whose quiet static laughter is always appropriate, conscious, complicated by an automatic and sophisticated concern for the special sensitivities of everyone present.

Viz. Bonnie laughs only *with;* Carlina was so conceived and constituted as to laugh only *at.*

E.g. Representative Laughter-Scenario: B. F. Tagus:

Envision dinner party—B. F. Tagus filling her self-imposed quota of one family anecdote that will 'tickle' our guests: "And Joshua gets his piece of pie from the waiter, and his eyes are getting bigger and bigger' (uncanny imitation here) 'he looks at it, and he says to me, he whispers when the waiter's left he says Momma, why Momma there's ice cream on this pie, and I say but Joshua, the waiter asked you if you wanted your pie a la mode honey and you said yes; and Joshua looks at me he's about to cry almost the poor love and he says A la mode? Momma I thought he said *pie all alone.* Is . . . what . . . he . . . thought . . . he . . .' (hand to mouth, eyes frighteningly wide, unaffected, shoulders moving up and down in sync, laughter full of love, good will, etc.).

Vs. Representative Laughter-Scenario: C. R-Cruz:

'Len, Len, what is different between beer nuts and deer nuts. I hear this in a club on the Loop' (The Loooop.) 'Beer nuts are fifty cents and yet deer nuts are just under a . . . buck!' (Becoming here crumpled, other, helpless in the grip of the nasty (*grip of the nasty*).)

Not to mention an utterly deadly accent, a fellation of each syllable through the auto-lubricated portal that is at once a deep garden and a tall jagged city. A planet.

'OH LENITO I WILL *EEET* YOU!'

(Congress, by the way, has revealed itself here to be a loud and exquisitely goy affair—cries from Carlina and accessory of a desperation only partly channeled; mad twined scrabble of a search for something key hidden at a system of bodies' center.)

And so ungodly *precise* about it all:

'Len, Len, how many of the girls known as Jewish American Princesses are needed for the screwing in of a light bulb?'

'Princesses?'

'Answer is *two* of them I heard. One to call a Daddy and one to buy the Tab!' contorting into wherever she sits. (Wicked. There is a wickedness in the corners here, and it is good. see below. (though I must say I found that particular joke offensive.))

Further,

MIKEY AND LOUIS

"So what's the point of even calling him, then?"

"Advice, Tagus. He's older. He's been around. He's been there. He can put the thing in some perspective for you."

"He's a pecker in situations like Carlina and me, is the thing. He talks down to me when I let him know I want advice."

"He saw how you were treating her good and how she was acting like it was going to last."

"It wasn't like I wanted it to last forever or anything."

"Len's a smart guy, Mikey."

"It's just if I'm going to stop sleeping with somebody I want it to be my decision to stop it, is all. Or to at least talk about it first."

"He'll understand, probably. You said he met her. He'll tell you to not sweat it."

"I really think I'd rather hit somebody."

"Tagus."

"Line's busy anyway."

"Have a beer. At least it means they're home."

"Maybe I should just go ahead and call Carlina."

"I wouldn't."

"I'm predicting right now he'll be a pecker about it."

LEN

I have told the cinnamon girl how I will never be forgiven for this. Never. How by the time you reach a certain history and situation you're bound up with people, part of a larger thing. How the whole constellation becomes as liquid, and any agitation ripples. She asked me who it was who first said never say never. I told her it must have been someone alone.

She is silk in a bed of mail-order satin. Complete and seamless, an egg of sexual muscle. My motions atop her are dislocated, frantic, my lone interstice a trans-cultural spice of encouragement I smell with my spine. As, inside it, I go, I cry out to a god whose absence I have never felt so keenly.

She wears Catholic medals, a jingle all their own. I have apologized for invoking god's name at such a moment. She touches my hip. There are no atheists in foxy holes. She laughs into my chest; I feel her eyes' squeeze.

She is *wrong* for me.

LABOV

I have arranged Mrs. Tagus's chair so that she is able to use my wall-telephone on the wall of my kitchen to talk to Lenny, her son, without having to stand—which in her conditions, at a time like this, with family and stomach trouble, standing would not be good. She is on the phone with Lenny. There is much bravery here as Mrs. Tagus listens without crying to things Lenny is saying on the wall-telephone. My heart is going out. I love Mrs. Tagus like a man friend loves a woman friend. She is my last true and old friend in this world except for old Schoenweiss the dentist who is too deaf now to converse about weather with even. As I drink my own tea and I look at Mrs. Tagus in her fine and well made coat and fine old wool dress with some small section of slip showing over heavy dark stockings and then the soft white shoes with the thick rubber soles, for her arches, which fell, her thick eyeglasses for her eyes and still mostly dark hair in color under a beaver hat which it breaks my heart to be remembering her late Arnold Tagus wearing just that hat to Bears football games with me, in the cold of old autumns, I know, inside, I love Mrs. Tagus, who I called Greta to her face while I helped her to the chair I arranged under the wall-telephone and strongly urged her, as a friend I said, to make for the sake of her stomach the telephone call that could maybe clear up some of the total misunderstanding. I am a dry and yellow snarling animal who loves another animal.

There is by my wall-telephone a large and wide section of flowered wallpaper, from the wall of my kitchen, which has been peeling since Jimmy Carter (try talking to my landlord about anything), and it is curving over Mrs. Tagus's hat and head like a wave of cornflower-blue water, with flowers. I do not like the way it appears to curve over Greta Tagus.

Anger from me at her Lenny, however? This I could not manage even if I could understand quite this trouble which keeps Mrs. Tagus crumpled over her stomach under my telephone. Lenny Tagus is a nice boy. This is a thing I know. I know the Lenny Tagus who put himself through a college, with a doctorate even, and all the time was helping the finances of Arnold and Greta Tagus when Arnold Tagus's office got bought by State Farm and he got put on commission only, which if you ask anybody is what killed him. The Lenny who would have helped also put Mikey through a college if Mike had not received the scholarship in college football to the Illini of the University of Illinois, but dropped out when it was revealed how he had never learned enough about reading, and went instead to work for the Softball Department of the Chicago

Park District, where he is doing a fine and solid job, although anybody could see how winters would be slow, in terms of softball business.

The Lenny Tagus who calls his mother, Mrs. Tagus, twice a week, like my clock, "just to talk," is the excuse, except really to always let his mother know how she's loved by him and not forgotten alone in her and Arnold's quite old cold apartment. Not to mention how Mrs. Tagus, often myself in addition, gets invited into Lenny's home and family for such a dinner cooked by Bonnie Tagus! Once a month or more. Josh Tagus and Saul Tagus and little Becky Tagus in pajamas with pajama-feet attached, yawning over milk in plastic mugs with cartoons on their sides. Lenny smoothing their fine thin child's hair and reading to them from Gibran or Novalis under a soft lamp. You know from warmth? There is warmth in the home of Mr. and Mrs. Leonard Tagus.

"So I should meet this person?" Mrs. Tagus is questioning under the wave of wallpaper into my phone. "Us and Mike and Bonnie and this person should just sit down and talk like old friends?" She broaches to Lenny the possibility that his mind is maybe temporarily out of order, maybe from stress and tension from middle age. She respectfully mentions just so he'll know that she can hear Becky, and also it sounds like Bonnie, crying in Lenny's telephone's background. She expresses disbelieving shock, plus all-new and severe stomach trouble, at Lenny's revealing that a certain girl who was not Bonnie was right there, he said, now, in his and Bonnie's master bedroom, under a sheet, with Lenny, and that Bonnie: when Lenny last saw her she was in the spray-cleaner closet of the utility room, crying.

The Len Tagus with a crewcut and Bermuda shorts with black socks who mowed the building's lawns when the super was under the weather from gin, to save the Tagus family a little rent. Who I remember refused to let Mike (Mike is four years younger but at ten even he already had inches and pounds over Lenny, over everybody—Mike may be five years younger, it's four or five) who would not let Mike fight a fight on his behalf when wicked boys broke Lenny's French horn and kicked him in the back with shoes as he lay on the ground of the schoolyard and left yellow bruises I can still with my eyes closed see on the back of young Lenny Tagus, who wouldn't let Mikey know who to fight.

The Lenny who did my wife Mrs. Labov's shopping for months when God knows he had work of his own and plenty of it to do in school for his degree and doctorate, when Mrs. Labov's phlebitis got extreme and I had to be at the shop tailoring and the elevator in the building was broken and the landlord, even during Kennedy and Johnson he was trying to get us out, he took criminal time in getting to repairs, and Sandra would give Len a list.

Mrs. Tagus is telling Lenny on the phone to just hold it right there. That she has things to tell him, as a mother. There is the fortitude of the person who carries around stomach trouble every day in her voice's tone. The cold of my kitchen makes for a pain in my hands and I put them under my arms, under my lined coat, like Arnold Tagus's old coat, that I made.

LENNY

As I spoke and listened to my mother, envisioning her hand at either her stomach or her eyes, the two physical loci of any of the troubles she gathers to her person and holds like shiny prizes, Mr. Labov doubtless at his black teapot, baggy old pants accumulating at his ankles and sagging to reveal the northern climes of his bottom (god I feel pathos for people whose pants sag to reveal parts of their bottom), envisioning him clucking and casting, from a cloak of tea steam, glances at my mother, at the phone, my mother no doubt leaning for support against the lurid peeling wall of Labov's prehistoric kitchen; and as I reviewed the letter, undoubtedly couched somewhere on the person of my mother, the letter a doomed exercise in disinformation I could not even finish before sending it from me, rabid with a desire that things be somehow just *known,* that it be out, the waiting over and trauma-starter's gun's sharp crack—

—I found myself raw and palsied with the urge, in mid-conver-

sation—the conversation consisted as usual chiefly of pauses, the
wire's special communication of the sound of distance, electric and
lonely—the urge . . . to explain. To explain. And as I urged my
mother to come to my home, to help the edible girl and me extract
Bonnie from a darkness of brooms rags and Lysol, and to hash this
all out, we five, together—I found rising in my hickied throat the
gorged temptation to explain, excuse, exhypothesize, extinguish in
and for myself the truth, the flat unattractive and uninteresting
truth that came concrete for me via nothing other than a small and
shakily faint line written in quick pencil over the southernmost
urinal in the men's room of my office's floor at University, the line
simply

    no more mr. nice guy

amid the crude tangle of genitalia that surrounded its eye-level
run. . . .

Instead, in electromagnetic communication with my flesh, amid
the sounds of Becky and Bonnie and the burble and chuckle of
Carlina's bare coffee back bent before a bong hidden somewhere
on the femininely held side of the Tagus bed; on the phone, instead,
I found roiling out of me a torrent of misdirections, like releases
of bureaucratic flatus, calculations derived from an ageless child's
axioms about what his mother wishes to hear, arguments twirling
off the base clause that Bonnie and I Are Just Not Right For Each
Other Any More Mom, that We've Grown Apart, with Nothing
But The Kids To Hold Us Together, and Is That Fair To Of All
People The Kids?

Which mr. nice guy knows is manipulative, empty, and testa-
mentally wicked.

Though there was an episode, too unbeveled to have been a
dream, in which one wee-houred morning, last last year, Bonnie
and I both half-awoke. In sync. In this bed. Half-awoke, sat up,
and looked at each other's thick outlines in the green glow of the
alarm's digital spears; we looked at each other, first with recognition,
then a synchronized shock: looked shocked at these each others

and shouted, in unison, *'WHAT?'* and fell on our pillows and back to a puffy sleep. Compared notes at breakfast and both came away shaken.

This Mom understands, this sort of unified moment's revelation of separateness; it's marriage trouble as opposed to person trouble, troughs in the ebbing and flowing sinal flux that attends all long-term life-term emotional intercourse. She says,

'Every marriage gets its ups and its downs, or else it's not a marriage. You I need to tell about the years me and your late father?'

Yes Mom.

But, see, also no.

I could respond honestly with the kind of interior paralysis that also attends any sustained intersection of two people's everyday stuffed-together practical concerns, and how this restricts the breath of a man. The way Bonnie's conversation condenses each and every evening around *issues.* The cost of re-covering the love seats in the family room. The quality of market x's cut of meat y. The persistent and mysterious psoriatic rash on Josh's penis that is causing him to scratch in a way that simply cannot go on.

Vs. this partner, who is in best and worst ways still a child: either sulking, overcome, silent, screaming *Yes* (*Sí!* Yes! [God!]); or offering on her Sears sofa, to a tie-loosened teacher pummeled into catatonia by the day's round with the near-Soviet bureaucracy that is this university's German Department, offering to me a cool twittered river of such irrelevant and so priceless insights as 'I hate my hair today; I hate it' (how can one hate one's hair?); or 'I notice on the television last night that the nose of Karl Malden resemble the scrotum of a man, no?' (*Yes*); or 'Fahck you man is not funny I get my period in my god damn pair of white jeans at the right there checkout line at Jewel'; or 'Will Mike beat you when he finds out' (were it only that simple); or 'I never love anybody ever'; 'You want me to feel sorry for your wife who you don't love anymore' (were it only).

Yes Mrs. Tagus weary of navigation, exigency, *routineschmerz,* mid-life angst rendered. A unit of cinnamon milk, on fire with love for no one ever, vs. exhaustively tested loyalty, hard-headed realism, compassion, momentum, a woman the color and odor of Noxzema for all time.

Vs. vs. vs. : the reasons that center on others are easy to manipulate. All hollow things are light.

Because I just tire of being well. Of being good. Maybe I'm just tired of not knowing where in me the millenial expectations of a constellation leave off, where my own will hangs its beaver hat. I wish a little well-hung corner. I wish to be willful. I will it. It is not one bit more complicated than no more mr. n. g.

That's no more mr. l. s.

Then no more bullshit, if I can send even myself only halves.

If only Bonnie'd stop scratching at the closet door.

LABOV

"A *good* boy Lenny," Mrs. Tagus says truthfully to my phone. "You're a good man, and we love you, Bonnie and Mikey and I. Even Mr. Labov," she looks my way and the bravery which has held on so long in Mrs. Tagus's case gives up, and Mrs. Tagus weeps, weeping like you can imagine whole nations weeping, and I turn away, for respect. I put my aching hands with arthritis under my arms in my coat and look across the fire escape across the courtyard of my building at the window my window faces, which has a shade down which has never recently come up. The shade has been down since the Viet Nam era and I do not know who lives in the apartment. I notice how there's no more talking and Mrs. Tagus behind me has hung the wall-telephone up on the wall by the piece of wallpaper that curves. She is weeping like a nation, her eyes squeezed tightly from the pain of such stomach trouble I don't even want to imagine. I go to Mrs. Tagus.

MIKEY AND LOUIS

"Mikey, all I said is where, is all I said."

" . . . ."

"If I get grabbed and I have to go somewhere in such a hurry I like to know where I'm goin', is all."

" . . . ."

"You won't say where you're going, you can at least tell me why that brake light on the dash stays on all the time like that."

"The brake light?"

"In the dash here. Long as I can remember that thing never goes off. You got brake trouble, I can give you some names of places."

"It's a thing in the dash's guts. It's the connection. It never goes out. Ever since I got it. It's kind of like an eternal flame to me by now."

"Never goes out?"

"And it ain't the brakes, either."

"That'd probably give me the creeps a little bit."

"I don't know. I think I like it. I think I think it's reassuring a little, somehow."

LEN

Though even the novice alone can see quickly that a life conducted, temporarily or no, as a simple renunciation of value becomes at best something occluded and at worst something empty: a life of waiting for the will-be-never. Sitting in passive acceptance of (not judgment on) the happening and ending of things.

I will wait for the arrival of those whose orbits I've decayed. I will wait through the publicness of the thing—the collective countenance, the conferring, recriminating, protestations of loyalty, betrayal, consequence. And then that too will end. The hurt will take the harmed away. My constellation will be outside my ken.

But they will wait, because I will wait. We will wait for the day when the puncture and cincture of Carlina Rentaria-Cruz becomes for Leonard Shlomith simply part of the day. And we will wait for that inevitable day when silent whistles sound and my one siren leaves me for a man the color of a fine cigar.

And do not say then that I will wait for something to wait for.

LABOV

"Go on out of here with yourselves and leave the lady alone!" I shout at a mobster gang of boys in leather who are taking up all the space of the plastic shelter of the El platform and who are whistling and making with comments at the tears which are frozen by the wind on the thick spectacles of Mrs. Tagus. I can feel in my cold feet on the platform (feet: arthritis also) the fact that the train is coming.

I tell Mrs. Tagus to call when she needs a late taxicab home. I will meet her at home.

A vagrant beside a burning ashcan for trash is singing the national anthem across both sets of the tracks, but the song comes to us and then goes in the strongly blowing winter wind on the platform. All the snow is frozen in rigid positions. I give to Mrs. Tagus the Thermos vacuum bottle of the tea for on the train, the ride takes three quarter-hours except for thank God no transfers.

I tell Mrs. Tagus to tell her boys to call my apartment. We'll drink something hot, talk the whole matter out.

So here comes the train. Mrs. Tagus feels her way. She never talks when she cries, Greta. We pretend how it's not happening, for dignity. She is inside the door of the train. She gets a seat alone, but facing away from where the train's going, which I'm worried is bad for stomachs. Greta takes her gloves from her hands and puts her yellowed hands, which I can remember when they were white, she puts her hands up to remove her frozen eyeglasses. Without her glasses Mrs. Tagus is older. The doors close themselves before

I can walk with my stiffness to tell Mrs. Tagus through the opening to face where the train is going. There is so much noise I can't stand the noise. I have my hands in my gloves I bought over my ears and I see Mrs. Tagus pulled away north on a track. In our building in my kitchen I look at my kitchen and see the train pull her away.

EVERYTHING IS GREEN

SHE says I do not care if you believe me or not, it is the truth, go on and believe what you want to. So it is for sure that she is lying. When it is the truth she will go crazy trying to get you to believe her. So I feel like I know.

She lights up and looks off away from me, looking sly with her cigarette in light through a wet window, and I can not feel what to say.

I say Mayfly I can not feel what to do or say or believe you any more. But there is things I know. I know I am older and you are not. And I give to you all I got to give you, with my hands and my heart both. Every thing that is inside me I have gave you. I have been keeping it together and working steady every day. I have made you the reason I got for what I always do. I have tried to make a home to give to you, for you to be in, and for it to be nice.

I light up myself and I throw the match in the sink with other matches and dishes and a sponge and such things.

I say Mayfly my heart has been down the road and back for you but I am forty-eight years old. It is time I have got to not let things just carry me by any more. I got to use some time that is still mine to try to make everything feel right. I got to try to feel how I need to. In me there is needs which you can not even see any more, because there is too many needs in you that are in the way.

She does not say any thing and I look at her window and I can feel that she knows I know about it, and she shifts her self on my sofa lounger. She brings her legs up underneath her in some shorts.

I say it really does not matter what I seen or what I think I seen. That is not it any more. I know I am older and you are not. But now I am feeling like there is all of me going in to you and nothing of you is coming back any more.

Her hair is up with a barret and pins and her chin is in her hand, it's early, she looks like she is dreaming out at the clean light through the wet window over my sofa lounger.

Everything is green she says. Look how green it all is Mitch. How can you say the things you say you feel like when everything outside is green like it is.

The window over the sink of my kitchenet is cleaned off from the hard rain last night and it is a morning with a sun, it is still early, and there is a mess of green out. The trees are green and some grass out past the speed bumps is green and slicked down. But every thing is not green. The other trailers are not green and my card table out with puddles in lines and beer cans and butts floating in the ash trays is not green, or my truck, or the gravel of the lot, or the big wheel toy that is on its side under a clothes line without clothes on it by the next trailer, where the guy has got him some kids.

Everything is green she is saying. She is whispering it and the whisper is not to me no more I know.

I chuck my smoke and turn hard from the morning with the taste of something true in my mouth. I turn hard toward her in the light on the sofa lounger.

She is looking outside, from where she is sitting, and I look at her, and there is something in me that can not close up, in that looking. Mayfly has a body. And she is my morning. Say her name.

WESTWARD THE COURSE
OF EMPIRE TAKES
ITS WAY

"As we are all solipsists, and all die, the world dies with us. Only very minor literature aims at apocalypse."

—Anthony Burgess

"For whom is the Funhouse fun?"

—*Lost in the Funhouse*

BACKGROUND THAT INTRUDES AND LOOMS: LOVERS AND PROPOSITIONS

THOUGH Drew-Lynn Eberhardt produced much, and Mark Nechtr did not, Mark was loved by us all in the East Chesapeake Tradeschool Writing Program that first year, and D.L. was not. I can explain this. D.L. was severely thin, thin in a way that suggested not delicacy but a kind of stinginess about how much of herself she'd extend to the space around her. Thin the way mean nuns are thin. She walked funny, with the pelvis-led posture of a man at a urinal; she carried her arms either wrapped around her chest or out and down at a scarecrow's jangly right angles; she was slatternly and exuded pheromones apparently attractive only to bacteria; she had a fatal taste for: (1) polyester; (2) pantsuits; (3) *lime green.*

Vs. Mark Nechtr, who was one of those late-adolescent chosen who radiate the kind of careless health so complete it's sickening. Ate poorly, last slept well long before the Colts went West, had no regimen; however strongly built, well-proportioned, thick-necked, dark. Healthy. Strong. (This was back when these qualities revealed things about people, before health-club franchises' careful engineering of anatomy disrupted ancient Aryan order and permitted those who were inherently meant to be pale and weak to appear dark and strong.) Not handsome in a to-die-for way, just this monstrous radiance of ordinary health—a commodity rare, and thus valuable, in Baltimore. We in the writing program—shit, even the kids over at E.C.T. Divinity—could love only what we valued.

Also because D.L. was also weird, and conspicuously so, even in an environment—a graduate writing program—where neurosis was oxygen, colorful tics arranged and worn like jewelry. D.L. carried Tarot cards, and threw them (*in class*), would leave her loft only on her psychic's endorsement, wore daily the prenominate lime synthetics—a lonely onion in a petunia-patch of carefully casual cotton skirts, tie-dyes, those baggy pastel post-Bermudas, clogs, sandals, sneakers, surgeons' clothes.

Also because she also seemed greedy and self-serving, and not near naïve enough to get away with the way she seemed. She idolized Professor Ambrose with a passion, but in a greedy and self-serving way that probably turned Ambrose himself off right from the very first workshop, when she brought a conspicuously battered copy of *Lost in the Funhouse* for him to autograph—at East Chesapeake Trade something One Did Not Do. Was thus, for our interpretive purposes, right from day one, a sycophant, an ass-kisser.

Also because she actually went around *calling* herself a postmodernist. No matter *where* you are, you Don't Do This. By convention it's seen as pompous and dumb. She made a big deal of flouting convention, but there was little to love about her convention-flouting; she honestly, it seemed to us, couldn't see far enough past her infatuation with her own crafted cleverness to separate posture from pose, desire from supplication. She wasn't the sort of free spirit you could love: she did what she wanted, but it was neither valuable nor free.

We could all remember the opening line of the first story she turned in for the very first workshop: "Nouns verbed by, adverbially adjectival." Nuff said? Professor Ambrose summed it up well—though not without tact—when he told the workshop that Ms. Eberhardt's stories tended "not to work for him" because of what he called a certain "Look-Mom-no-hands quality" that ran through her work. You don't want her facial reaction described.

At least she produced, though. She was fiendishly, coldly fertile. True, certain catty coffeehouse arguments were advanced concern-

ing the preferability of constipation to diarrhea, but Mark Nechtr
never joined in. He spoke rarely, and certainly never about the
kids he studied under Ambrose with, or the overall promise of
their work, or their neuroses and tics, or their exchanges of bodily
fluids. He kept his oar out of other people's fluids and minded his
own healthy business. This was interpreted by the community as
the sort of dignified reticence only the valued can afford, and so
he was even more loved. It was actually kind of sickening—D.L.'s
fellow McDonald's alumnus Tom Sternberg, the diplopic ad actor,
had Mark pegged as one of those painfully radiant types whose
apparent blindness to their own radiance only makes the sting of
the light meaner. Sternberg had Mark so pegged by the time they'd
all met as arranged at Maryland International Airport and departed
via red-eye for Chicago's O'Hare, thence by complimentary LordAloft
copter to Collision, Illinois, and the scheduled Reunion of everyone
who has ever been in a McDonald's commercial, arranged by J.D.
Steelritter Advertising and featuring a party to end all parties,
a spectacular collective Reunion commercial, the ribbon-cutting
revelation of the new Funhouse franchise's flagship discotheque,
and the promised appearance of Jack Lord, dramatic Hawaiian
policeman, sculptor, pilot, and—again under the aegis of the
same J.D. Steelritter who'd put Sternberg and D.L. together as
commercial children thirteen years ago to the day whose start
I've interrupted—director of a new and deregulated helicopter-
shuttle franchise, LordAloft, that was going national as of today,
Reunion day.

All that may have seemed like a digression from this background,
and as of now a prolix and confusing one, and I'll say that I'm sorry,
and that I am *acutely* aware of the fact that our time together is
valuable. Honest. So, conscious of the need to get economically to
business, here are some plain, true, unengaging propositions I'll
ask you just to acknowledge. Mark Nechtr is a suburban Baltimore
native, young, and (another thing he didn't ever talk about) a trust-
fund baby, heir to a detergent fortune. He is enrolled in a graduate
writing program at the East Chesapeake Tradeschool, where he

turned down the offer of financial aid, for obvious reasons, but pretty gracious ones. He is a fair competitive target archer, has been shooting competitively ever since he lost his technical virginity to a squat sweatshirted Trinitarian YWCA instructor who prose-lytized him on the virtues of 12-strand strings, fingerless leather gloves, blankly total concentration, dead release, and the advantages of arrows fletched by hand. Mark tends to walk almost tiptoed—something about exaggerated arches—has vaguely oriental eyes, radiates the aforementioned radiance, though he has glove-paled hands and a proclivity for neckless, rather effeminate surgeon shirts—slight imperfections that enhanced the overall perfection of the etc. etc.

How he was civilly married to Drew-Lynn Eberhardt was, quickly: one fine day he witnessed the lime-clad postmodernist write some-thing really petty and vicious on the seminar room's green black-board, right before the first bell rang for Dr. Ambrose's workshop; she saw him see her—shit, he was sitting right there, the only one of the eleven other students in the room that early; but D.L., seeing him see, still didn't erase the thing, wouldn't; she was on her way out of the whole Program by then; tactfully cool receptions from Ambrose always broke the hottest bulbs' thin skins first; she didn't care what the unproductive big-necked object of the seminar's love saw; he could go on ahead and rat on her, tell Ambrose what he'd seen her write, or erase it, since you two are on such great good pedagogical terms. Well and she fled, in her pelvis-led way, in tears, as the bell rang, clutching her own polyester chest with a pathetic vulnerability that stirred something in this boy who, underneath a sunny hide-brown healthy surface, saw himself as pretty vulnerable and fucked up in his own right. But so he didn't move to erase the petty critical limerick, and didn't rat to Ambrose, to any of us, about who'd written it. He was unworried about us thinking he'd written it, so we didn't, and anyway authorial identity was obvious—D.L. was the only student AWOL that day, and the thing had her dry, sour spite all over it (besides being self-conscious and bad). Hell hath no fury like a coolly received postmodernist. And Pro-fessor Ambrose, though he said nothing, didn't even use the eraser at first, was nevertheless visibly hurt: he had the reputation of being a pretty sensitive guy, off the page. Actually he was devastated, was what he wrote J.D. Steelritter, but he never told Mark Nechtr that.

By now Mark and D.L. were being seen together. Why? You can bet that question got asked, the subject of their fluids receiving the attention of many oars.

She because Mark was healthy and loved, and hadn't ratted, had minded his own business, even in the face of what he'd seen and what we all wanted from Ambrose. He hadn't ratted, which D.L. couldn't understand and so genuflected to as mystery, as something deserving of respect, as *virtue* (she loves the word *virtue,* and even manages, as the coptering three of them sneeze in a harmony with the abrupt Midwest dawn, to pronounce the word vaguely as she sneezes: vuh, vuh, vuh*rshoo*—the habit drives Mark quietly up the wall).

Yes and but he, Mark: why? Well, first because, that fine sea-breezy day, Mark had thought he'd maybe seen a little true thing, a tiny central kernel of illumination in that failed limerick D.L. had composed and graphed critically over Professor Ambrose's—and American metafiction's—most famous story, an accidentally-acute splinter that got under Mark's skin and split wider the shivers and cracks inside him, as somebody being taught how but not why to write fiction. He had, quietly, stopped totally trusting his teacher, inside, by then. Mark was down, blocked, confused then about what he was even doing at E.C.T., not producing what he was supposed to be producing. This condition was not helped by the respect—love, really—that came at him from everywhere in the Program, except from D.L.

Well and Mark saw D.L. around—he was a demon for coffee, and D.L. always sat there, in coffeehouses, alone, with a notebook for trapping little inspirations before they could get away. To make it short, they eventually hooked up—more or less because of something she'd written and something he'd not said. Just hooked up, in that gloaming territory between just friends and whatever isn't friendship. They'd rap, do the beach, collect the odd shell, she'd tell him about the day's troubles, she watched him place third in the Atlantic Coast 30-yard Championships, Young Adult Division. One rainy day, when the breeze off the bay didn't smell like anything at all, when she'd had word about something vague and parental and was just awfully down, she propositioned him. They happened to make love. But just once. They were lovers one time. There nevertheless took place, as D.L. liked to put it, a little miracle. The sort of miracle that transubstantiates the physical (blood) into the spiritual (certain claims on Mark as an honorable lover). It's very important to Mark that he be able to see himself as a decent and responsible guy, and so he sucked up the objections of practically all his friends and did right by a one-time unloved lover. Most in the Program thought it was the kind of rare unfashionable gesture that these days only someone of incredible value could afford to make. The little miracle—basically from *one* fuck, *with* protection, *his*—is now close to the third trimester, though the way D.L. carries herself you'd never know it was that far.

Invited to the civil ceremony are twelve guests, among them D.L.'s psychic and Mark's old Trinitarian archery coach. Mark's Dad gives them a Visa card with no limit, in the Dad's name, to help establish credit. Her psychic gives D.L. a quartz crystal way too big and phallic to be taken seriously. The proselytizing coach gives Mark a Dexter Aluminum target arrow with a nock of Port Orford cedar. Top of the line. The BMW of target arrows. Though D.L. makes no secret of her distaste for BMWs, the Dexter Aluminum's the best arrow Mark's ever had, and (sadly?) the main reason why the ceremony was, for him, the high point of a not at all promising marriage, so far.

OK true, that was all both too quick and too slow, for background—both intrusive and sketchy. But please, whether your imagination's engaged or not, please just acknowledge the propositions, is all. Because time is *severely limited,* and *whatever might be important lies ahead.* So, as we say in the nation's flat green gut, Hibbego, without further hemming or ado, in an uncompromisingly terse flash-foward, straight and without grace or delay to

THE DAY OF THE MOMENT WE'VE ALL BEEN WAITING FOR

For lovers, the Funhouse is fun.
For phonies, the Funhouse is love.
But *for whom,* the proles grouse,
Is the Funhouse a house?
Who lives there, when push comes to shove?

was the piece of anti-Ambrose doggerel the poor sensitive birth-
marked guy walked into the seminar room for his MF 3–5 to find
drawn onto the slateboard with the kind of chalk you almost got
to wash off. He was *devastated,* said the long letter Ambrose had
sent Steelritter to threaten about why he was maybe as a client and
entrepreneur pulling out of the whole Funouse franchise idea. Kids
and students are a shitty and shifty bunch, in J.D. Steelritter's
opinion. Like dogs, that you have to worry about getting bit when
you hold out the meat they whine for. Ambrose said he'd been
devastated: there it was, he'd said—when you rendered all the
flourishes and allusions and general crap out of his letter—there it
was, *criticism,* right there, even where you ought to be able to least
expect it. Criticism: it never left him alone. It lowered his quality
of lifestyle. So why go ahead and try to build a Funhouse in every
major market, for people to criticize, he'd realized, he said. Who
needed the grief? Ambrose needed not grief, he'd written, any
more than brave Philoctetes of yore had needed that snakebite.

What snake? J.D.'d cabled back. What yore? Relax, he'd cabled.
Cool off. Unwind. Read some of that Stoic shit you like. Have a
Lite. Dip into some of the roses I sent sub rosa for *you alone,* friend.
Reflect. Think over the totality of everybody's investment in the
thing so far. Of time, money, money, time, spirit. Don't do anything
hasty. Trust me, who's earned your trust. Cold feet are natural, as
the day draws near.

The super-sized ego of an arrogant pussy, is what J.D. had really
thought. Of course you need it. Spare me chumpness about this.

Criticism is response. Which is good. If J.D. lays out a campaign strategy nobody criticizes, then J.D. right away knows the idea's a dink, a bad marriage of jingle and image, one that won't produce, just lays there, no copulation of engaging gears, no spin inside the market's spin. You need it. Eat it up. It's attention. It engages imaginations. It sells. It works off desire, and sells. It sold books, it'll sell mirrored discotheque franchises. The criticism'll be what fills the seats with fannies. J.D.'d bet his life.

Standing there, past weary, his whole fine face, which tended to rush toward its own center anyhow, centered around a cigar he waits to crunch and spit the tip of, a fried-flower taste hanging like fog on his palate, standing at a window of the bunting-bedecked (WELCOME McDONALD'S ALUMNI WELCOME JACK LORD WELCOME PLEASE SEE NEAREST STEELRITTER ALUMNI ASSISTANCE REPRESENTATIVE FOR INSTRUCTIONS AND DIRECTIONS WELCOME!) and redecorated (in Mrs. Steelritter's favorite muted grays and dusty plum) Central Illinois Airport, waiting for sunrise and the LordAloft 5:10 A.M. shuttle from O'Hare to descend with the very last couple of alumni kids, J.D.'d bet his life. Admen do this. Bet their life on criticism, attention, desire, fear, love, marriage of concession and market. Retention of image. Loyalty to brand. Empathy with client. Sales. On life. *Life!*

Life goes on. You're empty, sad, probably the least appreciated creative virtuoso in the industry; well and but life just goes on, emptily, sadly, with always direction but never center. The hubless wheel spins ever faster, no? *Yes.* Admen approach challenges thus: concede what's hopelessly true, what you can't make folks ever want to not be so; concede; then take your creative arm and hammer a big soaked wedge, hard as can be, into whatever's open to interpretation. Interpret, argue, sing, whisper, work the wedge down into the pulp, where the real red juices be, where folks feel alone, fear their genitals, embrace their own shadows, *want* so badly it's a great subsonic groan, a lambent static only the trained adman's sticky ear can trap, retain, digest. Interpretation, he's fond of telling DeHaven, is persuasion's driveway. Persuasion is desire. Desire is the monstrous pulse, the trillion-hearted river that is the care and

feeding of J.D. and Mrs. J.D. Steelritter and their clown of a son
DeHaven. Meat on a table already groaning under meat, festooned
with homegrown food. This is J.D.'s way since the Lucky Strike
campaign, the first, in '45. Then McDonald's, through Ray, in '53.
Coca-Cola. Arm & Hammer. Kellogg's. The Funhouse. LordAloft
Shuttles. The American daydream, what made Us great: make a
concession, take a stand.

So then why waste time even thinking cold artistic feet and
Funhouses? There's a Reunion coming, and it will cap things, put
them right, for J.D.'s forever. He can hardly wait. Behind him, in
the terminal, DeHaven, his spawn, is greeting the second-to-last
bunch of alums, just off a Dallas Delta, he's checking off names of
every creed, passing out Reunion nametags: two little gold-filled
arches, to pin on, a peel-off sticker printed HI! MY NAME IS and
then with room for a name and year of appearance. DeHaven sleep-
deprived too, but stoned, too—on reefers, doobers, whatever they
called it now—eyes red as his yarn wig and violently rouged mouth
slack and dry and a smell off his clown suit like oily ropes way
below deck. Why the waste of time, the feeling like worry stands
just to J.D.'s left? Because *For Whom,* the little bastard has kept
repeating, intoning, for two solid days and nights, while he and a
J.D. who believes in the personal touch have driven back and forth,
outlasting their cars, shuttling folks to the revel site, finally reduced
to DeHaven's own souped-up hoodlummy car, the clown who loves
to drive, drives with just one wrist hooked over the wheel in that
way J.D. hates, that look-how-little-I-care way, back and forth,
father and son, personally touching, meeting, greeting, orienting,
shuttling impressed and eager alumni to Collision, Ill., a decent
little hike, on roads rural and dangerous, plus ugly; and the shitspeck, for reasons J.D. cares about even less than he understands,
he kept repeating it, *For Whom*, over and over, West and then back
East, useless to scream at the kid to shut up, today J.D. needs a sullen Ronald like a kidney stone. *For Whom,* intoned, toneless, zom-
bily stoned; and the little *For Whom* jingle—J.D. Steelritter has an
ear nonpareil for jingles—has stuck and sunk through that sleep-

deprived ear and is there, rattling, unfindable-penny-in-drier-like, in the head of J.D. Steelritter, a head that is fine, perfectly round, freckled of brow, scimitarred of nose, generous and wet of lower lip, quick to center on anything oral. DeHaven, who knows zero from any plans or big pictures, has worked the jingled line in there, an angry bee in J.D.'s bonnet; it's now detached from his harlequin son and plays without cease in a held, high-C idiot note, the note of a test pattern, a test of Emergency Broadcast Systems, the whine of no real sleep for maybe five days, a whiny question, from an ego in tweeds, a question the smug old avant-gardist had clearly asked just so he could right away answer it, the most irritating-type question, self-conscious, rhetorical, a waste of resources and time . . . and J.D. tells most folks don't waste his time, just start the fucking show.

OK but in that malicious little prodigal spiteful ungrateful jab at his delicate client, who he'd finally soothed and signed but couldn't induce to appear, today—was there not maybe a something there? Something true and sad and hubless, that goes on? Does a Funhouse need to be more than Fun? More than New and *Improved* Fun? Are actual house-considerations at work in this campaign, unseen? For whom is the Funhouse an *enclosure,* maybe? Does he, J.D., live in anything like a Funhouse? J.D. lives at the J.D. Steelritter Advertising Complex in Collision, Ill.; J.D. lives on and manages the few-acre rose farm his own itinerant father had stuck in the lapel of a corn-green state and then plowed himself into; J.D. lives deep inside J.D., marrying images and jingles, poking his sword of a nose out at isolated and alone moments to sniff the winds of fashion, fear, desire—the Trade Winds that blow overhead, moving between Coasts. J.D. has built the second-largest advertising agency in American history from the fringe that is the country's center, from a piss-poor little accidental town, smashed and stuck deep, corn-surrounded, in a flat blanket of soil so verdant and black it is one of only two things he truly fears. J.D. is of Central Illinois. Central Illinois is, by no imaginer's stretch, a Funhouse.

But neither is it enclosed. Enclosed? It's the most *dis*closed, open place you could ever fear to see.

He remembers the historical graphics Ambrose's agents had produced when they first, '76, ran the franchise idea up J.D.'s pole. Ocean City, off Baltimore, with laureates and tides and fish-stink— one of the last great true undeodorable stinks—the Amusement Park little Ambrose had mooned around in Depression-time and then bronzed in that infuckingsufferable story J.D.'s tried hard to read, to understand the client—that Ocean City Park was enclosed, though. The park was enclosed, and not by mirrors or ticket windows or dj booths. So then well.

But where was his head? The Park had burnt down, he'd traveled to personally research and found it down. Everything, turns out, fried crisp and hollow before the big-deal story even changed hands, back in the '60s, just when J.D. was building Ray Kroc into myth. How must it feel for Ambrose now, looking at it, burnt? Sad. J.D.'s never seen a no-shit fire. J.D.'s never been in a house that is not still a house, as far as he knows. Even his father's farmhouse and greenhouse, his mother's incorporating car, still stand and sit, intact. So is there a whispered worrisome something behind that rattling whined *For Whom?* Say you're standing by the gutted skeleton of a former Funhouse, with the door's grinning face a ruin, the plastic Fat Lady melted and then frozen lopsided, a blob, maybe supine, her drippy frozen laughing eyes now upward at a dead-white crabmeat sky, the House itself gutted, open, a bunch of black beams crossed and curved and supporting nothing, no roof, say there you are, and say maybe you say, *I was in that, once,* pointing; were you? If the that's down, burnt open, disclosed, Fat May's legs of plastic hilarity twisted and apart, yes the whole enclosure disclosed, kind of naked? No wonder the poor bastard tried to write the roof back on, put the whole thing erect. But J.D. almost smiles around the wet shaft of a cigar he cannot taste: the Tidewater boy will have his House back, in the West, a thousandfold. All he wants. Every wish come true. Big time.

J.D. stands brooding at the terminal glass. Jesus, Ocean City, in the past: gull sounds, rotty kelp waving like a big head's just underwater, a drowned giant with sluggish hair; and the homes: wharf-colored, pale gray and off-white. Rich dead salt smell. Slow.

Vs. Illinois, in the present, the here and now, looking: black sky; then licorice sky; maybe a crow's caw: *dawn.* Very little time wasted about dawn in Illinois. It's because it's always been so open. J.D. looks out the terminal window over the tarmac at the LordAloft landing pad, the underwater blue of landing lights in a circle under a by-now licorice sky pricked with fading stars, trillions of them, the corn tallishly black and still, even with wind, and wet with precipitate dew. Facing Eastward like this it's almost hard to even look: flat right to the earth's curve, East: never a hill, no western skyline of Collision's silos and arches and neon; the East from here is one broad sweep—there's nothing to hold your eye, you have to pan back and forth, like a big No, your eyes so relaxed and without object they almost roll. It can be scary.

But this moment, now: he holds, stabs his cigar into an ashtray's fine sand, no *For Whom*'s for now, this one moment. This one instant, no more, each eastern rise: there's a certain pre-dawn fire about everything. The distant commuter planes and refueling trucks, the stars fluttering to stay seen, the shuddering corn, the very *oxygen* of Illinois seems, in this one moment, to shiver as on the point of combustion. Just one daily moment, like that, the flat East drenched in deregulated gas and somehow . . . waiting.

And the fragile pre-ignition shimmer is gone. With nothing vertical between you and the horizon, the sun's just suddenly up. No rosy fingers, just an abrupt red palm; the Reunion day's ignition is spasmically brief: the sun seems to get all of a sudden just *sneezed* up into the faded sky, the eastern horizon shuddering at what it's expelled. A helicopter appears, one of Jack Lord's slope-head pilots, riding out of the instant sunrise.

J.D. should turn his broad back. To business. The kids are on that thing; they'd promised. The LordAloft 5:10 from O'Hare settles like a great gentle hand, a blur of bubble and blades, and its tornadic wind throws chaff and odd crap and shakes the corn— green, now, dusky, food for animals—and dew glitters, the corn one ocean, check that J.D. one cornfield, one hand passed over, producing one wave. Not sluggish and dead, but gentle and—

—but this landing and de-ignition gets to him, too, this change in the rate of the blades' spin. J.D. stares, rapt. You stare into a spinning thing, stare hard: you can see something inside the spin sputter, catch, and seem to spin backwards inside the spin, against the spin. Sometimes. Sometimes maybe four different spins, each opposite its own outside. Watching what spins: it's a hobby, but J.D. knows it has to do with desire, so the time spent's not shot. Even though he loves it. Anything with a circular spin and clearly marked axes, speeding or slowing: spoked wheels, helicopter blades (the real reason he's put so much time into LordAloft, admiration for Jack Lord and recognition of a void in the market aside), windmills, fans' spiraled petals. Any wheel without hub or constance. The best was a liveried carriage's right front wheel, once: a blur of delicately stretched spokes, then a perfect backwards spin, inside the spin, as trot became canter and the thing clopped away on a London street, spinning. On leave from the War. The big one. It was J.D.'s first spin.

By the way, not too much of this is important, either. But it's true, and J.D. is here at the broad smeared C.I. Airport window, not helping DeHaven greet the next-to-last, so he can scan for the final alumni children: Eberhardt '70, Sternberg '70. They're supposed to be among these folks now de-coptering, bent low under blades, hands to headwear against a swirl of chaff and dawn-fog. But no kids. Everyone coming off the tarmac and into the lei-strewn gate's entrance looks far too adult, purposeful, neither shifty nor shitty.

Shitty? Adult? J.D. Steelritter's own DeHaven Steelritter is a professional trademark. A clown. *The* clown. Been the campaign's Ronald a year now, ever since that last Ronald's indiscretion with that Malay girl (Oh Lord though skin like cream-shot coffee, and *eyes?*) in the Enchanted French-Fry Forest forced J.D. to see to it that that particular clown would never work in the industry again. Ever. The smears of lurid lipstick on that child's *au-lait* belly! The red nose clapped, with the obscenity of adult force, over her own! The goose-bruises—though thank *God* no poke-bruises, so no concessions needed, whole thing explainable to Malay stage mother as Stage Fright as she led the little thing away, the girl's legs shaky like a new foal's. Sweet Jesus never again one of those grizzled circus clowns, any man you can get twelve of in a Honda Civic you don't trust them, no? *No.*

But so DeHaven Steelritter? adult? putative son? possible heir? usurper? Who could love this DeHaven K. Steelritter—age: needs a shave; height; slouches, with intent; weight: who could know under either leather or this big-hipped dot-pocked outfit and swim-fin shoes; education: as school is not a hundred percent easy and pleasurable it's "bogus"; aspiration: atonal composer (alleged), to accept prime wages for doing the bare minimal and spending the rest of his time fucking off (apparent)? He represents the Product. Is Ronald McDonald. Professionally. This son, this sty on the cosmic eyelid, this SHRDLU in the cosmic ad copy, *represents* the world's community restaurant.

And but gratitude? This job is a plum, clown-wise—veteran clowns would have given left nuts for even a giggled audition. But the fix was in, after the Stage Fright snafu. J.D. Steelritter controls, and since the one-Collision-Illinois-Ray-Kroc-burger-stand beginning has controlled, the image and perception of McDonald's franchise empire.

No alumni on this LordAloft. They missed it. Children. The fly in every fucking machine's perfect lubricant. DeHaven is looking over at J.D. and shrugging, checking his fat clipboard, shrugging with that what-are-you-gonna-do apathy he directs at every imped-iment. J.D. ponders. What is his son? Those Jews have a word for it, no? Schlemiel is the clumsy waiter who spills the scalding soup? Schlamazl is the totally innocent hapless guy who gets spilled on? Then J.D. Steelritter's son is the customer who *ordered* that soup (on credit), and now *wants his goddamn soup,* and wants *quiet* from that screaming scalded guy over there so he can eat his soup with all the peaceful quiet enjoyment he hasn't earned. A child who exited a womb *inconvenienced.*

To avoid misunderstanding or prejudice, J.D. is sad, but not usually this bitter. Most of all this is sleep-deprivation, anxiety, an almost

Christmas-Eve-like anticipation, plus extended proximity to a son, which let's face it taxes even the most richly patient parent. DeHaven's not a bad kid, J.D. knows. He's good with the commercial children. Brings out a gentleness that would have surprised a lesser adman. The kid'll sure never give anybody Stage Fright.

But he's an apprentice clown who gets to be the third Ronald McDonald in American franchise history, and yet it's clear he doesn't appreciate it, he doesn't like the job—and, worse, doesn't like the job like a sleeping person dislikes things, with a torpid whimper and an infant's total frown—the latter he's doing now, and the frown disturbs J.D., rattles him, his son's skin's frown under a manic painted grin . . . it looks grotesque, a kind of crude circle of lip and lipstick, so your impression, that you should *never* get from a mouth that represents a restaurant, is just of a hole, a blank dime, an empty entrance you'd only want to exit.

Sternberg '70 and Eberhardt '70 are late. They missed the LordAloft 5:10. There's another at 7:10. J.D.'s idea to have them run regular as trains. So wait and hope for the next LordAloft? Fuck around with O'Hare's Kafkan bureaucracy and have them looked for and/or maybe paged? But everyone else is here, on the way into Collision and Funhouse 1 and McDonald's 1 to await the high-noon appearance of LordAloft 1, and the revels until then have been carefully structured. And J.D.'s got this obsession that everything like this he structures has got to be tidy, complete, fulfilled, enclosed. Not a single no-show except for two late kids who promised 5:10, in the contract. What's to do?

J.D. jumps a bit as DeHaven's voice appears next to his sensitive ear.

"Done," the big clown says, popping off the costume's red plastic battery-lit nose with a kind of fuck-you-in-Italian gesture he likes. "Couple no-shows, though, Pop."

J.D. snaps at him to put his nose on, in public, for Christ's sake, still looking squinted at what the East's expelled. That little worrisome sleep-deprived *For Whom* rattles, still, at that high-static idiot pitch.

WHY THE KIDS ARE LATE

After the flight from M.I. Airport, after luggage roulette—try packing a seventy-piece bow plus quiver—Tom Sternberg edged furtively into an O'Hare men's room and stayed in there for a really long time. Mark Nechtr got distracted watching a guy with long soft hair and beard, and a clipboard, who was giving away money in the commuter terminal. The man was well-dressed, respectable. The treasury notes were crisp. Mark couldn't determine what the scam was. He ruled out Cult because the guy had an utterly ordinary expression: no Krishna glaze or Bagwanite's pirate squint; no Moonie's mannequin cheer. Yet people kept avoiding him. He kept asking them what they were afraid of. Beefy types with holsters and field radios eventually led him off. What was the scam? The guy was maybe thirty, tops. Mark, a born watcher, watched, from a distance.

MORE QUICKLY WHY THEY'RE LATE

The LordAloft pilot, a Polynesian in a just bitching three-piece and mirrored glasses, wouldn't allow Mark's disassembled bow or quiver on the helicopter. The twelve shuttle passengers all sit together in a big plastic bubble: all luggage on LordAloft is accessible in-flight. Target arrows are deadly weapons, after all. There are FAA regulations that even the deregulated might not make, but must obey, *koniki?* A serious archer doesn't just leave his equipment, so what's to do. The helicopter ascends without them, sprays them with dark tarmac crud. Cases and carry-ons and almost-full quiver are spread out on the landing pad. Drew-Lynn is half-asleep, tranquilized, treating Mark's arm like a banister. Sternberg has his thumb tentatively against his forehead, where there's a bit of a poison-sumac cyst that's developed. Their reserved seats ascend; they recede. Sternberg's a bit honked off at Mark for being the sort you don't leave without. It's clear what's to do. They go back inside O'Hare's commuter terminal and transfer to the LordAloft 7:10. They kill time. D.L. sleeps in a weird chair whose attached TV wants quarters. Sternberg rehaunts the men's room after loud requests for a comb. Mark stows his bow's case and strings, quiver and wooden arrows, fingerless archer's gloves, tincture of benzoin (for calluses) and fletcher in a tall rental locker. The key he keeps for his four quarters is unloseably huge. He was supposed to try to maybe write a bit, but mostly shoot, at whatever YWCA's to be found downstate, while D.L. and her pen pal Sternberg, who's pegged as a furtive but so far generally OK sort, are reuniting, reveling, and appearing in a panoramic commercial, and awaiting Jack Lord.

HOW THE COMPLIMENTARY FLIGHT TO CHICAGO WAS

Not complimentary for Mark, who's just along.

And in general not great at all. Drew-Lynn is neurosis in motion, and simply cannot abide take-off if certain cards show up on the pre-flight Tarot she spreads on the fold-down tray. Death is actually OK: that card just means change. But the Tower, the Nine of Swords, any really charismatic non-Death arcana—these do not reassure, from the tray. D.L. claims that every possible option this throw betrays is cataclysmic, even with the crystal to focus negative ions and positive karma, and so things get off to a shaky start, as they leave M.I.A. behind.

AURAL ILLUSTRATION OF THE FLIGHT'S SHAKINESS FROM THE CONTEMPORARY ACTOR AND CLAUSTROPHOBE POINT OF VIEW OF TOM STERNBERG, TRAGIC

"I suppose I should apologize, Mark."

"It's OK, Sweets."

"I'm bad at will, I've decided. Postmodernism doesn't stress the efficacy of will, as you know. Although you can't deny I tried."

"D.L., screaming 'This thing's going down! We're all toast!' be-

fore we've even started moving doesn't seem like trying all that
hard, Sweets. . . ."

"See, you're mad."

"But it's OK. How you doing over there, Tom?"

"He's trying to sleep."

"I can't sleep, I hate these fucking things," Tom says. The inside
of his head has been a disappointing view. "They're too big outside,
too small inside. Hard to even breathe." He lights a 100 and holds
the long thing way away from D.L., for whom smoke is antimatter.

"Like to take something?" Mark asks him.

"Something?"

"For tranquility, I mean. D.L's not taking anything, because of
the baby, but she's got everything from chloral hydrate to Dalmane
fifteens," Mark says.

"We'll see. I don't think I want to be stumbling around O'Hare,
when we land. It's probably a fuck of a hike to the LordAloft gates.
I hate airports maybe even worse than planes. They're all the same."
He closes both eyes.

D.L. to Mark: "I took something, darling. I'll say I'm sorry. I
promised, then I went and took something. That Nine of Swords . . ."

"I know you took something."

"How do you know? You didn't either know. I took them in
the lavatory."

"You took thirty milligrams of chloral hydrate and a Dalmane
fifteen. It's in the way your head is wobbling."

What's *contemporarily* tragic about Sternberg is that he has a fatal
physical flaw. One of his eyes is turned completely around in his
head. From the front it looks like a boiled egg. It won't come back
around straight. It's like an injury. It's incredibly bad for his ambitions as a commercial actor. He doesn't talk about what the backward eye sees. He's offended that D.L. in person asked him right
off the bat.

He has other flaws, too.

"I'm bad at will, Mark, I've admitted."

"And then you drank a screwdriver. Right now the little miracle is probably rolling around in there totally stoned. It probably has no idea where it is or what's going on."

"You *are* mad."

"I'm not mad."

"But if you're mad just *say* so. Just *express* it. Don't be all anal all the time. Even *Ambrose* would express it."

"Why don't you just get some sleep, since you and the baby took something."

"There's a word for people like you, Mark. 'Minimal.' You never really *react* to things. Even art. You hardly ever give me feedback, even."

"I feed back, Drew. I gave you feedback just yesterday. I said I liked the ambiguousness of that 'FIRM DOCTORS TELEPHONE POLES' title. Why you're pissed is that I only said I thought a twenty-page poem that's *all* punctuation wouldn't be much fun for anybody to actually read. That's feedback. It's just not the reaction you want to hear."

"You persistently confuse reaction with this antiquated insistence that . . ."

Sternberg whimpers, pulls from his back slacks pocket a seat-warm Reunion brochure and unfolds the square it's in. The brochure is screamingly colored, high-tech, glossy except where it's faded from being folded into a square. It details the attractions and itinerary of the Reunion of everybody who's ever represented McDonald's.

HOW THEY ALL KNOW EACH OTHER

Sternberg out of Boston and D.L. out of Hunt Valley were both in the same McDonald's commercial on the McDonald's-site-turned-set in Collision, Ill., in 1970. They were small children in 1970. They've corresponded since around puberty. So Mark and Sternberg are connected through D.L.

WHERE THEY LIVE NOW

Tom Sternberg lives with his parents in Boston's Back Bay while he attends cattle calls and pesters agents and tries to break into the adult commercial industry. Mark and D.L live in an airy and utterly Yupster Baltimore condo complex, in a spacious suite D.L. has fashioned into as close to a squalid garret as circumstances permit (given that their housekeeper's a Philistine).

WHY D.L. AND TOM HAVE NEVER ONCE GONE HUNGRY AT MEALTIME

Not well known is the fact that anyone who has ever appeared in a McDonald's commercial receives a never-expiring coupon entitling them to unlimited free hamburgers at any McDonald's franchise, anywhere, anytime. It is a fringe benefit bestowed on commercial alumni by J.D. Steelritter Advertising in a stroke of sheer marketing genius. It allows McDonald's to proclaim, beneath each set of golden arches, exactly how many billions and billions and *billions* of hamburgers have been "served" so far. Of course the franchise is under no FCC or FTC obligation to mention that a decent percentage of these served burgers are in fact not paid for. The higher numbers breed higher numbers. Consumers are impressed, naturally, by the inflated number of items consumed, and consume even more. Actors are digestively secure, and so McDonald's gigs are regarded in the industry as plums. And the enormous (partly free) volume of service actually conduces to what microeconomists call economies of scale: the flesh is shipped from Argentina by the megaton and cooked, turned, and served according to timers. The food is the same from Coast to Coast. Dependable. Soothing. It's that rarest of transactions: everybody wins. We regard the How-Many-Served sign as just what our interpretation makes it: the sign of the world's community restaurant. It was J.D. Steelritter's second-greatest stroke of marketing genius. After the Reunion and Reunion commercial it will be his third-greatest.

For Tom Sternberg, airports are not fun. They blur and do not
hold his eye. Central Illinois Airport is no exception. For the contemporarily tragic, all airports are the same: orange-faced blondes,
slit-skirted stewardesses with luggage they can pull, college boys
with Nazi cheekbones, the inevitable green vest of the airport-
lounge bartender. Black-haired women in yellow. P.A. announcers
just one mouth-marble short of incomprehensible. Blankly harried
junior-executive types, the kind who are made by their employers
to travel, hauling complicated cases and what look like over-the-
shoulder body bags for their identical shiny-seated uniforms. College girls, with cheekbones, in gym shorts with Greek letters on
the ass. Crowds, people hugging. Ashtrays beneath No Smoking
signs. A rabbi runs for a missed connection. A pale woman totes
a limp infant. A lone and disoriented Oriental's black bangs ride
his forehead, fencelike. Latino men in bell-bottoms walk in con-
spiratorial two's, one holding a metal suitcase.

"Can't say as I like the look of that suitcase," he tells Mark, who
is pacing tiptoed in the C.I. Airport commuter terminal, waiting
for D.L. to take aspirin and wash her post-tranquil face in the
women's room. She's had sleep, though, at least. Said it just made
her more tired.

They're late, and so no Ronald or coincident Personnel to meet
them as foretold in brochure. Sternberg is now officially sleep-
deprived. For him this is not fun, either. It affects his vision. The
morning colors have the over-bright primacy of movies filmed pre-
Panavision. Fluttery hallucinations dance in his outward eye's pe-
riphery. An armless statue on a skateboard. A cyprus swamp, milky
water swirling in pockets, drooling over exposed roots. A rainbow
snapping like a whip. Except it turns out they're not even real
hallucinations; they're posters: "Visit This Art Gallery"; "Explore
Louisiana"; "Buy a Lawnchair at This Store and Get Ready to
Check Out a Genuine Midwestern Thunderstorm." And so on. Not
real. The closure of Sternberg's reversed eye tickles—eye-

lashes against raw nerves. A high pitch sounds in his skull—a sleep-dep test pattern, something persistent and shrill in a very small box.

"Is that all corn?" Mark asks, pointing past the terminal window.

"Sure as fuck green, isn't it."

"It's all there is. It's all you can see. I've never seen so much of anything."

"This is farm country, man. Serious farmers. D.L. and I were here as kids, for the commercial. Then it was white. Mom brought me back for an audition the next summer, though. Still has nightmares about all the corn. She wakes up, sometimes."

Mark Nechtr stares, slackly intense, at whatever he looks at. He doesn't even seem sleep-deprived to Sternberg. Radiantly perfect fucker. Creepy stare, though. Has the look of somebody in the front row of a really absorbing show all the time.

Eyes the broad-shouldered faceless character that symbolizes Men's Room, does Sternberg, and struggles with himself. He's needed a bowel movement for hours, and since the LordAloft 7:10 lifted things have gotten critical. He tried, back at O'Hare. But he was unable to, because he was afraid to, afraid that Mark, who has the look of someone who never just *has* to, might enter the rest room and see Sternberg's shoes under a stall door and know that he, Sternberg, was having a bowel movement in that stall, infer that Sternberg had bowels, and thus organs, and thus a body. Like many *Americans of his generation in this awkwardest of post-Imperial decades,* an age suspended between exhaustion and replenishment, between input too ordinary to process and input too intense to bear, Sternberg is deeply ambivalent about being embodied; an informing fear that, were he really just an organism, he'd be nothing more than an ism of his organs.

Thomas Sternberg is thus, like the Historical Idealists of yore—to whom, if the locutionally muscular and forever *terrible enfant* Dr. C—— Ambrose were fabricating this, he could (and so would) make frequent and explicit and intellectually-fruitful-no-matter-how-irritating reference—Sternberg is thus preternaturally fascinated with the misdirecting pose of bloodless abstraction. Ideas. He's an

idea man. It has nothing to do with how intelligent he is, or isn't.
Ideas, good and bad, but always bloodless, just kind of inform his
whole character and outlook.

He and Mark are both looking around the commuter terminal.
Things are clearing out. Emptying. It's a bit creepy. The terminal
has that too-suddenly-hushed feeling of the moment after loud
music stops. Curt-looking men in custodial white are tearing down
the WELCOME WELCOME bunting. Posters launch themselves at the
tourist trade from every wall. One glassed-in print advertises a
family bowling center, another a forty-eight-hour continuous showing of "Hawaii Five-O" episodes in the airport's lounges, in honor
of Jack Lord and J.D. Steelritter and the LordAloft shuttle service's
national kick-off.

One huge poster just dominates the wall opposite Sternberg: an
enormous J.D. Steelritter is shown next to an enormous Ronald
McDonald, one who resembles J.D., under the greasepaint, in the
strange way that, say, rugby resembles football—the enormous
Ronald's holding an only slightly less enormous promo-poster of
the prototype Funhouse discotheque, of which Sternberg's eye can
make out only what looks pretty much like an ordinary house, one
you could expect to see lots of in any bedroom community anywhere, except for the enormous cadaverous grin that represents
the Funhouse's door. The expression on J.D.'s face is ingenious,
already makes you feel deprived not being there with them.

"We're late," D.L. says, returning and immediately clinging to
Mark in a way you can't tell if he minds. "They've left, I'm afraid.
Those janitors just shrugged when I asked them where anybody
is."

Sternberg touches his forehead lightly. "We were supposed to
get greeted with nametags, with real gold arches, the brochure said."

"Look at the *fields*," D.L. says, gesturing at outside, rotating her
small head South to North.

We could rent a car, I guess," Mark muses.

"Ever rented a car?" Sternberg asks. "Unbelievable hassle. Like
applying for citizenship to someplace. Forms to fill out. Identity to

prove. You have to have a fucking *credit* card. Incredible lines. Picture Moscow on fresh-meat day."

"You got a better idea?"

"I almost thought I saw a kid with a nametag from a McMuffin spot going into the men's room just now," Sternberg says, wanting very much to smoke a 100, eyeing the filters and lone wet-tipped cigar butt in the window's ashtray's sand, but not lighting up, because smoking really makes him have to shit, if he has to shit.

"You want to go in and have a look?"

NO. "We could just cruise around and look for somebody," Sternberg says nonchalantly. "There's no way this place can be as empty as it looks."

It looks pretty empty, though. "Maybe I'll look," Mark ventures.

D.L. loves to put her hands on windows. "Can you even remember which way Collision is, from here?" she yawns. She can't see anything but land, the LordAloft's return to Chicago a blurred and receding dot exiting the window's left border. "If Collision was out there, close by, wouldn't we see it? There's certainly nothing in the way."

"Collision's West of here. That's East, out that window."

"So you don't see anybody to ask," Mark repeats quietly.

"Why are there like *no* windows facing West in here?"

Mark sighs, cracks pale knuckles, rubs his face. "I do not know. We could try Hertz or something. We've got a credit card. Or we could just walk around and find somebody. Or we could eat. You hungry at all, Tom?"

No *way* Sternberg is going to eat anything right now. He rarely eats around people anyway. And obversely.

Speaking of speaking about shit: Dr. Ambrose, whom we all admire with a fierceness reserved for the charismatic, could at this point profitably engage in some wordplay around and about the similarities, phonological and then etymological, between the words *scatology* and *eschatology*. Smooth allusions to Homeric horses pooping death-dealing Ithacans, Luther's excremental vision, Swift's incontinent Yahoos. Neither D.L. nor Sternberg, nor J.D. and De-

Haven—who're pulling up outside in the pay lot, arguing about something to do with DeHaven's car's ignition—have the equipment to react to opportunity in this particular manner. Mark now feels as though he distrusts wordplay.

So basically they're just standing around, as people will, their luggage a vivid jumble at their feet, kind of bogged down, tired, with that so-near-and-yet type of tension, a sense of somewhere definite they must be at by a definite time, but no clear consensus on how to get there. Since they're late. As Dr. Ambrose might venture to observe, they're figuratively *unsure about where to go from here.*

HOW THE CENTRAL ILLINOIS TOWN OF COLLISION CAME TO BE INCORPORATED

Fact: all Illinois communities, from well-built Chicago down to Little Egypt, have their origin and reason in the production of nourishment. The soil of Illinois is second only to the Nile delta in terms of decayed-matter percentage, fertility. Illinois has also always been known for its uncountable number of tiny, shittily maintained, shoulderless rural highways, against and alongside which corn grows quickly and thickly and tall. Tall, dense, the gorged corn obscures drivers' ability to see, at intersections of the little roads, whether anything's coming. And the funding necessary for CAUTION signs just never has quite come through.

And so in the early Great Depression era, during which Central Illinois' soil got not one bit dusty, the corn no less verdant, there was an unmarked intersected collision between a wealthy Chicago woman on her way South in a big touring car and a farmer on a small tractor who was crossing the road East to West to get to his other field. The car won the day. The farmer was thrown ass over teakettle into his field, where, hidden by corn, he expired. Loudly. The woman couldn't get to him because her car had knocked him so far into the green, and the humus-clotted soil made the woman's high-heeled shoes just impossible. The woman, who had a cut on her forehead and had killed somebody by knocking him way farther than any person was meant to fly, was traumatized beyond belief or reason. But she had will; and she vowed, right then and there, according to J.D., never to travel again. Ever.

Her vow, plus strength of character, yielded certain implications. Her slightly dented touring car stayed right where it had stalled, and the woman lived in it. Pretty big car. Farmer Kroc's family, across the field, was rather honked off, at first, about the collision and death and disappearance (utter) of their breadwinner's body; but the woman, out of guilt, paid them more than the farmer himself would have brought in in a lifetime; and not only was there no litigation, but the woman became almost an extended Kroc-family member, from her home in the motionless car. Various farm kids, at first out of minimal bare human charity, brought her food and basic essentials, appearing from the walls of corn as out of nowhere with the things she needed to live.

And but in return, plus out of gratitude and guilt, she reimbursed them, for these essentials. In fact she paid anybody who brought her anything she wanted. Inevitably, given the way the world wags, a kind of market was quickly established: here was this urban person in this big car at an intersection equidistantly central to rurally Depressed Champaign, Rantoul, and Urbana, who wanted things, and would exchange money for the things. The area was substantially transfigured. Misery, guilt and charity became prosperity, redemption, market. Itinerant Depressed poor, but with things, and entrepreneurial drive, flocked to the intersection where her tractor-smacked car sat inert, she inside. The redeemed poor built lean-to's, which became perma-tents, which became shanties, thence a kind of *nouveaux-bourgeois* Rooseveltville, clustered around the site of the collision.

A handsome scimitar-nosed itinerant peddler, bicycling through from back East, where things were just not in good shape at all, bearing East-Coast flora he'd purloined from the lavish funeral of a recently suicided banker, was the one who got in on the ground floor, so to speak. He saw the woman, in the car, and in that kind of ingenious marketing epiphany from which American legend grows, insisted on selling the woman his very top-of-the-line tea-rose bulb. *At cost.* The bulb was planted in the world's second-richest soil and in no time at all begat a bush. The bush begat countless other bushes, through fertilization, and an irruption of Valentine red began to impose its beauty on the green utterness of the farmerless field's own beauty.

In a parallel development, the destitute itinerant peddler and the wealthy inert woman fell in love with each other, in the big car, eventually begat a child, and then moved out of the car (a car being no place for a child) into a sprawling farmhouse the peddler designed and the woman underwrote, a house from which they never budged again, sustained by those in the surrounding shanties whose origin and reason was sustaining the guilty wealthy woman. The irruption of rose bushes became an actual tea-rose farm, a central dot of red on the state's black-and-green, camouflaged face, and Jack and Mrs. Jack Steelritter raised their well-fed children on the sheltered intersection Jack had discovered between beauty, desire, and discount.

Across the cornfield-turned-rose-farm, the Ray Kroc, Sr., farm family, minus a patriarch, but plus a settlement way beyond legal, and with a son who, once out from under his hard-working father's shadow, discovered he had vision, began to engineer a rotation, shifting the emphasis of their labor and capital in the direction of cattle, potatoes, and sugar. And it became good.

For whom is the Funhouse a house? Maybe for liars, creative types, campaigners, tree surgeons having at the great Saxonic tree. For Tom Sternberg, the Funhouse is less a place of fear and confusion than (grimace) an *idea,* an ever-distant telos his arrival at which will represent the revelated transformation of a present we stomach by looking beyond. A present comprised by fear *of* confusion.

OK true, Funhouse 1, like all the foreseen and planned national chain of Funhouse franchises, is, in reality, just a discotheque. A

watering hole and meat market and gathering place where the spotlights tell us where and how to swing to the beat. One big enclosed
anarchic revel—a Party: where we, via Party rule, gather and pretend with grim Puritan fortitude that we're having just way more
fun than anybody could really be having.

OK now but the Funhouse *also* represents, to Sternberg—as
hero, as Protagoras—the Funhouse represents the *future*. As of
right now, the prediction here is that Sternberg will arrive, through
the inexorable internal logic of his choice and circumstance, at
Collision's Funhouse, as a tagged and registered part of the foretold
and long-awaited Reunion of Everyone Who's Ever Represented
the Product in a McDonald's Commercial; will unite and interact
with the crowd of actors there; will have numerous insights, rev-
elations and epiphanies; and will, ultimately, at the end of the time,
confront his future. An implication will be that Sternberg, as an
emblem—or synecdochical appendage—of *his generation,* will
countenance, in his future, *The Future.*

All this is being made explicit both to avoid any possible appearance of Symbolist/New Realist coyness, and also because the
true tension of any record of Reunion day just doesn't rely on this
stuff, and so hopefully isn't compromised or tranquilized by being
made, as Dr. Ambrose told the workshop just before Memorial
Day, "desuppressed, anti-replenished, exhausted, *in full view.*"

He'd tell us yes friends and neighborhood association the textual
tension and payoff here lies in the exact *sort* of late-twentieth-
century Future this introverted aspiring product-representative will
confront. Ambrose explained—and it's all in Mark Nechtr's notes,
in a precise crabbed hand—Ambrose held that there are numerous
types of potential futures flapping and honking in man's conceptual
pond. Specifically that there's differences between the trinity of: a
future within time (history & prophecy); a future beyond time
(resurrection & eternity); and a future that *ends* time (eschaton &
apocalypse). Which did we find most attractive? he'd asked rhe-
torically, finally wiping the nastily critical poem off his green black-
board.

Three other things Dr. Ambrose told the workshop (that Mark

Nechtr doesn't have in his tiny crabbed notes because his attention
had strayed to the loveless pathos of the postmodern Drew-Lynn
Eberhardt and the thing she'd scrawled before blowing off class):

"The *subject* of a story is what it's about; the *object* of a story is
where it's going";

"Do not confuse sympathy *for* the subject and empathy *with* it—
one of the two is bad."

"Yes, he, Ambrose, the author, *is* a character in and the object
of the seminal *Lost in the Funhouse;* but he is not the main character,
the hero or subject, since fictionists who tell the truth aren't able
to use real names."

Since and as J.D. and DeHaven Steelritter are *still* arguing about
whether it's more efficient to shut off DeHaven's growling car, out
there in the pay lot, and since no one connected to today is in sight
in the terminal or rest room (Mark went in and checked for col-
legiate cuffs and footwear under the stall doors) to guide them,
still, the trio of Mark and D.L. and Sternberg are to be seen making
their way toward the arrowed signs for Ground Transportation,
their object being to rent a Datsun, Mark carrying both his light
bag and D.L.'s bag, a stabbing sensation in his thorax which full
hands prevent him from verifying as his special Dexter target arrow,
which he's attached to, and hid from the LordAloft 7:10 pilot in
his shirt, and is still carrying there, D.L. walking with arms crossed
over a lime-green-jacket-enclosed chest whose dimensions remain,
to Sternberg, disappointingly vague, her pelvis preceding her by at
least a couple steps. Sternberg is lugging the bag his parents bought
him, casting his castable eye this way and that for anyone with a
gold parabolic nametag, an expectant expression, a clown's face—
eye casting over a Semitically modest set of cheekbones but a rather
snoutish Gentilic nose, a full if somewhat ill-defined mouth, his
face itself unfortunately one big chaos of poison-sumac cysts, infections and scars, dimpled as a metal roof post-hailstorm; and of
course a pleasant blue forward-looking eye and an unnatural dead-

white backward-looking eye. Ironically, a good part of his anticorporeal stance (it was his idea to call having a body Corporeal Punishment) derives from his *non*fatal flaw, the skin trouble, the skin trouble itself deriving from a weekend years past, just before a cattle call for a Wisk spot he didn't get, a weekend of solo camping and getting-into-collar-soiled-character, alone, with a tent, in the Berkshires, West of Boston, during which he'd contracted a mild spatter of poison sumac, and had purchased a discount generic brand of poison-sumac medicine he curses now and forever (like most terse-labeled generics the product was untrustworthy, turned out in fact to be medicine for the *sumac,* not the sufferer therefrom, but if the label says MEDICINE FOR POISON SUMAC what the fuck are you going to think, standing there?) that had set his face, neck, chest and back aflame: pulsing, cystic, volcanic, allergic, clotted, almost sacredly scarred. The sumac is so bad it hurts—which of course is a constant reminder that it's there, on his body—and it won't go away, no sooner healed by brand-name antitoxin than reinfected. The whole thing's just pretty loathsome, and you can bet Sternberg loathes it. He's unhappy, but in that comparatively neat and easy way of those who are at least pretty sure they know why they're unhappy, and what to curse, now and forever.

They walk, with luggage, Mark bobbing slightly, D.L. loin-led and probably pregnant, Sternberg trailing and casting. Onto the escalator's shaver-head steps, down. Here's that Oriental again, with the tattered black bangs, ascending at them. The Oriental's still alone. Sternberg ponders: how often do you see just *one* Oriental anyplace? They tend to move in packs. The sun is early-to-midmorning. Lots of Eastward windows glide diagonally up as they deescalate. The sunlight is both glaring and impure. Dew-turned-humidity rises as one slow body from the green sweep of corn, the mist breaking Swiss-cheesily into patches as it heats and ascends to mess with the purity of the light. Mark could tell Sternberg how most Occidentals don't realize that Orientals do often appear in transit alone, do often pronounce liquid consonants at least as well as your average airport P.A. announcer. That their eyes aren't any smaller or wickedly slanted than our own: they just have a type of uncircumcised eyelid that reveals slightly less total eye. The eyes in Mark's healthy face appear vaguely oriental; they have that boxer-in-the-late-rounds puffiness, especially when he hasn't slept. But he's occidental as they come. He's a third-generation-German Baltimore WASP, though lately converted, D.L. wrote Sternberg, by an insidious pedagogical Mesmer of an archery coach, from an ambivalent parental Catholicism to Trinitarianism, known also as Mathurinism or Redemptionism. D.L., who is postmodern, and so atheist, wrote bitterly to Sternberg during her then-just-friend's formal conversion: the whole thing was savage, medieval, cannibalistic, lust-ridden, "This bread is my body" transformed into factitive verbs and epithetic nouns, a linguistic bewitchment, a leximancical fraud: how can three things be both one thing and three things? They just can't be, is all. But Sternberg thinks he gets the idea. If you can just want something bad enough, "to want" *becomes* factitive. Sternberg wants to heal himself. To act. He wants it more than anything.

The opposing escalator carries the Oriental up at them. Mark declines to meet the man's uncut eye. D.L. actually walks down the downward glide of their conveyor, the sort of girl who treats escalators like stairs, behavior which has always frightened and confused Sternberg. Her ass is disproportionately wide, flat, ungentle.

But so they're in motion, at least, notice, though the going is slow. It's undeniable that they don't even yet have transportation *to* the Funhouse, and that it's awfully slow going, here. Not one of them would deny this, and they're tired, and D.L. coming off meds, and Mark hungry and his bloodstream crying out for coffee. And Sternberg needs a b—— movement like nobody's business.

But and so things are slow, and like you they have this irritating suspicion that any real satisfaction is still way, way off, and it's frustrating; but like basically decent kids they suck it up, bite the foil, because what's going on is just plain real; and no matter what we want, the real world is pretty slow, at present, for kids our age. It probably gets less slow as you get older and more of the world is behind you, and less ahead, but very few *people of our generation* are going to find this exchange attractive, I'll bet. Dr. Ambrose himself told Mark Nechtr, over beers and a blossom at the East Chesapeake Tradeschool Student Union Bar & Grill, that the problem with young people, starting sometime in about the 1960s, is that they tend to live too intensely inside their own social moment, and thus tend to see all existence past age thirty or so as somehow postcoital. It's then that they'll relax, settle back, sad animals, to watch—and learn, as Ambrose himself said he learned from hard artistic and academic experience—that life, instead of being rated a hard R, or even a soft R, actually rarely even makes it into distribution. Tends to be too slow.

Meanwhile, oddly, here's another of these well-dressed young guys, in the lower terminal, near Ground Transportation, young and bearded and groomed, giving away money like it's going out of style, checking things off on a clipboard so full his slim hands strain to keep it together. Mark approaches him. He wants to verify the scam; he feels like he's figured out who these guys are: they're Mormons, it's some irritatingly altruistic Mormon thing. He wants to check it out before giving D.L. their Visa card, but D.L. is edgy, coming off Dalmane, a member of the Valium family. And a surprisingly sharp-voiced argument ensues, about schedules and reliability and lateness and who's responsible for what, in terms of various fuck-ups. It's the kind of public-place argument between married people you don't listen to, if you're polite.

A REALLY BLATANT AND INTRUSIVE INTERRUPTION

As mentioned before—and if this were a piece of metafiction, which it's NOT, the exact number of typeset lines between this reference and the prenominate referent would very probably be mentioned, which would be a princely pain in the ass, not to mention cocky, since it would assume that a straightforward and anti-embellished account of a slow and hot and sleep-deprived and basically clotted and frustrating day in the lives of three kids, none of whom are all that sympathetic, could actually get published, which these days good luck, but in metafiction it would, nay *needs* be mentioned, a required postmodern convention aimed at drawing the poor old reader's emotional attention to the fact that the narrative bought and paid for and now under time-consuming scrutiny is *not* in fact a barely-there window onto a different and truly diverting world, but rather in fact an "artifact," an object, a plain old this-worldly thing, composed of emulsified wood pulp and horizontal chorus-lines of dye, and *conventions,* and is thus in a "deep" sense just an opaque forgery of a transfiguring window, not a real window, a gag, and thus in a deep (but *intentional,* now) sense artificial, which is to say fabricated, false, a fiction, a pretender-to-status, a straw-haired King of Spain—this self-conscious explicitness and decon-structed disclosure supposedly making said metafiction "realer" than a piece of pre-postmodern "Realism" that depends on certain an-tiquated techniques to create an "illusion" of a windowed access to a "reality" isomorphic with ours but possessed of and yielding up higher truths to which all authentically human persons stand in the relation of applicand—all of which the Resurrection of Realism, the pained product of inglorious minimalist labor in countless ob-scure graduate writing workshops across the U.S. of A., and called by Field Marshal Lish (who ought to know) the *New* Realism, prom-ises to show to be utter baloney, this metafictional shit . . . plus *naïve* baloney-laced shit, resting on just as many "undisclosed as-sumptions" as the "realistic" fiction metafiction would try to "de-bunk"—one imagines nudists tearing the poor Emperor's clothes to shreds and then shrieking with laughter, as if they didn't go home to glass-enclosed colonies, either—and, the New Real guys would argue, more odious in the bargain, this metafiction, because it's a slap in the faces of History and History's not-to-be-fucked-with henchman Induction, and opens the door to a fetid closetfull of gratuitous cleverness, jazzing around, self-indulgence, no-hands-ism, which as Gardner or Conroy or L'Heureux or hell even Am-brose himself will tell you are the ultimate odium for any would-be passionate virtuoso—the closest we get to the forbidden, the taboo, the odium, the *asur . . .* —and so the number of lines between won't be mentioned, though its ass-pain would have been subordinate to and considerably more economical in terms of severely limited time than this particular consideration and refusal— there's to be, today, a Reunion of everyone who has ever appeared in any of the 6,659 McDonald's commercials ever conceived and developed and produced and shot and distributed by the same J.D. Steelritter Advertising that has sent myriad and high-technically seductive invitations, information packets, travel vouchers, brochures, and carefully targeted inducements and duressments (no maps, though, oddly) to everyone who's ever appeared. And get this: the Reunion's been so well conceived and promoted that *everyone who's still alive has promised to show up.* One hundred percent positive response is, J.D. knows, no accident. This Reunion's been in the works a long time. Besides things that spin, this gala's conception and arrangement have been J.D. Steelritter's central passion for years. He was predicting something like this right from the beginning. Converging on the sleepy, rose-scented town of Collision are close to 44,000 former actors, actresses, puppeteers, unemployed clowns: thousands of pilgrims from each of the great twelve market-determined classes of commercial actor: Caucasian, Black, Asian, Latin, Native American/Eskimo, plus finally those who wear bright mâché heads and costumes; with a dittoed six categories of child actors from child-spots aimed like cathode revolvers at the wide-eyed Saturday-morning and late-weekday-afternoon market. Free plane fare; complimentary LordAloft shuttle from O'Hare to Central Illinois Airport; clown-car transportation to the Reunion grounds (for the punctual); gold nametags, for keepsies; access to the flagship discotheque of a franchise that promises to thrive like carcinomae, to be *the* place to be seen, in the millennium ahead; free food (natch); a chance to meet and pal around with J.D. Steelritter and Ronalds 1 and 3, to chuck baseballs at the targeted dunk-tank over which will be suspended Ronald 2, to engage in general orgiastic *Walpurgisrevel* that would have just shot Faust's rocks; and finally the appearance, at 12:00 sharp, directly overhead, of Jack Lord, star, with a bullhorn and plastic rifle, Jack Lord, a fucking *icon,* aloft, in a helicopter, waving. It's going, the glossy brochure promises, to be a Reunion to end all reunions. Exclamation point. And it's going to be made into the biggest McDonald's commercial of all time. And they're going to get paid *all over again.*

Besides, New Realism, being young, and realistic, is pretty slow, too. Ask Ambrose. Ask Mark; he's checked it out. It diverges, in its slowness, from the really real only in its extreme economy, its Prussian contempt for leisure, its obsession with the confining limitations of its own space, its grim proximity to its own horizon. It's some of the most heartbreaking stuff available at any fine bookseller's anywhere. I'd check it out.

At the point of a surprisingly patient parallel line, at the C.I. Airport Avis counter, a very big farmer, in overalls—so big he unconsciously treats the counter like a footstool, has his boot on the counter and his elbow on his knee—is trying to barter an entire thousand-bushel crop of prime Illinois feed corn, plus his '81 Allys-Chalmers thresher/harvester, for just three weeks' rental of anything foreign. Anything foreign at all, is what's sad. It's for his oldest kid, apparently. His kids and our kids watch the negotiations. The Avis attendant, who clearly recognizes a number-two's imperative to try harder, explains that while she doesn't make policy, and can only relate that policy to the public, and must decline the barter, she empathizes with the farmer a lot.

"Datsun or nothing," D.L. iterates to the two, and Mark Nechtr grits his teeth, producing a fine tight smile. D.L. is seen only in Datsuns. It's a neurosis, for sure, but one so powerful as to dictate acquiescence in many amusing instances we haven't time for. Sternberg, all this time, is peering outward around the big farmer's thigh at yet another poster, this one for that Central Illinois bowling and family-fun center. Though Sternberg has lived with his parents all his life, and has in fact kissed only them, ever, he's puzzled by this term, "family fun."

The Avis representative's refusal of the big farmer's bartered offer has pity and empathy in it, however not compassion or sympathy. The absence of sympathy is probably due to the fact that her mouth is full of a sweet bite-sized Breakfast DoughNugget as she patiently explains Avis's unbendable remittance policy of cash, locally drawn check w/ guarantee card, and in any case at least data on a national credit card, which in this awkward age means MasterCard, AmEx, Visa, CitiCorp, or the new, convenient, and option-widening Discover Card. The farmer has only raw grain, and (weirdly) too much of it for it to be worth anything. And Avis's profit projections on thresher rentals out of airports are understandably bleak. Surely the farmer recognizes that the situation is no one's fault.

He does. The huge farmer.

Sternberg points the big poster out to D.L. "ENJOY A WHOLE NEW DIMENSION IN BOWLING" is its basic pitch.

He's puzzled about family-fun, and the poster makes him somehow fearful. "Bowling's pretty darn three-dimensional already, isn't it?"

Mark smiles. "Four-dimensional bowling?" D.L. laughs. Her laugh tends to sound like a cough. And obversely. Sternberg peers at the two-dimensional image, scanning the ad's family of models for flaws. Mark stands tiptoed, flexing his ankles, his arrow a little vertical wrinkle under his surgeon's shirt.

And they're all of a sudden at the counter's long line's front, Sternberg sees. What's happened to the big old farmer who's unable to trade a whole season's sweat and effort, in the tradition that made the U.S.A.—nay, the whole evolution from hunting-gathering nomadism to cultivation and community—possible and great, for a lousy three weeks of flashy transport? Has he gathered his flat-faced brood around him, raised the bill of his seed-company cap to rub his own tired brick-red face, and gone off to try even harder at car rental's number one agency? Mark feels as though he ought to be depressed about it: the car was for the farmer's eldest son's potential wedding to a loan officer's daughter. But Sternberg can see neither farmers nor broods anyplace, and his evacuation-imperative has now become a sick ache in his lower gut, and he draws out a fag, a 100, a type of cigarette he likes because it not only burns forever but also emits its light at a comfortable distance from his body. Again, the preceding generation of cripplingly self-conscious writers, obsessed with their own interpretation, would mention at this point, just as we're possibly getting somewhere, that the story isn't getting anywhere, isn't progressing in the seamless Freitagian upsweep we should have scaled by this, mss. p. 35, time. They'd trust, though, à la their hierophant C—— Ambrose, that this explicit internal *acknowledgment* of their failure to start the show would release them somehow from the obligation to start the show. Or that it might, in some recursive and above all ingenious way, represent the very movement it professes to deny. Mark's fix on these Gamarahites is that they're basically a sincere lot—critics, really, instead of the priests they want to be—and that it's ironic that it's because of their very critical integrity that these guys get captured by the very pretend-industry they're trying to regulate. Mark Nechtr is unfashionably patient, in line. T. Sternberg embodies a different generational story. Gray clouds roll in slow pain against half his sight. As the nicotine becomes a bright blood-tide, crashing against sleep-dep, ugly ideas descend on Sternberg, and are recorded here w/o comment. Fucking pathetic farmer. Fucking pathetic Midwest Avis girl with anvil-shaped hair and a translucent wart on her brow and sugary-shit at the corners of her mouth. The black girl-hair on her arm, like, *gleams*. Fucking Mark with his hypnotized stare and sensitive lashes and stink of health and his lone aluminum arrow, attached to the phallic little guy or what, terrific hiding job inside his neckless effeminate surgeon's shirt so the tip shows just under his throat. The clot can't even tell how he looks to other people. Fucking D.L. with her trim trimestered belly and limbo pelvis and too-clever pout, her failure to match memory, a dog-eared copy of something Progressive held across her chest in lieu of the jiggle of any discernible tit. Fucking Tom, varnished with a light oily sweat in the absence of one lousy visible flaw on the poster of these bowlers having family fun in a new dimension. We just want to ride, dude. Gratis. To the Reunion. We just want to do the bare unavoidable minimum. Pay taxes, die. Sternberg has resentment even he can't see, it's so deep inside. So an ugly mood, and a desperate need to evacuate his body. It's loathsomely real, I'm afraid. But what's to be done?

Avis girl w/ translucent wart and glazed DoughNugget behind aluminum counter: "How can we help you, today?"

Across the lower terminal is the lower lounge, mostly empty, the plastic tables round sprouts supported by single central stems, atomic clouds with tops shaved flat, the bartender in his green vest hanging washed glasses by their stems beneath the huge TV raised to its tavern-height in a corner on the side Sternberg can't see out of—though his other eye is marvelously keen, the eye of a marksman, really.

"I feel we should tell you right at the outset we'll be needing a Datsun," D.L. says, the counter at what ought to be breast-level.

"Hawaii Five-O" and the bartender are both on their last of forty-eight straight hours. The bartender is grim, has to hear Danno being told to book somebody just one more time. . . . But it's an episode Sternberg knows, moving his head to see. He just loves episodes he already knows.

"No more Datsuns? Mark, she seems to be saying there are no more Datsuns."

Looking at Sternberg and the distant elevated TV: "Datsuns are Nissans, now, Sweets. Ask if they have Nissans." Mark's broken this news to D.L. before. It never sinks in.

It's the first bit of violence, here, in this episode. Jack Lord's antagonists always get introduced through violence inflicted on the innocent and cameo. See these menacing oriental men enter a beauty salon where an occidental and male hairdresser is alone, putting receipts in order, soon to close. Menacingly they draw the shades and flip the window's sign over so its OPEN side faces Sternberg and the surprised hairdresser, who tries to explain that they don't do men, in this particular shop; one Oriental drawing a flicked stiletto, *weltschmerzian* end-lust aglitter in eyes far smaller than good old familiar occidental eyes, announcing, "We do"; and the revelation dawns on victim and viewer alike as "Hawaii Five-O" cuts to shots of an almost tidal-sized wave, a wave that conveys far better than realism the total disorder and -memberment taking place in that occidental Honolulu hair salon; as Mark, too, succumbs to the *familiar enchantment of popular culture,* leaves transportation negotiations to his bride, and drifts with Sternberg like flotsam toward the lounge and the syndicated television program "Hawaii Five-O." Numerous references to popular culture pervade the art which all three of these sexually mature children consume and aspire one day to produce and re-present. Popular culture is the *symbolic representation of what people already believe.*

But so they have a coccyx-hostile chair at a table's wood-grained circle, the boys, in a lower lounge almost empty, as morning lounges ought, Sternberg ordering a Jolt cola and fishing for fags in his shirt, Mark having to remove his arrow as he sits, since the tip's at his throat; and his throat wants coffee, and he can't believe the bartender's terse suggestion that he go up to the cafeteria, if he wants something hot. Meanwhile, across the terminal, in view of Mark but not Tom, who's into reruns, stands Drew-Lynn, edgy as only a tranquilizer hangover can make you edgy, trying to negotiate the legal rental of a Nissan, as the line behind her grows too long to really even be observed. Mark withdraws from a surgeon's shirt of surprising storage complexity a thick Ziploc bag one-third full of oily and darkly red things. Sternberg is witnessing Che, the Five-O M.E., trace a kind of chalk ectoplasm around the tastefully unfocused cadaver of the hairdresser; the first he sees of the roses is when Mark offers him one.

"Bit of fried rose, maybe?" reaching pale fingers in, bending as if to sniff coffee.

"Fried rose?"

Mark holds a petal so greasy it makes his fingers shine. "It's like a delicacy. You behead them and fry them in oil, and eat them."

Tom stares at both Mark and himself, lighting a 100 the way a cigar is lit, torching it, so that the end gets ravaged.

"Try one. I get them from somebody pretty trustworthy. They're better than they look. Try one. It'll pick you up."

He looks at it. "I think I'd rather drink bong-water than eat something that looks like that."

"Bong-water's a totally different issue."

"You're sure?"

"Just one. Try it. You look like hell. You can wash it down with Jolt, won't even taste it."

No inappropriate comestibles for D.L., though. D.L.'s psychic was dead-set against fried roses. Hors d'oeuvres to a meal you don't even want to think about, she'd called them. It was she who told D.L. she might be seen only in Datsuns. That the Death card was basically an OK card. But to consult her before ever leaving home. To wear amber resin instead of perfume, it's good karma, opens the third eye, plus smells good, like distant orange cake. D.L. wears amber:

"Excuse me? I heard only doughnut. A Nissan, then. We will, no, not be driving it out of state. We'll be taking it only to Collision, just West of here. Is Collision just West of here? Steelritter, yes. We're here for the Reunion of Everyone Who's Ever Appeared in a McDonald's Commercial" (caps hers). "The ultimate McDonald's commercial. A kind of logarithm of all other McDonald's commercials, a spot so huge the brochure, here's the brochure, the brochure says 'New equipment will have to be designed even to try to countenance the union of all the thirty years' actors consuming, to attempt to capture a crowded and final transfiguration that will represent, and so transmit, a pan-global desire for meat, a collective erection of the world community's true and total restaurant.' I know, Steelritter Advertising tends to talk that way. And Mr. Steelritter wasn't here to meet us. We were late. We. My husband and friend are both"—looking—"my husband is in the lounge, just across, facing the window, you can just see him. Mark Nechtr, spouse. With a *ch* and no vowel. He should go down first. Next D.L. Eberhardt, introduction of the McDonaldLand outdoor-eating and family-fun areas, winter, 1970. I sliding down a compactly curved slide, my possibly bare little bottom shrieking frictionally against very *very* cold metal. I innocently offering the Hamburglar a burger he doesn't even chew, swallowing it whole as I recoil. The poor man was bulging out of his costume by the time Steelritter was satisfied with the shot. He was a perfectionist.

He and the actors who wore costumes didn't get along well, was
our impression. Our. A Thomas Sternberg should go down, too,
as a possible driver. He's from the introduction of the Drive-Thru
option, winter, 1970. He petitioning a smiley-faced intercom for
a FunMeal while the actor at the wheel reaches down to tousle his
hair. Relishing the break he'd deserved that day. That's probably
more information than you need. It's just that we're tired, we've
flown in all the way from the East Coast, we haven't had quality
sleep, or been met, and we would so much just like to *get* there.
With minimal hassle. We are late, and have transportation needs,
and the credit to satisfy them. And our national credit card of choice
is: Visa. You're right, that's not technically our name on the card.
The card's technically in my husband Mark Nechtr's father's name.
He's in detergent. Steelritter doesn't handle his firm, I'm afraid."

There is narrative movement. Sternberg sits, fearful, trying to lift
his shoes from view. He fingers his forehead in further fear and
indecision as the smell of what what he's consumed produces rises
around him. Elsewhere, red-toothed, Mark idly flips his arrow up
and over and down and into the lounge's round table, where the
razor-sharp Dexter target-tip sticks. He's good at this—it's a lounge
trick—just hang the nock and part of the cedar shaft over the table's
edge, give it a carefully casual slap from below, and the thing goes
up, end-over-end, and comes down straight, to stay. The bartender,
who wouldn't be pleased at punctured tabletops, is however en-
grossed in what the menacing Orientals, now in leather, are doing
to an occidental nun.

"Is this because J.D. Steelritter, who probably owns this whole
airport and everything in it, doesn't handle detergent?" D.L. demands. "Well no I'm trying to tell you it *is* our card, it's just in his
father's name. Wedding present. We're practically newlyw——but
why does it need to be in our name? I'm over twenty-one, I'm
twenty-*five,* for Christ's sake—look at the license. I'm *pregnant.* I
have a *spouse.* No, Mark does not have a Visa in his own name.

He's just a graduate student. We're only just now establishing credit. Tom Sternberg I *know* doesn't have a credit card. He uses only money. Not even a checking account. He pretends it's a political idea, but really he's afraid he'll get confused, overextended."

The Avis representative chews empathetically as she explains that renters need cards in their own names. That she's only relating company policy. That there it is in black and white. Legal thing. Have to establish that you're accredited adults who can assume responsibility for someone else's high-velocity machine.

"But Miss this Visa has *unlimited* credit. Look—it's got 'LIMIT: SKY' printed right on it. *Embossed.*"

On Mark's table are his upright Dexter aluminum, his Ziploc of Ambrose's fried roses, a tall thin bar-glass of cola, and an untended 100 that refuses to die in its ashtray.

"Let me understand you," D.L. tells the anvil-haired Avis attendant as the mood of the line behind her moves beyond ugly and restless into something more like at peace and sort of awed, watching the exchange. "Though the credit is unlimited," she says slowly, "it's not *ours,* you're saying. It's unlimited, but it's not about responsibility, and so in some deep car-rental-agency sense isn't really credit at all?"

The Avis lady, whose name is Nola, chews a bit of chocolate glaze, nodding with the genuine empathy that got her the job in the first place.

D.L. turns to no one in particular: "This is an outrage."

And it is, sort of.

"Can I help, perhaps?" It's the young man with the soft beard, crisp bills and crammed clipboard, holding a vending machine's paper cup of coffee by its flimsy fold-out handle, exchanging pleasant nods with Nola, of Avis.

"Are you affiliated with the Reunion of Everyone Who's Ever Appeared in a McDonald's Commercial?" D.L. asks.

"No," the guy admits, sipping.

D.L. turns her lime-green back. "Then no," she says. "Miss," she says, "what then do you propose we do? Is there any sort of public transportation in Central Illinois? Don't laugh. We're in real trou-

ble. We have a severely limited amount of time to get to Collision
and the Funhouse discotheque that J.D. Steelritter, who just by
the way *does* own this airport, doesn't he . . . ?"

"J.D.?" the mild-eyed man asks.

"J.D.," D.L. says, not turning around, too pissed even to rec-
ognize recognition. "And we're not even sure where Collision is,
from this airport. How far West of here is it? Is it walking distance?
Is there a road? All we've seen is corn. It's been disorienting, wind-
blown, verdant, tall, total, menacingly fertile. This entire area is
creepy. We have transportation needs. I'll bet the insects here are
fierce. Is your state bird the mosquito? Is this snake country?"

"Fears?" the man with the money to offer is saying, idly working
those near the line's front. "Fears here?"

By the way, for whom would perpetual union with this person
yammering bad-news-customer-like at Nola be fun, I'll bet you're
asking. Perhaps the most direct and efficient and diplomatic answer
is that a rented Datsun is not in the offing.

Mark looks up at what's raised to public view. Jack Lord's helicopter
slowly ascends, wheeling gracefully into Hawaii's electric blue, Lord
at the helm, in a fine and no-bullshit-whatsoever business suit,
Danno riding shotgun with his marksman's rifle, in a slightly less
fine but still all-business suit. Where is Tom Sternberg? He'll give
Sternberg till the next commemorative commercial, Mark thinks,
trying to swallow a second gulp of soda against the rising gas of
the first. Something almost imperceptibly furtive about Sternberg
discourages the idea of contact in bathrooms. Mark is enormously
sensitive to these sorts of things, in general. There's still the tiniest
bit of cooked flower between his teeth, which he works slowly with
his healthy but sort of narrow tongue, in which irritated taste buds
are visible as individual buds.

Well and then he sees the probable Mormon, the money-giver,
with D.L. and the hairy-armed Avis girl, at the counter, across the
terminal, past the totally superfluous lounge window, which is itself

past the next table, now occupied by a blonde, orange-faced flight attendant and an effete narrow-faced man in an age-glazed corduroy suit. Mark rises in alarm. They *don't* need Latter-Day charity, Reunion or no. There's always a Mormon around when you don't want one, trying your patience with unsolicited kindness.

"Stop me if I'm wrong, but what I sense here is conflict," says the bearded man, who it turns out isn't a practicing LDS, but rather works for J.D. Steelritter Advertising in some research capacity unrelated to the McDonald's campaign or revel. "Stymied desire," he muses. "It's clear that there's something you *want,* and an obstacle, a what's the word a cheval-de-frise, to your actually *having* it." He's writing this stuff down on a clipboard whose poor clip is holding far too much print-out paper. "Doubtless in the confrontation and potential resolution of this conflict you'll undergo changes in experience, outlook, personality, possibly even in the makeup of the desires . . ."

"Needs. We have transportation *needs."*

". . . themselves. Maybe changes that'll be of interest not only to you, but to others. You'll have something to *interest* the Reunion, when you arrive."

"If."

"When," he emphasizes, his face like an ad for blind faith, happy karma.

"Maybe then you could get your own credit card," the Avis woman says helpfully, genuinely sorry that she does not fashion, but only communicates, company policy. The complimentary box of DoughNuggets is empty, its wax paper greebly and smeared. Honestly, though. Even bartering farmers are better than kids without real credit. And there is simply no way this person is only twenty-five, or pregnant, she thinks, as everyone else in the line all seems to lose his patience at once and she turns back to begin handling something that looks even worse than the commodities-trading center she'd left to get a job closer to her own family's roots. If ever a person has looked infertile, she thinks, why then—

J.D. Steelritter and DeHaven Steelritter are *still* out in the airport lot, if you will—their initial argument about ignition having metastasized into a really killer row about DeHaven's less than fastidious records of just which alumni have arrived when. Turns out they're missing three, not two, alumni. And is J.D. pissed.

"I *said* I was sorry."

"That's just *it!*" J.D. shouts over DeHaven's loud idle. "You *say* things. But you never *show*. Show me some pride, just once. Some *desire*. You have a *job*, shitspeck. Define for your old man what 'job' means. What does it mean to you: 'job'?"

"These things happen, Pop," DeHaven says, smoothing his yarn wig with a cotton-gloved hand as his malevolent car growls. The car can't ever be turned off, if it's to run right, was what started the row. "I'm sorry, and I'll try not to ever fuck up anything ever again" (pissed himself, DeHaven). "But I can't promise you I'll never fuck up, because these things happen, Pop. Maybe to everybody except a genius like you."

J.D. looks for sarcasm, but it's tough, what with sleep-dep and all; he can't read much in the ingenuous bloodshot flutter of the big clown's mascara.

Though, not to take sides, but sometimes things *do* happen. Even in reality. In real realism. It's a myth that truth is stranger than fiction. Actually they're about equally strange. The strangest stories tend, in a way, to *happen*. Take for example the single solitary piece Mark Nechtr has thus far been able to produce for discussion in Dr. Ambrose's graduate workshop at East Chesapeake Trade. Its conceit is lifted and carried off right out of a banner headline in the Baltimore *Sun*. Nothing as richly ambiguous as FIRM DOCTORS TELEPHONE POLES, but a simple MURDER-SUICIDE IN DOWNTOWN ELEVATOR BAFFLES AUTHORITIES. And details of the story are traceable directly to the voluminous correspondence between D.L. and Tom Sternberg, who's maybe about the most claustrophobic individual in the history of his generation.

The elevator at issue is in a mental-health professionals' building in downtown Baltimore. The setup is that a mental-health professional, the kind that can't write 'scrips, a Ph.D., is treating two different guys for debilitating claustrophobia. And the treatment of both patients starts at the same time and proceeds more or less in sync, though neither patient ever meets the other. Until, that is, it becomes that time in treatment for each of the guys to confront the true beak and claws of his phobia head-on. Yes it's *elevator-time.* They're to be put in the building's elevator and made to ride up and down repeatedly. But see now *together,* for support (the psychologist being a follower of the head-on-confrontation-but-with-support school of phobic treatment).

So in they both go, and they're riding up and down repeatedly. . . .

Except the elevator eventually stalls, possibly from all the phobic energy swirling around in there, and it gets stuck between floors, and the buttons don't work, the thing's just broken down. The two claustrophobes are trapped, together, in a tiny elevator in a thin shaft in an enclosed building in the center of a crowded metropolis. For a while, true, they support each other. But, in the fullness of time enjoyed by all stalled things, of course, they eventually totally lose it.

"YAAGH!" one screams at the other. "You're closing in!"

"No! No! *You're* closing in!"

"YAAGH!"

"GAAH!"

"Get very far away!"

"You're swelling! You're taking up the whole elevator!"

"Stop closing in!"

"GAAH!"

"YAAGH!"

"You're breathing both our air! You're consuming *my air!* Stop that breathing!"

"Leave me *alone!* Get *away!* Oh my *God!*"

"Nothing left! No more breathing!"

"YAAAAAAGHURGHLURGHLURGHLURGHL."

And so on. Their worst fears, which they'd slowly, supportively

come to see were fiction, came true. The whole piece was kind of
a go-figure story. Mark never showed it to D.L. D.L. had bagged
the Program by then, and nuptials were closing in.

I think what it was was Mark felt guilty, the story being basically
just a pastiche of truths and everything. Plus ghastly and loathsome.
Dr. Ambrose was surprisingly receptive, though, considering it
turned out he'd written a very similar story, way back when, one
about a fire in the bungalow of an elderly couple who are both
wildly pyrophobic and cripplingly agoraphobic. Mark claimed he'd
never read that story of Ambrose's. The whole stuck-in-elevator
thing had been his idea. With some help from the truth, admittedly.
Ambrose had fingered the port-wine stain on his temple absently and told Mark that of course he believed him. He trusted
Mark.

And there is something trustworthy about Mark Nechtr. Like,
if he promises to do something, you know the only way it won't
get done is if he just can't do it. Like, even if he's hooked up with
somebody he doesn't really desire or want to be hooked up with,
if he's given his word, the only way he won't stay hooked up with
that person is if he just truly cannot do it. If he promises to get
D.L. and Sternberg to this Reunion they've been looking forward
to for so long, he'll try. Though it doesn't look like he's trying too
terribly hard right now—his big flaw is that he's extremely easy to
distract and fascinate, and now he's fascinated with this beardedly
distinguished non-Mormon Steelritter janissary (who puts in a call
to Steelritter Advertising's Collision office complex, where he says
a Midwestern twang had promised they'd send an emergency van
right over, J.D. and DeHaven Steelritter and Eberhardt '70 and
Sternberg '70 and somebody down as Ambrose-Gatz '67 *all* being
late, now, and the alumni getting restless, somewhat sloshed, and
of course hungry) and who, he tells Mark, passes out free money
as part of an ingenious J.D. Steelritter marketing-diffraction-test
scheme.

As Hogan, the money-giver, tells the rapt Mark what the scam
really is, Tom Sternberg is *still* in the men's room, just destalling,

to give you some tantalizing idea of the laxative might of a quick-fried flower. Sternberg's now confronting the cracker-sized mirror stamped into the wall over an automatic airport sink. The sink spurts automatically at his approach. Step back and it stops. Saves water, but still. Disconcerting. Boy is he tired. Beyond tired—something behind that face in the mirror signals post-dire fatigue with the hissed whine of something inflatable in his head's center, inflating. D.L. would point to the obverse eye and ask what it saw, if it saw anything of the baggy thing slowly taking shape in his head. Well screw you, D.L.

Cause it's only dark, generally, back there in his eye's guts. Sometimes a spidery system of synaptic color, if he tries to move the bad eye too quickly. But usually nothing. But it'll heal, anyway. It'll come around. It's all in his head, he knows. Youthful-rebellion injury. Mrs. Sternberg warned from day one that the boy that does a forbidden thing, such as like for example crosses his eyes just to hurt a mother: that boy finds they stay like that. Well-known fact. Look it up in whatever resources orthodox mothers with lapsed sons access. Like early to bed: it's the *sleep before dark* that's most important. Like don't cry: you're better than whoever laughs at you. Like try this lotion, for sumac.

Here's the fresh sumac cyst, though, here, boy, between his eyes. It's darkened richly since the last cyst-check in O'Hare, matured from that tomato pink to the same plum shade as the airport lounge. The mirror does not lie.

Your average deformity sufferer has a love-hate thing with mirrors: you need to see how things are progressing, but you also hate it that they're progressing. Sternberg's not at all sure he likes the idea of sharing a mirror with a whole lot of actors. He's not sure he wants to rent a bureaucratic car and head West without sleep or soap for a Funhouse the brochure says is carefully designed utilizing mostly systems of mirrors. A crowded, mirrored place . . . Sternberg ponders the idea as the automatic sink fills gurgling to the slit of the emergency drain at its rim. This sumac cyst between his eyes feels fucking *alive*, man. Pulses painfully with the squeak of his head's blood. The cyst is beginning to show a little bit of

white at the acme. Not good. Clear evidence of white blood cells,
which implies blood cells, and so a bloodstream. From there it
doesn't take genius to figure out that you've got a body. A bit of
white at an infected cyst's cap is pretty much embodiedness embodied. No way he's messing with the fucker, though. It would
just love to be messed with. Would feed on it. And the stage after
plum is eggplant, big and dusky and curved, like a new organ in
itself, to be an ism of. And D.L. is here, after all. Who as a child
he loved. Though what a personal letdown, in terms of D.L. Her
being now married and knocked was OK—that was an attainability
issue. The letdown is how fucking undesirable, how *unlovable* she's
turned out, in person, after time. Three years of letters since his
dreams got wet and he'd written her care of Steelritter Advertising,
drunk with bright hormone, to confess to this girl whose whereabouts he didn't even know the *effect* she'd had on him as a child a
whole decade back, during the filming of those spots at the very
first McDonald's, in Collision, Ill., preserved and converted to a
commercial soundstage. The little men's-room mirror's image does
that blurred, swimming, memory thing. He nine, she twelve. She'd
seemed so . . . well, *developed.* Her bottom had made the slide's iron
sing. Her breastlets had been a maddening horizontal regularity in
a jumper-top's wrinkle. Sternberg in shorts and black socks, agog,
glands kick-started, though he then still only halfway to puberty
(low pituitary function). A winter afternoon in Illinois, the dead
fields' total snow like a well-ironed sheet, the sky blue as lit gas,
shallow and broad as all outdoors, a saucer with ungentle black
edges. The astringent classroom light of the elaborate McDonald's
set, D.L. sharing something deep-fried with Tom under the aluminum counter as stage mothers twittered and children and clown
and -Burglar were choreographed just so, for an indoor shot. A kind
of Beatrice in saddle shoes, she'd given birth to some of Sternberg's
first ideas. Her pubescent letters (she'd answered his letter, which
was just plain nice) had started out so lilting, warm, putting-the-
reader-at-ease. The poems and stories she later sent were less so;
they seemed cold, coy for coyness's sake, he never forgot he was

sitting in a chair in his parents' living room, reading print on paper; but they appeared deep and ambiguous and full of ideas in a way that, say, a Wisk spot's cattle call sure didn't. And but the photo she'd sent him: was that supposed to be of her? If so, something damned unsavory's happened in the time between the taking and the looking. Now she seems so . . . well, *under*developed. Like a total reversal. It's frightening. And has she really smiled once, yet, the whole time, since they met at M.I. Airport? Has she even once really looked at him when he says something? Nechtr looks at him, but that's almost even creepier: this Mark guy looks at you with the kind of distanced concentration you use to look at something you're eating.

Sternberg washes his hot face without soap. Way too much time has gone by in here, without question. Maybe everybody's out there waiting, deducing the activity and so presence of bowels.

He's got Nechtr pegged. Nechtr's that radiant distant type that it's just impossible to tell if he's putting you on, usually. So what the hell is he doing with this unsavory girl who looks way worse than her photo and says she's currently working on a poem consisting entirely of punctuation? Who has a face like a . . . a *long* face? Who wears synthetic green? Was it a planned pregnancy? Shotgun wedding? The shotgun has yet to be invented that could get Sternberg to marry the D.L. this D.L. has turned out to be, somebody one eerily fuck of a lot like Mrs. Sternberg, the sort of person who, if you visited her house, she'd smile the whole time you were there, then clean vigorously after you left. A cosmic nyet to that. Plus her tits it turns out can't be any bigger than they were that one childish day, that one single commercial either of them have ever been alumni of. Why didn't Nechtr just offer to pay for the abortion? Are Trinitarians pro-Life? Plus she smells weird— orangy on top and then a whiff of something dead and preserved underneath. Let's face it. She looks like her vagina would smell bad. He'd be long gone, personally, dude. Abortion or no. He'd be a red sail in the sunset by now if she tried—

The sink, with a gurgled sigh like almost mercy, overflows, emergency drain-slit and all, Sternberg's spent so unmercifully so much time in here. The water gurgles over the rim and onto the crotch of his gabardines. Great. That's just great. Now it looks like he's maybe wet himself. And what's he supposed to say. Or even if he doesn't say anything. Either way, explanation or interpretation, he comes out embodied. He demands compassion from a mirror he's backed away from, hoping to make the water stop. But it doesn't. Maybe it's been on too long. It's spilling onto the floor. Great. He demands compassion. Except of whom, though?

"J.D. bases the principle on the same principle animal researchers use to tag and track animals. Each bill is tagged with this teeny little silicon transmitter, see?" Hogan points out to Mark and D.L. what looks vaguely like a monocle over the eye that separates *Annuit* from *Coeptis* on The Great Seal. "Simultaneously," Hogan explains, "I ask the person who's taking the money to name, right off the top of their head, what they fear most in the whole world. Their one great informing fear."

Hogan, into it, extends the heavy clipboard, flapping it open to a plain print-out sheet headed simply FEAR. Mark goes down the page:
"Bomb."
"Meltdown or Bomb."
"Cancer—slow kind."
"Hyperinflation."
"The Greenhouse Effect."
"That my wife wife will scald me in my sleep."
"Hyperinflation and Attendant Fiscal Collapse."
"If the whole population in China all jumps up and down at once."
"Russian Bomb."
"Confusion."
"My father's voice."
"Ozone depletion."
"Apocalypse."
"That phone call in the middle of the night."
"Slow kind of cancer from Meltdown or Bomb."

"The dark."

"That I'll scald my husband while he's asleep."

"Nuclear Winter."

"If we get leaders over there in the U.S.S. of R. that are too young to remember what World War II was like, over there."

"Overextension."

"Fear itself."

"Bombs of all kinds."

"The Contamination of the White Aryan Race from nigger fag subversion."

"Scalding."

"The light."

"Nuclear terrorism."

"Confusion."

"Myself."

"That there's no God."

"Discomfort."

"My genitals."

"A sequel to *Three's Company.*"

"That I die and get to go to heaven and I get there and it stops being heaven because I'm there."

"Death by Water."

"Bombs that can fit in metal suitcases."

"That there's a God."

"That the people who invented Max Headroom are busy now inventing something else."

"And so on," Hogan says, flipping the clipboard closed, "with some similar distributions on the Desire end, when we did Desire. J.D. figures this—that anybody who'll take money from a stranger, in an airport, for free, with no idea of who we are or what if any scam is at work, who'll reveal his number-one fear and desire to a clipboard, for money, is a born consumer, a micromarket all to himself, full of desire and fear and vice versa, the perfect target for the next wave of targeting campaigns. And we want some kind of targeting of his spending patterns. And so the bills are tagged."

"Jesus," says Mark, rapt.

"Mark darling," D.L. says through grit teeth.

"Relax. I told you I called a van," Hogan says, hiking over backwards to get at the paper cup's good but cold last drop. He hands the frantic Avis lady the cup to throw out for him and looks the two kids over. "You two've worked with J.D. before, right? The Reunion and everything?"

"Well," Mark starts, "I—"

"So you know this is a genius I get to work for. This man is a genius. It's an honor to even do market research for J.D. Steelritter. Even in this God-forsaken place." He looks around as if for eavesdroppers. "This is the man, this is the legendary man, I'm sure you two know, who eventually got Arm and Hammer baking soda customers to start *pouring the stuff down the drain.* As . . . get this . . . *drain freshener!*" He licks a bit of sweetener off the heel of his hand. "Is that genius? Is that *textbook* planned-obsolescence, or what? And all off fear. J.D. eventually figured out that anybody who'd buy a box of baking soda out of fear of refrigerator odor wouldn't hesitate one second to shell out for another box to prevent *drain* odor." He laughs a marvelous laugh. "*Drain* odor? What's that, for Christ's sake? It's just fear. Very careful research, fear, and the vision of a genius. The man is a legend. I even had a poster of him on my wall, in ad school."

D.L. spots Sternberg creeping curiously and furtively from the men's room with its broad-shouldered symbol back to the lounge, moving serpentine, shoulder-first, trying somehow to keep his back to everything at once, his hands cupped before him like those of the suddenly nude. She raises her arm to him, to fill him in on potential transportation developments, but he doesn't even look their way. He eases gingerly back down at their round table and now low-level cola and *still*-going cigarette just in time to hear "Hawaii Five-O"'s last Jack Lord give Danno his last instructions, ever, to book certain people, Murder-One. The nock of Mark's Dexter Aluminum arrow overhangs the round table's edge. The table's wood-grained surface is pocked with holes, from Mark's lounge trick.

"These all seem like adult fears," Mark is saying to Hogan. "Are any of those younger people's fears? Is there a different list for kids?"

Hogan's eyes go cold. He mashes down the clipboard's metal cover and latches it. "Not at liberty," he says shortly.

"Why isn't fear just fear? What does it matter whose fear?"

"And by the way," Hogan indicates the crisp treasury note D.L. is snapping into her wallet. "Can I get your fears, please?"

"You want our fears?"

"No such thing as a free lunch, kid," Hogan shrugs.

"That's *just* the kind of fear I'm talking about," Mark says. "I don't see why you—"

At this point somebody like Dr. C——— Ambrose would probably interrupt to observe that it seems as though a pretty long time has passed since his last interruption on the general textuality of what's going on. But it seems almost like too little of true import has been going on to irritatingly interrupt and reveal as conventional artifact. Except but now some things really do start to go on. Two figures, one a long-awaited clown, round the broad carpeted curve of the lower terminal, passing the crowds at luggage roulette, bearing down. J.D. has gotten off DeHaven's slouchily apologetic good-for-nothing-shitspeck back, and has had a look at his watch, and they've rushed inside upstairs and had a look at the flight manifests for both the LordAloft 7:10 and the BrittAir 7:45. All three alumni and -ae are accounted for, in these manifest documents. J.D. and DeHaven have been scouring the whole of C.I. Airport. The last alumni are going to get a ride.

WHY J.D. STEELRITTER GAVE HIS SON DeHAVEN THE RONALD McDONALD JOB IN THE FIRST PLACE, "STAGE FRIGHT" INCIDENT ASIDE

Because DeHaven Steelritter, son, has unwittingly given J.D. some of J.D.'s most creative and inspired ideas. It was DeHaven who

first poured Arm & Hammer baking soda down the drain of the
Steelritter farmhouse kitchen, in Collision, to try to erase the in-
delible odor of two marijuana roaches mistakenly washed down
there along with the remains of something sweet. What happened
to the fridge's baking soda? asks Mrs. Steelritter, who fears the
noisomely oily smell of the fried roses that festoon the second-
to-the-bottom refrigerator shelf. Where's my Arm and Hammer?
she asks, as they sit down to a giant Midwest supper. DeHaven—
who, like anybody who smokes dope under his parents' roof, is
quick on his feet when it comes to explaining wild kitchen in-
congruities—delineates a deep concern for the impression the odor
of the Steelritter drain could have made on the next houseguest
who just might visit the kitchen and have occasion to get a whiff
of a drain that, he declares, dry-mouthed, had smelled like death
embodied.

The rest is ad history.

ANOTHER EXAMPLE OF HOW SOME OF J.D. STEELRITTER'S MOST POWERFUL AND LEGENDARY PUBLIC-RELATIONS CREATIONS ARE REALLY NOTHING MORE THAN A SLIGHT TRANSFIGURATION OF WHAT REALLY JUST GOES ON AROUND HIS OWN ROSE FARM'S FARMHOUSE

One fine winter morning, *years* back, J.D. Steelritter was getting
ready to go off to work at the J.D. Steelritter Advertising Complex,
just across the snowy, greenhouse-dotted fields and intersection
from home. But anyway he's heading for the door, and little DeHaven,
home from sixth grade (his second shot at it) with one of those
mysterious feverless colds that just cry out to be nipped in the
bud—he tells J.D., in complete innocence, the innocence of a child
before a television, to have a nice day.

The rest, as they say.

HOW, EVEN THOUGH J.D. STEELRITTER AND RONALD
McDONALD ARE BEARING DOWN, FULLY INTENDING
SIMPLY TO MEET, GREET, FORGIVE ALL DISRUPTIONS OF
SCHEDULE, AND SHUTTLE THE AWAITED ALUMNI WESTWARD,
TOM STERNBERG THREATENS, TO THE IMMEASURABLE
CHAGRIN OF EVERYONE INVOLVED, TO DELAY EVEN
FURTHER AN AT-LAST DEPARTURE FROM THEIR AIRPORT
ARRIVAL AND A HOPEFULLY QUICK TRIP TO COLLISION,
ILLINOIS, AND THE STILL-ON-IMPATIENT-HOLD FULFILLMENT
OF THE PROMISE OF REUNION AND PAYOFF

Sternberg sees brown natives paddling against the final episode's
tide of closing credits, listing all who've ever appeared. He sees
Mark in deep conversation with a guy who looks a hell of a lot like
Sternberg's personal idea of what Jesus Christ in real life probably
looked like, while D.L. stands on one foot and then the other,
green and diffident and unsmiling. Sternberg's crotch is still very
wet, and now warm, and just not comfortable at all. He sees Mark's
bag of fried flowers on the tip-pocked table. Funny thing about
those flowers. Who'd voluntarily cook and eat a rose? It's like
planting and watering a breadstick. It's perverse, and even sort of
obscene, eating what's clearly put on earth to be extra-gastric. Didn't
taste all that hot, either. And there's still a piece stuck with the
intransigence of the flimsy between two molars.

Except, after he'd washed the thing down with a Jolt and a grimace, he suddenly felt like he could go expel what he needed to
expel. He was still afraid, but it was as if the level scale that had
held his desire to evacuate and his fear of discovered embodiment
in a mutual and paralytic suspension had been not so much tilted
as just yanked out from under consideration. He was still very
afraid; but, post-rose, the fear had seemed somehow very tangent
to his desire to go. His need to have gone. He feels empty, better.
And gets cocky, as the empty will sometimes get.

Basically what happens now is that he tries but utterly fucks up
Mark's trick with the target arrow. He'd seen Mark do it a couple

times, a nonchalant and perfect bar trick, the fucker. Sternberg, maybe barely even consciously, has always wanted to do a nonchalant bar trick, the kind involving spoons and eggs, glasses in pyramids, knives and spread hands, syringes and dip. And here's his fag and his cola and ashtray and the flowers, fried, and the arrow, extended over the table's edge. And before he even knows it the arrow's aloft. By his hand.

The thing is that the esoteric arrow-in-table trick requires that the overhung nock be knocked upward, from *below,* so that the arrow goes forward and up and down into the table before the nonchalant trickster. But however Sternberg, maybe out of ignorance, or pride, whacks the arrow's overhang from *above:* hence its parabolic transmission backward, over his shoulder and ass-over-teakettle into the air behind him, only to hit the thickly anomalous window of the indoor lounge, rebound, and land javelinlike in the pear compote of the effete, narrow-faced, corduroyed pesticide salesman who's wangled a tête-à-tête with the blonde orange-faced flight-attendant who served him on his commuter flight from Peoria and who'd let slip, en route, while making change from the coin-cartridge at her belt, that she had to stick around C.I. Airport after descent, waiting for a ride of some sort, and whom the pesticide salesman wants very much to ball, age- and face-color-considerations temporarily on hold, because things haven't been going well for the pesticide salesman, lately, at all, given that this year's generation of corn pests seems to have developed a genetic immunity to—worse, more like an epicurean *taste for*—his company's particular line of pesticides, cornfields soaked in this pesticide now sought out by the most discriminating-palated pests, who have been observed under research-laboratory magnification using their little legs and mandibles actually to spread the stuff with the even care of marmalade on a leaf or kernel before digging in, a horror, the pesticide company's best hope for salvaging the fiscal year now being to take a suggestion from their marketer at J.D. Steelritter Advertising and pitch the stuff as a pest-*distractant,* new brand name Pest-Aside, to be sprayed on untilled or infertile fields as a red pickled herring to divert and so prevent entomological inroads into the more verdant and condiment-free cornfields; but it's a bit late in the game for this ploy to do more than cover some losses, and the pesticide salesman is angst-ridden and red-eyed and effetely low on self-esteem, and wants very much to ball this ageless but oddly sexy orange-faced stewardess, as further coverage against estimable losses. The stewardess is brittlely blond, her face orange, though stained port near the temple. She owns luggage that can be pulled instead of carried. Her name is Magda, with the *g* being silent and the *a* accordingly diphthongulated into something like the *i* in "child" or "lie."

And but so the narrow-faced pestidor, poised over his compote, reacts to the sudden and quivering and doubtless low-on-his-list-of-expected-appearances appearance of the big wicked Dexter target arrow with a shocked spasm that sends Magda the flight attendant's morning brandy straight into her lap.

"What the hell is *that?*" Sternberg hears the salesman cry behind him, and winces a why-him wince.

"Oh, *gee,*" cries Magda, instantly up—trying, as the spilled-upon try, somehow to back away from her own clothes. Sternberg, who like most people of his *generation* tries to brush eye-averted and shoulder-first past whatever disorder he causes, and also not anxious to confront anybody right now, what with an ominously dark gabardine crotch—and seeing, right that very minute, a polka-dotted and loose-limbed Ronald McDonald come galumphing up to deposit a butt in the Avis ashtray and a golden-arched nametag to both D.L. and Mark Nechtr, the latter declining to be tagged and directing the attention of clown, Avis lady, guy who looks like Jesus, and holy shit *J.D. Steelritter* himself toward the lounge, toward him, Tom Sternberg—tries to brush shoulder-first past the little disorder Mark's arrow has caused. However, the understandably pissed-off pesticide man, compote punctured and love-object brandy-stained, arrests Sternberg's flight with a wedding-banded hand and aims an isoceles system of nose-pores at Tom's good eye.

Sternberg tries the brusque variety of a "Sorry about that," moving shoulder-first, hands cupped before him.

"I'm afraid sorry won't quite do, here, young sir."

"Young sir?"

"Look at my *skirt*." Magda sighs.

"You've . . . *stabbed* my breakfast."

Though brandy in the lap isn't a completely downer-type sensation, really. Not on a par with cold water on the groin of the ambivalently embodied. Water from the automatic sink is still gushing defective, by the way, from a faucet below and just South of a woman whose white face, frozen in a photographically forevered climax, adorns the wall's condom concession; and the overflow is just beginning to shine at the base of the men's-room door, to spread a dark arc against the thin industrial carpet of the lower terminal.

"It was an accident, dude," Sternberg says, forehead aflame as Ronald's giant floppy tread lounge-ward sounds. "I'm late for this real important ride that's finally just here, so maybe we could just . . ."

"I am not a dude, and you are not riding off anywhere without some kind of significant gesture of apology."

"What's up, gang?" the clown asks from the nearby lounge door, a cool clown, making a fist to look at nails that are obscured by cotton gloves. Behind and beyond, J.D. is illustrating some wide remark to Nola (she of the translucent wart) at the mobbed Avis counter.

"I *said* I was sorry, man," Sternberg says, deciding equally-pissed-off is the way to play this one.

"There a Sternberg and or an Ambrose-Gatz here?" DeHaven asks, nodding briefly over at the pouch-eyed overtime bartender, who's punching out, shedding his inevitable green vest as the elevated screen goes peacefully static for the first time in days.

"Yes that's just it you have *said* you are sorry, and only then when I stopped you." Red-eyed and somewhat blue-balled, the salesman, who manages to be effete in corduroy, no mean feat, hears his own night-flight sleep-dep signal, the sound of an infinity of mutated little jaws munching, little legs patting contented little thoraxes. "But you've made no *gesture*."

"I got a gesture for you, if you want a gesture."

"He's *said*, but not *demonstrated*," the pesticide man appeals to the stewardess.

"I'm Magda Ambrose-Gatz," says Magda, at herself with a moist napkin.

"And I'm Thomas Sternberg."

DeHaven's painted smile broadens over a smear of abortive beard, to which particles of pancake makeup cling, as he distributes the Reunion's very last tags. He looks Sternberg over. "Mean zit on the old forehead, there, big guy."

"It's poison sumac. It's not a zit. And this on my pants is *water*."

DeHaven has turned to the salesman, looking intimidating as only a professional clown can. He sizes the effete man up. "Think you're pretty hot shit, don'tcha."

"The temperature of shit doesn't enter into it. This . . . *apparition* of a boy has deliberately spilled Rèmy on my date."

"It's not a zit."

"And I'm not a date," comes Magda's quiet-when-calm voice from Sternberg's inverted side.

Sternberg is struggling to restrain his rose-fed desire to jab the effete man's still-arresting hand with the fruity tip of Mark's arrow, which Magda, still on Sternberg's blind side, has removed and is inspecting. But the restraining hand is removed by the fine plump hand of J.D. Steelritter, who at this moment intrudes on Tom's sight as a cigar, a stomach, and a hand from above, freeing him. J.D. clears his throat.

Some people can ask whether there's any trouble here in a way that ensures a correct negative. Imagine the obverse of a greedy lover's midnight query:

"YOU AWAKE?"

The writer and academic C—— Ambrose, with his birthmark and cheery smile and a maniacal laugh the whole workshop has decided we associate most closely with Gothic castles and portraits with eyes that move, exerts an enormous influence on Mark Nechtr's outlook. Even when Mark doesn't trust him, he listens to him. Even when he doesn't listen to him, he's consciously reacting against the option of listening, and listens for what not to listen to.

Ambrose tells our graduate seminar that people read fiction the way relatives of the kidnapped listen to the captive's voice on the captor-held phone: paying attention, natch, to what the victim says, but absolutely *hanging* on the pitch, quaver, and hue of *what's said,* reading a code born of intimacy for interlinear clues about condition, location, outlook, the likelihood of safe return. . . . That little aside cost Mark two months.

But Dr. Ambrose isn't immune to this kind of stuff either. He's clearly obsessed with criticism the way you get obsessed with something your fear of which informs you. He told us all right before Thanksgiving to imagine you're walking by the Criticism Store, and you see a sign in the store window that says FIRE SALE! COMPLETE ILLUMINATION, PAYOFF, UNDERSTANDING AND FULFILLMENT SALE! EVERYTHING MUST GO! PRICES GUTTED! And in you scurry, with your Visa. And but it turns out it's only the sign in the window *itself* that's for sale, at the Criticism Store.

D.L. claims Ambrose ripped even that obsessive little image off, that the professor's whole "art" is nothing more than the closet of a klepto with really good taste.

And yet the stuff exerts a kind of gravitylike force on Mark Nechtr, who distrusts wordplay, who feels about Allusion the way Ambrose seems to feel about Illusion, who regards metafiction the way a hemophiliac regards straight razors. But the stuff sits on his head. D.L. doesn't. It's really kind of a wonder he produces at all, back East.

In a related development, as you stand shoulder-first across thirty orthogonal meters between you and the red ring that encloses the gold chroma, and draw your 12-strand string to the tip of your nose, the point of your arrow, at full draw, is somewhere between three and nine centimeters to the left of the true straight line to the bull's-eye, even though the arrow's nock, fucked by the string, is *on* that line. The bow gets in the way, see. So logically it seems like if your sight and aim are truly true, the arrow should always land just to the left of target-center, since it's angled off in the wrong direction right from the beginning. But the straight-aimed and so off-angled target arrow will stab the center, right in the heart, every time. It is an archer's law that makes no sense. How is this so?

In a related fashion, occasionally a writer will encounter a story that is his, yet is not his. I mean, by the way, a writer of *stories,* not one of these intelligences that analyze society and culture, but the sort of ignorant and acquisitive being who moons after magical tales. Such a creature knows very little: how to tie a shoelace, when to go to the store for bread, and the exact stab of a story that belongs to him, and to him only. How to unfurl a Trojan, where on the stall door to carve BEWARE OF LIMBO DANCERS, how to give the teacher what she wants, and the raw coppery smell of a scenario over which he's meant to exercise, not suffer, authority. And yet occasionally the tale is already authoritatively gutted, publicly there, brightly killed, done by another. Or else menacingly alive, self-sufficient, organic, sounding the distant groan of growth, trading chemicals briskly with the air, but still outside the creature who desires to take it inside and make a little miracle. How is this so?

The explanation for the latter lies way beyond anyone presently inside DeHaven Steelritter's frightening car, unless you want to buy Tom Sternberg's post-Murphy axiom that life sucks, then spits you out into a Dixie cup, then you pay the tab, gratuity, and Massachusetts sales tax.

The explanation for the former is as obvious as the nose we look beyond: it lies in what happens to the well-aimed arrow when it's released; what happens *while it's traveling* to the waiting target.

Things roadside keep mangling and reconstructing the car's shadow. C.I. Airport recedes behind them, Southeast, still clearly visible, should anyone care to look back. Its control tower's light rondelles, shining with the pale weak quality the sun lends manufactured lights. They pass road-kill, a Corrections Facility sign interdicting any stops for hitchhikers, unmarked gravel roads, the odd mailbox, and the odder fallow field, cropless but boiling with pests in a frenzy Mark can't figure.

They do not pass so much as are entunneled by corn, two walls of green that loom right up flush against what Sternberg hopes is a straight quick blacktop shot to Collision and Reunion. DeHaven drives with just one wrist, his white glove tapping something brisk and martial on the top of the dash. He occasionally and for no clear reason exclaims "Varoom!" D.L. humps it between the clown and J.D. Steelritter, who's on shotgun. Magda has the hump in back and is flanked by Sternberg and Mark Nechtr, who's now so impatient with D.L. over the whole Datsun thing that he's afraid someone might lose his temper, here.

They were just past the pay lot's attendant's booth, J.D. flashing a voucher that raises any gate, when they got passed screamingly on the right by two young men and a blur of beard in something low to the ground and exquisitely foreign that treated the lot's speed bumps like moguls.

Mark comes to the sudden realization that he doesn't have his Dexter Aluminum target arrow. The one that's been under his surgeon's shirt, stabbing. Sternberg has left it back in the lounge, in that sad-looking guy's compote.

"What about the van?" D.L. is shouting into DeHaven's too-white ear.

"Whut?"

"Mr. Steelritter's money-and-fear man said he called for a van for us!"

"Huh?"

"He lied!" yells J.D.

"What?"

"He *lied!* Close that fucking window, kid!"

DeHaven complies. Sternberg whimpers softly as they're sealed in.

"He lied," J.D. says. "Also doing fieldwork in false reassurance. Strategems and effects."

"That guy who looked just like Christ lied?" Sternberg asks.

"He looked like a Mormon," says Mark.

D.L. turns. "Mormons don't wear beards, darling."

Mark doesn't even bother to mention Donny Osmond's new beard. He's close to feeling upset as hell. His best wedding present, erect in heavy syrup. His prized inexpensive possession.

"No vans left," J.D.'s explaining, crunching a Rothschild's tip with gusto. "No limos left. Everything's worn down, all down at Goodyear, with Mr. Wrench." J.D.'s head is fine and utterly round, his hair rigid, thick, fitted snugly over forehead and some very red ears, trailing close-clipped sideburns. His hair suggests the squat immovability of the best Romanesque façades. No telling, of course, about DeHaven's real hair, though his yarn has been window-blown the wrong way, slightly over its bright slight central part.

J.D.: "My own car, down with Mr. Wrench and company. We've been shuttling and shuttling. Everything's in the shop."

"Three straight days *Varoom*," says DeHaven.

"Three virtually nonstop days of supervising and shuttling, thousands of people, most of them personally," J.D. says. In enclosed spaces his voice is much smaller than he, utterly without resonance, and seems to issue from a smaller person in his pharynx somewhere, a square root of Steelritter.

"You were late as hell, you two," he adds, producing a lighter with a tall flame.

"Problems with LordAloft." D.L. sniffs.

"Hey, man, three miles," the clown says, squinting past the furry steering wheel's axis. "Three more miles, then the odometer rolls over. To all zeroes. That's two hundred thousand on this baby. That's a big varoom, when the odom—"

"Shut up, shitspeck."

"Shit, Pop." Voice of a whiny sullen hood, Mark thinks.

". . . hate this car," growls J.D. He turns to those in back, his face a red planet impaled by a cigar, his eyes bloodshot. He's looking at Sternberg's bad eye. "On behalf of McDonald's I apologize for this car. This was our last car. Collision is not big on transportation."

"Plus try to get an alum to part with his car," DeHaven says.

"It's not that bad a car," D.L. says, smiling at DeHaven, whose lipstick dooms him ever to appear to be smiling back. He lights a cigarette with a complex nonchalance that confirms what Mark's suspected.

The car sat idling in a Forbidden Zone as the six approached. Sternberg pulled Magda's luggage for her. D.L., still groggy, was almost epileptically out of step with the other five, half hanging on her husband as he looked curiously at Magda and her stained skirt.

The car itself looked like a car for neither adults nor children. It was a huge, ageless, jacked-up, malevolent sports car—practically a car with fangs. Its crude paint job was the kind of gold-with-silverish-glitter-in-it one associates with postwar Formica. The interior was red. The car was a pastiche, home-assembled from scrounged parts, complex, rimed—much like the kind of cars assembled, maintained, and cruised in by Maryland hoods who roll cigarette packs into their sleeves and beat up sensitive heirs to detergent fortunes just on general principles. Mark narrowed his eyes at DeHaven: there may've been a pack up there in the polka-dot sleeve of that Ronald costume. One tough clown.

The deposit of a trunkful of heavy luggage didn't change the car's jacked-up posture one bit, either.

"This isn't a Datsun," D.L. had stated flatly, crossing her arms and advancing a foot to tap. Mark's now being in the back seat, and she in front, is directly traceable to this remark. Sternberg, whose tongue tasted metal at even the thought of riding six in a car, had rolled his eye. This girl was too damn much. On the plus side, his slacks had dried in the white sun almost instantly. Brandy being a tougher nut than automatic water, Magda's brown flight-attendant skirt was still stained. Also tight and slit, and sexy. J.D. Steelritter's walk resembled the noiseless glide of her pulled luggage.

"I'm seen only in Datsuns," D.L. said.

"This car's built from parts." Ronald McDonald slammed the loaded trunk hard, so that the dice suspended from the rearview did a jagged dance. "I built this baby from scratch. It's not technically an anything. It's a me, if it's anything."

"Shut up, shitspeck."

"I'm under instructions to avoid cars that aren't Datsuns," D.L. said firmly.

"Jesus fucking *Christ*," Sternberg moaned.

Mark now had his hands out before him, apart, palms opposed, his eyes cast upward.

Magda looked over at him. "Prayer?"

"Mosquito." He clapped, looked at his red palms. "Full, too."

J.D. Steelritter was looking D.L. over speculatively. They were all perspiring in the humidity by now, though Sternberg led the field in gabardine slacks and a forehead full of tributaries. His sumac throbbed in the sun.

"Let me guess," Steelritter said, looking D.L. over speculatively, supporting a big lower lip with a finger and that finger's elbow with his other arm's crook. "Artist," he speculated. "Free-form sculptor."

"Writer. Poet. Postmodernist. Regionally published."

"I'll take the hump," Magda Ambrose-Gatz volunteered. She got prettily in the back of the growling car and slid over.

"Tell you what, Eberhardt." J.D. Steelritter knows you have to know when to concede the easy concession. She'll get hers. "We write DATSUN in the shameful no-pride dust on the kid's rear window, here," scrawling a big NISSAN next to the WARSH ME! that was already there. He made a voilà with his hands, one finger dark. "Now it's a Datsun."

Mark laughed. Pretty resourceful.

It both relieved Sternberg and gave him the creeps. "An instant Datsun?"

After an interval of further interpretation and persuasion, a kind of undignified scramble for places ensues, resultant positions appearing above. DeHaven grinds gears—the gearshift in this car is up next to the steering wheel, where Mark has before seen only automatic shifts. DeHaven's manipulations of the idiosyncratic shift summon images of fencing.

He guns the car, which, instead of shuddering or rattling the way
home-assembled things are supposed to, seems rather to gather
itself more densely into its wedged shape. He guns it. We seem to
be minus a muffler.

"Varoom!" shouts the clown, rolling down his window and laying
quality rubber.

"Hibbego!" shouts J.D. Steelritter, thinking how if the speck of
shit says *For Whom* one more time he's gonna . . .

To the Egress. To the Funhouse.

And as they drive more deeply into the Central Illinois countryside,
which encases them in a cartographic obelisk, walled at the sides
and tapered to green points at the horizons front and back, Magda
Ambrose-Gatz—who, way back, newly divorced, just twenty-one,
way, way back, before recorded history as understood by the *four
young people here,* had represented the very first housewife on the
then-embryonic McDonald's national campaign to realize and reveal
through interpretive tap dance that, hey, she deserved a *break* from
the vacuum and hot stove her equally tap-happy husband had remanded her to, a break, today—Magda starts up a conversation in
back, that hard kind to carry on from the hump, flanked by boys,
her head swiveling like a tennis spectator, in answer to Sternberg's
awed remark that he'd no idea there was this much corn on the
whole *planet.* She explains that the usually awfully generous U.S.
government won't reimburse Illinois farmers for leaving their fields
fallow—the soil's too rich here, and the macroeconomics of the
nation's richest fields dictate maximum tillage—and but that, in the
dark screw *micro*econ drives into the agricultural picture, that very
fertility produced so *much* corn—so thick and tall that DeHaven
must (as was in a way foretold) downshift and pump distressingly
vague brakes at every rural intersection they pass, slow way down,
scan for vehicles whose perpendicular approach the crops' sheer size
would obscure—so much corn that it's literally worthless, oodles
(her term) of bushels of Supply that intersect the market's super-

(Sternberg's term) elastic Demand curve down near the base, where Supply equals oodles and Price equals the sort of coin you don't even bother to bend over to pick up if you drop it. There's agronometric bitterness in her voice, which resonates even at low volume—the result of breasts of high caliber, Sternberg figures—as she sketches with broadly historical strokes the unworkable marriage that sent her West from Tidewater regions, postwar, in time to marry a speculator in Illinois land, and then but how the land got so fertile it's worthless, if that makes sense, but how the speculator—presumably a Mr. Gatz?—was married to the land, and wouldn't leave, even after a foreclosure that forced them to live in his car, a car with tailfins, cervically pink (embellishment Mark's), so that soon she was having to do commercials, in nearby Collision, to supplement income; and then but commercial offers withered up as she aged (gracefully), and her face got sort of orange (inference Mark's)—and the speculator's attachment to land and car got to be . . . well, she divorced the speculator, who now dabbles in pesticides, though not the unfortunate brand currently viewed by pests as incentive, and now she's a flight attendant—an aloft waitress, she terms it—for a commuter line, with turboprops and unpressurized cabins, though she still cameos in the occasional Steelritter BrittAir ad, though always from the rear, a rear which is shapely and not at all orange (inferences and embellishments flying like unspoken shrapnel all over the inside of the menacing car), and is touching, ever so lightly, Sternberg's own gabardine leg through Magda's brown skirt, though there's a good-sized gap of red vinyl seat between her other ham and the leg of Mark Nechtr.

And, in a way, there's a sort of colored gap between Mark Nechtr and everybody else in DeHaven's homemade car. He has no historical connection to where they're going, has never appeared in a McDonald's commercial, has no connection to anything here except D.L., through a mistake and miracle and the ethical depth to try to do what ought to be right by her, although shouldn't she be showing by the end of six months? And but nobody at the Reunion will know him, or want anything from him, and he's left his equipment in an O'Hare locker and a dish of overpriced fruit. He feels unconnected, alone, sort of alienated, in transit, tightly enclosed, surrounded by a vast nothing that's alive.

He asks Magda the obvious question about to whom the remark about the unworkable Maryland marriage had been a reference, given her hyphenated name, but the question is forfeit in a great high-velocity wind as J.D. torches another Rothschild, and his cracked window positively roars, and also admits a lot of odd little gnats, and Sternberg behind J.D. lights a 100 in retaliation and also cracks *his* window, and D.L. coughs significantly and flips on the Heathkit radio DeHaven has built into the deep-red dash of the car, loudly. The static of the radio as D.L. scans for something contemporary sounds, to Mark, like Atlantic surf. The mixture of J.D.'s and Sternberg's lit offerings is a kind of violet gas that swirls frantically around in the sunlight that lights the eastern half of the homemade jacked-up car.

Sternberg asks, with a barely hidden pathos, if they're almost there yet.

D.L. homes in on an audience-participation-call-in program on a crime-and-gospel station that identifies itself in three-part slide harmony as Wonderful WILL. The program, at near the top of DeHaven's 110-watt capacity, is something called "People's Precinct: Real-Life Crimes," today's installment entitled "Murder or Suicide: *You, the Audience,* Decide." A stormy Midwest love affair ends in the impalement and death of one of the lovers. The other lover was at the scene, but only the dead lover's fingerprints are found on the weapon. "You," the announcer says, "the Audience, Decide." Giving a 900-number. Certain evidence is presented, and Mark feels the stab of a story that is his own, yet true about others.

Sternberg is asking Magda just where they are. The car moans on turns and clicks on smooth tar. They've already turned onto small rural roads several times. The two open windows are yielding still more little insects as they pass a rare night-black fallow field. The insects are weird, small, have transparent wings, seem not to fly, but just sit there, all over the windows' insides, inviting squashing; and, when squashed, smell.

D.L. looks up from her notebook and poem—the only person Mark's ever seen who can produce anywhere, even when being jouncily propelled—assumes her mean-nun posture at the radio's presentation of hideous crime, and shouts into J.D. Steelritter's red ear that one of the best indications that some sort of apocalypse is on the way is the fact that violent public crime's scales of practice are tilting: how it seems like, each year, violence reveals itself less and less as the capacity, and more and more as just the raw bare opportunity, to harm. DeHaven responds by shouting that the only really sure sign of cataclysm's coming is if the Cubs actually win the pennant, as this year they're in danger of doing. J.D. asks him to shut up, waving irritably at a tailgating car to pass. The car does pass, a Chrysler, crammed with Orientals. It's doing about 100.

J.D. Steelritter says goddamn slopehead Orientals. They're taking over the planet. It'll be either them or insects on top, at the end. And precious little difference either, he might add. He smashes some of the gnats that sit stoically on the jouncing dash. Smells at his fingers. They're all over the place, he says: fucking Orientals. Doing their calculus at age eight and working their blank twenty-hour days. Realizing their only strength is in numbers. He asks when was the last time anybody in this car ever saw an Oriental alone, without a whole ant-farm of other Orientals around them. They travel in packs. The Chrysler that's passed them had a bumper sticker that asks you to be careful: baby on board. J.D. is able to talk, gesture with his hands, and smoke all at once.

Mark pinches a smelly gnat and gazes out his window. DeHaven's driving fast enough so the rural highway's broken center line looks almost solid. The corn is stunted right here a bit, and Mark's view goes sheer to the earth's curve: dark green yielding to pale green, to dark green, to just green, with some tight white farmhouses and wind-breaking trees clumped at the seam of the southern horizon.

J.D. Steelritter, like many older adults, is kind of a bigot. Mark Nechtr, like most *young people in this awkward age,* is NOT. But his aracism derives, he'd admit, from reasons that are totally self-interested. If all blacks are great dancers and athletes, and all Orientals are smart and identical and industrious, and all Jews are great makers of money and literature, wielders of a clout born of cohesion, and all Latins great lovers and stiletto-wielders and slippers-past-borders—well then gee, what does that make all plain old American WASPs? What one great feature, for the racist, brings us whitebreads together under the solid roof of stereotype? Nothing. A nameless faceless Great White Male. Racism seems to Mark a kind of weird masochism. A way to make us feel utterly and pointlessly alone. Unidentified. More than Sternberg hates being embodied, more than D.L. hates premodern realism, Mark hates to believe he is Alone. Solipsism affects him like Ambrosian metafiction affects him. It's the high siren's song of the wrist's big razor. It's the end of the long, long, long race you're watching, but at the end you fail to see who won, so entranced are you with the exhausted beauty of the runners' faces as they cross the taped line to totter in agonized circles, hands on hips, bent.

In a related development, Mark Nechtr is now revealed by me to have professionally diagnosed emotional problems. He's actually been in and out of places, something that would astonish the kids at E.C.T. who value and love him. It's not that Mark's emotions are disordered or troubled, but that he is troubled in relation to them. That's why he usually appears cool, neutrally cheery. When he has emotions, it's like he's denied access to them. He doesn't ever feel *in possession* of his emotions. When he has them, they feel far from him; he feels disembodied, other. Except when he shoots, he very rarely feels anything at all. And when he is shooting, pulling slowly on his complicated bow, his statued hands in fingerless black archer's gloves, the 12 strands singing and wicked shaft whistling as it starts left of where it ends, he stands somewhere outside himself, eyewitness to his own joy.

I.e. either he doesn't *feel* anything, or *he* doesn't feel anything.

Magda Ambrose-Gatz's predicament is the obverse, and way more noble and tragic. And but *no one can ever know this*. Because where Mark's makeup is that of a subject, Magda's own character—

female, and precontemporary—is that of an object. Mark affects
that of which Magda is an effect. She has always been an object:
of child Ambrose's prepubescent, femininely-rhymed longing; of
adult Ambrose's cold postmodern construction; of the land speculator's need for *läbensraum;* of the unfeeling hand of agricultural
mac- and microeconomics; of J.D. Steelritter's desire to sell desire;
and now of Mark's own speculative machinery. There's neither
claustrophobia nor egress for this ageless alumna, this lovely seaside
girl whose errant trainer-strap built a flat Funhouse, who probably
wouldn't know the betrayed taste of a cooked flower if it bit her
on her ageless orange nose. But she never objects. She takes it
awfully well. She never has to *affect* neutral cheer, or health. Unlike
the young Mark Nechtr.

The sunlight gets quartzy, the sun Southward; its slant creeps
across Magda's dappled Orlon skirt, toward him. Mark Nechtr is
just way luckier than she. He, silently, objects to just about everything. He has *desires,* though he doesn't yet know what for. He
wishes he had the arrogant balls to just sit down and make up a
story about the adult Magda, about the Reunion and the Funhouse
franchise, Jack Lord, about Ambrose's supply of fried roses, his
perverse reward for eating beauty, the special arrow he's lost but
can't throw away. A song of tough love for a generation whose eyes
have moved fish-like to the sides of its head, forward vision usurped
by a numb need to survive the now, side-placed eyes scanning for
any *garde* of which to be *avant.* In the story he wants to make up,
the one that doesn't stab him, he'd be just an *object*—of irritation,
accusation, desire: response. He wouldn't be a subject. Not that.
Never that. To be a subject is to be Alone. Trapped. Kept from
yourself. Nechtr and Sternberg and DeHaven Steelritter all know
this horror: that you can kiss anyone's spine but your own. Make
love to anybody or anything except . . .

But Mark can never know that other boys know this, too. He
never talks about himself, see. This silence, for which he is loved,
radiates cry-like from his central delusion and contemporary flaw.
If his young companions have their own special delusions—D.L.'s
that cynicism and naïveté are mutually exclusive, Sternberg's that

a body is a prison and not a shelter—Mark's is that he's the only person in the world who feels like the only person in the world. It's a solipsistic delusion.

"I'd describe my current thinking as a sort of progressive minimalism," DeHaven is telling Drew-Lynn, who's killed the radio drama to hear the clown's description of his ambitions as an atonal composer with a bitchingly expensive Yamaha DX-7, to replace his outmoded Moog. "What I'm aiming for is a kind of fusion of the energy and what's the word *verve* of popular music with the intellect of like a Smetana or a Humperdinck."

J.D. snorts, but is otherwise strangely quiet, as if brooding. The car roars and the wind roars. It's too hot even to mention.

"I detest any and all kinds of minimalism," D.L. says firmly.

DeHaven shrugs and removes the illuminated red nose and yarn wig, revealing a curved Steelritteroid nose and dark hair of surprising brevity and lustre.

"Well minimalism in music just means the repetition of these real simple chords. Except the minimal attractiveness comes from simplicity of the repetition and not the simplicity of the chords."

"Put it back on," J.D. growls, shifting the cigar in his mouth to indicate without looking at the red tangle that now lies, like a yarn wig with a glowing nose, resembling nothing, beneath the rearview's dancing dice.

"Pop, for Christ's sake—"

"Am I unbent? Did we not have a conversation just now back there? Did we not both make concessions? Did we not arrive at a negotiated settlement about what a *job* was?"

"But Christ Pop it's *hot,* and I—"

J.D. stares straight ahead. "Define for me, speck of mine, the negotiated meaning of the word 'job,' again."

DeHaven stares icily at a black highway he's long stopped having to see, replacing the red wig but leaving it askew. The red nose, heavy with AA cell, slides toward the defroster-crack between windshield and dash and is lost from view.

Between teeth DeHaven says: "A job is where, when you take

on a job, you do things whether it feels good to do them or not, because you promised, by the fact of taking on the job."

"What a memory. Makes a father swell with—"

"I don't see how anybody here gives a shit if I wear a red wig or not."

"You represent *McDonald's,* shitspeck. It's not you who's driving. You represent the world's *community restaurant.*"

"*It is* awfully hot, Mr. Steelritter," Magda says, leaning forward to make herself heard. Mark hears her. The only evidence of a bra is a kind of knob at her back's center, under her brown Orlon blouse, over her spine.

J.D. ignores her. "Have some fucking pride, DeHaven."

"We there, just about?" Sternberg pipes up, his hands in his lap as he stares reluctantly at Magda's blouse's knob, where hooks that men can't undo and women can undo with just one hand behind their back lie engaged in complexly-imagined relations.

"No," says J.D.

"Umm, long way?"

"Odometer's just about ready to roll," says DeHaven, watching the numbered wheels' implacable spin.

J.D. broods, removes, crunches, and reignites. The red interior fills again with the green stink of cigar. Sternberg goes back to being ignored. D.L.'s cough sounds like a laugh, and is also ignored. A classy no-nonsense scarecrow of black woven iron, more like a decoration than a real scarecrow, right up flush roadside, messes nastily for an instant with the car's shadow. Mark's just as glad about the wig's being back on, not out of any special ill will toward this Ronald kid—

"Anyway, my music I want to do has affinities with the work of like a Glass or a Reich, but with more . . . *progression.* Harmonically it's even more atonal, and rhythmically it's got this kind of fascist quality I'm drawn to, a kind of jackboots-marching-on-a-small-Polish-town quality."

"Hush," J.D. says absently.

"It's music that grabs you by the lapels and says give me all your land or I'll gut your livestock," DeHaven sums up quickly. "Though in a much more cerebral way. And with percussion out the *ass*."

—but because its removal had revealed that the clown's heavy garish makeup simply *ended*, right around the top of his neck and the curve of his round cheeks, yielding to regular red wind-burned Steelritter skin with an abruptness that Mark just didn't like at all.

"Don't you even remember?" D.L. has turned to address Sternberg. "Don't you remember how out of the way the McDonald's set was, back then?"

"Collision's in the middle of nowhere, kiddo."

"C.I.A.'s the closest airport and helipad, but it's still no laughing matter, how remote Collision is."

"On purpose," J.D. says, balancing his cigar on his heavy lower lip. "You don't go to client. You make client come to you. That way the cap's in *his* hand. Client comes a complex series of long ways to see you, has a tough journey, encounters bad roads and no maps and detours: client's convinced already, en route, that your services have value, for him to be wandering all over hell's half acre like this just to find you." J.D. beams grimly. Mark notes that DeHaven can silently lip-sync his father's whole speech. Plus his summation:

"A-very-wise-guru-at-the-top-of-a-tough-to-climb-mountain strategem," J.D. says. "It's no coincidence it's the gurus on *mountains* who're wise. You get to the top: you're already theirs."

Everyone lets this sink uneasily in.

Sternberg clears his smoker's throat, directing this sound somehow at the flight attendant beside him. "Sorry about your skirt, and stabbing your date's fruit."

"It's all right," Magda says, smoothing yellow hair back behind her ears. "And he wasn't my date."

"Except what about my Dexter?" Mark asks flatly.

"He was just a passenger," Magda explains.

"My arrow, Sternberg," Mark says, leaning a bit to look across Magda's front at Tom's boiled-egg-colored eye, trying to feel angry. "You left it back there, didn't you."

"I have it," Magda says.

Mark shifts his gaze to her. A sudden jounce—pothole; "Shit," DeHaven exclaims—makes his stomach rise in that rapid-descent way.

"It's in my carry-on." She smiles. "In the trunk. I'll give it back to you when we're there."

Mark looks at her orange face. "Thank you. It's kind of my favorite. It's the only one I can get through Security. It's aluminum." He pauses. "Thanks again."

She laughs. "It looked pretty obscene, just sticking out of that compote. I thought one of you'd want it."

"Well thank you," Sternberg says.

"Yes. Thanks." The thing cannot be lost. Even shot it at the sea once. Off an old wharf. Except it *floated,* though, glinting; hung in the water by its cedar knock; came in on the sluggish tide within hours.

And Mark had waited for it. On the crumbled wharf that smelled of fish. The fact that the arrow can't disappear is both a comfort and a worry. It makes Nechtr feel special, true. But from special it's not very far to Alone.

Although we all, Mark would know if he bothered to ask J.D. Steelritter, who'd done solipsistic-delusion-fear research back in the halcyon days of singles bars, we all have our little solipsistic delusions. All of us. The truth's all there, too, tracked and graphed in black and white—forgotten, now that fear of disease has superseded fear of retiring alone—sitting in dusty aluminum clipboards in a back archive at J.D. Steelritter Advertising, in Collision, where they're headed. We all have our little solipsistic delusions, ghastly intuitions of utter singularity: that we are the only one in the house who ever fills the ice-cube tray, who unloads the clean dishwasher, who occasionally pees in the shower, whose eyelid twitches on first dates; that only we take casualness terribly seriously; that only we fashion supplication into courtesy; that only we hear the whiny pathos in a dog's yawn, the timeless sigh in the opening of the hermetically-sealed jar, the splattered laugh in the frying egg, the minor-D lament in the vacuum's scream; that only we feel the panic at sunset the rookie kindergartner feels at his mother's retreat. That only we love the only-we. That only we need the only-we. Solipsism binds us together, J.D. knows. That we feel lonely in a crowd; stop not to dwell on what's brought the crowd into being. That we are, always, faces in a crowd. It's Steelritter's meat.

O the sadness of J.D. Steelritter, a man who brings crowds into being! A crowded planet would lie right down for love of the men who build what they want built. But for the man who builds their *wants?* A drink on the house? God forbid a pat on the back, ever? A hug? A television Movie of the Week, the "J.D. Steelritter Story," sponsored by his sponsors, J.D. portrayed as the type of hero who *overcomes?* A sensitive novel from C——— Ambrose in which J.D., manipulator of image and sign, succumbs via epistasis to the be-witchment of the Mesmermaze he spins and is forced via resolution to transcend, to come of age, to see? *Something,* no? But no. TV about bodies politic and people with dying bodies or robbers and cops puncturing bodies or doctors resealing bodies. Novels about novelists writing novels about novelists, who never succumb. Cute stories that slouch, sullen, clever, coy, no hair on the chests forever.

Though let's not get a wild hair up anything: he has no real bones to pick with Ambrose-as-builder, -entrepreneur, -*Consumer.* And why think of anything except what's just ahead? The Reunion will be huge. Larger than life. Beyond belief. Forty-four thousand ac-tors, endorsers, celebrities, former actors, returning. 44,000 who will—photorecorded—reunite, greet, meet and eat. *Eat.* An irrup-tion of ninety-nine-and-forty-four-one-hundredths percent pure consumption. The cameras' shots will be panoramic. You'll need the side-placed eyes of a deep-depth fish just to even hope to take it all in. The enormous crowd J.D. hath wrought over thirty years of time purchased second by expensive second will come together, lose the supplicants' courtesy that atomizes crowds, and desire past all earthly care the rendition of fat, the sigh of oil, the sparkle of carbonation, the consumption of government-inspected flesh. They will revel in meat, lips stained purple with the fried blood of Steel-ritter's floral tonnage.

Still-distant Collision is a madhouse. Frantic, clotted, teeming with alumni begging to stay. The obverse of Saigon's fall. The townspeople, descendants of an accidental market, have learned to change big bills—everywhere there are souvenirs, homemade concession stands. Twin arches of plated gold have been erected, each the size of St. Louis's Gateway, and below their giant twin paraboloid zeniths a gemmed altar that demands, recorded, to let it give you a break. The predella itself a lawn-sized golden patty. And everything that's been built—arches, altar, predella—has been perforated and filled to spurt and shower U.S.D.A. Grade A blood at the ecstatic moment of Jack Lord's helicoptered approach. The sight will be halcyon, chialistic. He will watch desire build to that red-and-gold pitch, that split-second shudder and sneeze of thirty years' consumers, *succumbing,* as *one.* And this is the one secret of a public genius: it will be the Storm before the Calm. Gorged with flora and the fauna their money's killed and shipped frozen to serve billions, the alumni will give in, reveling, utterly.

And that, as they say, will be that. No one will ever leave the rose farm's Reunion. The revelation of What They Want will be on them; and, in that revelation of Desire, they will Possess. They will all Pay The Price—without persuasion. It's J.D.'s swan song. No more need for J.D. Steelritter Advertising or its helmsman's genius. Life, the truth, will be its own commercial. Advertising will have finally arrived at the death that's been its object all along. And, in Death, it will of course become Life. The last commercial. Popular culture, the U.S. of A.'s great lalated lullaby, the big re-mind-a-pad on the refrigerator of belief, will, forever unsponsored, tumble into carefully salted soil. The public, one great need, will not miss being reminded of what they believe. They'll doubt what they fear, believe what they wish; and, united, as Reunion, their wishes will make it so. Their wishes will, yes, come true. Fact will be fiction will be fact. Ambrose and his academic heirs will rule, without rules. *Meatfiction.*

And Steelritter, in what he's foreseen? He'll retire to the inter-section where everything started. At peace in the roaring crowd's center. Maybe have a long-needed nap, stretched out on the intersected road, each limb a direction, cigar a sundial. He'll relax and feel the great heavy earthspin beneath him stutter, flicker, oppose.

He will be the object of appreciation. He will be not just needed. He will be loved. Beloved. Because he will *Re-Present the Product.*

He broods, riding shotgun. He's smoked his cigar down to the point where he feels the heat of the thing on his lips. The woven-iron scarecrow recedes in no time. He pegs his butt out the window and, because he wants it so, ceases to brood, his great forehead smoothing like a smartly-snapped sheet. Soon they'll make the last turn West.

They're passed by a chicken truck in a tremendous hurry. Its sides are like the sides of a crate. Its passage is a spray of feed and feathers against DeHaven's windshield. The action of the home-made wipers (furious) sends the clown's redly pulsing nose all the way inside the crack between glass and instrumentation. The nose falls completely out of anybody's notice, resting somewhere inside the dash.

Our six in turn pass an enormous old farmer who's hitchhiking on the barely-there shoulder of the county road. You can see his old harvester disabled and listing tiredly to starboard in the waving corn behind him. On the moving car's other side, the very tops of the two giant arches glint, just visible, inclined like a child's severe eyebrows just over the countertop line between land and the baby-blue iris of a sky that looks down all day at food. J.D. is the first to make out the arches' tops—give that man a cigar, he smiles—because the other five are all looking at the big farmer, hitching, motionless, a statue rushing toward them. He's huge; his thumb casts a shadow. The malevolent clown's car sprays him with gravel.

"Not enough room for a farmer that big in here, dude," DeHaven says.

"You don't usually see big old men," D.L. says speculatively. "Big men seem to die young. Have you seen many big old men? It's rare. Usually they die."

This is kind of thoughtless. Both Steelritters are pretty big. So's Mark Nechtr.

DeHaven uses maybe two fingers to turn the car left, his other white hand scanning the FM dial. The car moans on the turn. A bit more of the giant blond arches appear, now dead ahead, still distant but revealing more of themselves, the Nordic eyebrows spreading, getting less severe, as the jacked-up car moves toward them. The intersection's road sign had said 2000W. All roads seem to be identified only by numbers and directions out here in the country. J.D. coughs richly. The car's six panes of glass are still speckled with some surviving but still motionless little insects— unkilled, Mark figures, killing one, because they make the killing uninteresting, plus loathsome.

A neglected fact is that a black line—obsidian, really—appeared when they turned truly West on straight-shot 2000W. These are possible storm clouds. They appear as a Semitic hairline above the golden brows.

In a development, DeHaven's gloved fingers have plucked from the tides of daytime static the FM avatar of that same Wonderful WILL station, now deeply into a mid-morning Pentacostal old-time gospel hour. The preacher—you can tell he's a charismatic, a Re-vivalist, because he can do to English what the Swiss can do to French: every syllable gathers to itself a breathy suffix—the preacher addresses himself to the issues of eyes and motes and beams. Al-ludes to the seasons that inform rural spirituality. Makes reference to tight cycles of life, passage, death, passage, life. He holds a mono-tonic high-C idiot note throughout, repeating one or two very simple themes. The high steady whine and breath ring wincingly against the sleep-deprived tuning forks of everybody in the car except Magda, who nightly sleeps, unmedicated, the sleep of the dead. The only variation at all is in the preacher's audience-response; he repeats each epithet three times. His tone is almost frantically la-conic, if that makes sense. Mark cops an image of Camus on speed.

J.D. Steelritter, whose own spirits now vary inversely with the car's distance from the still-distant but at least now visible and spreading arches, from the idea of the revel beneath them, tries absently to recall where and how he hired these particular troublesome, late-to-arrive kids, as children. Eberhardt he remembers spotting as he'd toured, with a guide, the gutted ruins of Ambrose's Ocean City Park. She'd been with her father, a really solid, sturdy-looking man, a Volvo of a man, in a crew cut, muscular under a black satin jacket whose back showed a blue Southeast Asia encircled by a red Kekulian serpent, sucking at its own sharp tail, with the white legend I DIED THERE below. It was the *way* she touched the melted lurid shell of the ruined Funhouse's Fat May, palm to its big sagged forehead, a tiny mother with a giant fevered child, that had excited J.D.—here was a kid at her gentlest with the luridly disclosed. The father had proffered his amputee's hook as J.D. introduced himself. Eberhardt'd been a well-developed, attractive kid. The Sternberg kid he couldn't remember just where he picked that kid up, or why, though he remembers all too well the metal twitter of his mother's voice, the way she kept fucking with the kid's hair and clothes, smoothing him into something seamless and false after J.D.'s time and care had gone into fashioning him as the kind of sad, rumpled kid who orders from intercoms and then eats while he plays.

"I see arches!" D.L. sings out.

The odometer gets extremely close to rolling all the way over.

"Varoom," says DeHaven, watching the dash's numbers. Then he sees something else.

The arches tumesce with maddening slowness, and above the golden rainbows the West's black line has grown to a broad smear. Possibility of rain.

DeHaven's being passed again, this time by a cylindrical fuel truck positively flying toward Collision. Its big silver tube of a rig veers and falls in ahead, wobbling from side to side, red signs on its ass advocating flammable caution and telling exactly how many feet long the thing is. It recedes.

One reason it recedes so quickly is because DeHaven has slowed a bit, because the dashboard's oil light's little red eye is now on.

This is a pretty dreadful development. D.L. sees the red, too. J.D. doesn't. But D.L. doesn't say anything about it to anyone in the car. Why not? Why not? Maybe she likes DeHaven Steelritter, since he's told her about his atonal ambition. You'd have thought ambition like that would sound absurd, exiting the red mouth of a clown. But it didn't, somehow. DeHaven and D.L. now share a bit of a sidelong look that Magda Ambrose-Gatz sees, using the rear-view from the rear. The car seems to roar even more at this new, slightly lower speed.

J.D., even from shotgun, can see the solid line of the rural high-way's broken line break up a bit, now.

"Thump it, kid. We're late. What are you doing? We're aiming for noon at the very outside I said. Here, I know. Take 'em in from the North. We'll shave ten minutes. But thump it. Pedal, metal. *Go.*" He runs both hands through his hair, which is unaffected by hands.

DeHaven turns abruptly right onto something dismally tiny and shoulderless, something called 2000N that looks to Mark almost freshly invented: new tar and mint-white gravel that clatters maniacally on their big sticky tires and hot wells. The big twinned arches reestablish themselves, after a clump of wind-breaking trees, out Mark's own window. He sees them, not surprisingly, as an initial.

Sternberg's voice, shrill and barely controlled: "We're going North?"

"Pop's going to bring you guys in from the Northeast, to save time," DeHaven says, eyeing the red oil light. "Whole South part of Collision's fucking mobbed. Traffic beyond belief. Fuel trucks, chicken trucks, Coke trucks, tourists, concessions, meat trucks, blood trucks. You name it."

The car seems to roar louder the slower it goes. Sternberg thinks the roar plus the clatter of gravel might drive him mad.

D.L. sniffs. "This car is louder than any Datsun."

"What *is* this with you and Datsuns?" DeHaven says, shooting his father a sidelong look and again removing his sweaty wig. Mark looks to J.D., but Steelritter seems to have something on his mind.

"Datsuns are all hype," DeHaven continues—looking, once again, different and abrupt. "Chickenshit engines. Plastic and alloys. No steel. No soul. And you have to like take the whole engine apart to get at anything to fix it if it breaks down. Which it does. They're cars for what do you call them Yuffies."

"I think you mean Yuppies," Mark says.

"I mean Yuffies, man. Young Urban Foppish Farts, is what we call them out here. Yuppies without the taste for quality that's maybe a Yuppie's one redeeming quality. We've heard about Yuppies and Yuffies. Illinois isn't another planet, man."

And for the first time Mark can hear a Midwestern twang in DeHaven's sullen voice.

"Not to mention even credit cards, in terms of young fartness," J.D. says. "You all none of you have one lousy credit card? That's what Nola said, over at Avis."

"Credit cards aren't toys," Sternberg says loudly. Assertively. This can be explained very briefly. Sternberg's emotional state is now officially one of panic. And the panic is on *top* of the claustrophobia. Source of panic: the car's jouncing, and the almost prosthetically firm push of Magda's right breast—they're that close together—have given him the sort of erection that laughs at the restraining capacity of gabardine the way a hangover laughs at aspirin.

"Credit cards aren't toys, to be rushed right out and bought and played around with," he says aggressively, but with a kind of deliberate calm and adult gravity, the sort of tone you use when grandparents ask about plans for the future.

"We have use of my father-in-law's Visa card," D.L. says.

"But we pay the bill when it comes," adds Mark.

"Credit cards need to be thought about," Sternberg insists, hunched, hand a little too casual over his tented lap. Mark sees the anomaly in the gabardine, and Magda seems diplomatically to be avoiding looking down at all. Sternberg closes his good eye, looks deeply within, and battles all-out with an autonomic function that has always defied his will. And obversely. Basically, of course, what he tries to do is sublimate, and he does this the best way kids who don't do sports or abstract oils or major CNS depressants know how.

"Credit is *political*," he pronounces. "It's a tool of the elite. You use credit without thinking, you're unthinkingly endorsing a status quo."

"Oh, Jesus," groans DeHaven—also, interestingly, sublimating his fear of a different mechanical function, one out of *his* control. "Another one of these politically correct ones, Pop. We've had it to here with this correctness shit from alumni, the past few days."

"Ease off, boy."

DeHaven produces a blank dime of a frown, turns a half-human and half-Kabuki cheek to Sternberg's tight corner. "You are one of those correct ones, aren't you. Do you pronounce 'Nicaragua' without any consonants? Pronounce 'Nicaragua' for us."

"I told you to leave the kid alone, shitspeck."

In a development that turns out to be pretty dramatic, Mark brings the Ziploc bag (which he *didn't* forget and leave in the lounge, which gives one pause) out of his complex surgeon's shirt. J.D. sniffs the interior's air almost immediately. The blackness to their left, West, now covers a good half the sky, a lid over something set just on simmer. It could be his imagination, since he's pretty intent on what he's holding, but Magda seems to be looking at Mark with a kind of orange horror. As if in response to something dire.

"And of course that's a zit on your forehead, dude. What is that sumac shit? Can bet *you* won't be in the front row when they start shooting the thing, am I right?"

"Where do you live," Magda says.

Mark looks at her, half-confused. "Baltimore. North Baltimore. Hunt Valley."

She opens her mouth slightly.

"*Everything's* got political implications, for crying out loud," a disgusted J.D. aims loudly sort of halfway between DeHaven, who's wanting to kick somebody's ass on general rural principles, and Sternberg, who's hunched in his corner, sublimating like mad.

"Not anymore," D.L. disagrees firmly.

"Amen and varoom." DeHaven's grin becomes voluntary.

Sternberg, right on the edge, sees Mark's Ziploc, too. Magda
has gone a bit yellow. Ideas now blow through Sternberg's high-
pressure sleep-deprived head like chaff, a kind of beveled lattice
of roses, oil, bodies, amber, sumac, hamburger, shit, Nechtr, Magda,
sex, erections, will, and, yes, politics.

"You're full of it, Drew," Sternberg says. "Mr. Steelritter is right.
Politics is everywhere. Except thank God in stuff like popular culture. That's why entertainment's so important. That's why TV's the
total balls. When it's vapid. Like it's meant to be. Screw PBS. Right,
Mr. Steelritter?"

"It is pretty much the only escape," Mark agrees quietly.

There are nods from everyone but J.D. and Magda. DeHaven
has slowed the malevolent car a bit further.

J.D. turns, smoking, shaking his fine head, disgusted. "I don't
know who of you's more full of what, kid. TV's not political? What
about that "Hawaii Five-O" Nola said you two were watching all
slack-jawed, so taken in you weren't even blinking?" Hiking an
elbow onto the front seat's back to level a centered face and heavy
cigar-supporting lip at Sternberg and Nechtr. "You saying there's
no politics going on on that show?"

The boys' response is immediate and unanimous and negative.

"Pure entertainment."

"Like a blanket so old it's falling apart. Soothing."

"Like blowing bubbles with your saliva. Mindless. Fun just for
the sake of fun."

"Especially in reruns, syndication, that you've seen before,"
Sternberg says, into it, feeling, feeling disembodied, other, flaccid.
"Incredibly comforting. You know just how the universe is going
to be for the next hour. Totally secure. Detached but connected.
A womb with a view."

Steelritter just cannot believe the naïveté of these cynical kids.
He'd trade looks with the older flight attendant in the rearview if
D.L.'s slender head weren't in the way. D.L. and DeHaven are
watching the odometer finally roll all the way over. It's exciting

and gorgeous. There's a slot-machine feel about it, which they share, together, and know they share it. The oil light has settled into a kind of stuttered flicker, which is even more dreadful, if you know your oil.

"I cannot believe these kids today," says J.D. " 'Hawaii Five-O' is not political? We're talking about the same show? The show that ran from '65 to '73? That had helicopter imagery in every episode? Helicopters full of wooden-faced, purposeful white guys in the kinds of business suits capitalism's all about? White guys flying around in helicopters restoring order to this oriental island that can't seem to govern itself, that's overrun with violent and bad and indigenous Orientals? The cop show where all the head guys are white and all their lieutenants are good Orientals in suits, and they all cooperate and co-prosper shooting at the bad Orientals out of helicopters? With this constant reference all the time to a 'Mainland' that seems close to the island and in peril from the island's disorder and in need of what's the word immunization, but which calls Jack Lord's every shot, and justifies all the shooting of natives out of helicopters?"

"Are you trying to draw a Vietnam parallel?" Mark asks.

Disgust and disbelief wrestle for control of J.D.'s big face. "Christ, you poor shitspeck, that show was the most blatant piece of politics ever," he says, imagining just how the Reunion will be, pegging his thick Rothschild, feeling at a crinkling pocket, trying to decide between a petal and a slim Dutch Master.

"He might have an idea there," says Sternberg to Nechtr. "Like those Clint Eastwood Westerns, with the Man with the Gun called back from the Wilderness to save the same threatened Community that out of fear chased him into the Wilderness in the first place?"

"The Deliverer-Hero, with a Weapon, on a Horse?" says Mark.

"The tough but loving tutor who tempers him like fine blue steel? The Bush? Kinobe? Yoda?"

D.L. is utterly silent throughout this exchange, watching the odometer begin slowly to lose its magic. There is a reason for her silence that is in a way parallel to the historical U.S. conflict in Vietnam. For her, Vietnam does not exist except as complicatedly cancelled letters and hissingly connected phone calls, a completely flat-eyed father whom she first met on a tarmac at nine. Who had a hook. Who dropped at automobile backfires (Datsuns never backfire—too little power), who gazed dully and accepting at the mosquito feeding at his one big bicep. Who's long gone, now. Who left a note.

LANCE CORPORAL LYNN–PAUL EBERHARDT'S NOTE, THAT HE LEFT

Dear Void:
The chances of living in the present seem good today.

Yrs.,

From D.L., Mark Nechtr knows only that Lieutenant Colonel Eberhardt is long gone to unknown locales. Never pressed her for details that clearly pained her. Actually, D.L. had started to tell her first and only lover all about it, that night, that time they'd gone (protected) to bed. But Mark, postcoital, had fallen asleep. She's never forgiven him for it. Will never. She was forced to do the whole rehearsed dialogue mono-, playing both parts, Ophelia-like: the only time in her life she's laughed so hard she had to bite her arm to stop:

"My Daddy's long gone. He's whacked. Looned. Zoned. Where all rooms are white and all shoes noiseless. My father has left the planet.

"Well as long as he waves, occasionally.

"I think the only thing he waves at is his food.

"Well, as long as it doesn't wave back. . . .

"I think that's why he waves in the first place."

Took her exclusively to ruined amusements. Liked boarded windows and walks chocked with crabgrass. Read her *Moby-Dick* at ten. One sitting. Whale trivia and all. Told her to call him Lynn.

Bought her a forest-green classic '70s fashion outfit she's had altered and cleaned so often it's lime. Told her she was loved. Would sit only with his back to walls.

He's never once asked for painful personal details, Mark. He'll take what you give him and just nod. He sees and won't cross uninvited this unbroken center-line between your business and his. Keeps his own counsel. Never ever presses. It's one reason he's so universally loved. Plus it's why, within a year after the time when the little miracle should appear but won't, she's going to scald him in his sleep. Bad business. But assault or defense? You decide.

This has, yes, been a digression. But if it's irrelevant, then ours is that part of town you want to make sure you drive through quick, windows sealed and doors locked tight, oil thoroughly checked, and nothing fishy in the dash.

Great lover, though, Mark. Healthy fucker. Energy right out the bazoo. Can fuck her into a sleep only the Dalmanated usually know. Tireless. Hard or flaccid at will. Comes only when he wants, like a cat. D.L. thinks she knows: it's the fried roses the tactful old klepto gives the pupils he's decided to gather to his arbitrary wing. The hors d'oeuvres her psychic pukes at the thought of. Healthily evil. Marries desire and fear into a kind of privately passionate virtuosity.

Mark has kind of a problem with the roses now, she thinks. She sees him getting dependent. They don't talk about it, Mark keeps his own counsel, but the problem with the flowers, she thinks, is what, ironically, keeps him from producing the way he wants.

D.L. simply refuses to eat beauty. It's defilement. A kind of blasphemy for atheists. Aesthetic Murder-One. D.L.'s got some desires, but says no thanks to eating what stands outside you, red and eternal, shouting that it's not food. She won't do it. Not even to be a better postmodernist. This makes her kind of heroic, in a tight-assed, grad-school way. Old fashioned, ironically. She does like the word *virtue. Honor* is even a noun to her, sometimes.

"I thought you knew Jack Lord personally," she says, seeing

through DeHaven's windshield what looks like imperfect tint. They
are thunderheads. "Yet but now here you are, talking down his
show. So why represent LordAloft?"

"I never talk down, Missy. And I do know Jack." J.D. flicks the
dice with a finger while DeHaven keeps his arm on the gearshift,
between J.D. and the stuttered red oil light, his face under the
happy face grim. The oil light's red stutters when the car jounces.
The sound of the gravel is unendurable.

"But Jack is a complex man," says J.D. Steelritter. "I've known
at least three different historical Jack Lords, since I've been in this
business. That was the first Jack Lord, up over paradise in a helicopter, firing blanks at underpaid natives. Then there was a retired,
artsy-fartsy, politically correct-type Jack Lord, back in the Seven-
ties, who sculpted free-form and did gratis spots for Easter Seals.
The new present Jack Lord doesn't fuck around. He's a business-
man. A professional pilot and franchiser. A kind of ideal Yuppie
with start-up capital and entrepreneurial drive and more balls than
are presently in this whole entire rotten car, which by the way did
or didn't I say to step on it, shitspeck. And don't think I don't see
that oil light. Quit with the elbow in my face. Screw the oil light.
I don't trust homemade instrumentation. Go. You've got till noon.
Our shadows get short, I want these folks to be reveling."

"Varoom," DeHaven says, but without conviction. The car leaps
forward a bit, quieting. The golden arches are sort of toward the
rear of Mark's window now. The homemade car is definitely Northeast of Collision. Mark would like a rose, but his stash is low, and
there's nothing he especially wants, except arrival and several cups
of coffee and a shower and sleep. And arrival is not a scenario
anybody can influence, it's starting to seem. It's unbearably slow.

"And shut *up* with that *For Whom* business," J.D. growls at his
son. "Gives me a pain." He extracts and unwraps still another green
Rothschild and crunches the tip and stows it in the wadded plastic
wrapper, all with one hand. The other hand is inflicting absolute
entomicide on the mass of dull, slow, stoic gnats that sit on the
cracked red dash. Those gnats are creepy. Lemming-like. Nihilistic.

Plus dull. An old hand, an actual chain-smoker of cigars, J.D. can also light a cigar with a match (lighter out of fluid) forefingered from its Ronald-emblazoned book and thumbed against the flint paper without being detached, all the while crushing tiny insects. This is not a safe procedure for ignition. Close cover before striking. Why not just use the dashboard lighter DeHaven fashioned out of a high-resistance iron mattress spring?

Because the lighter flies out. It gets way too hot, and suddenly'll just pop out, into J.D.'s fine lap. His son the atonal engineer. Defectively effective homemade dashboard lighter. Represents a product, won't keep a nose on, lets the nose fall into the dash, then whines about red oil lights. J.D. sometimes looks at DeHaven with this sort of objective horrified amazement: *I made that?*

"What do you mean, 'For whom'?" DeHaven is saying to J.D.

"You've been saying it. Repeating it. Two solid days. Back and forth. *For Whom.* Gets in my head. Gives me a pain. Quit with it."

"*Varoom,* I've been saying, Pop. *Varoom.* It's something atonal I'm composing. It's gonna involve engines, speed, lightning-war. It's a title. *My* title."

" 'For whom' are the first couple words of Dr. Ambrose's best story," Mark Nechtr says. D.L. snorts. J.D. draws at his cigar. The car is Cubanly redolent and greenly fogged. Mark is subjected, via crosscurrent from J.D.'s cracked window, to the main exhaust path of the stogie, but does not object. "It's the first bit of his Funhouse story. 'For whom.' "

J.D. grunts the noncommittal grunt of a father who's been mistaken about a son in front of that son. Even a violently rouged son.

"I compose my own stuff, man. I don't go around using other people's stuff. That's for bullshit artists. I'm no bullshit artist."

D.L. nods over her notebook in support.

"Half right, anyway," J.D. chuckles. His chuckle is like neither Ambrose's maniacal cackle nor D.L.'s mucoidal laugh. Has Sternberg laughed yet, ever?

Mark has been more comfortable with the general drift of a conversation before, lots of times. What if the stories that really stab him are really other people's stories? What if they're bullshit?

What if he alone isn't clued into this, and *there's no way to know?* He's afraid he does want a flower.

Plus he has other obvious troubles coming. Magda is asking to have a look at his Ziploc. Her hands are hairy-knuckled, but not orange.

"*Varoom,* I was saying." DeHaven shakes his head, lighting an unfiltered with the same nonchalant ease as his father. He holds the cigarette between thumb and forefinger as he drags, which looks pretty suspicious. Sternberg, too, lights a 100, which because of the eye trouble appears to the side of where it is. And Magda is holding Mark's smeared baggie up to the way-back window's southern light. The light through the NASSIN and !EM HSRAW is clean and penetrating. The arches, too, are now completely behind them.

There's the sort of silence in the loud car that precedes a small-talk question. Conversations between adults and kids tend to be punctuated with these silences a great deal. Then adults ask about present or future plans.

DeHaven, hurrying gingerly in the face of unreliable lubrication data, is no longer even bothering to slow at the dangerous corn-obscured intersections. (There's still lots of corn, by the way.) He fishtails suddenly West onto a 2500W. Again the golden *M* lies left, now fully revealed above a fallow stretch of soil.

"So then what are you kids doing now?" Steelritter asks, smelling the proximity of the last shuttle's end, doing something oral to the great cigar in his mouth so that it recedes, protrudes. He flares the slim nostrils of his hooked nose. A splatter of distant thunder sounds. The air through the cracks cools noticeably. Magda is looking at the side of Mark's face. J.D. manipulates his burning protrusion:

"Any actors left among us?" he asks.

"*Me,*" Sternberg says, swimming briefly into J.D.'s rearviewed ken. DeHaven snorts something about horror movies, and D.L. gives the padded shoulder of his costume a rather over-familiar hush-pinch.

"I'm still in the business, Mr. Steelritter," Sternberg says, voice up an octave as he tries to be casual but courteous. Sometimes J.D. Steelritter actually uses Clout as his middle name, when he signs contracts.

"Well good for you, kid."

"I'm based in the Boston area."

"Damn nice area."

"You bet. I like the area a lot."

"Working steady? Who've you got representing you? Do I know any of the people you're under?"

"I'm kind of still in the exciting breaking-in stage," Sternberg says casually. "I'm waiting for a callback on a Bank of Boston gig. I'm up for the part of a really helpful teller."

J.D. exhales at his own tip, holding the thing up, inspecting it coolly for an even burn.

"I have call-forwarding, for callbacks."

J.D. smiles to himself. "Maybe I can introduce you around to some of the more important folks, while you're all reveling."

"Gee."

"The way I see this business going, after this McDonald's thing, you could have a real future."

"Hey, that's really encouraging to hear, sir."

"Bet your life it is, kid. That's what I do."

"What do you mean that's what you do?" Sternberg asks, confused.

Magda clears her throat demurely against the oxides of three different brands and asks about Mark Nechtr's plans.

"Yeah, Nechtr," J.D. says. "You look like the acting type. Photogenic. Natural. At ease in designer jeans and that doctors' wear. Any acting in your future? Your father's in laundry, Nola said back there?"

Needing very much to exhale anyway, Mark explains that he's really just a graduate student. When DeHaven laughs and asks what in, Mark gets really interested in the floor. Sort of English, he says.

"In creative *writing*," D.L. amends, mostly to DeHaven, who still holds his cigarette like a joint, squinting against smoke between dashlight and road. D.L. turns slightly on the front hump. "He's

actually embarrassed to tell people what he really studies, when
they ask. He actually lies. Why do you do that, darling?"

J.D. chuckles that chuckle. "Hell, Nechtr, no need to be shy
about it. A lot of writing teachers make good solid incomes from
teaching creative writing. There's a demand for it. Sometimes over
at Steelritter Ads we get copywriters who're just coming out of
creative programs. Ambrose himself makes good solid steady money
over at East Chesapeake Trades."

"That's where Mark is. Mark's under him."

J.D. ignores this girl. "Creative programs are one reason the
whole Funhouse franchise thing's finally gotten off the ground.
Writing teachers don't press. They know when to concede. They
defer to people who know what's what in an industry."

"Technically part of English Department . . . technically a degree
in English," Mark mutters indistinctly into the roar of the window
he's opened. Smoke is drawn out the big crack, sliding like the last
bits of grainy stuff down a drain. The combined smokers' smoke
is the same general color as the clouds that have drawn past the
Westward arches and are moving visibly this way. Threads of bright
light appear and then instantly disappear in the clouds' main body—
filaments in bad bulbs. The air cools further, and there's that rain's-
coming smell through the window's crack. Magda leans a bit over
Mark with the flowers and breathes deeply at the roar of the crosscurrent:

"Rain," with a sigh.

And they pass a sudden and alone farmhouse, right up next to
2500W, with its trees and little skyline of silos, and tire swing, and
rusted machinery at angles in the dense grass of its limitless yard.
The fields around the house are full of odd grass-or-hay material.
A big-armed woman in a lawn chair waves from the gray porch, a
wet scythe and styrofoam cooler at her feet. The house's mailbox
has a name on it and is yawning open, waiting for mail. The woman
waves at the growling jacked-up Reunion car. Her wave is deliberate and even, like a windshield wiper. She's a storm-watcher. A

spectator sport in rural Illinois. Obscure elsewhere. But storms move like the very wind out here, no fucking around, building and delivering very quickly, often with violence, sometimes hail, damage, tornadoes. Then they move off with the calm even pace of something that knows it's kicked your ass, they move away, still tall, bound for points East, behind you. It's a spectacle. Mark would normally be more interested in the implications of the lawn chair and wave. He'd kind of like them to stop at the house and try to get some definite directions. Surely they can't be lost. The Steelritters live around here. And if they've been shuttling for three solid days and nights, as J.D. says, the precise way to go should be a deep autonomic wrinkle in DeHaven's brain by now. But they're *circling.* They are not, by any means, creating for themselves the shortest distance between C.I. Airport and Collision, Ill. Mark does know about straight lines and shortest distances. Maybe J.D. and DeHaven are the kind of people who can't navigate and talk at the same time. Mark feels in his designer hip pocket the giant key of the O'Hare rental locker.

"Except he never writes anything," D.L. says. "He doesn't produce. He's blocked. He's thinking of leaving the Program. Aren't you, Mark."

J.D. directs his scimitar and ember at Mark with real interest. "You're paying to go to school to write and you don't write anything?"

"Varoom," says DeHaven.

"I'm not terribly prolific," Mark says, wishing he could wish harm to the back of D.L.'s tightly knotted head.

"He only produced one thing all year," she tells the Steelritters. "And it was so bad he wouldn't even show it to me. Now he's blocked. These things happen in programs. That's why I've decided I detest all—"

"You're blocked?" Sternberg asks Mark.

Mark decides on maybe just one petal, to tide him over against arrival.

"Probably a standards problem," J.D. says, nodding as at the familiar. "I get a creative type under me who's blocked, it always

in the end turns out to be just a problem of unrealistic standards.
Usually."

D.L. and DeHaven snort together at the use of the word *realistic*
as yet another foil-bright fuel truck banshees past in the left lane,
a spigot in back, next to its signs, dribbling amber fluid.

"So what do I do I call them in on the carpet and bitch them
out about how all they've got to do is adjust their standards," J.D.
says, his cigar now just protruding, staying there, saliva-dusky, balanced on his lower lip, so that it moves with the nonchalant grace
of his speech, on that lip. "Adjust themselves downward and forward," he growls. "Adjust their creative conceptualization of, what's
the word attainable felicity."

D.L.'s head snaps up at this.

"That art-school crap's bogus, man," DeHaven muses. "Only
bullshit artists move in packs."

"Silence and speed, shitspeck," says J.D., hiking an elbow again
to look back at Mark Nechtr, the unconnected kid, for whom J.D.
shows a strange but genuine fondness. He gestures paralytically, if
you will: "Adjust this paralyzing desire they have to create the
perfect and totally new ad, is what I tell them," he says. "I ask
them—and remember this, kid, it's free advice—I ask them, do
they think it's any accident that 'perfectionism' and 'paralysis' rhyme?"

DeHaven rolls his mascara-circled eyes. Gravel clatters. A number of blank looks are exchanged. D.L. begins:

"But—"

"But they're goddamn *close enough,* is what I tell them," J.D.
laughs, the laugh of a small enclosed person, his forehead again
snapping clear. DeHaven lip-sync'd this whole thing. J.D.'s laughter
sends his cigar pointing in directions. There's a perilous tilted mountain of ash. His laughter becomes a meaty coughing fit.

Mark, too, laughs, liking this man, in spite of his tough son.

Sternberg deposits his smoked filter in a back-of-the-front-seat
ashtray you do *not* want described and clears his own throat:

"Nechtr, could we maybe discuss the possibility of some of those
flowers, you think, for a sec?" gesturing with his forehead's extra

organ at the Ziploc Mark and Magda somehow both hold below
J.D.'s headrest-limited view.

Steelritter's whole face lights up. The arches are now extremely
near. He's starved.

"You a flower man, kid? What kind? Violets? Roses, maybe? I
manage a little rose-bush farm of my own, back home. We get
there—which we will—you alumni are going to see a greenhouse
to end all—"

Magda quietly interrupts, trying to point out that they haven't
heard about Drew-Lynn's present or future yet; but and then D.L.
interrupts *her,* telling DeHaven and J.D. and Magda that she, D.L.,
is no longer a graduate student but now a real struggling artist. A
postmodernist.

"A postmodernist?" DeHaven grins.

"Yeah, well, we handle Kellogg's," Steelritter says gruffly. "I say
get out of here with your Post products."

"Specializing in language poetry and the apocalyptically cryptic
Literature of Last Things, in exhaustion in general, and metafiction."

Puzzled, DeHaven scratches his scalp with the furiousness of the
recently de-wigged. *"Who'd* you meet?"

Mark is embarrassed for Drew-Lynn. Figure someone has to be.

"In fact I rather wish Dr. Ambrose were coming for his discotheque's opening today, too, although I must admit I no longer
believe in him as a true artist. But I used to believe in him, and
I'd like to see him cut his own ribbon," D.L. says, yawning groggily.

Magda coughs, feels at her pretty throat.

"A genuine and pleasant guy," J.D. nods in agreement. "Never
any client-trouble over the whole long protracted Funhouse process. Doubts yes, but never an aggression, a press; never a real
cross word. Seldom an ego. Also a flower fan, photogenic kid back
there, by the way. You're under him? And he's got this wife who
just can't stop smiling," he says. "Ever met that lady? So pleasant
all the time it hurts. Dimples like bullet holes."

Behind a barbed-wire tangle can now be seen the Correctional
Facility whose sign, way back at C.I.A., had said not to give rides.

The Facility has slit windows, is low and squat except for guard
towers on stilts, and anyway is just on the whole huge, taking several
seconds to pass. Another sign, this one in red, says the area is
Federal and Restricted. There's no sign of movement Mark can
see. The wall of towering storm clouds is now flush up against the
(*very*) late-morning sun, giving the Southwest sky the appearance
of a nighttime wall, but with a night-light. Sternberg is gesturing
persistently for one of Mark's fried roses; Mark ignores him, listening, rapt.

"Gotta tell you, in confidence, though," J.D. says, craning to see
the sun finally get taken. "Never could get all the way through a
single one of those things the guy writes. Not one of them, and
we're friends. Sent me the whole load of his stuff. Couldn't even
lift the box. Figured that was a bad sign right there."

There's thunder.

"And sure enough," J.D. says. "Un-get-throughable. Troubled
marriages all over the place. Hard as hell to read."

"Marriages?"

"Sometimes boring, too," D.L. says, nodding as if in admission.
"Indulgent. Cerebral but infantile. Masturbatory. A sort of look-
Dad-no-hands quality."

"Hey, now, Sweets."

"Or, in the opposite concept, too," J.D. Steelritter says, butting
his cigar in another clottedly ghastly ashtray, hearing in the corn's
pre-kick-ass-storm hiss that idiot-high *For Whom* he'd thought was
his son's idiocy; "too smart. Too clever for its own good. Makes it
too coy."

"Almost Talmudically self-conscious?" Mark says. "Obsessed with
its own interpretation?"

Magda has pressed against Mark in the asexual way of a stranger
next to you at a really scary film, her left shoulder muscular and
port-wine birthmark bright.

"Personally I'm a hundred percent behind your basic phenomena
of interpretation," J.D. says. "Interpretation is meat on my table
and burger coupons in you kids' wallets. But for instance this story

we had to use to blueprint the franchise campaign off of . . . that *For Whom* story, in Sixty-Seven. Liked the concept. Did *not* like the story. Do *not* like stories about stories."

D.L. snorts softly to herself.

Steelritter looks down at her. "Because never did and never will do an ad for an ad. Would you? A salesman selling salesmen? Makes no sense. No heart. Bad marriage. No value."

Mark has leaned forward, smelling cannabis and talcum and carbolic and amber from DeHaven and D.L.

"Stories are basically like ad campaigns, no?" J.D. says. DeHaven isn't lip-syncing this one. "Which they both, in terms of objective, are like getting laid, as I'm sure you know from trade school, Nechtr"—looking briefly back. " 'Let me inside you,' they say. You want to get laid by somebody that keeps saying 'Here I am, laying you?' Yes? No? *No.* Sure you don't. I sure don't. It's a cold tease. No heart. Cruel. A story ought to lead you to bed with both hands. None of this coy-mistress shit."

By way of a weather report: the dark fingers of scout-clouds have reached past the sun and are groping at the malevolent car's broadly shallow sky. Shadows fall in county-sized stripes, making gray bars in dull-green terrain, an oriental watercolor whispering muted color. And Tom Sternberg, whom Mark has been studiously ignoring, and whose debilitating claustrophobia you've probably forgotten because he's been just strength embodied, so far, in the speeding crowded enclosed car, has that erection, still, sees no way politics can be brought into the above discussion, is now dreadfully afraid of himself, wants one of those scale-of-stasis-yanking fried blossoms, except now can't get the distracted, rapt Mark's attention. And is clubbed between the eyes with an idea. He asks J.D. Steelritter whether his own rose-bush farm grows the roses the Maryland academic Mark trusts cuts and fries and turned Mark on to. This is a cataclysmic development: Magda's yellow silence is that horrified public kind of one whose seatmate has farted at the ballet.

FINAL INTERRUPTION

Mark Nechtr has taken a keen personal interest in J.D. Steelritter's informal criticism of Dr. C——— Ambrose's famous metafictional story, "Lost in the Funhouse." He thinks J.D. is wrong, but that the adman's lover/story analogy is apposite, and that it helps explain why Mark has always been so troubled by the story, and by Ambrose's willingness now to franchise his art into a new third dimension—to build "real" Funhouses. He believes now that J.D. Steelritter and the absent Dr. Ambrose have not just "sold out" (way too easy an indictment for anybody to level at anybody else), but that they've actually done it *backwards*: they want to build a Funhouse for lovers out of a story that does not love. J.D. himself had said the story doesn't love, no? Yes. However, Mark postulates that Steelritter is only half-right. The story does not love, but this is *precisely because it is not cruel*. A story, just maybe, should treat the reader like it wants to . . . well, fuck him. A story can, yes, Mark speculates, be made out of a Funhouse. But not by using the Funhouse as the kind of symbol you can take or leave standing there. Not by putting the poor characters in one, or by pretending the poor writer's in one, wandering around. The way to make a story a Funhouse is to put the story itself in one. For a lover. Make the reader a lover, who wants to be inside. Then do him. Pretend the whole thing's like love. Walk arm in arm with the mark through the grinning happy door. Shove. Get back out before the happy jaws meet tight. Reader's inside the whole thing. Not at all as expected. Feels utterly alone. The thing's wildly disordered, but creepily so, hard and cold as windshield glass; each possible sensory angle is used, every carefully-taught technique in your quiver expended, since each "technique" is, really, just a reflective surface that betrays what it pretends to reveal.

Except the Exit would never be out of sight. It'd be brightly, lewdly lit. There'd be no labyrinths to thread through, no dark to negotiate, no barrels or disks to disorient, no wax minotaur-machina to pop out on springs and flutter the sphincters of the lost. The

Egress would be clearly marked, and straight ahead, and not even all that far. It would be the stuff the place is *made* of that would make it Fun. The whole enterprise a frictionless plane. Cool, smooth, never grasping, well lubed, flatly without purchase, burnished to a mirrored gloss. The lover tries to traverse: there is the motion of travel, except no travel. More, the reflective surfaces in all directions would reflect each static forward step, interpret it as a backward step. There'd be the illusion (sic) of both the dreamer's unmoving sprint and the disco-moonwalker's backward glide. The Exit and Egress and End in full view the whole time.

But boy it would take one cold son of a bitch to write such a place erect. A whole different breed from the basically benign and cheery metafictionist Mark trusts. It would take an architect who could hate enough to feel enough to love enough to perpetrate the kind of special cruelty only real lovers can inflict. The story would barely even be able to be voluntary, as fiction. The same mix of bottomless dread and phylogenic lust Mark feels when he bends to the pan's sizzle to see what . . .

Except Mark feels in his flat young gut, though, that such a story would NOT be metafiction. Because metafiction is untrue, as a lover. It cannot betray. It can only reveal. Itself is its only object. It's the act of a lonely solipsist's self-love, a night-light on the black fifth wall of being a subject, a face in a crowd. It's lovers not being lovers. Kissing their own spine. Fucking themselves. True, there are some gifted old contortionists out there. Ambrose and Robbe-Grillet and McElroy and Barthelme can fuck themselves awfully well. Mark's checked their whole orgy out. The poor lucky reader's not that scene's target, though he hears the keen whistle and feels the razored breeze and knows that there but for the grace of the Pater of us all lies someone, impaled red as the circle's center, prone and arranged, each limb a direction, on land so borderless there's nothing to hold your eye except food and sky and the shadow of one slow clock. . . .

Please don't tell anybody, but Mark Nechtr desires, some distant hard-earned day, to write something that stabs you in the heart.

That pierces you, makes you think you're going to die. Maybe it's called metalife. Or metafiction. Or realism. Or gfhrytytu. He doesn't know. He wonders who the hell really cares. Maybe it's not called anything. Maybe it's just the involved revelation of betrayal. Of the fact that "selling out" is fundamentally redundant. The stuff would probably use metafiction as a bright smiling disguise, a harmless floppy-shoed costume, because metafiction is safe to read, familiar as syndication; and no victim is as delicious as the one who smiles in relief at your familiar approach. Who sees the sharp aluminum arrow aimed just enough to one side of him to bare himself, open. . . .

But here's a development. Recall that the regulation competitive arrow, at full draw, is aimed a bit left of center, because of the dimensions of the bow—the object that does the shooting, and which gets in the way—but which, in the way, *resists,* is touched, moved, *irritated* by, the shaft's stubborn rightward push. Because, irritated, it resists, quite simple premodern laws come into play. The uncentered arrow, launched leftward by the resisting bow, resists that leftward resistance with an equal and opposite rightward shudder and spasm (aluminum's especially good, for the spasm part). This resisting shudder again prompts a leftward reaction, then a rightward reaction; and in effect the whistling arrow zigzags, moving—almost wriggling, really—alternately left and right, though in *ever diminishing amounts* (physics, law, gravity, stress, fatigue, exhaustion), until at a certain point the arrow, aimed with all sincerity just West of the lover, is on line with his heart. Someday.

Yes: it sounds less erotic than homicidal. Forget Renaissancemblances between fucking and death. In today's diseased now, everything's literal; and Mark admits this sounds deeply nuts. Like slam-dancing, serial killings, *Faces of Death Parts I–III,* civilian populations held hostage by their fear of foreign target areas. It is neither romantic nor clever, Mark knows. It is cold. Far colder than today. Colder than killing people because you need what they need. Colder than paying someone just what the market will bear. Than falling asleep while your bloody-armed lover weeps that you fall asleep instead of ever listening. Than splattering gravel on someone who's too big to fit.

And, worse, it sounds dishonorable. Like a betrayal. Like pulling out of what's opened to let you inside and leaving it there, fucked and bloody, tossing it away like a stuffed animal to lie twisted in whatever position it lands in. Where's honor, here, in what he sees? Where's plain old integrity?

I LIED: THREE REASONS WHY THE ABOVE WAS NOT REALLY AN INTERRUPTION, BECAUSE THIS ISN'T THE SORT OF FICTION THAT CAN BE INTERRUPTED, BECAUSE IT'S NOT FICTION, BUT REAL AND TRUE AND *RIGHT NOW*

If this were fiction, the cataclysm that prevents the six people in DeHaven's homemade car from ever actually getting to the promised Reunion in Collision would be a collision. DeHaven, out of a sullenly distracting attraction to the terse minimal girl beside him, or out of some timelessly Greek hostility toward his father riding shotgun with his big wet cigar, would close his eyes and put the accelerator to the floor at the very most verdant and obscure rural Illinois intersection—say, 2000N and 2000W—and collide three-way with the Oriental-crammed Chrysler and the foreign flashy car full of the big old farmer's corn-fed children. The Orientals, being expendable through sheer numbers, would be toast. The two cars full of shaken but unharmed Occidentals would end up somehow on top of each other, facing opposed directions, windshields mated like two hypoteni come together to blossom a square of chassis and crazily spinning wheels. Our six and their six would sit there, upside-down, looking at one another through patented unbreakable glass, their faces illuminated against the darkness of approaching rain by the flaming toaster of a foreign Chrysler.

If this were fiction, Magda would turn out in reality to be not Magda Ambrose-Gatz, but actually Dr. C—— Ambrose in disguise. It would turn out that Mark Nechtr had long ago been chosen

by Dr. Ambrose as the boy who would inherit clever academic
fiction's orb and gown, and that Ambrose has historically tracked
and kept tabs on and encountered Mark in any number of ingenious
disguises, à la Henry Burlingame of the seminal *Sot-Weed Factor*.
Magda/Ambrose would illustrate, via an illuminating and entertaining range of voices and dialects, the identities in which s/he has
kept atavistic watch on Mark's progress toward adulthood:

'Faith everlastin' me lad but you're growin' like the very hills'
heatherrrrr.'

'Father Costello? Mom's old priest, who heard her confessions,
and came for dinner every month?'

'Left at the next corner, please.'

'Officer Al? The officer who gave me my first driving test, in my
old Datsun?'

'Oh, that's not it. Not there. Let me . . . oh, there. Oh, yes. See?
Oh, *God*.'

'Charlene Hipple? From the YWCA? The archery coach who
took my virginity?'

And so on. Dr. Ambrose, who values the selflessness possible
only in the disguise of a voyeur, would be on the way with the five,
less to see the Funhouse open than to see the unfolding of the
Reunion—which he, like J.D. Steelritter the adman, views as the
American fulfillment of a long-promised apocalypse, one after which
all desire is by nature gratified, people cease to need, and enjoy
value just because they *are*. In the best kind of Continental-Marxist-
capitalist-apocalyptic tradition, the distinction between essence and
existence, management and labor, true and false, fiction and reality
collapses under the unrelenting dazzle of Jack Lord's aloft search-
light.

If this were fiction, the fried roses that unite J.D. as cultivator,
Ambrose as distributor, Mark as consumer and disciple, D.L. as
Manichee, Magda as apostate, and Sternberg as supplicant would
be rendered—by the magical process of quick-frying—all the *more*
lovely, as roses: crimsonly brittle, fine-spun red-green glass, varnished in deep oil and preserved in mid-blush for unhurried in-

spection, as trapped in flight as a gorgeous pest in amber. But the roses J.D. Steelritter has demanded that Mark Nechtr fork over this fucking *instant* are sootily dark, bent, twisted, urban, dusty, ugly and oily in the kind of smeared big Baggie junior-high dope comes in.

"What's the deal with these," the best in the business asks flatly.

"What deal?"

"You're saying Ambrose gave you these, aren't you."

Magda is giving Steelritter a look almost as steady as Mark's.

"I didn't know I was saying anything at all, sir."

DeHaven glances over with a son's special fear as J.D. gives suddenly in to an anger as total as the corn they drive through:

"Listen you little speck of shit these are *mine*. I plant them and care for them and kill them and prepare them. These, for you, are for *later*. Part of the whole Reunion package. That professorial fart and I had a negotiated gentlemen's agreement. These are for *his* fears. Not for him to pass out on streets. I'll ask you again. He gave you these?"

"Nechtr did say he got them from somebody he trusted a lot, Mr. Steelritter," from Sternberg's corner.

"I'll stamp him out. He's through in the industry. In every industry. Ambrose is dinked. He's zotzed."

"Of course he got them from him," D.L. says, her tone weariness over glee. "Just tell him, love."

"I got them under the condition I don't say where, if asked," Mark says quietly.

"That *rat*," J.D. says, his voice high with disbelief. "That hairless arrogant puss, that I brought up from a franchised nothing."

"Pop, this oil light's flashing kind of bright, right here."

J.D. is rapping his big forehead with the heel of his hand. "How fucking *untidy*."

"Nechtr said they give you an odd sort of self-control, sir," Sternberg says. Which Mark did not. Mark doesn't even look at him. He's staring at J.D. Steelritter's fine face.

"These things are the violent end of American advertising, kid,"

J.D. grimaces critically at the dusty, well-traveled crud in the blurred Baggie. "Advertising embodied."

Sternbeg horrified for real: *"What?"*

DeHaven's own distracting confusion sends a plume of talcum from a well-scratched scalp. "But we eat those suckers all the time," he says. "Fridge's full of them. Mom has to buy extra baking soda. They don't taste great, kind of corny. Mom says creative geniuses have perverse tastes, is all." He looks down at D.L. "What's the deal?"

DeHaven's oil light flashes OIL, illuminating redly each time the clown's lit nose is jounced with the car on the shittily maintained county road.

"They're obscene," D.L. says without expression. "That's the only deal they're part of."

"They make certain wishes come true, sir, don't they," Sternberg says.

Magda looks at Sternberg as if he's about five.

"Don't be an *idiot,*" J.D. shouts, as they nearly sideswipe that Chrysler, which has fishtailed out of a blind verdant intersection's gravel and is now going East, the wrong way. The sunlight's color through the clouds is that of quality licorice, and the air is chill. Lightning convulses in the sky's western flank.

"Make wishes come true," J.D. snorts. There's no cigar in his mouth. "They make *wishes.* There's a difference, no?" Yes, he thinks. Until the Reunion.

"They're obsce-ene," D.L. says in the singsong of the ignored.

"Take what you fear most and turn it to wishes. Ambrose doesn't know what he and you are into, kid back there."

Mark says he has no idea what Mr. Steelritter is talking about.

What Mark Nechtr fears most: solipsistic solipsism: silence.

What Tom Sternberg fears most: whatever he's inside.

What Drew-Lynn Eberhardt fears most: as yet unbetrayed, thus unknown.

What Dr. C——— Ambrose fears most: the loss of his object

and interpretive wedge: stained skirt, prostheses, pretend-history, blonde wig off its stem.

What DeHaven Steelritter fears most: see below.

"You think an ad's just a piece of art?" J.D. is saying. "You think it's not about what life's really about? That your fears and desires grow on trees? Come out of nowhere? That you just naturally want what we, your fathers, work night and day to make sure you want? Grow up, for Christ's sake. Join the world. *We* produce what makes you want to need to consume. Advertising. Laxatives. HMO's. Baking soda. Insurance. Your fears are *built*—and your wishes, on that foundation." He raises above his headrest Mark's stash, and his own. "These were my own Pop's. From a funeral, back East. They bring the two inside each other. Marriage of violence. Shotgun wedding."

"Cooking flowers is supposed to get you off?" DeHaven says. His half-and-half clown's profile pivots between creepy confusion and complete fear of his own instrumentation.

"They're a drug?" Sternberg says. "Except organic? An anti-fear pro-desire drug?"

"They're *wrong*," D.L. says in the strident voice of her Tarot tutor. "They *stand* for the fact that they're wrong. They're not only obscene symbols, they're *clumsy* symbols."

"Steelritter . . ." Magda begins huskily.

J.D. waves the rearview image of her orange face and askew wig aside, now so into what he's bet his life on that he's almost sublimated his utter dread about rain diluting the Reunion. Fucking Midwest weather. He says, "The Post-product missy's right, on this one. They're just symbols. They're about as subtle as a brick, for Christ's sake."

"Eating symbols?"

DeHaven's looking at the steady red light. "Pop?"

J.D. cannot believe the back-stabbing innocence of a man who'd pass out symbols like they grew on trees. He addresses the back through the rearview. "And you think how you appear, how you feel, are your adman's only levers? Your only source of fear? That Today has gone on forever?"

Sternberg's affirmative is ear-splitting.

"Then you've got some coming of age to do, Mr. Always-looks-at-himself-half-the-time. 'Cause the ad business goes way, *way* back. You've got fears so deeply conditioned they're ingrained. Built right in. Hidden in plain sight. You know you feel it, back there. This feeling it's so conditioned it's part of you. As in there's certain things that, no matter what, one *doesn't do those things*. You *don't* kill your father. You *don't* betray your lover. You *don't* lie. Except when absolutely necessary. You *don't* aim a loaded weapon. Except in self-defense."

You don't disappear," D.L. says tonelessly. "You don't scald people in their sleep."

"I'd go ahead and put those up there, too," J.D. nods seriously, grim. "And another one, see. You *don't* put what's beautiful inside you, as fuel, when the whole reason it's beautiful is that it's outside you. Supposedly certain things are in the world. To see. Not to chew up and swallow and expel."

DeHaven's point of view on all this is diffracted. He's thinking of the probably several tons of roses he's consumed, at the farm-house, over his childhood; and experiencing a growing affinity with D.L. Eberhardt, who's looking, as she hears the confirmation of her psychic's sagest advice, more and more like a cat hissing at the big shadow of some nameless and total threat—and has pretty well-developed canine teeth to begin with—and he's getting more and more afraid that a sleep-deprived J.D. is maybe off his fatherly nut, a bit, about the roses that have no, and I mean *zero,* historical effect on DeHaven; and the de-nosed clown is afraid that J.D.'s going to make him drive his malevolent car, that he built and lubricated with his own two ungloved hands, right into oil-depletion and sei-zure and breakdown; and begins to wish very much that they could simply stop, idle a bit, let J.D. calm down about what're only after all *snacks* and *commercials,* let DeHaven have a look at his own dipstick . . . that they could simply stop to check how things are, under the glittered hood; that they could suffer a brief interruption that would maybe probably ultimately *save* time; wishes they—

"Pop."

"But those deep-in-your-bones feelings are conditioning, too," J.D. says. "You know what the first real ingenious timeless ad campaign even *was?*" He sees in the rearview two blank stares flanking two closed eyes. "Jesus," he shakes his head in disgust. "But the *boredom,* at least: even you kids know you feel the boredom in your gut, right along with the fear. *'Do not do what is not right.'* Tired image. Hackneyed jingle. No marriage, anymore. Obsolete. Conditioning has obsolescence built right in. Like the Jew what's his name and his bells and dogs that drool. Dog hears the ching of that fucking bell over and over, plus his pups, generations of dogs, *ching, ching,* till the sound is like the sound of the dogs' own blood in their heads—they can't hear it anymore, don't listen—they after a while stop the drooling over meat the bell had started. Give them enough time and enough bells and they start *yawning,* at the ching. Over at Steelritter Ads we've done conditioning research up to here," holding one hand like a blade to his fine head's top, gently squeezing the flowers with the other, in the bag.

"Not doing what you know deep down is wrong to do is boring?" Mark says, feeling the stab of a particular numbness he associates with qualities that ought to make him glow.

J.D. hears nothing but his own small voice and *For Whom:* "So thus the same fears that inform your whole what's the word. . . ."

"Character," murmurs Magda Ambrose-Gatz.

". . . character: can't hear them, can't be moved by them, they're such old hat, by today," J.D. says. He turns, hiking an elbow. "Your adman's basic challenge: how to get folks' fannies out of chairs; how to turn millennial boredom around, get things back on track, back toward the finish line? How to turn stasis into movement, either flight or pursuit?"

"Make the listening unfashionable?" Mark says.

J.D.'s tired eyes widen as he nods. "But how to do that? How to do that? With *symbols,* is how. You make a *gesture.* You *show* you *desire* not to hear the ching."

"You behead an unsubtle image of what beauty is and fry it in lard and consume and digest and excrete it?"

"Turn your biggest fear into your one real desire?"

"Sounds pretty damn political," Sternberg suggests.

"Except what's everybody's biggest fear?"

"That Mormon researcher had whole lists of them."

"*Pop.*"

"No no *no*," J.D. shakes his head impatiently, gesturing with a cigar he does not hold. "The one *big* one. The one *everybody* has. The one that binds us up, as a crowd."

"Death?"

"Dishonor?"

"I'd go with death, darling."

"My vote still goes to having a body, dudes."

"*Pop.*"

"You *gesture*," J.D. says. "You sell out the squeak of your own head's blood. You sell out, but for selling-out's *own* sake, without end or object"—he looks above right, at the storm clouds, which are getting spectacular—"change the tired channel from life, honor, out of nothing but a *desire* to love what you fear: the whole huge historical Judeo-Christian campaign starts to spin in reverse, from inside."

"A campaign spins?"

"We're bored animals"—J.D. makes a summing-up gesture. "Even the naïve ones know that. Bored numb with the sound of bells, the taste of meat. But *ring meat*," he says, "and you can bet your life you'll *eat a bell*. And *like* it."

The unmuffled engine dies, the jacked-up car coasting in a sudden roaring absence of homemade sound and halting in the shoulderless space between rural blacktop and bare fallow field, by the field's ditch, in dirt, maybe a quarter-mile from where the road they're on takes its last curve left, West, dead into Northeast Collision. All that's there to hold your eye up ahead are three tiny rural shacks, shanties, up by the big broad leftward curve. The shanties keep you from seeing exactly where the curved road goes.

The complete silence in the quiet car, as it rolls to a crunching stop in the dirt, is like whole *minutes* of that second right after loud music stops. "*Like* it" ricochets around in the red interior as the malevolent car gives up the ghost in the roadside dirt, coming to rest perpendicular to a barbed fence between a lush verdant healthy cornfield and a rich black fallow field, boiling with confused pests lured by a taste for quality.

"Varoom," the clown says to himself weakly, squashing a placid gnat.

J.D. is suddenly very calm. He has a wristwatch. Jack Lord is scheduled to arrive over Collision *soon.* He is afraid. Sadness and anger and disgust at Ambrose's not-worth-it betrayal are scattered like the dust the car's halt has made, all before the great cold wind of a genius's fear. J.D.'s two great sheet-wrecking nightmares are missing his own Reunion and being stalled in someplace sweeping and panoramic and unenclosed and ever-growing.

There's a great ripping fart of thunder.

"Fix the car, please," he says softly as the first fat drops hit the windshield.

DeHaven is out with a stiff whimper. The windshield yields a sudden view of glittered hood.

"Could we just walk?" asks D.L.

"Not getting out of the car," J.D. says calmly. "Still two total miles or more. Rain. My suit will run. I can't preside wet. We'll stay here. The kid's got a way with machines."

Streaks of DeHaven's real face can be seen through the trademark face as the clown slams the hood shut in the spattered rain. The dice under the rearview jump at the slam, and the oil light pulses.

"Filter's a gem," he says, reentering. "My dipstick's clean as a whistle."

"I'll let that pass," J.D. says coolly.

"The lubrication seems totally OK," the clown sums up in a voice that makes you think he wishes it weren't.

"So start the car," J.D. says, managing at once both to clap his hands and look at his watch. "Hibbego. Let's go. Couple more miles. It'll be tit."

DeHaven shakes his head miserably, his lipstick rained into

something sad. The trashcan clatter of more thunder is now in-
distinguishable from echoes of that thunder. Big Midwest drops
start hitting the car's roof in that rhythmless, tentative, pre-serious
way.

"Start the *car!*" Sternberg screams, so that Magda jumps on the
hump. Mark closes his eyes, silent, lost in his own counsel.

DeHaven hooks a begrimed wrist over the fuzzy wheel and lights
an unfiltered with maddening deliberation. He shakes his head:

"This car doesn't just stop and start. The engine's Detroit and
the ignition's foreign. It's an admittedly ad hoc combination. You'd
call it a bad marriage, Pop. But those were the parts I could get
deals on. So I have to just keep it running all the time. Can't let
it stop. A motherfucker on gas. You wouldn't let me park it by the
greenhouses, Pop, remember? Because of the exhaust? It doesn't
even need a key, see?"—pointing a grease-tipped glove-finger at
the empty slant of an ignition receptacle where a key should be.
"Because if it stops, when you try to start it, the engine goes like
out of control." He exhales smoke with force. "Plus it was the oil
light made it stall, Pop," indicating the little plastic window that
covers his costume's nose. "I'm sure we've got internal problems
somewhere. I'll fuck up the belts."

"Try it, please."

"I'll make the timing belt jump if I do. We'll jump time. We'll
fuse cylinders."

"Give it a try, please, son," J.D. whispers, as roof-rain sounds.

The empty ignition screams to life. And, true to the clown's
word, the car's idle is now wild, tortured; the engine revs crazily,
way too high, so that ancient needles flap spastically in the dash.
The malevolent car stalls the second the clown reaches up by the
furry wheel to put it in a forward gear. It shudders.

"*Great,*" Sternberg yells, having cadged the Ziploc J.D.'s left on
the front seat's backrest. "*Great.* Fix the *car,* you shitspeck rotten
clown." He feels too enclosed to bear.

The adman is looking through the shield's angled rivulets at the
three wharf-gray shanties up where the last road takes its final

Westward curve. The ancient askew shacks are interconnected by a system of corrugated plumbing pipe. J.D. breathes deeply and counts the three shanties out loud, willing the Reunion to remain temporarily on hold. They'll wait for him. Jack, aloft with his bull-horn, above a sea of red smiles, the cameras sweeping panoramic, looking for what to latch onto. The rain can be worked in somehow. Could enhance the whole conceit. Funhouse 1 will be opened and used, then 'dozered. J.D. Steelritter gets stabbed in the back by a client exactly once. No Funhouse franchise. No erection of memory for Herr Professor C—— Ambrose, rat. No angled systems of mirrors Windexed nightly by anally compulsive teams in white. No barrels and disks on the dance floor. No happy fellatory door. No parts that shine, burnished to reflect and refer to every other part. No whole new dimension in alone fun.

It's going to rain one fuck of a lot, they can all see. 2500W steams. The stuff seems to fall in bright curtains that close and part at the discretion of gusts. The rain threatens to enclose the stalled car. Sternberg's bad cheek is right up next to his smeared window, pressing against it, bloodlessly white. He's sure he's going to puke. The clouds before the curve and car are huge. They have an almost Trump-like architectural ambition. Mark can see still more rain coming, off to the West, but coming, braids of it hanging from the sky and whipping back and forth like tinsel in wind, the real meat of the thunderstorm now probably over Collision and the now-obscured giant arches and the sheltering tight-roofed Funhouse club, where all the adults and former kids are in out of the elements, waiting, raising flashcards emblazoned with the word GLASS, drinking the symbolic health of the very idea of toasting itself. He's sure now they've got it all backwards.

"Look, kid. Three shanties up there," J.D. points. He squeezes his son's pastel shoulder pad. "I want you to go have a look and a knock, see if anybody's home. Somebody rural, with a way with a homemade idle."

"The car's going to go down in this mud, Pop," DeHaven sniffles across D.L. "We'll get stuck sure, anyway. The fucker's already

level, in back." He wipes clotted talc off his cheek. "God am I
sorry, Pop."

"Hush, kid. Not your fault. Just go have a look. Please. Here,"
handing him the noseless yarn tangle from the dashboard. "Wear
the wig. Keep your head dry. Don't catch cold. No sniffling Ronalds."

DeHaven keeps his chin up. "Right." He's out of the car and
behind the silver curtain of serious rain—you can hear the hiss as
his cigarette's hit and extinguished—and he's off up the road, his
orange yarn held to his scalp like a hairnet, riding-habit hips jouncing under his orange trousers, big red shoes sending water everywhere, up the steaming rural blacktop road and out of sight into
the breath-mist that collects on the windshield of the utterly enclosed, sheltering, rained-upon car.

This is pretty much the climax of the whole journey, by the way,
pending arrival. The final impediment—reimbursement and revelry
and meat and fried roses, all the roses anyone could want, roses
right out the bazoo, just up ahead: past the impediment.

Drew-Lynn Eberhardt can tell DeHaven Steelritter and J.D. love
each other, deep down, and this affects her. She is enormously
sensitive to who is loved by whom.

While J.D. Steelritter settles back cigarless, letting condensation
collect unwiped over a watch-face which why worry if worrying
won't serve purposes; while D.L. flicks at the dice that hang from
the rearview; while Tom Sternberg snacks, watching his gabardines
go up and down like a derrick at his discretion alone; Magda uses
an initialed cotton hankie to wipe at Mark's window, and they look
out at the fallow field to the left of the fence, the black muddy
field fallow and empty right to the skyline but for Pest-Aside-
maddened pests and one old, rickety, blue-collar, and totally superfluous scarecrow. The scarecrow looks somehow both noble and
pathetic, like a stoic guard standing sleepless watch over an empty

vault. Mark and Magda both look at the field and scarecrow and all-business Illinois rain like people who are deprived. Magda feels an overwhelming—and completely *non*oracular—compulsion to talk to somebody. Mark, a born listener, right from day one, feels nothing at all.

ACTUALLY PROBABLY NOT THE LAST INTRUSIVE INTERRUPTION

Mark Nechtr's ambivalent artistic attitude toward his teacher Dr. Ambrose—the fact that Ambrose is warm and tactful and unloverlike aside—and the fried-rose business completely and totally out of this picture altogether—really derives from Mark's new Trinitarian distrust of the fictional *classifications* that Ambrose seems to love and has entered, curling, looking for shelter from the very same cold critical winds that, in the fullness of time, had carved Ambrose's classified niche in the first place, see.

See—Mark tells the orange-faced flight attendant as they part a briefly-open-anyway curtain of water and enter the rain comparatively unseen, she shoeless and brown-skirted, his fashionable surgeon's shirt soaking quickly to a light green film over much health—dividing this fiction business into realistic and naturalistic and surrealistic and modern and postmodern and new-realistic and meta- is like dividing history into cosmic and tragic and prophetic and apocalyptic; is like dividing human beings into white and black and brown and yellow and orange. It atomizes, does not bind crowds, and, like everything timelessly dumb, leads to blind hatred, blind loyalty, blind supplication. Difference is no lover; it lives and dies dancing on the skins of things, tracing bare outlines as it feels for avenues of entry into exactly what it's made seamless. What Ambrose's "different" fictions do are just shadows, made various by the movements of men against one light. This one light is always desire. This is a truth so true it's B.C. If you're going to make lists to hide inside, he tells the stewardess—referring now to the D.L. he would love to hate—if you're going to classify everything, you might at least divide by the knife of what is desired, of *where* in the sky to look for the nothing-new sun. Divide from inside. Homiletic fiction desires peace. Eleemosynary fiction desires charity. Iconodulistic fiction desires order. Prurient fiction desires desire. Apocalyptic fiction desires the inevitable change it hides behind fearing.

Mark, if he were ever a real fiction writer, thinks he would like to try to be a Trinitarian writer. Trinitarian fiction, distinctively American, desires that change which stays always the same. It's cold as any supermarket—probably more economics than art—tracing the rate of a rate of change's change to a zero we pretend's not there, lying as it does behind Newton's fig leaf. It's an art that hides, tiny and fanged, in the eyes of storms, the axes of spins, the cold, still heart in the lover's pounding heart. It is triply subject, and good.

(Another reason Mark tends to keep his own counsel is that he can be a crashing chattering flap-jaw, once he lets go. His real friends suck it up, though, out of a kind of blind loyalty I'm afraid I can't help but admire.)

Yes Mark as Christian sees himself as would-be artist seeing himself as archer; baby Cupid; sick, bit Philoctetes, lover beyond time or compare. It is, he says, his one desire, the one beyond conditioning or obscene cuisine.

Except he tells Ms. Ambrose-Gatz it's beyond him. When he shoots, he feels it so. He feels, in his guts, that it would take three archers really to pull it off, to leave the reader punctured and spent and red. And American children shoot alone: it builds character.

"Three?" she asks, whole stewardess uniform now dark as her stained lap, shoes in a hand that balances her path through mud so fertile it stinks. Gorged insects have drowned in the milky Pest-Aside runoff, and bob.

One, he says, to aim just left and so impale the target's center. Another, he says, to betray the perfection of his comrade, to split the first arrow in two, with his own shaft.

And the third?

To be the beloved. The willingly betrayed. To wear the bright bull's-eye, and dance, under one light. To invite the very end we object to, genuflecting. To be aimed at: the at-long-last Reunion of love and what love loves.

Well and this old not-at-all-classy scarecrow is on the job: there are no crows in the rain. The malevolent car is visible through the undulating downpour, above, past a roadside ditch roaring with runoff. Sternberg's hands are at his window, and his face, looking out. J.D. and D.L. are fogged from sight. The colorful clown is on the crooked porch of the third and most distant shanty, knocking at an open door.

The potent abandoned scarecrow they stand by is just a crude cross of slapdash timber dressed up in faded military fatigues. It has no subtlety at all. The name on the military jacket's breast is obscured. The scarecrow wears a sodden Chicago Cubs cap on the not-fresh pumpkin that serves as a head, and, since it's a cross, has its arms straight out to the sides, though the arms' timber has been jaggedly broken, to simulate elbows, so that the fatigued sleeves droop earthward. The broken arms afford shelter, a bit, for the Magda who stands under an empty sleeve.

Mark can tell that Magda Ambrose-Gatz is smart. Not brilliant or witty or well-read. Not an idea man or a creative genius. She's just smart, the way simply hanging in there, as you, through all kinds of everyday tribulation and general shit can make you smart. She *was* in that story of Ambrose's, she tells Mark, though in there she was disguised and misrepresented, because even then her face was kind of orange. She had, yes, united with Ambrose, for a while, in holy matrimony. She still cared for him. Although they hadn't been in contact for a really long time. But she wished to speak to Mark Nechtr, here, she said, in the scarecrow's absence of shadow, because she thought she sensed underneath Mark's affected cool exterior a boy hotly cocky enough to think he might someday inherit Ambrose's bald crown and ballpoint scepter, to wish to try and sing to the *next* generation of the very same sad kids.

This storm's not a really bad Midwest storm, she remarks, as they stand by the scarecrow in the horizontal rain. Too windy to be really dangerous. The bad storms always hide behind a dead calm and a yellow-green sky. That's when you head for the cellar.

Mark should keep off the fried roses, in Magda's opinion. Not because they're fatal, or evil. Magda claims she'd used something similar, both with her Maryland lover and after, to preserve her orange face and voluptuous history against time's imperial march though a Depression, three recessions, a War, a Police Action, a Conflict, nine droughts, three plagues of mutagenic pests, twelve corn harvests so bountiful they were worthless, one airline deregulation, three (whoops, make that four) Presidential scandals, and the eventual erosion of agricultural price supports under pressure from the grocery lobby. And not because the dead snacks are advertising embodied, or clunky symbols, or obscene; or that they block Mark, shut him up alone inside the silence he dreads.

But just because they're not right. And right means more than ought. It also means *direction*. To try to digest fear into desire is to go backwards. Fear and desire are *already* married. Freely. One's impaled the other since B.C. What you're scared of has always been what moved you. And where you're heading has always been your real end, your Desire.

(This is all a summary, a what's the word a synopsis, and admittedly not in Magda's real voice, which cannot be done justice by me.)

That what unlocks you, even today, is what you *want* to want. In what you value. And what you value's married to those certain things you *just won't do*. And here's a cliché that's earned its status as a cliché: whether you're free or locked up depends, all and only, on what you want. What you have matters about as much as the color of your sky. Or your bars.

The rain makes the sound of rain. DeHaven's homemade car whines and roars above the flooded ditch and bare shoulder. The car's big rear wheels spin, screaming, sinking deeper into the mud. The car's acclivated shape is now a declivated shape.

Why using beauty for fuel is bad; why it's clumsy: it's superfluous: we *already* ache with desire for what we fear.

This sounds to Mark troublingly familiar: it's a seamless wave of muscular Anglo-Saxon ideas, it smacks of Dr. C——— Ambrose. Whom Mark no longer quite trusts, obviously.

Magda'll give Mark examples, then. Sternberg is obviously a bigtime claustrophobe—she can always smell claustrophobia on a passenger—so why's he still inside the steamy enclosed car, eating? J.D. Steelritter desires, more than anything, to be happified, at peace; so why, though he consumes enough roses to color a Tidewater spring, does he spend his whole life worrying, planning, conceding, debating, persuading, interpreting, manipulating a faceless Crowd into backward ideas of what *it* wants? Why is he trying to bring about a Reunion that will silence the very clamor whose whine in his head is that head's life and bread?

And Mark's bride. D.L. wanted to be pregnant, miraculous, so that Mark would love her, do her virtue honor; so why didn't she seduce him when fertile, instead of constructing a coy and obvious lie whose lifespan can't possibly exceed three seasons?

The rain on Mark, though violent, feels good, familiar, like the tattered imagined bedroom breezes of pre-sleep. It seems OK that this alive woman who'll live forever only as an object in Ambrose's story about passion should know the secret D.L.'s mother knows, Mark's parents know, Mark knows, that only D.L. still believes he does not know. Why she lied about the little miracle to this boy, who was loved.

"Because she's infertile; she cannot produce," Magda says. "She will tell you, when you ask, that it has to do with a past. With a father. She'll invoke Electra, Vietnam, amputation, Laing, Freud. But the truth is that—inside, where push comes to shove—*she* wants it so."

The rain reveals both their bodies, and the skeleton under the scarecrow's clothes. Magda is really not at all pretty, facially, except for the utter and unconsciously expressed pleasure she takes in the water's feel, the overhung sleeve's fungal smell, the milky mud between her toes.

"How do you know this?"

"Because it's true, Mark. Everybody who really wants to knows what's true. Most people just don't want to. It means listening from deep inside. Most people just don't want to. But the special people listen. You can hear what's true, inside. Listen. You can always hear it. In the rain. In the static between stations. In the magnetic whisper on tapes, right before the music starts. And in that sound that utter, complete silence has, in your ears—that glittered tinkle, like tiny chimes at great heights. I believe I know you, and that you're probably special. The chances are good that you're a born listener."

Mark listens. It's true: he's special. They're both special. (But I'm not special, and chances are you're not—shit, we can't *all* be special, obviously; not enough room for a crowd that big in here. Suck it up.) So but he's special, it's true. Magda's right. He's a born listener.

But he can't hear anything out of the ordinary, anything that sounds especially true.

Magda laughs at the sight of DeHaven galumphing back to the screaming car, his wig still clamped tight as a skullcap, leading a big old farmer in a military-surplus slicker. The farmer leads a big horse by a heavy chain.

"I'm afraid I can't hear anything, Ma'am. I hear rain, and the car, and the car's horn, and clopping, and a chain clanking. I can't hear anything that sounds especially true."

"You will. I promise. Trust me. I know. What's true never changes its tune. *He* heard it, once."

"Ambrose heard it with you?"

"And you're wrong about why he's wrong. You and Steelritter are both wrong. I'm no postmodernist, or artist. I can't lie. But I still know the center you want isn't in classes, or categories, or even in what kind of religion you choose to genuflect to. It's *here*." She doesn't gesture. "Wherever you are. It's all around you. Every minute. That sound you hear when it's quiet, without sleep. Or awake, listening. A great silence." Her eyes roll up toward her receding hairline, toward memory. "He used to love that silence. He'd just surrender, listening." She looks at Nechtr. "That was before you were even born. Before he wrote anything anyone but he and I would ever buy."

"Before Mr. Steelritter turned him on to meat and oil and metabetrayal?"

She smiles orangely, smooths her limply askew hair with a fatigue-sleeve.

"And what's true never changes, is what he said. From B.C. to this Very End you kids seem to worship. I believed in him, as an artist. I loved him very, very much. Enough to trust him even now.

"If you want," she says, "your whole life in the adult world can be like this country. In the center. Flat as nothing. One big sweep. So you can see right to the edge of where everything curves. So everything's right in front of your nose. That's why I sometimes throw cards. To show me my nose."

"You throw cards?" Mark says, making a face with his rosy face. "Jesus, D.L. throws them." Mark distrusts thrown cards: all those arcane categories, vague meanings, wish-fulfillment as prophecy. "I don't trust them," he admits. "They just tell her what she wants to hear. They're just vague enough so you can make them say what you want to happen or are neurotic about happening." He almost sneers, if there's such a thing as a numb sneer. "And then you and her psychic call it prophecy. It's *obscene,* is what it is."

Magda looks at him baldly from her side of the broken-armed cross in military surplus. The rain around them is letting up. The real heart of the sudden storm has moved off East, seeming coolly to strut, a bit tiptoed.

"Your lover doesn't *throw* cards," Magda laughs. "She carries them around probably wrapped in silk, probably even with a souvenir crystal; and she shuffles them and closes her eyes and spreads them out, afraid to look, the way people who make wishes are scared to tell you the wish, for fear the magic is fragile, sensitive to light."

(Again, I feel an obligation to say that this is synopsis, and not true to a voice I'm afraid I just can't do.)

"She tries to *use* them," Magda (more or less) continues. "She invests them with a power to change what they can only reveal. She wants shelter, a structure. A house of cards, with tiny furniture. Not the kind of great blind sweep you get when you *throw*." She makes a throwing gesture that's surprisingly deft and slight. "Not a mirror, that just shows you your nose." She looks at Mark. "When's the last time you saw your nose?"

FOREGROUND THAT INTRUDES BUT'S REALLY TOO TINY TO EVEN SEE: PROPOSITIONS ABOUT A LOVER

Maybe because she's never, never once, been made to be anything other than what others see, Magda Ambrose-Gatz has vast untapped resources of virtue and smarts and all-around balls. D.L. reads painted Elkesaite cards, knows her own rising sign, and consults media. Magda, who's been seen so often her face is pumpkin-colored, is never called on to see others, or to speak from the heart. So she listens. And sees, inside. Never called on to speak, she can actually love her own tongue, as those born to subjection may love their skin, ears, eyes. She can count the hairs in your head, hear the cries of my cells expiring. She can *see*. She can spread the whole outside flat, inside, throw the kind of colorless cards that reveal what cannot change. She does so for Mark, and does not condescend when the boy protests that she has no Tarot cards, only a regulation flight-attendant's skirt and a faded fatigue jacket taken from the super-fluous figure suspended above them and wrapped around her against the bland chill that always follows a storm's third act.

I am sorry. I have such respect for this woman that I just cannot show her to you in the light her shadow deserves. I am lovesick, and ungrown, and know no trope or toponymic topoi, no image worthy. I have to play the supplicant here; ask you simply to eat some raw bare propositions I can't prepare or flavor enough to engage your real imagination. We're all quite tired, and deprived, and it's getting pretty clear that we'll probably be asleep by the time the actual revel gets started; so I'm going to cease all fucking around and just tell you what Magda tells Mark—what she knows, from just her senses, which are never in demand.

Magda knows that the water D.L. finally boils will not be for any labor. Magda knows that D.L. will emerge, in time, unMarked, as the single best copywriter J.D. Steelritter Advertising has ever used. She will rise through the adman ranks, assume a management position, eventually marry J.D.'s atonally ambitious harlequinned son (who'll be a sensitive and surprisingly gentle father), and be the lone female pallbearer when the most creative mind in the history of American advertising finally succumbs to carcinoma of the lower lip and is buried in a plot that requires no floral embellishment. Drew-Lynn will, in time, *become* J.D. Steelritter Advertising, and discover that the key to all ingenious and effective and original advertising is not the compelled creation of all-new jingles and images, but the simple arrangement of old words and older pictures into relationships the consumer already believes are true. She will take root, blossom, and mature in an environment of responsibility, and will do her late mentor true honor in continuing the masterful orchestration of the two long-term, brand-building campaigns J.D. will die proudest of. She will live to see Ray Kroc's one little Collision concession stand truly become the world's community restaurant. She will see to it personally that Dr. C——— Ambrose's one flat gutted Maryland Funhouse comes truly to offer a whole new dimension in alone fun, become the discotheque where America can be themselves. She'll impose her will on awed, sleep-deprived, travel-weary clients with a dispassion born of an oracular instinct for What the People Want. A grown D.L., cardless, will divine a nation's post-postmodern economic future. Funhouses will eventually allow patrons to toast the idea of toasting with actual drinks: the consequent rise in patronage, consumption, Demand, and thus price of admission, will meet the Supply curve at profit. McDonald's will eventually suspend its free-food-forever-for-commercial-alumni policy, unmoved by scattered reports of hungry former actors wandering, pressing gaunt noses to windows warm as flesh—and will, in consequence, suspend its emblazoned pronouncements about how many trillions of burgers have been served since the beginning of franchised time. The public will interpret McDonald's new silence about the number of meat patties served as the kind of modest reticence only the world's true community restaurant could afford to display. P.R. And it shall be good.

Magda's Tower- and arcana-dominated reading of Thomas Sternberg I'll skip, out of respect for limitations of time and a general repulsion for all those like us. Know, though, that he'll eat what cannot be food, be prurient, have ideas, believe he wants to heal and act, neither heal nor act, will putter all his adult life around the house his dead parents leave standing, and generally become the sort of Back Bay neighborhood presence with whom you Do Not Fuck.

Mark's field of time is harder to survey; because, since he is, at root, still an infant, his future is not yet something that cannot change. He believes there's some simple, radical difference about him. He hopes it's genius, fears it's madness. Magda knows it's neither. She knows that in truth Mark is just a radically *simple* person, wildly noncomplex, one of the very few men she's read for who's exhaustively describable in fewer than three adjectives. She predicts he will, in the Eleemosynary period following a scarred divorce he wants to be depressed about, give away a detergent fortune to the United Redemption Charities Corporation. That he'll travel without cease—not in the way of his father or J.D. or Ambrose, who steer exclusively by their rearview mirrors, but with the forward simplicity of a generation for whom whatever lies behind lies there fouled, soiled, used up, East.

But since J.D. Steelritter is the type of parousia whose advent leaves exactly zero to chance, the bloody, chocked field of the Reunion's next five days cannot change. And Magda sees that, in that time, Mark, his complicated bow exchanged for a bulky rented key, will shut the Funhouse franchise doors against the reveled babble, sit his ass down, and actually write a story—though it'll be one he'll believe is not his own. He'll see the piece as basically a rearranged rip-off of the radio's "People's Precinct" episode they've heard just now, and of the whole long, slow, stalled trip in general. It'll be a kind of plagiarism, a small usurpation; and Mark will be visibly embarrassed about the fact that the Nechtr-story Professor Ambrose will approve best, and will maybe base letters of recommendation on, will not be any type of recognized classified fiction, but simply a weird blind rearrangement of what's been in plain sight, the whole time, through the moving windows. That its claim to be a lie will itself be a lie.

The story that isn't Mark Nechtr's by Mark Nechtr concerns a young competitive archer, named Dave, and his live-in lover, named L———. Dave, who is not nearly so healthy as Mark, believes that the only things that give his life meaning and direction are his competitive archery and his lover, L———, who is a great deal more attractive and sympathetic than D.L., with cheekbones out to here and a zest for life Dave cannot but share, through her. L——— is pretty much an emblem of Dave's generation, is deprived and aimless and mildly wacko, with moods that change like the shapes of the moon that obsess her. Dave stands witness to all of her faults, though only some of his own, and but anyway loves L——— anyway. It's implied that he's dependent on her, for support; she stands in the hushed tournament galleries when he stands perpendicular to targets and shoots competitively with his complex fiberglass bow and Dexter Aluminum arrows. Dave is a solid young competitive archer, but by no means the best, even in his age division, and at the piece's outset he feels like a true, born-to-be archer only when L——— is standing there, in the gallery, watching him stand and deliver.

But they fight, as lovers. L——— is self-conscious, neurasthenic, insecure, moody, diffracted. Dave is introverted, self-counseled, and tends to be about as expressive as processed cheese. When the hottest darkest mood in L———'s weather collides with his cold white quiet, they have violent arguments that seem utterly to transform them. Dave had never even raised his voice to a girl before he fell for L———, and hates confrontation's habit of making his hands (which he values) unsteady. But when she slips into the worst of herself, they scream and fight and carry on like things possessed. Pointy personal shrapnel flies. The air gets coppery with violence. In truth, Dave is often afraid to turn his back on L———, especially in their kitchen, when sharp things are handy; and he's ashamed of this, and of the fact that after a fight he's often afraid to go to sleep when she is awake and malevolent and boiling water is only a stove and kettle away. Nevertheless he loves his lover, and cannot understand the dark heat that fills him when they fight, or his need to lick his lips while she lists real and imagined grievances—or that his only really true deep concern during the screaming matches is that the neighbors in their community might hear her screams, or his screams, or her different screams as they reconcile, always via violent union. Though callow and beardless and not experienced, Dave loves L——— enough to maintain the form of excitement throughout broad stretches of heated lovemaking; and L——— believes, wrongly, that he is a born lover. She loves him physically with an intensity that is informed by her zest for a life she consumes. But the intensity of her loyalty to Dave is shot through with streaks of what can only be called a kind of greed. When she loves him, and cries out through the thin ceiling to maybe the whole neighborhood oh just how much she *loves* him, he fears that she means only that she loves what she feels. And he wishes, in the cold quiet of his archer's heart, that he himself could feel the intensity of their reconciliations as strongly as he feels that of their battles.

The workshop and Ambrose approve this overture, this setting-up, though they do point out that it goes on a bit longer than absolutely necessary, limitations of space and patience being a constant and defining limitation, these quick and distracting days.

And but yes there is something self-obsessed about L———'s love, we can feel. For example, she wishes Dave to tell her, instead of that he loves her, that she is loved. Her father used to say it as he tucked her gently into his USMC-surplus poncho-liner at bedtime, she explains; and it made her happy. That she was loved. That she is loved. Dave feels like not he, but rather her desire to be loved, to be beloved, is what gives *L———'s* life its direction and meaning; and some tiny targeteer's voice cries out inside him against telling her that she is loved just because the fact that *he loves her* isn't enough to stave off insecurity and self-consciousness and dissension and row.

Etc. etc. Dave, pretty darn stubborn when it comes to his tiny archer's cry, refuses, inside, to use the passive voice to articulate his love. And one fine day he actually *articulates* this refusal, and the reasonable arguments that lie behind it. He does this at significant personal risk.

For, articulated-to, enraged, L—— blows off her appearance at the most important junior archery tournament of the Tidewater shooting season. Dave shoots alone, unwatched, afraid—and but he *overcomes,* shoots so surprisingly well that he places an overall third in his age-division. His best finish yet. When L—— bursts into their loft at nighttime, darkly transformed by both his articulated refusal to use the passive voice and his subsequent failure to fail without her, Dave wills himself to appear cool and distant and emotionally mute, but is actually licking his lips furtively as a dusky heat inside him dawns and breaks into tributaries and attendant falls, spreading. Maybe the loudest fight in the history of this generation's verbal love ensues, with broken valuables and threats of a very great stabbing.

But L—— hates herself more than she loves or hates Dave, it turns out, is the thing. Which makes her climactic lover's thrust at him sort of perfect in both directions. Having de-quivered and brandished Dave's best and unlosable Dexter Aluminum target arrow, as if to stab her lover, L—— turns it shaft-backwards and, with a look on her Valentine face past all belief—a look that communicates perfectly her three true selves: the blindly loyal, the greedily past-impassioned, and the self-imprisoned hating—with this look, reflected bulgingly in Dave's TV's dead green eye, she unfortunately puts the Dexter arrow through her own creamy oft-kissed throat, right up to the nock. She falls and lies there, victorious and pierced, her pelvis moving and life a bright fountain around the boy's unlosable shaft.

So far it's a good graduate-workshop story, the rare kind that imposes the very logic it obeys; and plus it has the unnameable but stomach-punching quality of something real, a welcome relief from those dread watch-me-be-clever pieces—or, even more dread, a fashionably modern minimal exercise, going through its weary motions as it slouches toward epiphany. What "works least well" for Dr. Ambrose and Mark's colleagues at the E.C.T. seminar is the part that deals with why this guy Dave is subsequently arrested and incarcerated and tried and imprisoned for L———'s murder. The section's chattery, and about as subtle as a brick, but the gist is that picture this: L——— lies twisted and punctured and spent and moving and red before the mute Sony in Dave's shared room, losing blood with every pulse, self-stabbed with the high-tech arrow that had placed Dave third alone. She's clearly near death, and looks with supplication and a trust born of true love's blind loyalty at Dave, waiting for him to obey basic human instincts and leap to remove the wickedly intrusive shaft. But Dave, come suddenly of age, hears no ching of instinct's bell; he feels only the kind of numb visual objectivity that makes a born archer mature. He takes precious time out to look at the big picture, here. He takes the long view. He: sees that L——— has pulled crunchingly into death's gravel driveway, that no way can she be saved in time (tourniquet pretty obviously impractical); fears that their community's collective ear has heard the violent row he didn't start; concludes that if he takes hold of the aluminum shaft to remove the weapon, the whorled oil his fingers exude will establish itself as his forensic mark on the Dexter arrow; and then his lover will die anyway, and the whole thing will maybe be interpreted by others as exactly what it will look like. Crime of passion. Murder-1. Dave licks his lips absently as he tries to anticipate interpretation. This goes on forever, narratively speaking. L———, her eyes never leaving her lover's, finally, to pretty much everyone's relief, expires.

The workshop objects especially to two things, here. The first is the story's claim that all Dave's self-conscious caution about fingerprints is for naught, because the whorls of his oil are already on the arrow anyway—he had fletched, held, fitted, nocked, and shot the special arrow three times in that day's competition. Since explicit and verisimilitudinous mention is made on Mark's mss. p. 8 of the skin-thin leather gloves all serious competitive archers wear, though, the believability of Dave's fingerprints being on the shaft depends on an awareness that an archer's glove covers *only the wrist and palm* (protecting them from the shaft's explosive reaction to the bow's leftward pressure): the nakedness of an archer's fingers, Dr. Ambrose argues reasonably, is not a piece of information Mark can expect the average reader to have in the arsenal average readers bring to bear on average stories. Basically what you're doing when you're writing fiction is telling a lie, he tells those of us in the seminar; and the psychology of reading dictates that we're willing to buy only what coheres, on some gut level, with what we already believe.

Weaker still, Ambrose claims (though with tact and cheer), is the story's claim that the Tidewater coroner's inquest reveals that the cause of L——'s death, as she lay horizontal with the wicked shaft protruding, was neither trauma to aspirate organ nor loss of bodily fluid, but rather . . . *old age*. A collective "?!?" greets this move of Mark's. Though it's done lovingly.

Do some very simple cost-benefit analyses, Ambrose advises Nechtr, rubbing the red commas his glasses have imposed on his orange nose's bridge: Why compromise the tale's carefully crafted heart-felt feel and charming emotional realism with a sudden, gratuitous, and worst of all *symbolic* bit of surrealism like this?

Especially since the real meat of the story lies ahead, in the Maryland Facility for Correction, where a numbly shattered and even less healthy Dave awaits trial and a judicial retribution he cannot deny he deserves. The epistatic twist of the knife here is that Dave is Not Guilty, yet is at the same time *guilty* of being Not Guilty: his adult fear of the community's interpretation of his prints and shaft has caused him to abandon his arrow, to betray a lover, to violate his own human primal instinct toward honor. How ethically, craftedly clever is this double-bladed twist, Ambrose tells us as we take notes; and how charmingly unfashionable to hear *honor* actually used as a noun, today.

Meanwhile, inside the story we have all, as part of the class requirement, read and put copious comments in the margins of, we're told that exactly nothing in Dave's sheltered experience prepares him for the hellishness of the Facility where he awaits trial. He lives in a tight gray ghastly cell. And he is not Alone in there. He has a cellmate. His cellmate is horror embodied. A hardened career criminal awaiting sentencing on a counterfeiting conviction, the cellmate who licks his wet lips at Dave's arrival is a "Three-Time Loser," and under Maryland law can expect to receive the same Life Dave expects. The cellmate's body is loathsome, flabby, puke-white, fat-spider-like, flatulent, pocked, cystic, and carbolic. Dave finds him disgusting, and the evident fact that the counterfeiter, whose name is Mark, loathes his own body, resents the cell's two-thirds its confined storage requires, and is revolted by the sounds and odors that issue whenever he moves, breathes, or makes his unceasing use of the cell's elimination bucket—this Mark's self-loathing only increases the young archer's disgust. Plus horror. The cellmate is so cruel, bestial, hard, terrible, sadistic and depraved and repugnant (he actually sits on Dave's head, requiring that Dave play the part of bidet or else face the consequences) that Dave calmly considers suicide as maybe preferable to the possibility of Life in this cramped fetid cell with this hellish counterfeiter; but not for a moment, the story claims, does Dave feel ill-used by the universe in general, or doubt that he is not somehow precisely where he belongs: he cannot close his eyes without being subjected to the diplopic double image of his lover's steady, supplicating and aging (!?) eyes, and then his own eyes vertical above her, darting from side to side, more concerned with how he is seen than with what he sees. Yes, when he's not being savaged, violated, sat and shat upon, Dave has time to think; and he grows up all over again, in the Facility. He is, the story takes a risk by saying, "repentant"— which in its Franco-Latinate etymology, Ambrose reminds us from his station at the green blackboard, denotes a process, not a state. Dave accepts, numbly but not passively, his unacceptable confinement.

Yes but the counterfeiter, Mark, hates the tiny cell even more than Dave, though suicide never enters spider-minds unviolated by naïve romantic thoughts about things like honor or betrayal. But Mark does *(does)* have Ideas. He believes—and whispers, over and over, as Dave falls asleep brown-nosed and bloody in the violated bunk below—that if he, Mark, can just work out the kinks in his counterfeit key, can just *escape,* leave the tiny gray cell and the barbed, guarded Facility complex behind, return to the mythic and fertile Tidewater marshland he'd roamed as a ghastly child, he can be happy, whole, human. An idea man, he posits that the whole purpose of confinement in barred cells with tiny barred windows— the latter all the worse for the prisoner's ability to see a striped Outside which the bars render both visible and impossible to reach— the whole point is to *"dehumanize,"* and that he, Mark, as minimally human (Dave, no idiot, holds his peace on this point), has a right to escape analogous to any attacked man's right to defend, to kill for what he must have or retain.

Data: Mark has spent most of the latter portion of his life behind bars, in the Facility, and presides over a whole predatory school of demoralized Lifers who are the whole Facility's basic mandate for erection. Mark has underground tentacles that extend into even the blackest markets. He and his school of followers do unspeakable things to Dave, force themselves on the weak sickly repentant archer in complexly depraved ways that Nechtr, quite frankly, hasn't the nerve or dark imagination yet really even to describe. This lack of facility, though, is interpreted by a sensitive instructor and loving workshop as disciplined restraint, and is duly applauded.

Etc. etc. but so eventually, one night, after Lockdown and the muffled screams of pre-sleep rape, Mark makes good his prophecy of flight. Dave wakes from his one familiar diplopic nightmare to see, against the striped light of the cellblock's hallway, his bulbous cellmate manipulating a counterfeit key, one Mark has spent two months tempering in the Facility's license-plate metal shop, into their cell door's Lockdown mechanism. The key, which is surprisingly simple in shape and serration, nevertheless gives the hardened counterfeiter total control over the movements of all the Facility's state-of-the-art automated doors. The key, as key, doesn't look like much of anything: Mark's had the thing in plain sight by the elimination bucket for weeks—only Dave, he said, had been told what it really was, or what, if willingly used, it could do.

The barred door slides silently open on its reliably-oiled track. Dave hears Mark cock his floppy puke-white ear for sounds: there is only the distant whimpered symphony of unfree dreamers.

And in that familiar moment of hesitation, the one before all leapers leap, Dave's tormenting mate turns to survey the space he has filled and now would empty. The keen archerlight of Dave's open eye is reflected in the counterfeit absence of the bar-shadow that usually shades him. He, supine, and Mark, erect, stare at each other across that silent moment. Dave does not know, right then, whether what is spoken is aloud.

"You've known what I've made. You've heard me whisper. You see what I'm doing."

Dave nods.

"And you know where I'm headed."

Dave does.

"Don't rat. Do not rat."

Dave nods.

"Rat and I'll kill you."

Dave hears.

"Rat and I'll have the whole place up your ass. They'll fuck you bloody and feed you your cock. They'll dink you. Your weak little body'll be found in locations. Note the plural. Shitspeck."

"I hear you," Dave says, so flatly there's no hint of echo.

But Mark's voice always echoes. "Rat and you're a late boy. As in zotzed. Klapped. This is a promise. I have tentacles, and rights. I'll defend myself against you."

"I don't rat," Dave says.

"Poppa!" cries a compulsive exhibitionist down the cellblock.

"Don't rat."

"Go, man." Dave's glad Mark's going, who're they kidding. "Bon voyage. Godspeed. Wear a hat. Don't try to hitchhike."

Further echoed connections between ratting and violent death recede with the counterfeiter, who holds his key before him like a candle in the bright cellblock hall.

Understandably, though, the M.F.C.'s professional penal authorities are not at all glad that the three-time counterfeiter has gone. Is at large. Penal helicopters chop and chuff all night, aloft. Dave turns his back to the still-unlocked door, holds his window's bars in his fists, and watches searchlights shine from clouds to play the land outside; hears the whiny petition of eager leashed hounds, the sinal rhythm of the Facility's escape siren; stands there, watching, till the gradual Maryland dawn, when he's led by uniformed hands to the spare, spartan, no-nonsense office of the Facility's Warden.

Here a narrative risk is gauged and taken. The Warden is Jack Lord, of fame. With the sort of apparent inconsistency that makes creative writing professors such delightfully puzzling pixies, Ambrose *approves* this particular unrealistic/symbolic touch. Some of the rich ambiguity of realism is, he concedes, sacrificed. But since Nechtr's whole story is interpreted by the workshop as about a whole new generation's feelings of amorphous but deserved guilt, confinement, fear, confusion, and, yes, the place of honor in the general postmodern American scheme of things, his fictional use of a popular icon, forged in the medium that is (sadly? *sadly?*) this generation's unbreakable window on itself, this rings somehow true, Ambrose tells us. It also ties in with the vivid post-escape helicopter imagery, which creates a sense of unity, craft, care. Which is good.

Also good is the fact that Lord needs little description, since he is an image of fame. His hard square face—white as the face of a man keeping an iron grip on ever-recalcitrant reins—his improbable overt jaw, barely-there lips, black eyes and high dark hair, one lank askew, are stamped on the consciousness of a whole post-bellbottom generation. Dave needn't even raise his eyes to know his gaoler's mettle as he listens to Jack Lord, listens, and then lies, denies that he knew of Mark's plans to escape, or that he witnessed the escape, or that he knows anything at all about the counterfeiter's means of exit, or destination, or route, or rate of travel. Mark, Dave says, did not confide in him. Mark repelled, terrorized and violated him. He is, to be honest, glad the Three-Time Loser has gone, yes, but knows not where to; cares less. If he'd been privy to the whole thing, wouldn't he be gone, too? Don't all, facing Life, given the chance, flee?

Not if they're guilty, Lord replies. Not if they're one of the special few here who know just where they belong.

Jack Lord always knows more than those he questions suspect that he knows. It is the nature of his character. It is law.

Another law of character is that an escapee *always* blabs to his cellmate about where he's going. And Mark, like all confined compromisers of the Mainland's order, like all loathsome men whose every movement is not toward but away, is a chatterer. A born talker. And Dave here, Lord can tell just by looking, is a born listener. Jack Lord's pointing finger is that of a potent and manicured God. His eyes burn dark. He may not smile. Dave knows, and he must tell. The truth.

Dave stands there and lies and lies and lies.

"And even if I did know," he says finally, voice even as cheese, "I don't rat. I will not rat. And you cannot make me. I've got Life, coming. The community heard my lover's screams. Fluids from my body were on the shaft that killed her. I'm going to be sentenced to Life. I'm trying to accept it, and this Facility. I'm coming of age. It's a hell beyond Bosch's worst nightmares here, and I'm headed for tenure. What more can you brandish? There's nothing you can do."

Mark Nechtr's dialogue does tend to get a tad flowery, when he's carried away. But what the *fuck*. You know?

But Jack Lord is smiling his one permitted smile: the smile that finds no humor in what may not change. The ordered world he lives by steering is black-and-white. Dave's face yellows as Lord breaks the basic news. It's not a question of what the penal authorities can do. It's what *his cellmate,* even though absent, can do. Dave is the one stray thread in the counterfeit escapee's seamless weave. And this counterfeiter's a hardened pro: he knows one sleepy mumble could unravel months of craft. Perhaps—no, *un-doubtedly*—Mark threatened Dave about what happens to those who rat. Omitted from his presentation, though, Lord advises, was what happens even to those who do *not* rat. Dave represents an untidiness. A loose thread. An aesthetic problem. And counterfeiters are compulsive about the aesthetic integrity of what they've wrought. Lord makes a prediction. Mark is going to have Dave exterminated. Dinked. Zotzed. Jobbed. Mark has a circle, a ghastly following, here in the Facility. They will come, Lord predicts. Dave's only option is to rat, to reveal, to Jack Lord, Mark's means and route and velocity and end. Then and only then may Lord, who does not make the rules he only enforces them right up to the *hilt,* be allowed to shield and protect a helpful witness, Dave, an asset, with penal value. Only then will Jack Lord be empowered to preserve Dave's life. Let the archer eat and bathe, exercise and evacuate alone, in private, under trusted guard, away from Them. Perhaps even be able to work toward having Dave transferred to a different Facility. Let him make a fresh start, inside. Elsewhere. Clean penal slate. But Lord promises that all that, nay just plain old bare hand-to-mouth survival, can come to pass only if the archer reveals what Lord knows he knows. If not . . . well, things don't need spelling out in this sort of environment, do they. No one is Alone in a Facility.

Jack Lord smiles that monochrome smile we know. The matter's in the archer's hands, not the Warden's. Dave is invited to give the whole matter some unleisurely thought, back in the general population. In the prison community.

Sure enough. In no time, things come to pass. They come for him in the exercise yard, the shower, the license-plate shop, the cell. Dave is assaulted, savaged, violated, punctured with homemade weapons the more fearsome for their being homemade. The Word is out. The grapevine sings. Vague drums beat low. Something has been offered. A bounty beyond measure. A hundred cigarettes.

Jack Lord explains to his teutonic new Assistant Warden—in a

narrative interruption Ambrose says he'll let slide, just barely—
that the price of life in the penal system is low, because the Facility
is overstocked with lives, lives that wear only numbers, lives without
honor or value or end. There is no demand for them. The market's
invisible hand hefts a finger, damning the guilty to an existence of
utter freedom, freedom to choke and starve, alone in a riot.

Didactic little fucker, too. Nechtr. But Ambrose was being indulgent that seminar day. We could tell he loved the kid, deep
down.

But so here's the weak, sickly, and *badly* damaged archer, in the
run-down Facility infirmary, looking like death incarnate, a black-
eyed mummy of gauze, fed by tubes, relieved by tubes that often
run red. Jack Lord appears bedside, dressed all in black. That his
black pants are bellbottoms symbolizes what we already know: this
is a man above ridicule.

Lord asks Dave how's life in general, down there, these days.
It's the cold sort of question that is its own answer. The logic of
Lord's prophecy has been immaculate. Mark, who's still at large,
outside, though probably just long enough for someone in the
population to accommodate his tentacled demand, has put a hundred-
cigarette price on the archer's bandaged head. A hundred *100s*.
The good kind. The kind that burn forfucking*ever*. Word's out, kid.
Not even this infirmary is safe, what with Dave's life as simultaneously worthless and valuable as it now is. Lord invites Dave to
have a look at that Trusty of an orderly over there, grinning a
Grinch-grin and filling a blunt syringe with something that just
doesn't look promising at *all*; while out the hospital window's mesh
a fag-hungry population waits, implacable, patient, pounding their
own palms with socks filled with sand.

It's a matter of time, kid down there. Jack Lord won't waste it
repeating himself. He's terse; it's well known. Dave can get dinked,
or he can rat on the counterfeiter who sees him as a flaw, a smudge,
who has the capacity and capital, and his suppliers the opportunity,
to do the archer grievous and final harm. The Warden's helping

hands remain penally bound. Dave must *let* him help. He must give, to receive. There can be lunch, but it is never free.

Ambrose tells us that this conversation, this dialogue between Dave in white gauze and Lord in black fashion, is handled with a deftness that earns our approval, a lengthy economy born of a precision that promises Payoff. That it "rings true." And that the story's end, "like all true *apokes'* tragicomic *climae*" (which I'm still damned if I can find in any dictionary or thesaurus *anywhere*), is not the less triumphant for its pathos.

OK, Ambrose concedes—he's no pedant—the story here bends over backwards a little too far—limbos, almost—to argue that Dave's climactic refusal to rat has nothing to do with his guilty innocence in the impalement and death of his one true love. That there's way less self-hatred than selflessness being performatively rendered here. Selflessness is, of course, horror embodied; but the argument here is that it keeps safe in its ghastly silent center the green kernel that is the true self.

Ambrose concedes that there are some technical fuck-ups here, because the story cuts its own argument's legs out from under, viz. when Dave admits that his refusal to rat to Jack Lord, still, is deeply selfish in a way. That it has to do with Desire. That he, Dave, covets something, some one thing, even in the depths of injury and cut-rate anesthesia above which Jack Lord's famous and logical image swims.

It has to do with honor, see, the prisoner says.

Dave tells an icon of popular culture that he feels like his own experiences and fuck-ups and trial and tribulations and anguish, both on the Outside and in the Facility, have given him some insights—some sight-ins—that have helped him on his way, a way less toward "coming of age" than toward just plain old living in the adult world. The adult world, in Dave's opinion, has turned out to be a basically shifty, shitty place. It's risky and often sad and always wildly *insecure*. It beats him over the head, just how insecure and fragile is his place in his own lifetime. He knows, now, that nearly everything you call Yours in the world can be taken away from you by other people, assuming that they want it enough. They can take

away your freedom of location and movement, if there's judgment.
Men you didn't vote for can take your life with one red button,
Jack. The world can take your loved ones, your love, your one
beloved. Your dreams can be taken. Your manhood, integrity of
cock and bum: vapor before a gale. What's *his,* then, that he can
hold tight, secure?

This is the one thing, he says. He's had time to think, and he's
no idiot, and he's been able to come up with just one thing. They
can't take your honor. Only that can be only given. And it *can* be
given—with good reason, without good reason. But only given,
that. It *belongs* to him. His *be-longing.* The one arrow he just can't
lose, unless he lets it fly. His one thing.

Dave's thought it over, and he's decided he just does not rat.
He does not betray. Not even Mark. Dave is going to be greedy.
He's going to refuse to give away his last thing.

Get ready, because Jack Lord is . . . *nonplussed.* This weak kid's
own life worth less to him than some *idea?* The Warden, were he
younger, would be able to move his face's image into a surprise
Dr. Ambrose confesses he'd like to see shown. 'Cause there's no
logic here. No instinct. No sense. Some imaginary debt to a minimal
human who'd job you over a matter of freaking aesthetics? Jack
Lord's white face *does* move, a bit. What manner of beasts, these
kids today? Our future? Tomorrow's Mainland? This boy would
eat cock and die to honor some wacko abstract obligation to a
person with no, and here Jack Lord means *zero,* value?

The supine murderer would sincerely like to make the erect
peace officer understand. It is no matter, this *To Whom* the debt is
owed. Dave's just too fucking selfish to do it. He feels like his
bludgeon-blurred sense of obligation is all that's him, now. As much
what's him as his past and present and future. His past is spent,
cannot change; it's not in his control. God knows the future sure
isn't. The present is, yes, probably just waiting to get zotzed by a
market for endless flame. O Mr. Lord, but the fact that he *does not
rat:* this is his self's coin, value constant against every curve's wave-
like surge. Dave covets, values, hoards, and will not spend his

honor. He'll not trade, not for anything the cosmic Monty's got stashed behind any silver curtain.

(So OK, it goes on a little long. Nechtr's lover-cold passion, unleashed, will admit no minimalist imperative, Magda knows.)

But so no. He apologizes. He'd love to buy lunch. He'd love to see the counterfeiter who sat on his head hopping up and down on something pointy till the end of time. He'd love to help Jack Lord maintain order. The famous Warden may have anything but what is *his*. This is *his*.

This last number is, believe it or not, a monologue, a ring-tailed kitty of a bitch to pull off, made somehow more powerful for us in class by the pathetically unself-conscious *sentimentality* with which a healthy but simple and kind of fucked-up boy reveals to us colleagues, and to his teacher, Magda's old lover, J.D.'s crafty client, something as obviously hidden as a nose, today.

Except but so *does Dave rat?* is the question Mark Nechtr's unfinished and basically unfinishable piece leaves the E.C.T. workshop with. Does the archer maybe rat, finally, after all? Sure doesn't look that way. But Ambrose invites us to listen closely to the kidnapped voice here. This Dave guy is characterized very carefully all the way through the thing as fundamentally *weak.* It's the flaw that informs his character. Is this the real him, bandaged, prostrate before ideas so old they're B.C.? That shit with Jack Lord: that was just words. Could a weak person *act* so? Debate, before the bell rings, is vigorous and hot. The ambiguity is the rich, accidental kind—admitting equally of concession and stand.

Well and understandably Mark Nechtr wants to know, too. Does the archer who's guilty of his lover rat? Doesn't he, Mark Nechtr, have to know, if he's going to make it up? And how can he in good conscience just rip off, swallow, digest and expel as his what an alumnus with a streaked orange face and removable hair has clearly seen first herself? Would that be honorable, or weak? Don't make light of it. Don't laugh. Look at him, beseeching, soaked, scalded. He looks like a supplicant, one of us, the unspecial who burn without ever getting to ignite, as he lies, stabbed for real, finally, by this one gift that always returns, in Pest-Aside-milky mud, among gorged little corpses, before a scarecrow stripped of fatigues to reveal what it's been revealed as all along: two planks, opposed; a rotten orange head just stuck there, topped by a cap-usurping wig; and a power to strike contemporary fear into just those crows who've no stake or interest in a dead black lacuna between two fertile fields of greenly dripping feed.

And, in a related relation, Mark Nechtr won't rat. Will never tell of the realistic or sentimental compassion the poorly hidden and obvious Dr. Ambrose, warmed by fatigues whose sun-dried breast reveals only a suffix and number, arms strong as pine, fleshy of head, thin hair plastered across under the cap of some Chicago Cubs who this year *just might do it*—Nechtr never once will rat about the genuine feeling the cold genius used to cradle an infant's thick healthy neck, to bear an exhausted but replenished but still deprived detergent heir from an unenclosed place, toward the possibility of transport. Night crawlers boil confused at their feet, pests marching back into the fray like men with a mission, bearing tiny straws into furrows lactic with runoff from Pest-Aside, the Brand that Lures to One Side, as the academic man straddles a double, trampled path marked by impractical pumps, fruit-stained skirt, corporate jacket, fried petals, prosthetically engorged blouse. He is just nice, to carry both arrow and archer, and not even to mention about ratting.

Not that he's not irritating, of course. A born talker, he reminds my classmate of various obvious facts. That they have left the East Coast, have left the world's busiest airport, have left the world's least busy C.I.A. and its inevitable pay lot; that they've driven here and there and but are now not lost but only stalled, idled too high by a fearsome plastic nose, on the last road, one whose in-sight curve Westward leads straight to Collision. That the storm's worst has, once more, taken itself off East, where they've been. That they've left some awfully sore folks in a machine that's now dead-level in mud, but are returning via the path they've taken from them who sit bunched tight in a clown's car washed clean of plea or foreign brand, a homemade machine, attached even now by a length of chain to the chestnut mare of a big old farmer, harvester down, who'd wanted to hitch a lift only to the curve's third shanty, since his eldest kid's got the rented car; who has a surplus slicker, a flat-faced brood, a way with physics and chains, and the bare animal charity to pull a malevolent car from the earth and set it back on the road. That here's the public representative of Mc-Donald's, pastel hips jutting and legs bowed atop the foaming mare, which heaves and steams and gallops, muscles in bunches moving like whole corn-fed waves under a tight hide. That it all looks at once mythic and familiar, set against the new same sun's dripping green noon: J.D.'s perfect profile at the furry wheel, under hanging dice, cigar unlit, his window clean and down, while those of Sternberg and D.L. are up, since they like to feel what they look through, four hands on two panes; and the laboring horse game, galloping without purchase in the glassy mud, the enormous farmer pushing at the mare's ass, except without any friction for his big boots, so he is, yes, OK, in a way, walking in place; the car, J.D. Steelritter's accelerator pushed flat, the big car's idle screaming, higher and higher, its big rear Goodyears' hubs popped and spokes awhirl as the soaked earth, by not holding on, will not let them go.

That, tired, but in time, they'll arrive at what's been built. That it's way too late to go back on anything. So to the Reunion of All Who've Appeared, to the Egress, to the Funhouse, Ambrose's erect Funhouse, designed to universal standards to be—past all the hype that will support it—just that. A *house*. That, though Dr. Ambrose would rather be among those for whom it's designed, he'll eat with sad cheer the fact that he, as builder, is *not* among: not a face in the crowd of those for whom it's really there: the richly deprived, the phobically unenclosed, the in-need-of-shelter. Children.

Just a tad too long? Lovesick! *Mark'd!* I have hidden exactly nothing. So trust me: we will arrive. Cross my heart. Stick a needle. To tell the truth, we might already be there. The gleaming tar reflects our state's lidless noon. We can see ourselves in what we walk on. Jack Lord's promotional LordAloft chopper can even now be seen, reflected, aloft, in and out of the last of the clouds, probing with a white finger for all who are astray, stalled, behind schedules.

The light of his image's sun illuminates our homemade machine's rear tire, spinning in place, as the mare gallops in place, as the big old man shoves in place, without purchase. But the wheel! Bound by nothing, the Goodyear spins and spins, has lost its ringing hub, has disclosed a radial's spokes. Hold rapt for that impossible delay, that best interruption: that moment in all radial time when something unseen inside the blur of spokes seems to sputter, catch, and spin against the spin, inside.

See this thing. See inside what spins without purchase. Close your eye. Absolutely no salesmen will call. Relax. Lie back. I want nothing from you. Lie back. Relax. Quality soil washes right out. Lie back. Open. Face directions. Look. Listen. Use ears I'd be proud to call our own. Listen to the silence behind the engines' noise. Jesus, Sweets, *listen.* Hear it? It's a love song.

For whom?

You are loved.

Available in Norton Paperback Fiction

Andrea Barrett	*Ship Fever*
	The Voyage of the Narwhal
Rick Bass	*The Watch*
Simone de Beauvoir	*The Mandarins*
Anthony Burgess	*A Clockwork Orange*
Frederick Busch	*Harry and Catherine*
Stephen Dobyns	*The Wrestler's Cruel Study*
Jack Driscoll	*Lucky Man, Lucky Woman*
Leslie Epstein	*Ice Fire Water*
Leon Forrest	*Divine Days*
Paula Fox	*Desperate Characters*
	The Widow's Children
Carol De Chellis Hill	*Henry James' Midnight Song*
Linda Hogan	*Power*
Janette Turner Hospital	*Oyster*
Siri Hustvedt	*The Blindfold*
Starling Lawrence	*Legacies*
Bernard MacLaverty	*Cal*
	Grace Notes
John Nichols	*The Sterile Cuckoo*
	The Wizard of Loneliness
Craig Nova	*The Universal Donor*
Jean Rhys	*Good Morning, Midnight*
	Wide Sargasso Sea
Josh Russell	*Yellow Jack*
Kerri Sakamoto	*The Electrical Field*
Joanna Scott	*Arrogance*
Josef Skvorecky	*Dvorak in Love*
Frank Soos	*Unified Field Theory*
Jean Christopher Spaugh	*Something Blue*
Kathleen Tyau	*A Little Too Much Is Enough*
Barry Unsworth	*After Hannibal*
	Losing Nelson
	Morality Play
	Sacred Hunger
David Foster Wallace	*Girl with Curious Hair*
Rafi Zabor	*The Bear Comes Home*